MILLION STEP III
OUROBOROS

MILLION EYES III
OUROBOROS

C.R. BERRY

Elsewhen Press

Million Eyes III: Ouroboros
First published in Great Britain by Elsewhen Press, 2023
An imprint of Alnpete Limited

Elsewhen Press, PO Box 757, Dartford, Kent DA2 7TQ
www.elsewhen.press

British Library Cataloguing in Publication Data.
A catalogue record for this book is available from the British Library.
ISBN 978-1-915304-22-3 Print edition
ISBN 978-1-915304-32-2 eBook edition

Designed and formatted by Elsewhen Press

For Katy

PREVIOUSLY IN *MILLION EYES*

"HOW COULD YOU DO THAT TO THOSE WOMEN? IT'S UNSPEAKABLE!"

In 1888, eleven-year-old crossing-sweeper Harriet Turner and her mother, Emma, are living on the streets of Whitechapel when Jack the Ripper strikes.

After Jack murders his fifth victim, Harriet has an unexpected and grisly encounter with him in a church, where he introduces himself as Henry Van Deen.

When Harriet overhears Van Deen talking on a futuristic telephone about the 'timeline' and 'the future' before vanishing into thin air, she decides that the police never found Jack the Ripper because he time-travelled back to the future.

"I THINK SOMEONE JUST TRIED TO KILL ME."

Dr Jesus M. Hirschfield, a physician for the Twelfth Remnant fighting aliens called the Shapeless in 2222, travels back in time to the year 28. The last thing he remembers is taking cover in an abandoned building, and has no idea what led him to travel in time.

A woman called the Unraveller attempts to assassinate him the moment he arrives in ancient Nazareth. He is saved by the Hooded Man, who chases after the Unraveller.

Jesus begins warning people about the Shapeless and the 'Last War', which he records in a series of scrolls. He unwittingly becomes the Jesus of Christian theology after his message is distorted by his followers for their own ends.

"HE CAME TO SAVE US. HE CAME TO PREVENT THE LAST WAR. AND WE CANNOT LET HIM DOWN."

Jesus is betrayed and crucified, but survives his crucifixion and manages to escape his tomb. His friend, Joseph of Arimathea, flees to Britain with his scrolls and buries them in Glastonbury.

Nine centuries later, a monk called Cuthwulf unearths the scrolls and founds an organisation called Million Eyes to carry on Jesus's work, namely, finding a way of preventing the extinction of humanity at the hands of the Shapeless.

Million Eyes work their way into the halls of power in the 17th century, becoming an unstoppable political force.

"OUR SECRECY IS HOW WE PROTECT OURSELVES FROM OUR ENEMIES."

Following the disappearance of Flight 19 in the Bermuda Triangle in 1945, a Million Eyes-led investigation discovers that a mysterious red cloud composed of unstable chronotons has been transporting planes and ships across time. The cloud is dubbed the 'Ratheri' after the strange Morse code message it transmits.

Million Eyes extract and experiment on the chronotons, eventually creating the little red pills – chronozine – that enable people to travel through time. They begin using time travel to further the Mission, which is what they now call Jesus's scrolls and message.

With the invention of time travel inviting extra scrutiny, Million Eyes set about becoming the world's leading consumer technology company as a distraction and smokescreen.

"THE UNRAVELLER IS INTERFERING WITH THINGS THAT ARE *SUPPOSED* TO HAPPEN. WE CAN'T LET HER."

The Unraveller continues to try to undo Million Eyes' rise to power.

She time-travels to 993 to assassinate Cuthwulf. Ten years later, she tries to kill Cuthwulf again – along with several of his associates: Million Eyes' earliest members.

Thwarted both times by the Hooded Man, the Unraveller travels to 1605 and tries to ensure that the Gunpowder Plotters are successful in blowing up Parliament – and Million Eyes along with it.

"WHATEVER'S COMING, WE'LL BE READY FOR IT."

Following the excavation of a Cretaceous-era dinosaur with two human skeletons in its stomach, Dr Samantha Lester joins forces with Adam Bryant to take down Million Eyes, who they both believe responsible for a whole host of time-travelling crimes.

Million Eyes CEO Erica Morgan already knows that Adam and Lester are onto them. She and the mysterious Dr Neether are in possession of future knowledge and a device called the oraculum, which is set to offload its secrets by April 28th 2027.

But on April 27th, Miss Morgan receives information that could shatter Million Eyes' power and legacy, along with her own. She decides the information must go with her to her grave.

"IT'S THE AUGUR. IT'S BEEN DESTROYED."

In the early hours of April 28th 2027, the Augur – the machine that tells Million Eyes about forthcoming temporal incursions – is destroyed by a saboteur. Miss Morgan fears that someone is about to change history, and has a feeling she knows who.

Miss Morgan's fears are confirmed when the oraculum finally activates, telling her and Dr Neether that a time traveller called the Unraveller is about to cause a devastating temporal incursion by killing Jesus.

Armed with the oraculum's intel, Million Eyes send Adam Bryant back in time to stop the Unraveller and restore the timeline. Adam becomes the Hooded Man, saving Jesus, Cuthwulf and Million Eyes' founding members from the Unraveller's onslaughts.

"I'M THE WOMAN WHO SAVES THE WORLD."

When the Unraveller travels to 1605 to kill Tom Digby, the boy whose warnings led to the foiling of the Gunpowder Plot, she holds Adam at gunpoint in the street, telling him that Miss Morgan hasn't told him everything.

Their altercation leads to the Unraveller getting shot with a musket and fleeing through time once more. She makes one last attempt to stop Tom Digby's warning from reaching King James I, which Adam averts.

Having succeeded in restoring the timeline, Adam returns to 2027, only to be unceremoniously dispatched by Miss Morgan for knowing too much.

"YOUR LIFE IS OVER, DR LESTER.
IT'S TIME FOR YOU TO START A NEW ONE."

Miss Morgan sends Lester back in time five and a half years to fulfil the cycle of events that will enable Million Eyes to stop the Unraveller.

Lester has been going steadily mad with grief at the loss of her daughter, Georgia, and later the betrayal of her husband, Brody. She attempts to run over Miss Morgan's younger self with a car, the subsequent car crash leaving Lester with half a face.

Seeing a chance to use time travel to bring Georgia back from the dead, Lester reluctantly joins Million Eyes. She reverts to her maiden name, 'Neether', going on to become the same Dr Neether who will advise Miss Morgan on future events.

"THEY WERE A STEP AHEAD OF ME THE ENTIRE
TIME."

Million Eyes operative James Rawling, aka Henry Van Deen, aka Jack the Ripper, is stunned when the Unraveller returns to him at the facility where he is hiding out after destroying the Augur.

The Unraveller is Harriet Turner, the eleven-year-old who accosted him in a church in Victorian London, one hundred and thirty-nine years before. Harriet and Rawling are working together to bring down Million Eyes – and are failing.

Since changing history was their last resort, Rawling wonders what on earth they're going to do next.

1

February 9th 2219

"Now tell me, young man, how exactly does this thing work?"

It disassembles your atoms, converts them into data, downloads them into a generator, sends them to another generator, converts them back into matter and reassembles them. Not that Jackson Montgomery was going to tell the hundred-and-thirty-four-year-old great-great-grandmother any of that. He'd frighten the poor woman to death. No. As with every customer he teleported, he had to stick to the script.

Jackson smiled at Mrs Chatterjee and pointed at the oval-shaped pod in front of them, one of hundreds lining the enormous terminal. Just half an hour ago, the room was empty and quiet, the pods looking like petrified eggs that would never hatch. Now it was filled with the bustle and noise of the morning rush hour, labyrinthine queues of passengers being ushered through to the telepods by dozens of pastel-green-uniformed staff like him, the room sparkling like Christmas with the continuous flashing of the pods. Unlike many of his colleagues, who found rush hour stressful, Jackson rather enjoyed it. The quieter periods were boring.

"Basically, you step into that telepod there – Telepod 108 – and I'll push some buttons at my control station over there." He pointed at the console behind them. "You'll hear my voice from inside the pod and I'll start counting down from twenty. At zero, a bright purplish

1

light will surround you and you'll feel... lifted. It's actually really relaxing. A moment later, the light will disperse and you'll find yourself back in the telepod again. Only it won't be this one here, in Aberdeen. It'll be Telepod 14 at the Interstate Terminal in Bayside, Melbourne."

Mrs Chatterjee's prune-like face scrunched into a pouty frown. She leaned forwards on her walking stick, craning her neck to face him. "And what does the purple light do?"

Stick to the script. Jackson pressed his lips together and swallowed. This was the part where, if the customer was asking too many questions, the teleport operator's next move was to confuse them with the tech specs.

"It produces high-yield interphasic inversion radiation that quantifies matter-streams for subspace transference."

Mrs Chatterjee arched one eyebrow. "I've no idea what you just said." Then, "Will it hurt?"

Jackson chuckled inwardly. "No, ma'am. It's completely painless." When she didn't look convinced, "I promise."

Mrs Chatterjee nodded. "Okay. Let's get on with it then. I've been avoiding these infernal machines ever since they were invented. I make my busy great-granddaughter come and see me every time, when I'm perfectly capable – as she likes to remind me – of going there. Did I tell you she's the CEO of Chosen One, the space clothing brand?"

Yes, you did. Four times. "Is she? That's wonderful."

The tiny old lady shuffled towards the telepod, her walking stick keeping her steady. Partway there, she did a half-turn towards Jackson. "Will it even take the stick?"

Jackson smiled. "Of course, ma'am."

"How clever."

He was getting pretty good at persuading reluctant teleporters. It probably wasn't that different to flight attendants helping passengers overcome their fear of flying in the old days, although fear of teleportation was more common – perhaps because it was easier to imagine

2

being suspended thirty-six-thousand feet in the air than having your atoms scrambled. Most people still flew shuttles or took the Skytrain. Even Jackson's wife, Cara, refused to teleport.

As the automated doors to the telepod slid open, Mrs Chatterjee edged her head into the doorway and peeked into the big, brightly lit space. "Oooo. Very nice." Satisfied, she stepped inside, the doors hissing closed behind her.

Jackson triggered the initiation sequence and started his verbal countdown. Sure, the system could do the countdown for him. In fact, the system could do all of Jackson's job if it was set up that way. However, the executives at Next Phase – the company that had invented teleportation – had decided that a human element was necessary for making anxious customers feel at ease, and that they should continue to hear their teleport operator's voice right up to the moment of dematerialisation.

Jackson watched Mrs Chatterjee on his screen, listening for a potential last-second change of heart – those were common too and would mean cancelling the initiation sequence. This involved a lot of wasted energy and money, which was why teleport operators like Jackson were under pressure to make sure customers didn't back out.

Mrs Chatterjee stood motionless, eyes shut, as Jackson counted down, but she wasn't showing any signs of wanting to stop the process.

At zero, the pod was doused in a brief but vivid burst of purple-tinged light. It faded a moment later, the pod now empty. Jackson checked the data on his screen. It read **TELEPORT COMPLETE** with a note of the customer's arrival time and place.

Before attending to the next customer, Jackson accessed the voice message Cara had sent to his orb, the microcomputer in his head. "Hey darling. I've been asked to do a forensic consult, so I probably won't be home for dinner. Also, I have something to tell you. Speak later. Love you."

Something to tell him? Her tone was flat when she said that, so Jackson couldn't tell if it was good or bad. If it was good, then it could be that they'd had a response from the adoption agency after months of delays. If it was bad, it could be that her mum was ill again. For the rest of the day, Jackson kept his fingers crossed for the former.

Dr Cara Montgomery invited the next patient into her clinic room at Aberdeenshire State Hospital. She felt like she had seen a hundred patients today, but it was only because she was hankering to get home and speak to Jackson.

The patient, Andrew Harris, sat at Cara's desk and described how he had been experiencing frequent headaches, nausea, memory lapses and weakness in his left arm. Cara opened his file on her orb and telepathically transcribed his symptoms. When he had finished, she asked him to lie down on the bio-bed for a body scan.

Mr Harris went to lie down. Cara accessed the bed's controls and, like a metal creature waking and spreading its limbs, the machinery hanging above the bed shifted. Large steel arms clawed out of the mesh, connected to a cylindrical canister. The canister descended towards Mr Harris's feet and moved slowly up his body with a low hum. Cara analysed the readings it produced on her orb.

When the cylinder had finished scanning, the metal creature contracted and returned to its slumber, and Mr Harris sat up on the bed.

"So?" he said. "What's the damage?"

"You have a grade-four brain tumour that's spread to your spinal cord."

"Really?" Mr Harris's eyes were wide and fixed but as the news registered, they softened, his shoulders loosening as relief visibly skittered through him and blew past his lips. "Oh, thank goodness for that. I thought it might be Lassian's disease."

Cara thought about how her mum had battled Lassian's last year and *only just* beat it. It had been touch and go for a fair few months. "Count yourself lucky," she said, smiling. "Can you come back tomorrow for cellular reprogramming?"

Mr Harris nodded.

"Great." Cara arranged an appointment for Mr Harris at the cancer treatment centre through her orb. "I've booked an appointment with Dr Adelman for tomorrow afternoon at 3.20pm, and I've sent you a treatment card."

Mr Harris's eyes glowed yellow as he checked his orb. "Yep, I've got it. Thank you, Dr Montgomery."

"You're welcome."

Three more patients later, Cara was preparing to head home for the day when Dr Perrineau stopped by her room. "Any chance you can do a forensic consult before you go?"

"What case?" Cara asked.

"Dream theft," said Perrineau. "Scotland Police need us to confirm the brain wave patterns."

Cara would be late home, but she didn't like to turn work down, not when she was hoping for a promotion to senior consultant before the end of the year. Telling Jackson her news would have to wait. "Sure," she said. "No problem."

"Thanks. I'll get the files sent over to your orb right away."

Cara finished sterilising her equipment and sat down at her desk. She recorded a voice message on her orb to send to Jackson. "Hey darling. I've been asked to do a forensic consult..."

After the message was sent, Cara logged into Aberdeen State Hospital Forensic Service. Sitting at her desk and munching on a brownie, she spent the next hour analysing brain wave pattern readouts and determining that the accused man had hacked into and downloaded his now-ex-wife's sex dreams about her previous partners.

At 9pm, Cara finally logged off and made a dash through heavy rain to her shuttle in the parking lot. The shuttle flew over a wet landscape draped in moonless winter night and, sensors showed, a dense coastal fog that had drifted inland and was making it impossible to see any of the lights of Aberdeenshire. Her shuttle meeting some congestion in the airways, Cara took the opportunity to phone her mum.

Danica Montgomery's smiling face filled Cara's field of vision. A deep warmth rippled in Cara's chest. She was so glad her mum was still with them.

"Hi love," said Danica. "Another late one?"

"Yep. Good day, though. I had to do a dream theft forensic consult. That's why I'm late."

"I think your father stole my dreams once. Could never prove it though."

"I doubt it, Mother. Dad wouldn't do that."

Danica's eyes flared. "Your father was no angel, Cara!" Then her expression softened. "I did love him, though. The big idiot. I still miss him."

"I know, Mum. Me too." Her mum and dad had had a *complicated* relationship, that was for sure. She decided to move the topic along; she didn't want Danica getting upset, which tended to happen any time the conversation turned to Cara's father. "How was that symposium on faster-than-light reactors?"

Danica hesitated and said, "Er– actually, I didn't quite make it to the symposium." Her expression and voice were sheepish, like she knew she'd done wrong. "I've, er, just been in the hospital for a couple of days."

"What?" A flush of concern, mixed with annoyance, made Cara's pitch rise. "Why the hell didn't you tell me?"

"I didn't see any point in worrying you, darling."

Cara simmered down, realising she'd done exactly the same thing to Jackson and that this was where she got it from. "What happened?"

"Just a very teeny-tiny shuttle collision."

"What!"

"It's fine, darling. The doctors have fixed all my broken bones and my insurance will cover the shuttle. I'm fine. Hospital gave me a clean bill of health and discharged me this afternoon. Nothing to worry about."

Cara gave a heavy, disapproving sigh. "I'm glad you're okay. But you should've told me you were in an accident." Cara swallowed. *Just like I should've told Jackson.*

"You're right. I'm sorry. You know what I'm like. What about you? Any news?"

Cara took a slow breath in. She knew she was asking about the adoption agency. Things had changed so much since then. "None yet."

Yes, it was a lie. And a massively hypocritical one. That said, she had to tell Jackson first. She'd kept it from him for long enough.

As Cara's shuttle began its descent into the little seaside town of Roslaig, Cara wrapped up the conversation. Her shuttle landed on the driveway in front of the beachfront stone and waxiglass cottage where she and Jackson had lived for the past four years. The rain still coming down like a merciless barrage of lances, Cara ran indoors.

Jackson lay on the sofa, cuddling a cushion, a bowl of leftover vegetable casserole on the coffee table in front of him. His eyes were glowing yellow, which meant he was probably watching another episode of that alternate history show on his orb. It was about a world where the Global Accord never happened, the United States of Earth never formed, and the world still had national governments fighting over religion, territory, climate change and whatever else they could. It wasn't Cara's cup of tea. Too much war.

When Jackson saw Cara, he paused the show, eyes returning to their normal brown, and leapt off the sofa. "Hey!"

"Hey love."

His eyes darted all over her face, clearly trying to figure out whether the news was good or bad. "So? Out with it.

I've been on tenterhooks ever since your message."

Cara took a deep breath. "I'm pregnant."

Jackson's thick eyebrows shot up into his forehead, then plunged into a contiguous black V. "Wait– what?"

Cara nodded, repeating, "I'm pregnant."

"But how? How is that possible? You're... you're infertile!"

"I, er... I *was*."

"What are you talking about?"

"You remember that uterine reconstruction procedure we looked into?"

Jackson's frown deepened. "The super-dangerous one?"

"Yeah. Well, I... I underwent the procedure three months ago."

Jackson's voice rose. "What?"

"I just... I needed to give it a try. The important thing is, it worked. I'm pregnant."

"You underwent a life-threatening treatment without telling me?"

"Yeah."

Jackson's face flushed scarlet. "Why? Why would you do that? What about the adoption agency?"

"They... they rejected our application back in November."

Her husband's eyes almost popped out as he blared, "What!"

"I didn't have the heart to tell you. It broke my heart when they told me. I wanted to spare you the pain and find a way of giving us both a child. Now I have, and now I can."

"You could've died, Cara!"

"That's exactly why I didn't tell you. I didn't want you to worry." She swallowed, remembering that her mum had just said the same thing to her and she'd had a go at her for it.

Jackson shook his head in what looked like disbelief. "I'm your husband – it's my job to worry! Whatever happened to basic husband and wife honesty?"

"I just knew you would've tried to talk me out of it."

"Yeah, I would've. We could've tried other adoption agencies."

"I didn't want to get rejected again."

"Then we should've made that call together. This isn't just about you, you know."

A stab of guilt hit Cara in the chest. She knew in that instant that she'd made the wrong call.

"I'm sorry, okay. I am. I shouldn't have kept it from you. But shouldn't we be celebrating? We're having a baby."

Jackson brushed past her and stormed upstairs to their bedroom. Even though she knew he'd slam the door, she still flinched when he did.

Cara warmed up some of the vegetable casserole Jackson had made and slumped down on the sofa, kicking herself for not telling him, realising how selfish she'd been. They were married, after all. They were in this together. She should never have shut him out.

When she'd finished eating, she went into the kitchen to synthesise a cup of chamomile tea and a bowl of snow pudding, Jackson's favourite dessert. She also synthesised a dark chocolate heart with a picture of a hand clutching a penis and the words *I'm sorry for being a wanker* drizzled in white chocolate, which she set on top of the pudding.

She carried the tea and pudding upstairs, opening their bedroom door tentatively. Jackson was on their bed, eyes yellow and watching something on his orb again. This time he ignored her.

"Baby, I brought you something."

Eyes brown again, Jackson faced her. She put the tea on his bedside table and handed him the bowl of snow pudding.

A giggle escaped his lips and Cara felt a flood of relief. He said quietly with a smirk, "You *are* a wanker."

She nodded sheepishly. "A big wanker."

"Really big."

"Huge."

His smirk widened into a grin. "Let's hope our daughter is less of a wanker."

"She will be." Raising an eyebrow, "Wait– I haven't told you it's a girl."

"I know. I just have this feeling. Am I right?"

Cara nodded, smiling.

Jackson pumped his fist. "And she's okay? How many weeks gone are you?"

"Four weeks. And she's great. Still just a sack of cells at the moment, but the doctor ran a microcellular scan and said the cells are good and she's got strong, healthy genes."

Jackson nodded. "Good."

Cara stooped to kiss him. "I'm sorry."

He kissed her back. "Just promise me you'll *never* keep something like that from me again. We're supposed to be a team."

She sighed. "I know. I won't. I promise."

He kissed her again and she folded into his arms. The light in the room was low, shadows playing on every wall, easing their fall into the moment. Cara lost herself in his mouth, their warm tongues dancing together in perfect rhythm, her body throbbing with anticipation as he ran his fingers through her hair, across her neck and down her chest. Shirts, trousers and underwear slid off like the rain against the windows and soon they were making the kind of intense, rapturous love that they did on their early dates, lasting into the small hours.

The next morning, they awoke early and decided to go for a pre-breakfast walk along the beach. It was cold and drizzly and the thick fog from last night continued to press down on Roslaig. It was Cara's favourite type of weather. Jackson's less so, but after last night, if Cara asked him to run naked through a blizzard, he probably would.

Walking out of their paved rear garden onto the beach, they couldn't tell if the tide was in or out. The fog had completely engulfed the sea and the fractured red granite cliffs looming out over it like intentionally placed monuments, allowing them only a few metres of sight in every direction. Holding hands, they walked forwards to find the water's edge, the powdery white sand bracingly cool and damp beneath their bare feet. Behind them, their house faded like dust brushed away by the wind.

After a moment spent drinking in the spray in the air and trying to gauge how far the waves were, from the sound of their crashing, Cara looked at Jackson and smiled.

Jackson was already looking at something straight ahead and squinting slightly with confusion. "What was that?"

Her eyes followed his. She couldn't see anything but the grey-white curtain that encircled and moved with them as they walked. "What was what?"

"I just saw something."

She looked into the fog again. "A dog?" There were a lot of wild dogs around here.

"No." Then he stopped and pointed, whispering, "Look– there."

Cara ground her heels into the sand and peered forwards. She saw something – a flicker of movement ahead – but too briefly to even guess what it was.

"It's probably just someone out for a walk like we are." She tugged on his arm and they continued walking.

Something white – whiter than the fog – flitted past in front of them. Fast. Cara only glimpsed it, but it was long and slender, like a limb. A white limb. Whatever it was, it was running.

She stopped. So did Jackson.

"Did you see it?" he said.

She frowned, staring ahead. "I saw... something."

Cara's chest tightened as they glanced around.

A white shape moved quickly in the fog again – to their left. And again, to their right. With the movements came a soft padding of feet, or paws, or hooves. Or *something*. And then a strange clicking, like somebody cracking their knuckles.

Cara's breathing quickened. "I don't think we're alone."

"Let's head back."

They turned and started back to the house.

More footsteps behind them. More clicking. Louder. Closer.

They're right behind us.

Hand in hand, Cara and Jackson walked faster. The padding got faster too. They were following them, matching their speed. *Chasing them.* Cara threw a fleeting look over her shoulder, but their pursuers were still hidden by fog.

Cara's heart thudded. She and Jackson shot each other a quick glance, silently agreeing to run. Disentangling their fingers, they sprinted forwards, kicking up sand as they went.

The 'things' – whatever they were – ran after them.

They stayed close to each other, but Jackson was faster and every few seconds parts of him disappeared behind clumps of fog. He kept glancing back to check Cara was close.

Something sprang onto Jackson's back. A mass of jointed limbs – different lengths and thicknesses – flailing wildly. Cara didn't see a head or a body, but thought she saw a bunch of finger-like digits at the end of one of the limbs.

"Jackson!"

She stopped, feet submerged in cold wet sand. Jackson went down. He and the thing on his back fell behind a curtain of fog.

Cara walked towards Jackson, tentatively, jaw clenched, teeth squeaking.

Fog clearing, she saw Jackson on his knees and caught the briefest glimpse of the mass of limbs scuttling away. It was no taller than a dog.

"Jackson! Are you alright?"

She placed one hand on his shoulder, the other on his upper arm, and helped him to his feet. A grimace of pain and confusion twisted his face.

"Wh– what just happ– *aaaahhh!*" His question turning abruptly into a loud, deep groan, he doubled over, clutching his middle like he'd just taken a solid punch in the gut. He dropped to his knees again, his arm yanked out of Cara's grip.

"Jackson! Jackson, talk to me!"

On all fours, Jackson started retching.

Cara crouched down. "Jackson?"

He heaved, choked, trying hard to throw up, but nothing was coming out. His fingers clawed the sand desperately.

But then Jackson's throat started to bulge and swell. Something was travelling up it, distending it from the inside.

Jackson's mouth snapped wide. Wider than it should. Something dark and red erupted from his lips.

Oh my God oh my God oh my God.

The moist sound of flesh on flesh curdled Cara's blood. She watched, hand cupped over her mouth, as a long, red, sticky mass pulled itself from Jackson's throat and fell in a heap on the sand.

Jackson froze, staring at the thing he'd just vomited, his hands half-buried in the sand.

Every cell in Cara's body went cold. The red mass writhed out from underneath its host. The bleak daylight revealed it. Pouches of flesh, darkened by a crimson slime, entangled in what looked like thick strings of sausages, now slithering seawards across the sand, leaving a stinking trail of blood and bodily fluids in its wake. At first Cara thought it a creature. It wasn't. The sacks of flesh were a heart, a stomach, lungs, and the long snake-like appendages they were wrapped in… bowels.

Viscera. Jackson had puked up his organs. And they were alive. But not in the way that they should've been.

A moment later, Jackson toppled onto his side, eyes and mouth agape. His jaw looked broken, his mouth hanging wider than it should, his teeth, lips and chin smeared with blood and bits of flesh.

Cara wanted to vomit, cry, scream, pass out. Her body wasn't sure which to do first. In the meantime she just stood there, motionless, feeling all the blood drain from her face and her heart as she watched her husband's insides crawl slowly away from his corpse.

More padding and clicking. Her eyes shot up to the fog.

Her heart stopped.

Lots of long, white, gleaming limbs were scrambling about in the fog up ahead. It was still too thick to make out any shapes or features, or how many there were, but again she could see that some of the limbs terminated in finger-like protrusions. Some looked as tall as her, others as big as the one that had latched onto Jackson. Or perhaps they were the same, just bent low to the ground.

"*Should we kill her?*" a chorus of voices whispered. Dozens, maybe hundreds, whispering together in perfect unison.

"*She has an embryo inside her,*" more voices whispered.

Clicking behind her made her wheel round on her heels. White limbs scuttled fast over the sand, lost in the haze.

"*We should wait till it's born – then come back and kill them both!*"

Cara shivered.

The voices laughed.

"*Yes! Let's do that!*"

More laughter. Cara's fingernails dug painfully into her palms, tendons stretched white over her knuckles. A mix of fear, horror and anger coursed through her.

Then the laughter, the clicking and the padding started to fade into the crash of waves and squeal of wind. Whatever those creatures were, they were gone now.

Cara looked down. Jackson's viscera had disappeared into the fog, a patchy track of coagulating blood drifting towards the sea.

Cara knelt down next to his body, lifted his cold right hand out of the sand, entwined her fingers in his.

And stared emptily into the mist.

2

June 10th 1895

Seventeen-year-old Harriet Turner shook her head at the fascia sign above the new barber shop on Whitechapel High Street. Squeezing her hands into fists, she crossed the road and thundered into the shop, ignoring the 'opening soon' notice on the door.

A man in his forties, perhaps early fifties, in a grey, double-breasted waistcoat over a white shirt, looked up from behind a stack of boxes he was in the middle of unloading. The man, whose name, Harriet had heard, was Frederick Gleeson, looked like he was from the continent, with tanned skin and dark, dishevelled hair crying out for his own services. Harriet's eyes flitted to the barber's chair shadowed in the corner. Its frayed and dusty brown leather backrest and arms and tarnished brass footplate made it look like the dentist's chair at South Grove Workhouse, where she'd had a molar yanked out with pliers – one of the most awful experiences of her life.

"Er– sorry," said Mr Gleeson. "I'm not quite open yet. And, er, I'm afraid I only cut men's hair."

The man had an unusual accent. Having never left London or spoken to non-Londoners, she couldn't place it. Scowling fiercely, she replied, "You're not likely to be cutting anyone's hair, Mister."

Mr Gleeson looked confused. "How's that?"

"Because you've already offended half of Whitechapel. Including me."

He shook his head. "I–" His neck undulated in a nervous swallow. "Why? How?"

"Because of what you've named your shop."

"*Jack the Clipper?* I thought it was clever. My name isn't Jack, but I didn't think that would matter."

This man was either a heartless brute or very, *very* naïve. "It's less than seven years since Jack the Ripper stalked these streets murdering women. What in Heaven's name possessed you to name your shop after that monster?"

Mr Gleeson's face flushed crimson. Hopefully it was starting to sink in. He stepped out from behind his boxes and walked over to Harriet.

"Gosh. I– I didn't…" His eyes flickered with guilt. "I didn't think."

Harriet raised both eyebrows. "Clearly."

He sighed, looked at Harriet and held out a dusty hand. "I'm Frederick Gleeson – Fred. Pleased to meet you."

"I know who you are." She shook Fred's hand. "Harriet Turner. And I wish I could say the same."

Fred's eyes lit up. "You're the girl who recites the poems outside the Pavilion Theatre. I was passing the other night, heard a few of them. They're good. Sad. But good."

"Thank you." His compliment warmed her, but Harriet tried not to let any hint of a smile leak into her scowl. He couldn't have been a dunce if he was perceptive to the subtext-hidden sadness in her latest recitals. With her mother being so ill, her poems had become an emotional outlet for her – as well as a bit of extra coin.

Fred gave another nervous swallow. "So you're saying everybody round these parts already thinks I'm a shit-sack? That I've frightened off all my customers before I've even opened?"

"That depends on how quickly you replace your sign."

Fred nodded. "You're right. I'm not from around here. I came down to London for a change of pace. Heard about the Jack the Ripper killings when I arrived and the name just came to me. I guess I didn't think it would still be so raw for people."

16

"Well it is. Everyone remembers the horror of what he did, and everyone still feels the fear that one day he could come back. Especially me."

Fred frowned. "Why you?"

Harriet hesitated.

Fred picked up on her silence. "Oh, gosh. He killed someone you knew, didn't he? I'm so sorry."

"No, it's not that. I… met him. That's all." The words just came out. Even though Harriet had made a promise to her mother to stop telling people she had met Jack the Ripper, here she was, breaking it again. Honestly, though, she had no shame telling people about her encounter with Jack. If they didn't believe her, that was *their* problem. Because it was real; it happened.

Fred's eyes sprang wide and Harriet backtracked quickly. "Never mind. Forget I said that."

"You *met* Jack the Ripper? I thought he was never found."

"He wasn't. He disappeared right after I met him."

Fred stared at her with a soft frown. He appeared to be trying to make out whether she was telling the truth, but Harriet wasn't interested in trying to convince him. She had nothing to prove.

"You don't believe me," she said. "That's fine. No one does. I'll be going now." She turned to leave.

"I didn't say I didn't believe you, did I?"

Harriet stopped and half-turned to face him. "So you *do* believe me?"

"Well I don't know. I only met you two minutes ago and all I know about you is that you write nice poetry and you, well…" He looked her up and down, noting her old bonnet and ripped frock that was a dark enough green to hide most but not all of the stains, and her bare, dirty, calloused feet, and blushed slightly. "I assume you live on the streets."

"Sometimes, yes. Not always."

He smiled. "I must say, you're very well spoken for a *mostly* homeless person."

"I have my mother to thank for that. She's always made

sure I speak properly." And Emma Turner was only homeless because Harriet's rich grandparents had kicked her out – not that Fred needed to know that.

He nodded. "So tell me."

"About Jack?"

"Yes."

"Why are you so interested?"

"You were the one who brought it up. Would you expect me not to be interested after you tell me you met one of the world's most notorious serial killers?"

Harriet frowned. "I thought you said you only heard about Jack when you arrived here?"

Fred's eyebrows flickered. "I... did. It's just something... something I've heard people say."

Do people say that? To be fair, the things the Ripper did probably had made him 'notorious' in other parts of the world. And Fred didn't look like he'd been born in England.

"I should be going," Harriet said. "Good day, Mr Gleeson."

As Harriet continued towards the door, she passed an open box that seemed to be full of books. This man clearly had a lot of money to have afforded so many. Did barbers even make that much? He must have run a very successful business wherever he lived before.

A book lying on top of the stack drew Harriet's eye. *The Time Machine* by H.G. Wells. Harriet had seen it advertised in the window of a bookshop, with a sign beneath it reading: *Time-travel into the distant future for a marvellous adventure!* Seeing it had sent her thoughts hurtling back to her bizarre encounter with Jack the Ripper, in St Mary Matfelon church in 1888.

Before reaching for the door handle, Harriet paused. "Are you interested in time travel, Mr Gleeson?" she asked, turning round.

Fred's brown cheeks reddened. "Time travel?" he said uncomfortably. "Why do you ask?"

Harriet gestured to the box of books. "Because I noticed you have a copy of H.G. Wells' book."

He shot a puff of air through his nostrils and walked over to the box. "Ah, yes. Of course." He picked up the book. "It came out a week or so ago and everyone was talking about it, so I just had to get it. It's about an inventor who believes that time is simply another dimension, a fourth dimension, builds a machine to move through it, and uses it to travel into the far future to discover what has become of humanity. Here." He handed the book to Harriet and she traced her finger over the title, author's name and the drawing of a sphinx embossed on the front of its pale brown cloth cover.

"Do you think..." Harriet hesitated and spoke her next words more quietly, her reluctance to say them draining the vigour from her voice. "Do you think... it's possible?"

"Do I think *what's* possible?"

"Time travel. Travelling into the future."

Fred gave a slow, thoughtful shrug. "Well, I– I don't know. Could be, I suppose. Why?"

"Because I think..." She swallowed, again unsure whether to say it. Her mother would've scolded her if she were here.

But she isn't, Harriet, so what's the harm? "I think that's where Jack the Ripper went."

Fred frowned. "The future?"

"Yeah."

"Why do you think that?"

"Because I heard him speaking to someone on a kind of telephone, saying peculiar things about timelines and 'returning to the future', right before he disappeared."

Fred blinked several times, silent.

"You think I'm talking tommy rot." Harriet handed *The Time Machine* back to the barber and reached for the door handle. "Good day, Mr Gleeson."

He stepped forwards. "Wait. I'm just processing what you're saying, that's all."

She stopped before grabbing the handle and peered silently into his eyes, which stared off thoughtfully. She had told a number of people her theory about what happened to Jack the Ripper and although everyone had rebuffed her, she still clung to a slim hope that someone, someday, might *not* think she was speaking nonsense.

Fred looked at her, ready to give his appraisal. "It's an intriguing idea. If Jack the Ripper really did travel to the future, that would explain why the police still haven't found him."

Was he just humouring her or did he actually believe her? Harriet couldn't tell. His face was kind and amiable, but it told no secrets.

"Would you like a cup of tea?" Fred asked. "I haven't got to know many people since I arrived here and, well, it's the least I can do after you warned me about my sign and have hopefully saved me from an embarrassingly quiet opening day."

Harriet regarded him. *What an odd afternoon this is turning into.* But she could hardly say no to a free cup of tea, and replied after a brief pause, "Erm, yeah. Okay. Yes, please."

Fred pulled up a couple of dusty chairs that were in amongst the boxes and plonked them in the middle of the floor. Harriet sat down as Fred opened one of the boxes, dug through its contents, and pulled out a cast-iron kettle. He then found a couple of cups and spoons and went into a room at the back, evidently a kitchen. Harriet listened to the rumble and eventual whistle of the kettle as it boiled.

He brought her a cup that steamed enticingly and sat down in the chair opposite her. "So, what actually happened between you and the Ripper?"

It was funny. She had come in here expecting a fight – something she would never shy away from, not if a point needed making. Harriet had learned not to take shit from anyone. She'd had to, living on the streets, dealing with all kinds of ruffians and having to take up arms to protect herself and her mother. She found it easy now, confrontation. *Too* easy, sometimes. Harriet's mother often said that her mouth and her manner would get her killed one of these days.

But Fred... golly, he was a strange one. His kind face

and mild manner were not at all like she had expected, particularly after naming his shop 'Jack the Clipper'. Having met him, that really did seem a genuine act of naivety from someone not from the area.

"I went to my church, to pray for the soul of Mary Jane Kelly, the Ripper's latest victim," said Harriet, taking a gulp of her tea. "And I found him… He was… I found him doing something unspeakable in there. And there was a briefcase. He had a briefcase that had human organs in it."

"Oh my word," said Fred, his lips curling with the very horror Harriet still felt when she thought about it. "What did you do?"

"I confronted him. He told me his name was Henry Van Deen. I went to fetch a policeman but I stayed to listen to the conversation he was having on his – whatever it was. He spoke about returning to the future; then he went into the room at the back of the church and I followed him, and a big light flashed from inside the room."

"You must've been frightened out of your wits."

That night, still as clear as a bell, would never leave her, but she remembered being more appalled than frightened when she caught him fetching mettle over his gruesome trophies in a house of God, and more curious than frightened when he disappeared.

"Where do you think he went?" Fred asked.

"Well, I went inside the room after the flash and he was gone. And yet he *couldn't* have gone."

Fred frowned. "What do you mean?"

"There was only one door and the windows were too small for a person to crawl through."

"So where did he go?"

Harriet widened her eyes, waiting for Fred to answer that himself based on what she had said earlier.

"Ah," said Fred, realising. "You think he *did* return to the future."

Harriet nodded silently.

Fred stared at his teacup, nodding with her.

"I've always wondered how he could've done it," she said. "He certainly didn't have a machine with him, like in Mr Wells' book."

"Mmm," said Fred. "Maybe he had a different kind of machine."

"Maybe." Harriet couldn't tell if this was no more than an entertaining story to him, but in any case, she was enjoying talking about it with someone who was open-minded, or at least pretending to be open-minded about it.

She realised she'd been gone much longer than intended and stood up, handing Fred her teacup. "Anyway, thank you for listening and not telling me I'm mad, even if you may think it. I should be getting back." She strode to the door, pausing to peruse *The Time Machine* once more.

"You can borrow it if you like," Fred said unexpectedly.

Harriet looked back. "Really?"

He nodded. "I finished it a couple of days ago. Read it in one sitting."

"Why would you trust a homeless girl you've just met with a brand-new book?"

He arched a furry black eyebrow. "Are you saying I shouldn't?"

Harriet frowned. "I'm no thief."

He gave a single nod. "Then *that's* why."

Excitement fluttered in Harriet's belly. The last time she had access to books was during her very brief spell in school, before her mother got ill. All she'd got to read since were newspapers people threw away.

Harriet cracked her first smile since entering the shop. "I'll bring it back as soon as I've read it."

Returning her smile, "No hurry."

"Thank you." She slipped the book into the tatty leather satchel she carried everywhere. "Good day, Mr Gleeson."

"You're welcome. And please, call me Fred. Good day, Miss Turner."

She opened the door, glancing over her shoulder as she left the shop. "Harriet."

Harriet returned to her mother, Emma, who was sleeping upright against the wall of a stable yard under a dirty blanket. The stable yard stood next to Whitechapel High Street's cheapest doss-house, which they hadn't been able to afford a room in for a week now. Fortunately it had been dry and warm, otherwise Harriet and Emma would've been clamouring for a spot under the rank and crowded arches of London Bridge each night.

Harriet had to shoo away a rat chewing hungrily through the wicker seat of her mother's already partly broken wheelchair. Emma stirred momentarily but didn't wake. Harriet's chest ached at the sight of the shadows collecting in her hollowed cheeks, her weary, sunken eyes, the deep creases around her sagging jawline.

Emma had been unwell for as long as Harriet could remember. For many years she had been told, by every doctor around, that the disease she was suffering from was called laziness. Then, five years ago, during their brief return to the South Grove Workhouse, a doctor visiting from America had diagnosed Emma with neurasthenia. Harriet had thought the stars were aligning for her and her mother at last. The diagnosis explained Emma's fatigue, her aches and pains, her changeable appetite, her low mood – everything.

Only none of the treatments prescribed for Emma had worked, and Harriet's spark of hope never caught aflame. Before long, Emma and Harriet were on the streets again. Emma had always had good days and bad, but the good days were much fewer in recent months. Lately it seemed like she was getting weaker, thinner and paler by the day – wasting away before Harriet's eyes.

Harriet earned what she could as a crossing-sweeper and costermonger, the latter being Emma's profession before her illness. And, in the last couple of years, there was her poetry. Still, life was damned expensive. Some weeks they had enough for a few nights in the dosshouses, some weeks, like this one, they didn't. It was an existence Harriet was used to. But the idea that she might soon be living it alone filled her with dread and melancholy.

Harriet sat down next to her mother to read Fred Gleeson's copy of *The Time Machine*. A few minutes later, Emma sensed her presence and awoke slowly.

"What you got there?" she murmured, eyes sleepy and grey.

"It's a book called *The Time Machine*," said Harriet.

Her mother blinked several times. "Time machine?"

"It's about time travel. The new barber, Frederick Gleeson, said I could borrow it. I went into his shop to tell him off for putting up that sign–"

"Oh, Harriet," Emma interrupted. "I told you not to."

"Somebody had to. Anyway, I, er..." She hesitated and took a breath, knowing how her mother would react. "I ended up telling him about when I met Jack the Ripper."

"Oh, Harriet!" There was a bite in her voice. "You promised me you'd stop telling people that."

"It just came up." *All right, I brought it up.* "He seemed interested. He didn't just dismiss me like most people do."

Emma frowned. "I wish you'd leave this time travel thing alone."

"Why?"

"I just do."

Emma closed her eyes again. Harriet resumed reading. Within a minute, her mother had gone back to sleep, snoring gently.

Harriet got to a scene in the book where the unnamed English scientist unveiled his time machine to his dinner guests. *Parts were of nickel, parts of ivory, parts had certainly been filed or sawn out of rock crystal.* Harriet felt captivated as she read of its levers for going forwards and backwards in time, its dials for registering the vehicle's speed, its saddle in the middle for the time traveller to sit on. She found no mention of any pedals or what fuel it used and hankered to know how this thing actually worked.

By the time the scientist began recounting his journey into the far future, wherein he discovered an Earth quite different to the one he left, Harriet's real life had fallen away. She read the book in one sitting and, that afternoon, thought up a new poem about visiting the future. Theatre-goers that night seemed to enjoy it. She earned enough to be able to get some fruit and vegetables from the Spitalfields Market.

The next day, after selling enough to secure her and her mother a room for the night at Finney's doss-house, Harriet rushed back to Fred Gleeson's shop.

When she arrived, Fred was at the top of a ladder with a hammer and nails, erecting a new wooden fascia sign painted with the words: *Shaving the World.*

"Good afternoon, Fred," said Harriet.

Fred peered over his shoulder and down. "Harriet! Like the new name? It's like saving the world but–"

"Yes, I get it," she interrupted, letting a small smile flit over her lips. "Please could I talk to you inside for a moment?"

"Sounds ominous."

"Not ominous. Important."

Fred climbed down the ladder and showed Harriet inside. The small shop was coming along. A thorough dust and polish had made his tired-looking barber's chair shiny and inviting. It had moved from the corner to the centre of the rear wall, in front of a table laid with brushes, blades and a ceramic basin, and a wall-mounted mirror with a tiny crack at the rim. Shelves erected along the other walls held sharpening strops, piles of towels and various pots of creams and lotions, and the chairs they had sat on yesterday had been dusted and shined and positioned close to the door for waiting customers, along with a coat stand. Only a few boxes now waited to be unpacked.

"So, what's so important?" said Fred, setting his tools down on one of the shelves.

"I'd like you to help me find H.G. Wells," said Harriet.

Fred frowned. "The author?"

"Yes."

"Why?"

"Because I want to build a time machine. Like the one in his book."

Fred raised an eyebrow. "Harriet, that book is fiction."

"You don't know that. The science makes sense to me." Not that she knew anything about science, but it *sounded* sensible. "What if Mr Wells actually built the time machine he describes? What if *he* is the time traveller in the story?"

"It's possible, I suppose. Why do you want to travel in time all of a sudden?"

"Because I have to get my mother away from here. I have to get her to a better place. A better... *time*."

"You mean the future?"

"Yeah."

"And what makes you think the future will be better than this? I take it you haven't got to the part with the Eloi and the Morlocks."

"I have. I've read the whole thing. I wouldn't travel as far as that. Just a few years, maybe a decade or so. I'm hoping there'll be a cure for neurasthenia. It's what's killing my mother."

"K-killing?" Fred swallowed and shook his head. "Harriet, I'm– I'm so sorry. I didn't–"

"It's fine," she said quickly. She didn't want his sympathy, only his assistance. "I just need to know if you can help me find Mr Wells. Time travel is the only thing I can think of where my mother might have a chance."

"I'm worried you'll be disappointed, when– *if*– you find out the book's fictional and Mr Wells' time machine isn't real."

"I'm a big girl. I know there's a chance of that. I have to do *something*. Will you help me?"

Fred squinted one eye. "What's in it for me?"

Harriet came prepared for a bargain. "I'll tell everyone I know that your cuts and shaves are first-rate."

Fred grinned and nodded thoughtfully. "That sounds fair."

"Wonderful. How would you suggest contacting him?"

Fred paused to think for a moment. "What I would probably do is write to the publishers and ask if they can give you Mr Wells' address. Then you could write to Mr Wells himself. I have letter-writing materials you can use. And a stamp."

"Thank you. Can I give them this address to respond to?" She could hardly put *the pavement somewhere on Whitechapel High Street.*

"Yes, you may."

"And..." She looked down and fumbled with her hands. She didn't want to push her luck. "Do you think you could maybe write the letters for me? It's just that my handwriting is not good. I wasn't in school long enough to learn how to write well."

Fred blinked wide eyes.

Damn. I'm asking too much. She added, "If you do this, I promise to write a poem about you and your shop for my next recital, encouraging everyone to come for a shave or a haircut at *Shaving the World.*" She had no idea how such a poem would go, but she'd think of something.

Fred's eyes sank into friendly crescents and he smiled warmly. "Well I can hardly say no to that." He was probably just taking pity on a homeless girl, but who cared?

"Thank you," Harriet said. "You're very kind."

"Or just very pliable." He smirked slightly. "Do you have the book with you?"

"Yes." Harriet lifted *The Time Machine* out of her satchel and handed it to him.

He opened it, eyes flickering over the first few pages. "William Heinemann Ltd. Covent Garden. All right. I'll post a letter to them this evening. Come back at the end of the week and I'll let you know if I've had a response."

Harriet nodded, smiling. "I'm very grateful." She cast her eyes around the shop. "When is it you're planning to open? Your shop is shaping up nicely."

"It's getting there. Tomorrow, hopefully."

"Well, I will leave you to get on. Thank you again."

"You're welcome. Good day, Harriet."

"And to you."

Harriet left the shop and crossed the road, heading back to her mother. As she did, a man dressed smartly in a dark grey morning coat and top hat, with a monocle, stepped into her path. She shrank back.

"You a friend of his?" he said, nodding towards Fred's shop.

Harriet frowned. "You mean Fred?"

The man smirked. "*Fred.* So that's what he's calling himself now."

Unease balled in Harriet's gut. "What do you mean?"

"He said anything to you? About where he was before he came here? Or what he did?"

"No. I only met him yesterday."

The man leaned towards her and frowned, about a quarter of his monocle disappearing beneath his left eyebrow.

Harriet shivered and drew a sharp intake of breath. "What?" she asked with a trace of annoyance.

"I'd be careful if I were you. That man is not what he seems." And with that he swept past her, suspicious eyes fixed on Fred's shop as he strode up the road.

3

The ominous warning from the man in the monocle sparked instant speculation in Harriet about what Fred Gleeson might have been involved in before he came to London. Only she didn't have long to ponder. About fifty yards from the stable yard next to Finney's, her mother cried out for her, sounding in pain. Harriet's sense of emergency took over, every other thought scattering. She ran the rest of the way, finding Emma lying sprawled on her front, agony twisting her face.

"Mother!" cried Harriet. "What is it? What's wrong?"

Harriet lifted Emma into a sitting position and fetched their tin flask. Emma's face briefly uncreased as Harriet lifted the flask to her mouth, warping into a new grimace the moment it met her lips, the water spilling down the sides of her mouth onto her dress. She bent forwards, taking a sharp breath in, face reddening, her exhalation breaking into a scream.

Panic speared through Harriet. "Mother– where does it hurt?"

Emma straightened against the wall again, trembling, breathing fast. "H-Harriet... I need... I..."

Harriet's gaze flitted to her mother's legs, the corner of the blanket having come away. She gasped at the sight of her lower right leg and foot, the skin black and yellow, peeling and oozing pus. An awful rot had set in.

"Mother– your leg!"

Emma strained forwards to tug the blanket back over her feet. But it was too late. Harriet knew the truth.

She looked her mother in the eyes. "How long? How long has your leg been like that?"

Her mother squinted, her wrinkled throat rippling as she pushed down a swallow, gulped another breath and choked, "A while." Her voice was barely there.

So *this* was why she'd been so ill lately. "Why didn't you tell me?" Harriet couldn't help the anger that now laced her every word.

"B-because... because I knew... I knew you'd try and fix it."

"We need to get you to a doctor. I'll go and fetch Dr Johnson. He likes us. He'll help."

Emma shook her head, squeezing a firm, "No," past her gasps for breath. "Harriet, this– this is what I'm talking about."

"We can't just do nothing!"

"Listen to me." She tried to steady her breathing. "I've already seen Dr Johnson. A few weeks ago, when you were at a recital. He said" – she coughed and pulled in another breath – "he said I'd need to go to the workhouse infirmary to have my leg amputated. That's not– that's not happening. I've..." She shook her head. "Harriet, I've had enough."

A deep ache spread through Harriet's chest. "You've given up."

"My time has come, my darling. God has given me these precious extra years with you, but now– now I must go to him." Emma looked lovingly at her daughter, tucking a strand of hair behind Harriet's ear and cradling her chin in her hand. "Oh, Harriet, I'm so proud of–" Her words twisted into another cry of pain.

Harriet brought the water back to her lips for a second attempt. This time a small sip made it past them. "Please, mother. Just let me fetch Dr Johnson."

Emma wheezed a gravelled breath. "No, I– I don't... I don't have much time. I need to... tell you something."

"Tell me later. You need to rest."

"No. Harriet – darling – you have to know– the truth."

Her mother's strength was dwindling fast, her ragged

breath growing shallow, her voice fading. Harriet didn't know what to do. Before her eyes her mother's body was coming to a stop, a train chugging into its final station.

"It's… it's about…"

"Mother." Harriet's blood pumped with desperation. "Mother, stay with me."

"That book– that book you're reading… I have to tell you about… the… future…"

"Stay with me."

"I– I have to tell you… I have to tell you w-w-where…"

Emma's words fell into a breath, her head tilted to the side and her hand flopped into her lap. Harriet saw the light leave her mother's eyes and knew she was gone. And yet she still whispered, "Stay with me," over and over, even as the tears started to flow and she folded both arms around her mother in an embrace so tight that ten men could not have parted them.

All night Harriet lay wrapped in her mother's blanket, surrounded by her scant belongings, in the spot where she had died. Even though she could afford that bed at Finney's, and the evening brought spells of rain, she didn't want to move from this place.

Emma's body had been taken by the police to the Whitechapel mortuary earlier that evening. She would be buried in the closest cemetery, probably in a shared grave, with no headstone and no ceremony. Her mother had always told Harriet that, when the moment of her death came, not to be sad about such things. That her soul would go to Heaven and whatever happened to her body didn't matter. Still, it would've been nice to celebrate her life and have a monument to it somewhere, like the rich folk got.

It wasn't till the morning that Harriet's thoughts drifted back to the things Emma had said to her before she died.

She'd said she needed to tell her something. A 'truth', to do with the book she'd been reading and 'the future'.

Harriet looked at the leather satchel hanging from the back of her mother's wheelchair, hesitating. Emma had never let her see the things inside it; she had said that they were her private possessions and 'not for the eyes or hands of children'. Despite the constant itch of curiosity and there being many occasions when Harriet could sneak a look while her mother was sleeping, she had chosen to respect her mother's privacy.

But now she was gone. And Harriet was no longer a child.

She lifted the satchel off the back of the wheelchair and placed it in her lap. She unbuckled the metal clasps, opened the main flap and started combing through the contents.

She pulled out a beautiful silver hairbrush, a bejewelled hair pin, a handkerchief with a festive pattern and crochet lace trim, a string of crystal rosary beads and a leatherbound photograph album.

Anticipation fluttered in Harriet's belly. She didn't know her mother had photographs.

She unbuckled the clasp and opened the album. Most of the pictures were of a man and a woman with a child, a little girl. Harriet assumed that the girl was her mother, the man and the woman her grandparents.

Harriet pushed back the rush of emotion. She had grown up not knowing what her grandparents looked like.

Her grandparents were dressed to reflect their wealth – her grandmother in long gowns with hoop skirts and bustles, her grandfather in patterned waistcoats and bow ties. And their wardrobe was clearly extensive; in every photograph they wore a different outfit. How utterly lavish next to the couple of moth-eaten dresses Harriet and her mother each owned and endlessly switched between. A pinch of guilt wound through Harriet. This was the life her mother had before her. Before she fell pregnant with Harriet out of wedlock and got disowned by Harriet's grandparents, banished from the family home. Left with nothing.

Harriet's guilt morphed quickly into resentment. Resentment and anger. It wasn't Harriet's fault. She was a child. For years she'd blamed her mother's fornicating for their predicament. But God forgave sins, didn't He? And if He could forgive, then why couldn't Harriet's grandparents? Now their daughter was dead, their granddaughter all on her own, and they would likely never know. Because they didn't care.

So fuck them. Fuck them both.

Harriet flipped past any photographs of her grandparents, unable to look at either of their faces for a moment longer. There were some other photographs of people she couldn't identify. Perhaps uncles and aunties, or family friends. And there was a picture, only one, of a younger man with shoulder-length curly hair and a cheeky grin, wearing a light-coloured vest jacket. A stronger surge of emotion shortened her breath as Harriet stared at the man who could well have been her father. Emma had rarely spoken of him, and had never revealed what became of him when she got pregnant. When she had spoken of him, her words were fond, and she had mentioned two features she adored: his cheeky grin and curly hair.

Steadying her breathing, Harriet set the album aside. There were a couple of further items in the satchel at the bottom. Harriet pulled out the first and frowned.

What on earth is this?

Harriet fondled the small, grey, pyramid-shaped device. She shook it gently, close to her ear. Nothing moved inside and even if it did, there didn't seem to be an opening. Then she pushed her finger against the depression in the base and gasped as blue lights started flashing softly around the rim. She held it in her palm, waiting for something to happen, but nothing did, and the flashing stopped. *Curious.*

A final item lay at the bottom of the satchel. A small, lightweight pot with a printed label. This one *did* have something in it. A number of tiny items rattled as Harriet lifted it out. She popped the lid off the top and peered inside. Four capsule-shaped red pills lay at the bottom. She read the name on the label: *Chronozine.* Did Dr Johnson prescribe these?

Hoping for a clue, Harriet inspected the directions beneath the name…

Do not use without a chronode.
Take one tablet only.
Do not use for anything other than time travel.
Do not time-travel without authorisation from the Time Travel Department.
Active ingredient: chronotons.

Harriet's heart missed a beat. She turned the implications over and over in her mind, and as she did, the seeds of a plan began to germinate. She refastened the lid on the pot, piling all the items back into her mother's satchel and slinging it over her shoulder. She folded the blanket and stuffed it into her own bag, which she slung over her other shoulder. Leaving the wheelchair and items of clothing she would no longer need, she parted with the place where her mother's presence had already started to fade, and bolted up the road to *Shaving the World*.

She knocked at the door. Still early, most shops hadn't yet opened. But Harriet couldn't wait.

When there was no answer, she knocked again, for longer, with her fist.

"Just a minute!" cried a voice from inside.

Harriet heard the scratch and clunk of a lock. The door opened and Fred's bright, wide eyes instantly narrowed as they connected with Harriet's.

"Oh, it's you," he said, sighing. "I thought you were my first customer."

"Can we talk?" said Harriet.

"Actually, I–"

Ignoring whatever excuse he was about to raise, Harriet swept past him into the shop.

"Yes, of course, please come in," Fred muttered sarcastically.

"My mother's dead."

"What?" Fred's shoulders and eyes sank. "Shit. Oh, Harriet. I'm so sorry."

A lump of emotion formed in her throat; she swallowed it away. "Thank you."

"Do you... do you want to talk about it?" He looked nervous as he asked, like he was hoping she'd say no, which was fine, because she didn't.

"No." She opened her mother's satchel and pulled out the pot of chronozine. "I want to talk about *this*."

Fred squinted at the pot. "What's that?"

"Something I found amongst my mother's belongings." Handing Fred the pot, "Read it."

Fred's thick eyebrows rose and fell with surprise and confusion as he read the label, his first thoughts no doubt mirroring hers.

"No need to speak to H.G. Wells anymore," said Harriet. "I think I've just found my time machine."

Fred looked at her. "And you say these– these were your mother's?"

Harriet nodded. "Yes. Just before she died, she was trying to tell me something. She said it had to do with the book I was reading. And that she had to tell me about 'the future'." Harriet took the pyramid-shaped object from the satchel and held it out. "This was also amongst her things. I don't know what it is or does, but it doesn't look like anything I've seen or read about. I don't think it is of this time. Look." She pressed the depression in the bottom as she had done before, causing the rim of the base to flash softly.

Fred stared at the object and his face dropped, a deathlike pallor immediately washing over it.

"What's wrong? Have you seen something like this before?"

"I..." He couldn't seem to find the words.

"Fred?"

He shook his head, a bead of sweat forming on it. "No. I've never seen that before."

Harriet frowned. "Then why do you look like you've seen a ghost?"

35

He exhaled deeply, staring off, eyes strained with something troublesome and deep-seated. "It's nothing. Just– just reminds me of something, that's all." He shook off whatever was bothering him and refocused his gaze on Harriet, colour returning to his cheeks. "So you think... you think your mother was a–?"

Harriet nodded. "A time traveller. Yes. She must've used these pills before I was born." She gestured with the pyramidal device. "If this is future technology, then she must've travelled to the future."

"So why didn't she do what *you* were going to do – travel to the future and save herself? And why would she settle for a life on the streets if she had the power to change it?"

"I don't know. Maybe she couldn't. Or maybe she didn't want to leave me. Maybe someone was after her and she was hiding."

Fred gave her a funny look. She had chosen her words carefully, to try to trigger an admission. Although he stayed silent, his expression was admission enough. He was hiding from something too.

Fred popped the lid off the pot of pills and looked inside. He took out a pill and inspected it on his fingertip. He stared silently at the pill with an unreadable expression and Harriet would've given anything to be able to see inside his head.

He broke off his stare. "So what are you going to do?"

"Use them."

"What?"

"I'm going to use the pills to travel in time. Now that Mother's gone, there's nothing left for me here."

Fred dropped the pill back and closed the pot. "Travel in time to *when?*"

"I don't know. I don't know how these pills work. I could end up in the past and see my mother again. Maybe it will be before she got ill and I'll have a chance to save her. Or maybe I'll end up fifty years in the future."

"Or 800,000 years in the future," said Fred, referencing *The Time Machine.*

"Maybe. But any future would be better than here."

"You sure about that? Don't forget the Eloi and the Morlocks. The future could be worse."

"It can't get much worse than this."

"You'd be surprised." He cast a despondent stare around the room and Harriet had a feeling there was more he wanted to say.

"Well, if whatever place in time I end up in is worse, there are three more pills in that pot. Or... *two* more. If you were to come with me."

He whipped his gaze to Harriet, eyebrows beetling over his nose. "What?"

She hesitated and took a breath. "Come with me."

His face stretched in a wide grin and he snorted a laugh. Harriet stayed straight-faced.

His grin shrank quickly into a look of unease. "You're serious."

Harriet nodded, "Yes."

Fred gave a bemused shake of the head and handed the pot of pills back to her. "Why would I go with you?"

"To escape whatever it is you're hiding from."

He stared at her, throat expanding in an uncomfortable swallow, a deep shade of pink rushing to his cheeks. Though his face gave him away again, he continued to say nothing, probably waiting to find out what Harriet knew.

"There's someone in town asking about you," she offered. "He came up to me yesterday in the street, asked me if you'd said anything about where you were or what you did before you came here. He suggested that Fred might not even be your real name. And if that's true, it means you're hiding from something."

Fred pulled in a deep, sober breath but remained silent.

"Look, I don't care what it is. All I'm saying is, these pills could be a way out. For both of us."

Fred looked at her. "But why would you *want* me to go with you? Why... *me?*"

"Because you're the only person who hasn't told me I'm crazy for thinking time travel is real and Jack the Ripper went back to the future. The only person who's

37

ever really listened. Not even my own mother did that, although now I think I know why. Everybody always told me I was talking nonsense – till you."

"But how do you know I'm not lying to you? How do you know you can trust me? That I'm not dangerous? Particularly after what that man said to you."

"I've met a *lot* of bad people in my life. The worst. You're not one of them. I have a good sense about people. Trust me, you encounter all walks of life living on the streets of London. And this foul place has been my home a long time." After a moment, she added, "Plus, if you *did* try anything, I can take care of myself." She lifted her frock to reveal the knife she had strapped to her leg, the knife she had carried with her since she was small, that had saved her from many an ugly situation. "I did accost Jack the Ripper when I was eleven, remember."

Fred smirked. "That you did." Falling silent and pondering Harriet's words, he sat down on one of the chairs for waiting customers, a battle being waged on his face.

Harriet waited a few moments, then said, "Listen. I knew it was unlikely I'd be able to persuade you to come. But don't ask, don't get. I'll go alone if I have to."

Fred gave a vague nod. "I need to think. Give me some time to get my head around this."

"Of course. But I'm not going to wait too long. I don't plan to spend one more night here."

"Give me the day. Come back this evening. I'll let you know what I've decided."

Harriet nodded and left.

Harriet walked by *Shaving the World* a few times through the day. Fred hadn't opened as planned, which made Harriet wonder if he was actually contemplating going with her. She wandered the East End, sitting by the Thames and watching the steamers passing under Tower Bridge, re-evaluating conversations she'd had with her mother.

She remembered when she told her about the Ripper being a time traveller from the future, how uncomfortable her mother had seemed talking about it. At the time, Harriet had presumed it was because she just didn't believe her – that she didn't want her to get caught up in a wayward fantasy. But now...

Shortly before 4pm, Harriet returned to Fred's shop. It was earlier than they had agreed, and Harriet offered to come back later if he needed more time, but Fred let her in anyway – silently and without meeting her eyes. A travel trunk lay in the middle of the floor and a couple of shelves had been cleared, although most of Fred's barber paraphernalia remained.

Looking around, Fred said, "I guess I'll have to leave all this stuff here, which is a shame. Paid good money for it."

Harriet felt a flush of delight. *He's coming with me.*

"I'm taking this trunk of essentials, though," Fred said determinedly, frowning as he added, "If I can, that is."

Harriet wasn't sure if any of their belongings would go with them. Harriet hoped they would; she had her mother's satchel on her shoulder, containing the only things she had left of her. But who knew how these pills worked? Would their *clothes* even travel with them, or would they end up naked somewhere? *Let's hope time travel protects your modesty.*

"Thank you," said Harriet softly. "For agreeing to come with me."

He nodded, smiling without conviction. Harriet wondered if the only reason he was doing this was because of the man who had come asking about him, but reminded herself that Fred's motives weren't her business, or her concern.

She handed each of them a pill. Fred picked up his trunk and, on three, they swallowed them. Taking Fred's hand, Harriet prayed silently that the Lord would take her to a time where she might be reunited with her mother before she became ill.

A loud humming permeated her ears, her own voice drowned by it. The room fell into a whitish, dreamlike haze, suddenly and impossibly filled with dozens, maybe *hundreds*, of people. All blurry, indistinct, transparent – ghosts – walking into and through each other. She shook her head, dizziness billowing over her like a great wind.

I'm dead. This is Heaven.

She blinked several times, harder each time. The fog of ghosts remained. Her gaze sank. A thin mist coated the floor and her feet, although themselves still solid, couldn't feel it. It was like she was floating in midair.

She looked at the hand still entwined in Fred's, realising she was squeezing it. Both hands still solid. The rest of him solid, too. It looked like she and Fred were the only things that were.

"Are you all right?" Harriet shouted over the humming.

Fred nodded slowly, eyes roaming the room. He looked calm, considering.

Something in the corner of Harriet's eye tugged her gaze to the door. Or at least where the door used to be; right now it was a blur, overlaid with a cloud of ghosts and motion.

She and Fred *weren't* the only solid things in the room. There was something else.

Harriet peered into the haze.

Writhing around on the floor was a snake. A snake with shiny, blood-red scales and stark yellow eyes, cutting through the blur. Harriet blinked, rubbed her eyes with her free hand, stared. The snake was slithering slowly and mindlessly, round and round, in the same spot, its head getting closer and closer to its tail.

Then, as Harriet watched, the snake's jaws opened and clamped around its tail. It continued circling the floor, a solid hoop of snake. Harriet shivered. The hoop was getting smaller, the snake walking its jaws over its tail, ratcheting it deeper and deeper into its throat. Swallowing its tail like it would its prey.

"Fred… do you see that… snake…" Harriet murmured.

Before Fred could answer the whole room fell away, Harriet's head spinning into a vast mantle of white.

4

November 15th 2024

Dr Samantha Neether found it strange living in a world where there were two of her. In the same city. While she worked in, or rather, beneath, the imposing Brutalist skyscraper that was Million Eyes' headquarters in Central London, her five-years-younger self worked at LIPA – the London Institute of Palaeontology and Archaeology – just a few miles further up the Thames. But it was as comforting as it was strange. Dr Neether would still, on occasion, catch a train to her younger self's house, mainly so she could see Georgia, her daughter, whose death was still two years away. Sure, it meant seeing her husband sometimes too – the noxious piece of shit who would cheat on her and, deservedly, end up dead himself just months after they lost Georgia. But seeing her beautiful daughter alive again made up for that.

Dr Neether had been living in her past for three years now, working in Million Eyes' top-secret Time Travel Department, doing her bit for the Mission. Namely, saving the human race from destruction by the Shapeless in the 23rd century. Not that she cared much about that, not really. Humanity deserved to perish. But Georgia didn't. Changing her daughter's fate remained the secret drive behind her work. Finding a cure for necrocythemia and using Million Eyes' own time travel technology to save Georgia's life. *That* kept her from leaping in front of a train each day. Nothing else. Just that.

Still, she had to feign concern for the Mission. Pretend

to care about the Apocalypse. Pretend she didn't still loathe the woman in charge of everything, Erica Morgan. It was the only way to keep her job and remain in a position to save Georgia.

So far, Dr Neether had performed rather excellently. If she'd known acting would come so naturally to her, she might have gone to Hollywood in search of movie stardom instead of becoming a scientist. Sitting in her office in Time Travel that morning, chomping on a bagel, she laughed inwardly at the thought.

A knock at the door made her look up from her MEc.

"Come in." Her voice came out a gravelly croak. She was used to it now.

The head of Time Travel, Carina Boone, opened the door. "Morning."

"Good morning, Miss Boone," said Dr Neether. "How can I help?"

Boone came in and closed the door behind her. She stood in front of the door and let out a deep sigh. Clearly something was troubling her. "Morchower's back from 2222."

Dr Neether nodded. Boone's gaze drifted unsubtly across the side of Dr Neether's face that was missing – the skin-grafted cavity where an eye, ear and cheek used to be.

"Sorry, do I have bagel on my face?" Dr Neether pretended to brush off crumbs with her hand.

Boone met her one good eye again, eyebrows dipping slightly in confusion. "No."

Then stop fucking staring. "Good. Please go on."

Boone folded her arms and began tapping her fingers against her elbow. She sighed again, her gaze now wandering aimlessly around the room before returning to Dr Neether. "We're still losing the war."

Million Eyes made only rare trips to the time of the Last War. It was too dangerous and most operatives never returned. What little intelligence they had managed to gather from those years revealed one important fact. The Shapeless were real. For centuries all Million Eyes had ever known about these creatures was what was written in the scrolls of Dr Jesus M. Hirschfield, the man who had unwittingly bestowed Christianity on the world.

Actually, no. *Two* important facts. The other was that everything Million Eyes were doing in the present to defeat the Shapeless in the future... wasn't working. Because every time they visited the future, nothing had changed. Nothing substantive, anyway.

Not that Dr Neether much cared whether humanity lived or died. It was more a case of scientific curiosity; how their actions in the past were affecting events in the future intrigued her. If Morchower were to have found 2222 Earth war- and Shapeless-free, with humanity thriving, then it would mean that the Mission would ultimately succeed. Thus far, that had never happened. Every visit they made, Earth was still war-*torn*, humanity still dying. Did that mean they were doomed to failure? Or had they just not yet found the solution that would set them on the right path?

"Well – we keep going," said Dr Neether. "As we've always done."

Boone shook her head, her eyes glazing over with a look of defeat. She pulled the chair out from in front of Dr Neether's desk and sat down in it, unexpectedly. Dr Neether got the impression this woman was going to confide in her, something that had never happened before.

"Are... are you alright, ma'am?" Dr Neether said gently.

Boone sat slumped in her seat, shoulders drooped like someone had let the air out of her. "What if it isn't working? Everything we're doing? What if we can't change the future?"

"We *can* change the future. We've already made changes. We've seen them."

Boone shook her head. "But we haven't changed *that* future. We haven't stopped the Last War. The Apocalypse. Our destruction at the hands of the Shapeless. The whole reason any of us are even here."

Speak for yourself.

"Nothing we've done in the past thousand years has made one iota of difference to that future," Boone continued. "It still happens. What if we can't stop it? What if that particular future is written? Pre-destined?"

Dr Neether paused. "I suppose it is theoretically possible."

Boone frowned, and her eyes dawdled over the broken side of Dr Neether's face once again. "Doesn't that bother you?"

What bothers me is when you stare at my goddamn face. "I try not to lose sleep over the mysteries of time."

Boone arched her eyebrows. "That surprises me."

"Why?"

"You're a scientist."

It was a fair point. Scientists loved solving mysteries. And for the past three years, Dr Neether had been working closely with science's biggest one: the Ratheri – a red cloud of pure chronotonic energy that Million Eyes kept a sample of in a tank in *Chronozine Production.* However, the Ratheri, and time travel itself, defied so many scientific principles – not to mention basic logic – that Dr Neether had given up trying to understand all the whys and wherefores of it some time ago.

Boone's words made Dr Neether realise something else. Her enthusiasm for science wasn't what it used to be. To be honest, it had been waning a little bit each day since she lost Georgia. Maybe it might come back? Who knew. Right now, Dr Neether was going through the motions because, frankly, the only thing she really gave a shit about anymore was dead and buried. For now.

She spun some bullshit to cover her apathy. "Science is full of mysteries. I can't get hung up on all of them. Neither should you."

"I'm the head of the Time Travel Department. It's my job."

Dr Neether tried to clear her throat, but a thick lump of phlegm was lodged in it. "Alright. But all we know at this point is that our efforts aren't working *yet.* Somewhere down the line, I believe they will." Did she believe that? She wasn't sure. At this point, she just wanted Boone to get the hell out of her office. "But we don't know how far we have to get down that line before those changes happen."

Boone nodded but had discontent all over her face. She stood up and left Dr Neether's office without saying anything else. Dr Neether muttered sarcastically, "You're welcome. Great chat."

A little while later, Dr Neether found herself dwelling on her and Boone's conversation. She felt the scientist within her stirring awake as she contemplated whether the reason they were not yet on a path to a different future was because they were going about this all wrong.

She had an idea.

Parking her other work, she spent the next few hours cultivating her idea into a plan. Then she checked that Miss Morgan was available and went up in the lift to the C-Suite.

She knocked at the door to Miss Morgan's office. A low murmur, "Enter," came from within.

Dr Neether opened the door to see Miss Morgan partly hunched over her MEc and typing at speed, brow furrowed in concentration. An inch of deep amber liquid, probably bourbon, shimmered in the glass on her desk. "Afternoon, Miss Morgan. Do you have time for a brief chat?"

Miss Morgan straightened and looked at her, hiding discomfort at the sight of her facial injuries even less well than Boone. "Afternoon, Dr Neether. Yes. Please come in." She returned her gaze to her screen, continuing to type. Dr Neether closed the door and sat in the chair opposite Miss Morgan's desk.

A few moments passed, then Miss Morgan finished typing, leaned back in her high-backed chair and made a bridge of her long, thin fingers over the desk. She looked at Dr Neether with her signature disingenuous smile, glossy bronze lipstick catching the light. "Are you well?"

As Miss Morgan wasn't the type to enquire about her

employees' wellbeing, the question caught Dr Neether off guard. "Er, y-yes. Yes, ma'am. Fine, thank you. Yourself?"

Miss Morgan stared at the broken half of Dr Neether's face. "You're due another facial reconstruction surgery soon, aren't you?"

"It got delayed yesterday by two months."

She tutted. "No, no, no. Let me get onto them. The sooner we can get you looking less like a hideous ogre, the better."

Sparks of hate ignited in Dr Neether's cheeks. She imagined how satisfying it would be to spit in the woman's face. "Y-yes, ma'am. Thank you."

Miss Morgan thumbed the cartwheel of a silver Zippo lighter and lit a cigarette. She blew a ring of smoke in Dr Neether's direction and said in a smoke-choked voice, "Are you here about the oraculum? Has it activated?"

Sadly the oraculum, a timed data vault containing instructions for dealing with a future event, still lay dormant. Dr Neether had no idea what it was going to reveal and neither did Miss Morgan. All they knew was that *something* was going to happen, something that Dr Neether and Miss Morgan would face together, and that the oraculum was going to offload its secrets for handling it sometime on or before 28th April 2027. That was the day Miss Morgan's future self sent Dr Neether and the oraculum five years and six months into the past, precipitating the car crash that had left her with half a face.

"No, ma'am," said Dr Neether. "I'm afraid not."

"Then how can I help?"

"I have an idea. It pertains to the Mission."

Miss Morgan exhaled another ring of smoke, the end of her cigarette glowing bright. Dr Neether wrinkled her nose.

"I see," said Miss Morgan. "Good. *Excellent.*" She seemed delighted, but that was probably because hiring Dr Neether three years ago had been a huge risk that, thanks to her exceptional work performance, was so far paying off.

Dr Neether smiled inwardly. An exceptional 'performance' indeed.

"I'm wondering if we're going about this all wrong," Dr Neether explained. "I think there's been too much emphasis on changing the outcome of the Last War and not enough on preventing it."

Miss Morgan pursed her lips thoughtfully and tapped a clump of ash into her ashtray. "It's difficult to prevent something when we still don't know what causes it."

Dr Neether leaned forwards. "Maybe we don't need to know what causes it."

Miss Morgan frowned. "What are you suggesting?"

"That instead of waiting for the Shapeless to come, we seek them out. We know from Jesus's scrolls that the Shapeless came from the Guinan System in the Devidia Cluster, and that there may even be something in the Guinan System that's guiding or controlling them. We should go there. Go there and catch them off balance. Destroy them before they can destroy us."

"You have something in mind?"

She nodded. "Yes, ma'am. I call it Operation... Blue Pencil."

As she spoke the words, Dr Neether's mind bounced back to the day she travelled in time, when she and Adam Bryant were at the derelict office block hacking into Million Eyes' systems. They had got into a classified drive on the X9 Server, found a proposal document for an 'Operation Blue Pencil', titled *Recommendations for a Final Solution to the Last War.*

Dr Neether couldn't have known at the time that she was looking at her own work. Something she'd not yet written. Something she'd not yet conceived.

This was why she tried not to let the mysteries of time get to her. Because she wouldn't just lose sleep. She'd lose her fucking mind.

"Operation Blue Pencil?" said Miss Morgan.

"Yes," replied Dr Neether. "A final solution to the Last War."

5

May 26th 2219

At midday, Cara Montgomery finally dragged herself out of bed. Sunshine pierced through a gap in the curtains and painted a thin gold bar on the wall – another glorious day. The weather had been consistently and uncharacteristically good in Roslaig for weeks now. Cara used to love it. It used to make her want to skinny-dip in the freezing sea, wander the hills above the town drinking in that potent blend of heather, lavender and sea salt, or just sit in the garden of the Roslaig Arms with a pint. Now it made her want to stay in bed, buried deep in duvet.

Blinking the sleep from her eyes, she activated her orb. Then she padded to the mirror, the tiled floor cool against her feet, and stared at her naked figure. Was her belly getting bigger by the day? Felt like it. *Looked* like it. She sighed and smudged a tear across her cheek with her finger, her mind swimming with doubt, worry and indecision. She still didn't know if she even wanted to have this baby. A part of her did, because it was the only thing she had left of Jackson. Another part of her, the part that seemed to be growing as fast as the baby, didn't. Because she didn't want to raise her without him.

Sniffing, she pulled on Jackson's joggers and t-shirt, which she'd worn daily for weeks now and still hadn't washed. They still had his scent. She went downstairs to the kitchen to synthesise a cup of green tea and a bowl of porridge. Breathing in a whiff of apple and cinnamon that steamed from the bowl, Cara allowed a trace smile to play briefly on her lips. It made her think of home. Her childhood home. And her mum.

That reminded her. Danica called again yesterday to see if she was alright and, once again, Cara hadn't called her back. If she wasn't careful, her mum would be on her doorstep threatening to move in. She would call her this afternoon.

Cara slumped on the sofa and lifted a spoonful of porridge to her lips as her orb gave her the day's headlines. The warm, milky oatmeal tickled down the back of her throat, leaving a dreadful aftertaste clinging to the sides of her mouth.

Cara wrinkled her nose and glared at her belly. "Seriously? You're going to screw me out of my favourite porridge?"

The baby kicked as if to say yes.

As Cara went back to the kitchen to find something else to eat, a notification slid into the corner of her vision.

Cara had instructed the search engine, Spoggle, to notify her of anything posted on the database that was similar to the horrors she had experienced on the beach in February.

She felt a tightening in her chest – what had Spoggle found?

She opened the notification. Spoggle had sent her a link to a video of a man. Taking a deep breath, she played it.

The man was American, in his sixties, speaking directly to the camera from a dimly lit room. He looked tired and gaunt and his eyes were red, like he'd been crying. "I don't know what's going on." His voice shook. "I've talked to reporters but my story hasn't been published by anyone, which is why I'm making this video. Three weeks ago, something awful, *horrible*, happened. My husband Grayson and I, we were walking our dog in the woods. The dog saw something. Went hurtling after it. Grayson chased her but I– I've got a bad knee, see. Can't run."

The man paused and took a breath. "I lost Grayson for a minute and then... then I saw him, up ahead, on the ground. There was– there was something on his back."

Cara felt the blood drain from her face. *Something on his back.*

"I dunno what it was," said the man. "It was… white. I saw legs. Loads of legs. Fingers. I couldn't make out a body but I wasn't really close enough. And then, before I got near, the thing scurried away. I didn't see where it went."

Cara clutched her chest with one hand and leaned against the kitchen worktop with the other. Everything that took place on the beach in February came flooding back, like water through a burst dam.

"I caught up to Grayson, tried to help him up, but he was coughing, choking on something." His breaths got shorter and faster, his face more contorted. The still-raw pain of his memories was palpable.

"And then he started puking – not just normal puke. He was… he was…" The words caught in his throat and he shook his head, like he couldn't believe his own recollections. "He was fucking puking up his guts, man! His fucking organs! And they were– they were alive. They were moving like a crea–"

The video abruptly cut to black with a caption reading: *We're sorry. This video has been removed for rights reasons.*

Cara was confused. Rights reasons? This was just a man talking about the death of his husband. Whose rights could be in dispute?

Fortunately Cara had set up her orb to record anything Spoggle tagged as similar to the events of 9th February directly onto her PID – the personal internal drive in her orb. So she was able to replay the video up to the point that it cut off. Sitting down at her kitchen table, she did just that.

She couldn't believe it. Finally some evidence she wasn't crazy or a murderer. Since February she had been on bail for Jackson's murder and suspended from her job at Aberdeenshire State Hospital. Although Scotland Police had no idea how to pin Jackson's total evisceration on her, she was the only suspect they had. This video could change all that.

She phoned Dan Balfour, her friend who worked as a data analyst for the world government. Would he listen to her now?

The call rang for a while, then Dan finally answered, his face filling Cara's field of vision. He didn't look happy to see her.

"I thought you weren't going to answer for a second there," said Cara.

"I was considering not. What do you want, Cara?"

"Your help."

He nodded. "I was afraid of that. Cara, I've told you before. I *cannot* use my position to interfere with a murder investigation."

"Come on, Dan. Do you honestly believe I murdered Jackson?"

"I don't fucking know, do I?"

Cara fell silent. *That* hurt.

Dan sighed. A shadow of guilt crossed his face. "Okay. Honestly, no. No, I don't think you murdered him."

She swallowed. "Thank you."

"That doesn't change the fact that I—"

"I just want to show you something, okay?"

Tentatively, "Okay."

Cara sent him what she'd recorded of the video. "Please. Just watch this."

Dan's eyes glowed yellow as he watched the video. She waited, feeling her heartrate increase. When his eyes returned to their normal hazel, they stared at her in bewilderment. "I... w-what does this mean?"

Cara shook her head. "I don't know. But it's the same as what happened to Jackson. Are you at home?" Most of the data analysts for the world government worked remotely, and Dan lived in Rosdale, the next town on from Roslaig.

"Yeah," he said vaguely.

"Can I come over?"

He frowned. "Er..."

"I just want to talk. Something's going on, Dan. Please."

He nodded.

"I'll be there in fifteen."

Cara hung up and ran upstairs to change into clothes that were clean and not Jackson's, remembering as she undressed that she hadn't washed in three days. She hopped in the shower, which was cold. The hot water had been broken for a week and Cara still hadn't called anyone to fix it. She wasn't too bothered; cold showers soothed her.

Pulling on the last set of clean clothes she could find, she left the house and walked to her shuttle. She waved her hand over the vein scanner on the side and the rear hatch opened. Although the lights came on and environmental controls quickly flushed through the warm, stale air that had stagnated inside with a cool, fresh current, the low power message still flashed on the control screen. The shuttle's fuel cell ran on air, so there had to be a malfunction in the conversion matrix. Just another thing Cara hadn't got around to fixing.

Figuring she had enough power to make the short trip to and from Rosdale, she instructed the computer to fly to Dan's address. Five minutes later, her shuttle landed behind Dan's on his driveway. She exited and deactivated the shuttle and went to knock on the door of Dan's modest two-bedroom bungalow.

"Hi," Dan said gloomily as he opened the door and beckoned her inside.

"Hi. You alright? How's Mary doing?" Cara said brightly and off-topic in an attempt to put him at ease.

"We broke up."

Oh. Not the best topic to choose. "I'm sorry. I didn't—"

"It's fine. What do you want to talk about?"

Cara arched an eyebrow. "Come on, Dan. You *know* what."

He shrugged. "And what are you expecting me to do about it?"

"I don't know – give more of a shit than you seem to?

Jackson was your friend, wasn't he? Aren't you concerned about what happened to him?"

Dan sighed, shoulders sinking, a look of regret stealing over his face. "Okay. Come through. I'll get us coffees."

"Decaf for me, please."

Dan synthesised two cups of coffee and they sat down at his kitchen table. "So, what do you think is going on?" he asked.

Cara took a sip. "I'm not sure yet. But I bet what happened to Jackson and that American man's husband aren't isolated incidents. I also found it interesting what he said about the media not publishing his story. And then when the video was removed for rights issues – it felt like someone didn't want us to hear the rest of his account."

"Okay…"

"So are you able to run a search of the government database? See if there are any records of similar incidents that have been removed from the public database?"

"Cara, seriously, I told you I can't use my position to interfere–"

"I'm not asking you to interfere. This isn't about me. This is about finding out if other people are being attacked. All we're doing at this point is looking. Can you do that?"

Dan nodded reluctantly. His eyes turned yellow as he initiated a search cross-referencing details of Jackson and the American man's deaths with government records.

A few moments later, "Found something."

Cara leaned forwards silently, waiting.

"Several people have reported loved ones being attacked by creatures who make them vomit their" – he blinked several times, his throat rippling in a slow and patently uncomfortable swallow – "their organs. Similar to the American, and Jackson, there's references to the creatures being 'white', having 'lots of limbs'. A man whose wife was killed said he saw two of them, and each looked completely different, with different numbers of limbs. And no heads."

Cara swallowed the bile that had collected at the back

of her throat while he spoke. "Where? Where are these attacks happening?"

"Everywhere."

A horrible sinking feeling wormed through Cara's gut. "And where are you finding these reports? Why are they not public?"

"These accounts first appeared in discussion forums and a bunch of newspapers, in threads and articles that have since been removed by the Department for Media."

"Why?"

"I don't know. But... there's something else." His glowing yellow eyes narrowed.

Cara fell silent. A chill darting down her back made her squirm in her seat.

"A few people have reported seeing huge metal objects in the sky, around the time of the attacks."

"Objects? What kind of objects?"

"Spaceships. At least that's what they're assuming."

"Do they describe them?"

"Hold on..."

Suddenly Dan's eyes turned hazel again. "What the–" His whole face contorted with confusion.

"What?" said Cara. "What is it?"

"My orb just went dead." He looked at her, confounded. "I've lost my link to the database."

"I've never heard of anyone's orb going dead."

"Me neither." He concentrated, trying to get his orb to activate, but his eyes didn't change.

"Try yours," he said.

Cara took a breath and concentrated her own mind.

Nothing. Her orb wouldn't respond. What was going on? Orbs didn't just *stop*. They couldn't. The signals travelled through subspace. Something would have to disrupt subspace to interfere with them, which was impossible – *wasn't it?*

Coffees half-drunk and going cold, Dan stood up and bolted into the front room, Cara close behind. Peering through the window onto his quiet residential street, he said, "It's not just happening to us."

Cara trailed his gaze to the street. Several people had come out of their houses looking confused and disoriented.

Dan lurched out of the room, swung open his front door and stepped outside, Cara joining him. Already standing on her own doorstep, Dan's next-door neighbour turned and faced them as they emerged. "Daniel, is your orb working?"

"No. It just stopped."

"Mine too."

A burgeoning dread clawed at Cara's chest. A peculiar foreboding hung in the air. It prickled down the back of her neck, made the hairs bristle.

Something's wrong. Something's very wrong.

Dan looked at her, his eyes misty with worry. "What do you think's going on?"

Staring up at the sky, the sun now trapped and reaching out fleetingly through scudding grey bars of cloud, Cara replied grimly, "They're coming."

6

April 5th 2027

Life in the 21st century had proven something of a double-edged sword for Harriet Turner. There was less disease, wonderful free healthcare and a great deal more care and compassion shown to the poor and destitute. In her century, richer folk liked to pretend that people like Harriet and Emma didn't exist. Sometimes even Harriet's customers refused to speak to her or give her eye contact. Here there was decent housing, benefits – actual money the government just handed to you if you were in need – and dozens of charities trying to make things even better. Dosshouses and workhouses had been relegated firmly to the past, and the elderly received pensions from the state, and could be lodged in nursing homes, instead of going penniless to the workhouse to die. It wasn't perfect, nothing ever was, but by God was it better. If her mother had come here, Harriet had no doubts that she would have lived.

But then there was all this infernal technology. Harriet had entered a world of powerful electric screens displaying moving pictures on every wall, in every home, in the palm of every hand. She knew now that Jack the Ripper had come from a time like this, the thin black object he'd talked to in the church the same as the smartphones that everybody in this century seemed glued to. And computers here weren't people but machines, and nearly everything ran on them. Even after six years, Harriet still hadn't wrapped her brain around it all.

Supposedly computers and phones and this thing she still didn't totally understand called the internet made everything easier and faster. Well, fast was right – but easier? Certainly not. Not to Harriet anyway.

And a part of Harriet remained thoroughly Victorian. Sometimes she couldn't help but feel shocked at how crass everybody was, how scandalously the women dressed, how dreadfully children spoke to their parents. Worst of all, the godlessness. Even purported believers had very little room for the Lord in their lives. It saddened her, made her wonder what God Himself thought of this strange new world.

Several times Harriet and Fred had discussed travelling in time again. They still had two chronozine pills left. But Fred seemed content here and even Harriet had to admit, there were surely worse time periods they could have ended up in. Although she had prayed so hard to be reunited with her mother again when she swallowed that first pill, perhaps this was better. And Fred had quite rightly pointed out that if they travelled again, they'd be stuck there. 'What if we end up in dinosaur times?' he'd said. 'We'd be T-Rex fodder.' Harriet couldn't disagree. The most sensible thing for them to do was stay put.

These were the thoughts cycling through Harriet's head as she sat in her office at the Mystery History Museum, people-watching through the window, the morning rush hour in full swing with hordes of people weaving in and out of each other with haste in their step, and motor cars whizzing up and down Bermond Street. *All these damned motor cars are another thing.* There were none on the streets of Whitechapel in 1895; now they were everywhere. And so fast and frightening were these boxes of metal that the only one she would ever go in was Fred's, on the condition that he drove as slow as possible. She certainly couldn't imagine being in control of one herself. Some even drove themselves, for Heaven's sake! People putting their very lives in the hands of machines? *No, thank you.*

Harriet's computer wasn't working properly, partly the

reason for all these ruminations. She'd come in to the office an hour early to do some work on their latest private investigation, a missing persons case that the police had abandoned years ago. Harriet, thanks to some tuition, now knew how to use Google, a search machine – although she still preferred cases that required her to look at old paper records in libraries. But this morning everything Google took her to was in Spanish. She couldn't work out what she'd done.

At 8.55am, Harriet gave up. The museum would be opening soon, the first guided tour of the day starting at quarter past nine. *Where the hell is Fred?*

At two minutes to nine, Fred arrived, looking hot and flustered, just as Harriet was preparing to go and open up.

"Sorry I'm late," he said breathlessly.

"It's fine," said Harriet. "I'll do the first tour. You can have a look at my computer and tell me why everything's in Spanish." Fred had got the hang of computers much quicker than her. In fact, fitting in with 21st-century society had come naturally to him. Sometimes she felt like he belonged in the future.

"Sure," he replied.

Harriet went to open the entrance door. A man and a woman stood waiting outside. Harriet let them in to the museum gift shop and reminded them that the tour would start at 9.15. They browsed the museum's modest range of books and gifts, purchasing a souvenir mug and a book about Jack the Ripper.

At 9.15, five more people having arrived, Harriet led visitors through the turnstiles, where they scanned their electronic tickets on their smartphones. More clever technology Harriet didn't understand. When she and Fred had opened the Mystery History Museum, he had been in charge of installing all the technical stuff.

She ushered them into the *Mysterious Places* room, which had model recreations of the lost city of Atlantis and what Stonehenge might have looked like when it was built, along with information, photos and artefacts to do with the Nazca Lines, Loch Ness, magnetic hills, various haunted houses and castles, and the Bermuda Triangle. After introducing herself and the museum, Harriet took them through the mysteries they showcased, drawing their particular attention to a recent and exciting addition to their Bermuda Triangle exhibit: the handwritten account of an anonymous radioman at Port Everglades in Florida, who claimed, quite bizarrely, that the missing planes of Flight 19 were chased by a living red cloud before they disappeared. It had been posted to the museum a couple of weeks ago and could well have been bogus, but Harriet and Fred had decided to feature it anyway.

She took them next to the *Mysterious Deaths* room, which had exhibits on all the ones considered famous by people of this century: Princess Diana, Marilyn Monroe, JFK. A couple their visitors may not have heard of, like the mysterious shooting of William II in the New Forest. And one that Harriet had wanted to include because she remembered her mother talking about it: the Princes in the Tower. Technically, Edward V and his brother, Richard, went missing rather than died, but because some bodies were found centuries later that people at the time believed were the princes, it fitted. Now that Harriet knew her mother was a time traveller, her mention of the Princes in the Tower led Harriet to wonder if the princes had vanished without trace because they travelled in time, and that her mother had known more about their fate than she had let on. She'd talked to Fred about maybe transferring the Princes in the Tower exhibit to the *Time Travel* room on the next floor, but Fred had convinced her to keep it where it was.

"Did you hear about that dinosaur they're digging up in Tower Hamlets?" one visitor – the woman who had arrived early – asked. "The one with the kids in its stomach?"

Harriet had heard about that, although it seemed to have vanished from the news cycles now. "Yes, I have."

"You could do an exhibit on that here."

Harriet nodded. "Yes. We may well do." She'd already

been thinking about it, and if they did, where they put it – *Mysterious Deaths* or *Time Travel* – would again be up for debate. To Harriet's mind, the two human children discovered fossilised inside the belly of a sixty-six-million-year-old dinosaur *must* have time-travelled. She'd even suggested to Fred that *they* may have been the Princes in the Tower, although her level-headed co-founder had told her not to let her imagination roam too wild.

The *Time Travel* room, which Harriet took the group to next, was Harriet's favourite. Informing and entertaining visitors here was incidental. Really, this was a place for Harriet and Fred to collate evidence of supposed time travel cases in an effort to better understand what had happened to them.

A TV screen integrated into the wall showed black and white footage from the premiere of a Charlie Chaplin film called *The Circus*, at the Chinese Theatre in Hollywood in 1928. The short clip depicted a woman in the background talking on a mobile phone, decades before mobile phones were invented. Harriet explained to her tour that the woman had since been dubbed the 'Charlie Chaplin Time Traveller'.

She talked them through the photos they had displayed. One was of the 'Time-Travelling Hipster', a man photographed at the reopening of a Canadian bridge in 1941, dressed in a fashion that appeared much too modern for 1941. Another depicted three children at a goldmine in Canada in 1898, one of them bearing an uncanny resemblance to the climate change activist Greta Thunberg, even down to the same braided pigtails.

"Wait – you're saying you think Greta Thunberg is a time traveller?" said a man on the tour, eyebrow arched incredulously.

"Maybe," said Harriet. "What do *you* think?" She didn't want to pretend that she and Fred had all the answers; they wanted the museum to be a place where people could pose questions and come up with their own ideas.

A woman chimed in, "Maybe they sent her back in time to key moments in history to prevent the climate crisis."

Harriet nodded non-committally. She had wondered the same.

She went on to show them replicas of the items said to have been found on Rudolph Fentz, a man who turned up in Times Square, New York City, in 1950, looking lost and disoriented and wearing Victorian-era clothes, before getting run down by a taxi and killed. The items included obsolete banknotes, a bill from a stable for washing a carriage and feeding a horse, and a copper token bearing the name of a saloon, all of which had led authorities to believe that Rudolph Fentz had slipped forwards in time from the 19th century. Harriet loved this case in particular, Fentz having travelled from *her* time.

After talking them through a few further exhibits on lesser-known time travel cases, Harriet took the group to the second floor and final room of the museum, the *Jack the Ripper* room.

Privately, this was the museum's true *raison d'être* for Harriet. After arriving in 2021 from 1895, Harriet and Fred had rented this building (and for a time, lived in it), using a large amount of money Fred had managed to *acquire*. He hadn't revealed to Harriet where the money had come from or how he'd got it and Harriet, presuming it stolen, had decided to look the other way. Vowing to earn an honest living in this century from that point on, Harriet had proposed opening a museum about Jack the Ripper. In addition to living on the proceeds from ticket sales, Harriet had planned to fund their own investigation into the Ripper's true identity and whereabouts, particularly once she had figured out that he may well have originated from a time period like this one.

Fred knew they wouldn't earn enough with such a tight focus on the Ripper, so his idea had been to expand their remit on both fronts. Make the museum about historical mysteries generally, to draw broader interest. And become freelance private detectives on the side.

Harriet explained, after talking them through the room's exhibits, that she and Fred were looking at two Ripper suspects in the London area. She said that they were planning to test their DNA against the Ripper's, which had been lifted from the infamous 'From Hell' letter and the silk shawl stained with blood and semen found next to the mutilated body of the fourth victim, Catherine Eddowes.

"Which suspects?" asked the man in his early twenties, Harriet's age, who'd come with another man who looked like his brother.

"I can't say at the moment," said Harriet. *But they look remarkably like older versions of Henry Van Deen, the time-travelling creep I met in 1888.*

"How will you source their DNA though?" said the man. "Through their relatives?"

"We're hoping to get it directly from them," said Harriet.

He frowned softly. "So you're going to exhume their bodies."

"No."

Frown deepening, "I'm confused. Jack the Ripper murdered those women in 1888. He'd be long dead by now."

"The two men we're looking at are very much alive."

"But how is that possible?"

"Because I believe this case would also fit right in, in the room we've just been to."

The man's eyes widened in realisation. "Ooooh. I see."

The man who was probably his brother added with exuberance, "Cool!"

Harriet smiled.

The tour now over, Harriet told the group that they could look around for as long as they liked, before returning downstairs to the gift shop. Fred was just finishing serving a customer.

"Good group?" he asked as his customer started out of the shop with a replica of the t-shirt worn by the Time-Travelling Hipster.

"Yes. They asked a lot more questions than the last lot."

Fred smiled. "That's good."

"Have you been busy?"

"Not really. Sold some tickets for next week. Also picked up a new case. A woman who's convinced her nanny is breastfeeding her baby and wants her surveilled."

Harriet's face creased with shock. "As I live and breathe."

"I know. Oh, and I fixed your computer. It's no longer in Spanish. I think you must've downloaded something by mistake."

"More than likely."

Fred was so good at negotiating this technology, despite them having originated from a much simpler century, and it made her wonder. What if he had been to the future before? After all, her mother was a time traveller and Harriet had never known. There was a lot she hadn't known about her mother till she went through her belongings, and a lot she still didn't know now. But she had barely scratched the surface with Fred Gleeson. So many secrets he kept locked and bolted and out of reach. The fact that he had helped her survive this century made her want to keep him around, even though her friendship was with a skin-deep version of the man.

The following day, Harriet was walking to the Mystery History Museum from her tiny apartment a few blocks away, picking her way through the morning hordes of Londoners rushing about like they had rockets up their backsides.

Suddenly, she stopped dead, jamming the traffic of people. Those who had to change course around her shouted all kinds of foul remarks.

Normally Harriet would have lambasted the levels of rage on the roads and footpaths in this century compared to hers, but nothing they said went in. She stood frozen, her stupefied gaze clinging to the slender man in a grey suit strolling down the pavement towards her.

Can't be.

As the man got closer, she realised it *could*, and it *was*. Same long face. Same green eyes. Same dimple in his chin.

It's him. Henry Van Deen – Jack the Ripper.

There were so many people walking up and down that Van Deen didn't catch Harriet standing motionless in the middle of the pavement, staring at him. He may not have recognised her if he had; Harriet was eleven when they met and thirteen years had passed since then.

Thirteen years? A hundred and thirty-nine, technically.

His gaze pointed straight ahead, he strode right past her. She pivoted round on her heel, eyes refusing to let him go, even to blink.

But then her eyes were forced to as he disappeared inside a building. Her heart racing, she looked up at the green hanging sign.

Jack the Ripper's just gone into Starbucks.

Without thinking, Harriet unstuck herself from the pavement and followed him. Through the window she could see that he had joined the back of the queue of people ordering. She walked in without any kind of plan for what she was going to do next.

Immediately aware that she couldn't just stand there in the middle of the shop and stare at a customer, she decided to get in line. *But he's at the back – I can't stand next to him, for Heaven's sake.* Fortunately another customer, tutting at Harriet for standing in the way, joined the queue after Van Deen. Harriet stepped forwards and stood behind her.

Van Deen ordered a mocha with extra chocolate and a toasty, to eat in. Plucking a copy of *The Overlook* off an empty table, he went to sit by the window. Too busy wondering how and where Van Deen lived, who he worked for and how long he'd been in this time period, Harriet hadn't given a single thought to what to order when the barista asked her. She said tea, to drink in, although she didn't actually want one, and a tea wouldn't help her bone-dry throat. She should've ordered a juice.

A barista brought Van Deen's mocha and toasty to him just as Harriet sat down with her tea. There weren't many free tables, so she had to sit on the other side of the café. At least she could see him. As she was prone to doing, she had left her smartphone at home, otherwise she could let Fred know that she might be late to the museum. She was sure he would cope on his own for a bit.

So now what?

Van Deen read his newspaper with blank disinterest and sipped his coffee, as Harriet watched. Then, as he turned the page, his cup on its way to his lips, his face dropped. His cup returned to its saucer but didn't quite make the depression in the middle, resting at a slant. *What's he seen?* A moment later, he closed the newspaper and stood up fast, chair scraping the floor with an unpleasant screech. Leaving his toasty untouched, he swept out of Starbucks.

Harriet clocked his direction up Bermond Street, then made a dash for his table. She picked up the newspaper and draped it over Van Deen's cup, which she lifted with her other hand. Pretending to read, she used the paper as a shield as she walked to the nearest bin, poured away the rest of the liquid and stuffed the cup into her handbag. Folding up the newspaper so that it was easier to carry, she bolted out of the café.

Van Deen had walked in the opposite direction to the museum. Her eyes combed the road and after a moment she caught him, about a hundred yards away, now on the other side.

Harriet sprinted over the road at the nearest crossing, just as the traffic lights were switching back to green. A car blasted its horn at her, made her flinch. Despite hearing them every day, their awful sound still frightened the life out of her.

She followed Van Deen onto Puttenham Lane. He appeared to be heading for the glass and concrete monstrosity everybody called the Looming Tower, so tall it cast its unsightly shadow over half of London. It was the headquarters of Million Eyes, a technology company

Harriet knew little about apart from the fact that their products were everywhere.

Van Deen strode past the gold statue of an ugly fat man in the building's front garden and disappeared inside its huge glass entrance doors.

This meant one of two things. Van Deen worked for Million Eyes but was a member of a time-travelling cabal on the side. Or Million Eyes themselves *were* the time-travelling cabal on the side.

Harriet hurried to the museum. In the end, she wasn't late at all and wondered if Fred would even be here yet. She found him sitting at his desk in the office eating a Danish pastry. Looking up and frowning as she walked in, he said, "Are you okay?"

Breathless and hot, "I found him."

"Found who?"

Harriet pulled Van Deen's cup out of her handbag. "I need you to run a DNA test on this cup. Compare it to the profile we have for Jack the Ripper."

Fred took the cup. "You found *Jack?*"

"Yes."

"Where?"

"Starbucks."

Fred gave an incredulous shake of the head and fetched the handheld DNA scanner from their equipment cabinet. He ran it over the cup and analysed the results on his computer. Since she didn't understand how the process worked, and could make neither head nor tail of all the numbers and twisted ladder patterns that appeared on his screen, Harriet left him to it and started studying the newspaper that had made Van Deen abandon his lunch. She already knew what the results would show anyway.

Shit. A few pages in was a story about a murder in St James's Park. The article included a computer-generated mock-up of the prime suspect, based on a description given to police by a witness. The mock-up was simple and vague and could've been a hundred different people.

But those hundred people included Henry Van Deen.

Up to your old tricks again, are you, Jack?

"It's an exact match," said Fred, looking up from his computer. "It's him."

Harriet held up the newspaper. "And it looks like he's still killing."

"*That's* him?"

"It's not a very good image, but I'd say so. He got up and left the café in a rush, and I think it was after reading this."

"Which means he wasn't banking on there being a witness."

"That's what I'm thinking."

"Did you see where he went?"

"Yes. I followed him."

He looked down his nose at her. "Harriet, I hope you didn't put yourself in danger!"

She brushed off his concern. "He works for Million Eyes. I saw him go into the Looming Tower."

Fred's eyebrows prodded his forehead. "Do you think Million Eyes are something to do with his time-travelling?"

"I don't know. But I have an idea."

"What?"

"You're not going to like it."

"Why?"

"Because it involves putting myself in danger."

July 8th 2035

With so much of it owned by the military and inaccessible to the public, the vast plateau of desolate grasslands known as Salisbury Plain had been a source of rumour and conspiracy theory for years. Used for infantry training and live artillery firing and home to several classified military research facilities dubbed 'Britain's Area 51' at one time or another, the plain had become synonymous with secrecy.

However, the biggest secrets of Salisbury Plain weren't the military's. For underneath the plain sprawled a heavily guarded bunker belonging to Million Eyes, which only a select few in the company knew about.

One of those few was Dr Neether, who had been frequently stationed at the bunker, known as Facility 9, to monitor the construction of the Redactor, a machine based on her designs and the culmination of Operation Blue Pencil. Even more frequently in the past two years, since initial testing of the machine had begun.

Today, Dr Neether was in the Redactor chamber preparing for the first test of the machine on a live human subject. The positive results yielded by the last two years of tests on manmade objects, plant life and, later, animals made Dr Neether hopeful for similar success.

But that didn't stop the apprehension clawing like fingers with scraggy nails at the lining of her stomach as she waited for the human subject to be brought in. A lot was riding on this, including Dr Neether's future with

Million Eyes and her power to save Georgia.

As her colleagues prepared the machine, two operatives escorted a handcuffed and struggling Irene Jenkins into the room. They led her to the large 'X' in the middle of the floor and told her to stand on it or they would shoot her. The operatives retreated to the wall, making sure they were well out of the way but keeping their disruptors trained on her.

"Who the fuck... who the fuck are *you?*" Irene's eyes sprang wide with shock and fright as they landed on Dr Neether. A normal and anticipated reaction. She had long given up trying to repair her broken face. The reconstructive surgeries had been traumatic and mostly ineffective and even though new techniques had been developed and offered to her, she'd turned them all down. She had made peace with what she looked like. She'd adapted. And now, when she looked in the mirror, this face fitted.

"Good morning, Miss Jenkins," Dr Neether replied, stepping forwards. "My name is Dr Samantha Neether."

"Where the fuck am I and why did you bring me here?"

"I'm sorry for the inconvenience. This will be over soon."

"What will? What the fuck are you going to do to me?"

Irene took several steps forwards, immediately retreating back to the 'X' when the operative to her left blared, "Do *not* move!", his disruptor poised.

"Please stay calm, Miss Jenkins. You won't know anything about it. I promise."

"Know anything about what?" Panic scraped at the woman's voice. "What the fuck! Where are my kids? I want to see my kids!"

"That surprises me." Dr Neether said it with a very intentional bite.

Irene detected it. "What the fuck does *that* mean?"

The bleach-blonde-haired, benefits-scrounging mum of five by five different dads, who appeared unable to form a sentence without the word 'fuck', was starting to grate. If Dr Neether had any ounce of regret over what she was about to do, this boorish woman was making it vanish quickly. "Well it's our understanding that you're more interested in getting drunk and stoned and laid by every man you meet in the pub or the supermarket than you are in raising your children. Which is why your two youngest are *this* close" – she mimed a pinch with her fingers – "to being taken by Social Services."

"Fuck you. You don't know anything about me. You don't know how hard it's been, how badly people treat me. Nothing's ever gone right in my life."

Dr Neether felt her muscles stretch taut in disbelief as she walked up to Irene. "I'll tell you what I do know. I know that children are a gift. The most precious of gifts anyone can be given. There are some people in this world who can't ever receive this gift. And there are others who are lucky enough to receive it, but then it's cruelly ripped away from them in a blink." She swallowed, trying to conceal the trembling of her hands. "You say that nothing's ever gone right in your life, but life has given you *five* of these gifts. And you've squandered every one."

Irene stared at her through a glaze of tears, the hate and anger in her features softening with what Dr Neether hoped was realisation of the truth in her words.

Dr Neether didn't let up. Why should she? This woman didn't warrant any sympathy, certainly not from her. "You don't deserve your children, Miss Jenkins. And they don't deserve you. Which is why you're here."

Her loud mouth receded to a pitiful murmur. "I love them."

Dr Neether felt nothing but cold. "Then you should have shown it." She turned and walked back to the machine, telling her colleagues, "Begin the activation sequence."

"What are you doing?" Tears streaming down her cheeks, Irene gazed up at the Redactor. "What is that?" As the machine whirred, the rings around the giant central cylinder started to revolve, its large round midsection opening to reveal an enormous ball with wide vertical grooves and a deep depression in the middle, like an eyeball.

"Primary fusion matrix online," said Dr Neether's colleague. "Antitachyon injectors charged."

Dr Neether nodded. Looking back at Irene and pulling in a deep breath, she murmured, "Fire."

Irene stared, confused, as the 'pupil' of the weapon's core started to glow deep red. Then a powerful red beam of light surged from the pupil into Irene's chest. She froze as the beam hit her, face fixed in a gape of horror. When the beam stopped, she remained frozen, now surrounded by a soft red haze that made her look fuzzy and grainy.

Dr Neether chewed on her lip as the changes began. First to go were the clothes. Irene's gaudy purple tracksuit disintegrated, leaving her naked, bags of fat and cellulite hanging inelegantly. A moment later, her fat began to shrink, her skin tightening and lifting. Her bleach-blonde hair changed colour, length and shape continuously. Blonde, then brown, then streaky. Patched with grey. Blue. Brown again. Shoulder-length, a bun, long. Eventually her whole body started to shrink. Her arms and legs grew shorter, her facial features softened and her breasts flattened as she morphed into a child.

Dr Neether stepped forwards. The red haze continued to encircle Irene as she went from a schoolchild to a toddler to a baby. Dr Neether crouched down and peered into the haze as the baby shrank into a tiny foetus. Its fingers and toes disappeared inwards, its arms and legs reduced to buds, and its face became a smattering of dots and dips. Now a diminutive blob, an embryo, Dr Neether could no longer see it through the haze.

The haze dissipated, by which point the embryo had reduced to nothing, the 'X' on the floor where Irene had stood, bare.

Dr Neether straightened and breathed a long sigh of relief, hoping to God the results would bear out what they had just witnessed.

"Temporal incursion complete," her colleague read off

his computer console as she walked back towards the machine, now powering down, the 'eye' closing. "Full erasure confirmed."

Dr Neether nodded. "Run a sensor sweep."

"Yes, ma'am." A few moments later, "Irene Jenkins' children also erased."

A hand of guilt gripped and squeezed Dr Neether's heart in that moment, but quickly loosened. Yes, she had taken the lives of five children: an inevitable side effect of deleting their mother. But even if there had been some way of avoiding that, these would have been broken children. Children who had been suffering a mother like Irene, and would have continued to suffer getting bounced around foster carers. And despite everybody's interventions, they probably would've turned out exactly like their mother anyway. For their own sake, they were better off never having existed.

"Collateral impacts coming in now," her colleague said. "Nine new births. Four lives erased. None significant. Thirty-two personal histories have been altered. Again, none significant."

Relief flushed through her. Even though Irene Jenkins' children were gone, nine other *hopefully* more well-balanced individuals had taken their place.

"Any counter impacts?" she asked.

"None," he replied. "All changes minor and localised. No damage to Million Eyes or any of our key people."

Dr Neether looked at him, feeling a smile of triumph start to tug at the half of her lips that still worked. "Lower the Shield and notify headquarters that they are safe to lower theirs."

"Yes, Dr Neether."

Dr Neether left the Redactor chamber and returned to her office, where she spent a few moments looking out of the window over Facility 9's primary laboratory, and the huge glass tank that housed a swirling sample of the Ratheri. It was in this very room, way back in 1984, that the power of the Ratheri to manipulate time was finally understood. And now, all these years later, Dr Neether had gone a giant leap further, harnessing its colossal and complex energies to literally turn time into a weapon.

The next step would be to reconfigure that weapon for a much larger-scale erasure. It would take a year, maybe two – and a lot more money. But Dr Neether felt confident that as soon as the board of directors had heard about today's test, she'd have all the money she needed.

8

January 1st 2220

It didn't feel like the start of a new year. No one had gone from 31st December to 1st January expecting 2220 to be different because they knew it wouldn't be. There were no signs of a turning point, no faint glimmer of hope on the horizon, no reason to celebrate. So no one did. One day simply turned into another.

Many people didn't even know it was New Year's Day, Cara Montgomery included. Living in a pokey, rundown apartment in Deepwater, a town in South-East England, she and Dan Balfour had stopped registering what day it was ages ago. Actually, *living* was too strong a word. *Surviving.* They had managed to escape to England as the aliens laid waste to most of Scotland. Cara would never forget the view of Roslaig below, crumbling and on fire, as she and Dan sneaked through the bombardment in a shuttle.

Cara and Dan sat on a moth-eaten sofa in the lounge in front of an antique television, Cara cradling her three-month-old baby, Dina, in her arms. Her bundle – and only source – of joy. While the world ended outside, Cara could watch Dina coo, gurgle and blow tiny bubbles of spit, talk in adorable nonsense baby words to her toys, and see how many of her toes she could fit in her mouth all at once. Dina knew nothing of the horrors going on beyond these walls, and in those moments, Cara could pretend she didn't either.

As Dina suckled intermittently on Cara's breast,

fighting the growing heaviness of her eyes, Cara and Dan watched the latest announcement from the world government, or what was left of it, on the TV.

"The United States of Earth military, supported by our enhanced human unit, are continuing to fight the Shapeless with courage and determination," said the USE president.

Cara had never owned a TV before. No one had needed to before the aliens – dubbed the Shapeless by the government – disrupted subspace and disabled everyone's orbs, cutting them off from the database and each other. Orbs had long been the only way people communicated long-distance, and the database had been everyone's source of information and entertainment. After the disablement, which Cara had heard people refer to as the 'Silence', a global effort to reconnect had led to the recovery of old computers and web servers from museums in order to reforge the system that preceded orbs, known as the internet. Although it was widely believed that the Shapeless didn't have the capacity to monitor communications that used obsolete technology, all internet-based communications had been encrypted anyway, and encryption keys had been handed out in person to those who wanted access. Dan had managed to source a TV, and an encryption key, to be able to connect to this internet, so now they had a window on the world, albeit a small one, since the only things being transmitted were announcements from the world government about the war.

Fortunately Dan had managed to find some old – *very old* – movies, stored on a rudimentary hard drive he'd managed to link up to the TV. Most were from the 21st century, including all two hundred and seventeen movies in the Marvel Cinematic Universe. The newest movie was the twenty-ninth remake of *Murder on the Orient Express* from the early 22nd century, starring a hundred-and-one-year-old Millie Bobby Brown in her final film role. The oldest was a film from the late 20th century called *Independence Day*, which, although trashy and dumb, they quite enjoyed watching because it let them imagine a day where humanity turned the tables on the Shapeless.

"Unfortunately, the Shapeless are proving highly resilient," the USE's president continued. "Our weapons do not work well against them. If we were to capture one, alive or dead, we could seek to understand more about their physiology and endeavour to find a weakness to exploit – but we have not been able to do this. Even when we do manage to kill one, their bodies are immediately teleported away. The USE military has destroyed some of their ships, but only a few. And while our enhanced humans have fought bravely, many of them have already been killed and their interventions show no sign of making a difference."

This certainly wasn't the defiant and invigorating speech given by the fictional President Whitmore in *Independence Day*. The real president appeared tired, her eyes hollowed and dark, her words laced with lethargy, resignation, hopelessness.

"It is clear we are in a tenuous position. The Shapeless have already slaughtered millions of us in a relentless sequence of attacks and continue to refuse to participate in any sort of dialogue. My governors and I have been debating our options over the past few days and we have come to a decision."

A cold sliver of dread snaking up her spine, Cara straightened and sat forwards, her nipple popping out of Dina's pink, puckered lips. It didn't matter; Dina was already asleep and making wheezing noises. Dan sat on the edge of the sofa, chewing the skin around his thumbnail.

"It is with heavy hearts that we have decided to lay down our arms and issue an unconditional surrender."

Cara's stomach sank. Dan slumped back on the sofa.

They were giving up. The war was lost. It was over. She looked down at Dina, sleeping peacefully. Her cheeks had filled out, her hair growing fast, and she had definitely put some weight on in the past week. *Oh, little one – less little by the day. What world have I brought you into?*

The president continued explaining how she and her governors had arrived at their decision to throw in the towel. Then the transmission ended and the screen cut to static, and Cara and Dan stared vacantly at one another in silence.

After several minutes Dan broke the silence with a dispirited sigh. "Well that's that. I need a drink." He stood up, walked into the kitchenette and poured himself a whisky, something he was tending to do on a daily basis lately. "Want one?"

"No, thanks." Cara lifted Dina into her carrycot and stroked her soft head.

"I'll go out tomorrow, see if I can find her some more sleepsuits," Dan said. "She's barely fitting in those." Deliberately avoiding talking about what they'd just seen, he downed one whisky and poured another. He'd be drunk within the hour.

"I've got a couple of bigger ones," Cara said. "We're not desperate yet."

"Actually, maybe we won't need anymore." He poured a third whisky and brought it to the sofa to nurse. "Sounds like we don't have much time left."

Suddenly another transmission started cutting through the static on the TV. *Strange.* The government tended only to make one announcement a day.

A man appeared on screen, standing in front of a red background, the words *RESISTANCE IS NOT FUTILE* captioned in black capital letters along the bottom of the screen.

"This is a message for anyone who is receiving this. My name is Fabio Bonnich and I am here to tell you that even though the government is giving up, the people are not."

"Shit," said Dan, plunking the remote control off the coffee table and ramping up the volume.

"A few of us anticipated this move to surrender by the government," said Bonnich. "But do not be under any illusion that surrender will save us. It will not. The Shapeless want us dead. All of us dead. If we surrender, we are, in effect, turning our guns on ourselves."

Cara's heart started to race. This man, whoever he was, was right. How could surrender to these monsters be their only option?

"We are in the process of forming resistance groups all over the world," said Bonnich. "I am leading a group in London called the First Remnant. We will be gathering in a place the Shapeless believe they destroyed months ago and are no longer monitoring. Although we are using the government's encrypted channel to transmit this message, we are not taking any chances. We will reveal the exact time, date and location of this first meeting only to those who come in person to the underground checkpoints that were used by the government to hand out encryption keys. A member of the First Remnant will be at these checkpoints from 8am to 10pm tomorrow."

Cara and Dan's nearest checkpoint was in Basingstoke, a five-minute shuttle flight away.

Bonnich continued, "Please, if you are receiving this message and are in a position to help, come join us. The First Remnant will be gathering intelligence, looking for ways to find out more about the Shapeless and where they came from, and we intend to use stealth and cunning to combat them, instead of brute force, which the government has proved doesn't work."

The deep rumbling of Bonnich's voice had stirred Dina awake. Cara glanced over at her. She was chomping on her toes, happy as a clam.

Bonnich made a final plea. "This war isn't over. We are not defeated yet. I implore you not to let our president vanquish hope. We are not going to just hand over our lives to these creatures. We cannot let the future of humanity be erased. We must defend it." A moment later, Bonnich's image scattered into static.

Cara's stare roamed to Dina, goo-gooing at the various stuffed toys strung from the arch over her carrycot, bubbles frothing at her lips. Bonnich's words echoed in her mind. *We cannot let the future of humanity be erased.* This little button had barely begun to live. Her future had no roadmap yet, it could go in a million different directions. A huge abundance of potential and possibility lay swathed in that duck-covered blanket kicking excitedly and burbling sweetly. The Shapeless threatened to stop her bundle of joy's journey before it had started, and that wasn't something Cara was going to stand by idly and let happen.

"Wow," said Dan, switching the TV off and sitting down, downing the rest of his third whisky. "Well, good luck to them."

Cara looked at him. "Them?"

Dan frowned. "What does *that* mean?"

"It means I think we should go to the Basingstoke checkpoint tomorrow and find out where and when this meeting's going to be."

Dan's eyes flared. "Are you crazy?"

"Never saner."

"So– what? You want to join this resistance?"

"Yes."

Dan huffed. "Well that *is* crazy. What about Dina?"

Dina's teeny fingers fumbled with the jingle bell butterfly dangling above her, making a charming racket. "That's exactly why I want to join. You heard what that man said. Surrender's like turning guns on ourselves. I'm not doing that, and I'm certainly not turning a gun on my baby."

"We've survived this far. We should just keep doing what we're doing."

"Just sit and hope the Shapeless don't come, you mean? You yourself just said you didn't think we had much time left!"

"Because we can't win, Cara! You know that!" Cara knew that the acrimony in his voice stemmed from fear more than anger. "These resistance movements aren't going to change a fucking thing. I get that they want to instil hope in people, and normally hope is a great thing to have. But not in this situation. In this situation, hope is dangerous and stupid and it's only going to get people killed quicker. People like you, who get taken in by it."

"Dan, you're an amazing friend. You've done a lot for me and Dina. And I love you. But you're a pussy. You always have been. And if you want to lie down and die, I can't stop you. But I'm not giving up. Not on my daughter's future. I'm going."

Dan fell into an affronted silence, but she didn't regret calling him a pussy. It wasn't an insult if it was true, which deep down he knew it was. Later that evening, she asked him again if he would consider going with them. She didn't want to put pressure on him but she had to try. And it wasn't just because she could use his help keeping Dina safe, but because she wanted *him* to be safe. If he stayed here, he would surely die. If he went with her and joined the resistance, at least they'd have some semblance of a chance. Dan said he'd think about it.

The next morning, Cara awoke to the sound of the building's alarm and her heart plunged in dread. Dina was sleeping peacefully in her cot, arms above her head, mini fists clenched. The tiny tyke could sleep through a bomb blast.

Cara sprang for the window and threw open the curtain.

She froze. Her heart stopped.

The sun had barely risen, the sky milky, the town bathed in pastel hues. In the distance, hovering next to an apartment building, were two spacecraft just like the ones that destroyed Roslaig, each one a thick cylinder with huge arched prongs jutting out of its hull and a sharp narrow rod protruding from one end – like giant spiked screwdrivers. As she watched, one of the ships dive-bombed the building, thrusting its rod right through the façade, impaling it like a spear. A moment later, the other ship did the same. As both withdrew, twisted metal and concrete rubble tumbled down the side of the building. Again they smashed into the building's sides, stabbing the building in a frenzied knife attack. Even though they had energy weapons that could level a building in a few blasts, this was how they chose to attack. It was like they were *playing*. Cara winced as she remembered their laughs of twisted, sadistic joy on the beach in Roslaig right after they made Jackson's organs erupt from his throat.

Cara didn't wait for the building to become a Swiss cheese and collapse. She threw on some clothes and lifted Dina out of her cot. Now she stirred and cried. Cara opened her bedroom door to the lounge. Dan was dressed also, currently stuffing his feet into shoes.

"We have to get to the basement," he said.

There was no certainty that the building's basement would make an adequate shelter. Even though it had been reinforced and furnished with supplies and a food synthesiser in the event of a Shapeless bombardment, it couldn't defend against a ground attack if the Shapeless were to land.

"No," Cara said. "I'm going to get our shuttle and fly to the checkpoint in Basingstoke before they get here."

"But we still have a chance!"

Cara sighed. "No, we don't. The government's surrendering. That means there's no one to save us anymore. We have no chance – unless we make our own. Unless we save ourselves."

"And what if we can't?"

"Then at least we tried."

Dan shook his head hopelessly.

"Look." Cara stepped forwards and put her hand on his arm. "No one's making you do anything. You have to do what's right for you. And so do I."

Dan stared at her, glassy-eyed, features flush with fear. "I can't leave you and Dina. I'd fucking hate myself."

"Well me and Dina are going. So you'll have to come with us."

He huffed. "Fine."

She wasn't expecting that. "Really?"

"Yes. Fucking hell, yes! Let's just go before I change my mind."

Cara placed Dina in her carrycot and slung her bag of baby essentials over her shoulder. Dan packed a bag of food and spare clothes for each of them; it was looking unlikely they would be able to come back here.

There were queues of residents waiting by the turbolifts so Cara and Dan had to go down the access chutes. When they got to the shuttle park, they noticed that a few other residents had decided to eschew the basement option.

Cara activated the shuttle and they entered through the rear hatch. It was her shuttle they'd taken after Dan's was crushed when the Shapeless decimated Aberdeenshire. Cara took the helm, while Dan sat with Dina in the aft section. She instructed the computer to take them to the Basingstoke checkpoint and they flew out of the shuttle park, away from the building, not far behind another shuttle.

She figured the Shapeless ships were preoccupied with wrecking the town – but then sensors detected one ship turn and move towards them. *Shit.* Cara brought up a visual on her display. One of the vessels that had been leaving a trail of destruction on Deepwater's outer edge had moved to intercept the shuttles currently vacating Cara and Dan's building.

Maybe this *was* a bad idea.

Too late now.

Cara decided not to reveal the sensor data to Dan and said, even though she hadn't smelled anything, "Dan, I think Dina might need changing." Then she manually increased the shuttle's speed to six hundred kilometres per hour.

As Dan started changing Dina on the floor of the aft section, another ship appeared on Cara's sensors, this one a USE gunship, and hailed them. Cara responded and a black-haired woman in a burgundy military combat uniform appeared on her comm monitor.

"My name is Captain Shanthi," the woman said. "I need you to turn your shuttle around and go home. Get to the shelter in your building where it's safe."

"I'm not going back," Cara said defiantly. "It's not safe there. *Nowhere* is safe."

"Cara, you should listen to her," said Dan quietly

behind her. Of course he wanted to go back.

"There is a Shapeless vessel approaching your position," said Shanthi.

"What?" cried Dan. Leaving Dina naked and wriggling on the floor with a rattle, he leapt to his feet and launched forwards to check the sensor data himself. "Shit!"

"I know," said Cara. "We can still make it."

"I can't condone this course of action," said Shanthi.

"I'm not asking you to. But the government's signed our death warrants by surrendering to these bastards and I'm not sitting on my arse waiting for my sentence to be carried out. Not when there's still people out there who want to *do something*."

"You're talking about the Resistance. You're leaving to join them."

Cara looked at Dan, who shook his head in desperate hope that she'd relent and turn back. Returning her gaze to Shanthi, "Yes. I have to. I have to defend my baby's future, Captain."

"Your baby?"

"Yes. I have a three-month-old." Cara glanced at Dina, who'd discarded her rattle in favour of fervently sucking her toes again. "She's aboard right now, so please, just let us go."

Captain Shanthi gave a thoughtful sigh and nodded with resignation. "Alright. Go. I'll try and slow the Shapeless down, keep them off your tail."

"Haven't you laid down arms?"

"Some of us. Not all."

Cara smiled. "Thank you, Captain."

"Good luck."

The captain ended the transmission and Cara looked at Dan.

His eyebrows rose to meet his hairline. "Now even the military are telling us to go back, and we're *still* gonna go?"

"You heard her. She's going to slow them down. We can make–"

Boom. A metallic rumble ate the rest of Cara's

sentence. The shuttle lurched beneath their feet and Cara jerked in her chair. Dan, standing over the control console, slammed into the wall. Cara threw her gaze behind as Dina rolled across the floor and smacked into one of the aft seats.

"No!" Cara lunged to the floor and plucked Dina into her arms. The baby broke into a hysterical cry and Cara checked her for bruises or scrapes. She couldn't see any.

The shuttle still shuddering from the blast, Dan bolted forwards and tapped at the control console. "That Shapeless ship just fired on us! Wasn't a direct hit but it grazed one of our engine coils. What do we do?"

Cara harnessed a still-naked Dina into the secure baby seat. "How far away are they?"

She answered her own question, the ship now visible through the aft windows, the sharp point of the 'screwdriver' coming right for them. Another hit from one of their energy weapons and they'd be toast. Commercial shuttles didn't have weapons or shields. They were completely defenceless.

Dan yelled breathlessly, "I'm increasing speed but they're gaining on us fast. We can't outrun them – we're in a shuttle and they're in a *warship*!"

A panicked sweat broke out across Cara's body. She hadn't a clue what to do. When they escaped Roslaig, it was because the Shapeless were busy exchanging fire with the military and hadn't noticed their shuttle. But this ship had seen them. This ship was *after* them.

A blue light glowed at the base of the spiked cylinder section of the Shapeless vessel. It was preparing to fire again, which would undoubtedly reduce them to dust.

And then Cara's view of the fast-approaching spaceship was blocked – by Captain Shanthi's gunship. It had flown directly into the path of the Shapeless vessel.

"What's she doing?" Cara cried.

Dan tossed a glance over his shoulder at the USE gunship shadowing the aft windows. Returning his gaze to the console, "She's on a collision course with the Shapeless!"

The impact happened quicker than Cara expected. As she peered out, lips parted in horror, Captain Shanthi's vessel exploded against the spiked hull of the alien ship. Cara squinted into the blinding blaze of fire and smoke and spinning debris, and trembled. She and Dan gripped the handrails as a small, roaring shockwave rocked the shuttle. Dina's cries intensified.

After the shockwave had passed, Dan looked down at the sensors. "I think the Shapeless have lost propulsion. They've slowed right down. I'm not seeing any weapons signatures anymore either."

"She gave her life for ours," Cara murmured, words trailing a heaving sigh of relief mixed with sadness as she stared off into the empty blue skies ahead. "Let's keep going till we clear the area."

Dan nodded. Her heart beginning to slow, Cara leaned forwards, unlocked Dina's harness and collected the crying child into her arms, kissing her smooth forehead. "Sssshhh. It's alright. Mummy's got you. We're safe now."

She wasn't sure if she was saying it to comfort Dina, or herself.

9

April 6th 2027

Fred peered down at his watch again as he and Harriet sat on a bench opposite the Looming Tower. Harriet didn't care what time it was, though. She'd wait here all night if she had to.

"For all we know, Van Deen left ten minutes after you followed him here," said Fred. "And we've wasted three hours sitting here waiting for him to come out."

"It's not wasted if this is the only place we know he could be," said Harriet. "Maybe he's working late. Who knows what he does in there?"

If she and Fred had been sitting here for three hours, then it was just before eight o'clock. They had arrived shortly before five, closing the Mystery History Museum early with the expectation that Million Eyes workers would start leaving on the hour or half-past it. Which many had, just not the man they wanted to see. Since it was how he had got to work this morning, Harriet expected Henry Van Deen to be among those departing from the main entrance doors on foot, as opposed to those leaving in cars from the building's rear car park. So they had picked a bench that gave them a clear view of everyone who came out of the doors.

Dusk had fallen. A pale sliver of moon idled in the twilight, and shadows all around had grown deep and long. Not that Puttenham Lane could be called dark, the daylight having been replaced by a soft but consistent glow from all the streetlights, car headlights and interior lights that shone through the windows of buildings. That included the Looming Tower, much of which remained lit up with occupied offices. However, unlike most of the other buildings, whose unshuttered windows allowed a view of the illuminated space behind them, the Looming Tower used one-way glass panes which, lit from inside, looked like they were painted cream.

"Aren't you hungry?" said Fred. They'd had pizza for lunch – literally Harriet's favourite thing about the 21st century – and hunger for the next meal hadn't reached her yet. Eating more regularly now than she ever did for the first seventeen years of her life, Harriet rarely felt hungry, her body used to going much longer periods without sustenance.

"I'm not," said Harriet. "But you go and find something if you are. I'll keep watch."

"And what if he comes out while I'm gone? I'm not having you chasing after a serial killer without me."

Harriet smirked at him and shrugged. "I suppose you'll have to stay here then."

Fred sighed. "I suppose I will."

A few moments later, Harriet's heart leapt into her throat at the sight of the grey-suited slender man from earlier striding out of the Looming Tower.

"That's him," Harriet whispered, standing up and swallowing hard.

Fred stood and followed her gaze. "Shit. You sure?"

Harriet nodded. "Yes."

"Alright, so we should–"

Harriet had already started following him up Puttenham Lane.

"Wait!" Fred whispered loudly, catching up and leaning close to her ear. "We shouldn't get too close, remember."

"We won't."

Seeing Van Deen heading for the entrance to the Puttenham Lane Underground Station, Harriet quickened her pace and lengthened her stride, closing the gap between them and Van Deen to ten metres.

"We're too close," Fred whispered. "If he looks round…"

"We can't lose him."

They followed him down the steps at the entrance to the station. Harriet plucked her smartphone from her bag, which she had popped back home to get at lunchtime. Fred had configured it to make instant automatic ticket payments at the barriers just by hovering them over circular pads. It still seemed like magic to her, but she tried not to think about it.

Scanning their phones and pushing through the turnstiles, Harriet and Fred followed Van Deen down the escalators onto the westbound platform of the District Line, towards Ealing Broadway. Having to wait twenty minutes for the next train, they stood a good fifty metres or so from Van Deen, partially blocked by an old couple, so that Harriet could keep a subtle eye on her target.

The next twenty minutes felt like eternity. Apparently Underground trains used to be much more frequent than this, but with so many people using those terrifying driverless motor car things, trains were less in demand.

When the train pulled into the station, Harriet and Fred stepped aboard the same carriage as Van Deen but sat at the other end. Harriet nervously squeezed the handrail next to her seat. Straight-backed and straight-faced, Van Deen just stared at the floor with his hands clasped together in his lap. He seemed calm, but also deep in thought. Harriet wondered what was going through his head.

"Stop staring," whispered Fred. "He'll see you."

"I'm not staring, I'm… looking," Harriet said.

"Well stop *looking*. He's not going to do anything on the train."

Fifteen minutes later, the train pulled into Kingsgate and Van Deen stood and prepared to disembark. Harriet and Fred followed him up the escalators, out of Kingsgate Station. Van Deen crossed the road and strode up a long residential street.

Harriet's heart raced. *This is it. Somewhere round here is the home of Jack the Ripper.*

Van Deen turned down a different street with big, opulent houses on both sides, double-fronted with fancy bay windows upstairs and down. Jack the Ripper had some money.

The road dark and quiet, Harriet and Fred extended the gap between them and Van Deen and remained on the opposite side.

Halfway up the road, Van Deen opened the gate to the small, walled-in front garden of one of the houses. Harriet and Fred stopped. Harriet chewed on her lip. She heard Fred's deep breath.

Van Deen walked up to the front door.

And knocked on it.

"What?" Harriet whispered. "I assumed this would be his house."

"Could be visiting a friend for the evening."

"Damn."

The owner took a while to answer the door, so Van Deen knocked again. A moment later, a light was switched on in the hallway and shone through the window above the front door.

A woman in a green nightgown opened the front door. Her eyes snapped wide and Van Deen lunged at her, clapping his hand over her mouth to stop her from screaming and forcing his way into the hallway, the woman throwing up her arms to fend him off.

"Shit!"

Harriet bolted forwards but Fred grabbed her arm and yanked her back.

"Stop– don't," he said firmly.

Van Deen kicked the front door shut.

Harriet squirmed out of Fred's grip and sprang across the road. Fred launched into her path, blocking her, clamping his hands on both of her upper arms. "Harriet, stop! We can't do anything!"

"What do you mean? We have to help her! He's *murdering* her!"

"She's probably already dead by now. This man is fucking dangerous, Harriet, and we have nothing to defend ourselves. If we smash our way into that house, he'll likely kill us too."

Harriet's taut shoulders slackened but she clenched her jaw in frustration. "Then what do we do?"

Fred eased his hands off her arms and turned to face the woman's house. "I say we wait for him to come out, and we film him."

"Film him?"

"Yes. My phone can record video – at night. So, even though it's dark, we would likely be able to catch his face as he comes out of the house."

"And then what?"

"We take the recording to the police, and they'll arrest him."

Harriet heaved an angry sigh, the anger stemming mainly from the fact that they hadn't anticipated that Van Deen might *murder* someone on his way home. Although – would they have been able to do anything about it had they known? They could have gone to the police, but they wouldn't have been able to give them much to go on. DNA evidence linking a man who looked in his forties to murders from a hundred and thirty-nine years ago would've made very little sense unless you knew time travel was involved. But if they filmed Van Deen leaving as Fred had suggested, they would be able to give the police potent evidence that he'd murdered someone *tonight*.

The problem was, handing Van Deen over to the police would leave them without any explanation for why he time-travelled to 1888 and brutally butchered Mary Ann Nichols, Annie Chapman, Elizabeth Stride, Catherine Eddowes and Mary Jane Kelly. And those poor women would never, ever get justice.

Harriet shook her head. "But there's more going on here. He's a time traveller. He's murdered people in other *times*. I don't think the police are equipped to deal with someone like that."

"What do you suggest?"

Harriet stared helplessly at the house of Jack the

Ripper's latest victim and clenched her jaw. "That *we* handle this. That we follow this piece of shit home and find out where he lives as per our original plan." Only some of that was her feeling that two time travellers were better equipped to deal with a time-travelling killer than the police. The rest was that *she* wanted to be the one to take this monster down.

Although he seemed reluctant, Fred agreed.

As they stood and waited for Van Deen to emerge, Harriet wondered if the woman he had just murdered – *probably* just murdered – was the witness who had seen him kill that man in St James's Park. Maybe that's why he'd been working late; he'd been pulling all kinds of strings to find out who she was and where she lived.

Thirty minutes later, Van Deen emerged and Fred, his phone poised to film, hit 'record'. Fred filmed him exiting the front gate and heading back the same way he had come, and for a little longer as he and Harriet resumed following him.

They arrived back at Kingsgate Station and followed Van Deen onto a train heading eastbound. This time they had to sit even further away from him. If at any point he had noticed them earlier, seeing them again on the same train going *from* Kingsgate would've been an extraordinarily unlikely coincidence.

Van Deen didn't go back to Puttenham Lane. Rather, he got off at Barons Court and changed for the Piccadilly Line, going north. After about twenty minutes, he got off at Chalk Heath.

Harriet remembered as they followed Van Deen up Chalk Heath's long high street that she hadn't eaten a morsel since their late lunch that afternoon, yet her stomach still held off complaining about it. The turbulent mix of shock, anger, guilt and adrenaline currently coursing through her had probably sapped her appetite. It must've been the same for Fred, who'd expressed hunger earlier but had not made any further mention of wanting dinner.

Momentarily distracted by a woman of a similar age to

her who, despite the temperature having plummeted, looked like she was dressed for the bath, Harriet recoiled slightly as Fred barred her way with his arm.

With a flick of his head, "Look."

Harriet peered forwards. Van Deen was heading for an apartment building. *Damn.* If he lived in a building with flats in, they'd have no idea which flat was his unless they followed him inside.

Crossing the road and hiding behind a tree close to the building, Harriet and Fred watched.

Van Deen stopped next to the door to the building to open one of the metal mailboxes built into the external wall. They were too far away to see which number box it was. Harriet's fists tightened.

Van Deen flicked through a wad of post. Then he walked away from the building, to the bin flanking the pavement, and dropped one of the letters into it. A spark of hope made Harriet's fists loosen. Van Deen walked back to the door and let himself in, disappearing up a brightly lit staircase.

Harriet waited a few moments and made a dash for the bin.

"What are you doing?" Fred asked.

Harriet started figuring out a way of pulling the top off the bin so she could look inside. She was able to pull the entire plastic outer shell off a metal frame with a bag hanging in its rim. "What does it look like?"

She stooped to grab the letter sitting on top of the rubbish.

"Yes! We have him." She read the name and first part of the address aloud on what, judging by all the desperate advertising slogans on the envelope, was clearly a piece of junk mail: "Mr James Rawling, Flat 7 Borogrove House." She looked at Fred, "So that's who Jack the Ripper is: 'James Rawling'."

Fred nodded. "Assuming that's his real name."

Harriet felt an uncomfortable flutter in her stomach. *Because you'd know all about using fake names, wouldn't you, Fred.*

"So what do you want to do next?" Fred asked.

Harriet looked at the building. Her plan had been to find out where Van Deen – *Rawling* – lived, and then come back another day when he was out and break in, see if his home might yield answers as to who he was and what he was up to. And while they were a step ahead on the who-he-was front, getting inside this building to find out what heinous plots he was entangled with wasn't going to be easy. The building looked heavily secured and was probably packed with alarms and those security televisions that could record you.

"That man who got the DNA scanner for us," said Harriet. "Do you think he'd be able to source us a gun?"

Fred's eyes widened. "I don't know. Maybe. He seemed to have a lot of fingers in a lot of pies. But firearms are illegal in this time, remember."

"I know."

"What have you got in mind?"

"I think we should come back a different night, armed, and threaten Rawling to let us in," Harriet said. "Tell him we know what he did to that woman in Kingsgate and the man in St James's Park and that we have evidence. When he lets us in, we'll get him to tell us everything."

10

April 7th 2027

Harriet and Fred walked up to the front door and knocked. To Harriet's surprise, it was opened by a woman with kinky black hair and thick-rimmed glasses, wearing a navy blouse, smart black trousers and a knee-length white coat. Harriet had assumed that James Rawling, if that was indeed his real name, lived alone.

"Yes?" the woman said, frowning softly as she looked Harriet and Fred up and down. She was about Rawling's age, Harriet guessed, perhaps a bit younger. His friend? His sister? Eying her lab coat again – *his doctor?* "Can I help you?"

"We– we're here to see James Rawling," Harriet stumbled, swallowing a lump of apprehension.

"Whatever you're selling, we're not buying."

"We're not selling anything. We're private detectives looking into a murder."

The woman's frown deepened, eyes narrowing into slits. "And what's that got to do with my husband?"

Harriet threw a quick glance back at Fred, whose eyes widened. "Your husband? You're *Mrs* Rawling?"

"Dr Beverley Atkins, actually. James Rawling is my husband. And you are?"

"Please just tell your husband he's going to want to speak to us," said Fred.

"Excuse me?"

Fred sharpened his tone. "We know it was him. Just get him for us, will you?"

Her face suddenly lined with worry, she called over her shoulder, "Jim? You need to come down here now."

A man hurtled down the stairs behind her. It was him. Although, strangely, he looked different to yesterday. He wore a similar suit, but his face appeared fuller and a trim beard shadowed his jaw and upper lip. He'd grown a beard overnight? Maybe it was stuck on.

"What's going on?" Rawling asked, looking at his wife and then at Harriet and Fred. "Who are you?"

"We're private detectives," said Harriet. "We're here about the murder you committed last night."

Rawling's cheeks instantly flushed crimson, sweat beading on his brow. "What? *I* committed?"

"Yes. You."

His eyes flickered incredulously. "But– last night? Last night I was at a works function. There were at least two dozen others there who can vouch for me. I gave the keynote speech."

He was obviously lying so his wife wouldn't know what a monster he was. Harriet had no intention of keeping her in the dark any longer. "We *saw* you. We have evidence."

"Mum! Dad! I can't find my PE kit!" shouted a young girl from somewhere inside the house.

Jack the Ripper has kids?

Rawling smiled uneasily at his wife. "You go see to the kids. There's obviously been a mistake. I'll get this straightened out."

He wanted her out of the way. Face clouded with reluctance and uncertainty, Dr Beverley Atkins turned to go upstairs.

"I suggest you come in," said Rawling, motioning them inside.

Harriet and Fred stepped onto the plush parquet floor of the large hallway. Harriet noted two different pairs of trainers and school shoes on the shoe rack by the door. Rawling showed them through to a cosily furnished lounge with a wood burner and family photos on the wall and mantelpiece, several depicting two young girls. An enormous, wall-mounted television displayed an animation of that creepy Disney mouse character, with the big yellow shoes and white gloves, running from something. Rawling grabbed the remote off a table and switched it off.

"Now, I'm not sure what this is about, but–" Rawling started.

"Yesterday we followed you from Million Eyes headquarters to Kingsgate, where we saw you barge into a woman's house," Harriet said. "That woman was found dead this morning."

"Million Eyes? The computer company?"

"Yes."

"I've never worked for Million Eyes in my life. I'm the chief operations officer for Fine Locks, the Rawling family business. We're a shampoo manufacturer. Fine Locks is my uncle's company and before that it was my father's."

Harriet's gaze roamed to one of the photographs on the wall, of Rawling as a young teenager standing next to a man maybe twenty years older. She pointed at it. "Is that your father?"

"No, that's my uncle. My father died in a car crash when I was two. As did my mother."

Harriet looked at Fred. "Show him the video."

Fred frowned. "What video?"

"The one you filmed last night, of course! On your phone."

He looked confused. *Why do you look confused?*

"You filmed Rawling coming out of that woman's house in Kingsgate, remember?"

Fred shook his head.

"Look," said Rawling. "Someone's clearly got the wrong end of a very long stick. Let me give you the details of a colleague at my company that you can speak to. He'll be able to confirm my whereabouts last night." He got his phone out and started looking through his contacts.

"You're a lying, murderous fuck," said Harriet, baffled and seething at Fred's abrupt change of heart about

97

showing Rawling the evidence as they'd discussed.

Rawling put his phone back in his pocket without giving her anything. "And you have just outstayed your welcome. I'll show you to the door."

He ushered them back into the hallway and opened the front door, directing them out with his arm. Harriet and Fred exited onto the doorstep.

"You don't remember me, do you?" said Harriet, turning round.

"I've never met you before." Rawling's hand grasped the door handle and was moments from pushing it shut in their faces.

"But you have," Harriet insisted. "A hundred and thirty-nine years ago. We met in St Mary Matfelon church in Whitechapel, right after you murdered and mutilated Mary Jane Kelly."

"I've no idea what or who you're talking about."

"You're a liar! I know you're him! You're Jack the Ripper!"

Rawling snorted a derisory laugh. "Jack the Ripper? Sounds like a character in a low-rate crime novel. Good day, detectives." He slammed the front door.

Harriet and Fred walked to Fred's car, Harriet shaking her head in a mix of confusion, frustration and disgust. The pair were silent as they got in the car and Fred drove away. Then Fred turned to Harriet and said, "So who's this Jack the Ripper then?"

Harriet looked at him. "What?"

A wave of dizziness swept over her, Fred blurring into a whitish haze. Harriet clutched her head. Nausea rippled up her throat. "Stop the car."

"Are you alright?"

"Just stop the car. Please."

The car pulled up next to the kerb. Harriet took a series of deep breaths and was able to blink away the white haze over her eyes, her legs, hands and the car dashboard coming back into focus. The nausea dissipated.

She looked at Fred, also in focus again. "Sorry. I don't know what happened there."

Fred smiled. "That's okay. I know you hate being in cars. But if I drive any slower, I'll get pulled over by the police."

It was true, she would've taken the rattle and shake of a slow, clip-clopping horse-drawn carriage over these rapid and roaring (though admittedly smoother) metal boxes any day. But something else had caused her dizziness and she wasn't sure what.

She stared straight ahead. Whatever it was was gone now. Her thoughts circled back to their bizarre encounter with James Rawling.

"I think we should go back," Harriet said.

"Why?"

"I think we should go back and ask more questions. About his family."

"About whose family?"

"Rawling's, of course."

Fred looked down his nose at her with a puzzled frown. "James Rawling?"

"Yes."

He continued staring at her, lips pursed and slightly apart, as if he wasn't sure what to say.

"What!" she exclaimed, frustrated.

"Why would we want to ask Claire Flanders about James Rawling's family?"

"Claire Flanders?"

"Yes. The woman we just went to see. The one who thinks her nanny's breastfeeding her baby!"

"What?" Harriet felt every muscle in her body stretch taut. "We just went to see James Rawling. We went to his house."

Fred's eyebrows met in a heavy frown.

"We found out he had a wife and children," Harriet continued. "He denied murdering the woman in Kingsgate, said he worked for his uncle's company and was at a works function last night. Remember?"

Fred took a deep breath. "Harriet... none of that happened. We just interviewed the woman who called us yesterday and wants us to investigate her nanny. We went to see where Rawling lived last night, and he lives in a flat, not a house. In Chalk Heath. We said we would go back once I've sourced a firearm."

As Fred spoke, the realisation that everything he was saying was true crept over her like rising damp. She remembered their meeting with Claire Flanders and everything Ms Flanders had said about her nanny and she remembered feeling like Ms Flanders was chasing a villain where there was none. She glanced around at the pretty, mostly residential road they were in, the bright mid-morning sun painting the trees that lined it in resplendent splashes of gold. A dozen or so kids played in the playground at the front of an infant school they were parked outside of. *What on earth just happened?*

"Where are we?" Harriet asked.

"Dunford Cross," Fred replied softly. "Are you alright? Do you want me to drive you to a doctor?" He placed his hand on her arm, which had started to tremble.

Harriet shook her head. "No, thank you. Please just take me home."

Fred smiled. "Sure." He shifted the car into 'drive'.

As Fred prepared to pull away, Harriet looked out of the window at the pavement just outside the infant school's front gates, and her blood ran cold.

A red snake with glowing yellow eyes slithered in a circle on the pavement, walking its sharp-toothed jaws over its tail. Just like the snake Harriet had seen when she and Fred had travelled in time six years ago. Harriet blinked hard several times, wondering if she was seeing things. The tail-eating snake remained each time she opened her eyes.

Fred pulled away and Harriet kept her eyes on the snake as it got smaller and smaller, partly because they were driving away and partly because its body was disappearing up its own throat.

She thought about telling Fred but quickly decided against it. After everything that had happened that morning, he might well have driven her straight to a mental hospital if she'd told him that as well.

11

August 23rd 2037

It was a hot Sunday afternoon in the village of Llanderi in West Wales and most of its five hundred residents were either working up a tan in their gardens or sheltering in their air-conditioned homes and avoiding the sun altogether.

Jake Kotler, his two-years-younger sister, Gretel, and their friends, Billy, Aaron and Pablo, were on the village green having a water fight, all armed with various types and sizes of water guns and running around laughing and screaming.

Jake, however, was starting to feel a tad frustrated. He had a Super Saturator Double Soakage 3000 and Pablo only had a Drench Nation Floodinator X2, yet Pablo had one wet sleeve and Jake felt like he'd been dunked in a lake. It was because Pablo was so short and skinny and ran like a Whippet.

Jake had to get him. There was no way he was letting Pablo win. Not again.

Pausing from soaking the others, Jake fixed his eyes on Pablo, who kept sneaking behind trees, hedges and benches on the green and mounting surprise attacks while the others were distracted. *I know your game. Fool! You won't defeat me so easily.*

While Billy and Gretel chased each other around the duck pond and the war memorial, Jake used a succession of subtle gestures and nods to call a temporary truce with Aaron and instigate a silent conspiracy to turn the tables on their true enemy. Guns poised, they started to approach Pablo from opposite sides.

We have you now, Pablo. Prepare for maximum soakination.

Then, before they'd even got close, the sneaky little pipsqueak scurried between them and unleashed a torrent of water on his sister!

"Jake! Gretel!" called their dad from the path skirting the green, heading for the village shop on the corner. "Do you want ice cream?"

They were in the middle of a crucial battle, but a chocolate whippy with sprinkles and a flake seemed an excellent reason for a ceasefire.

"Yes, please!" Jake and Gretel shouted in unison.

Jake glanced back at Pablo, who grinned evilly at him. To be honest, he and Aaron still had a chance to get him before Dad brought their ice creams.

"Guys, look!" cried Billy.

Jake turned. Billy was staring skywards and Jake followed his gaze. A strange silver object, shaped like a giant jelly bean, hovered in the sky behind the Half Moon Inn. Other people on the village green had noticed it too and were staring and pointing.

"What is it?" said Pablo, lowering his floodinator. Now would've been a great time to drench him, but Jake was more interested in the object.

"I think it's one of those new drones," said Jake. "The Seed, it's called. I saw it on the news. It's the fastest ever and has a stealth field that makes it invisible to sensors, *and* a positronic super computer." Jake was a bit of a nerd when it came to drone tech.

"Cool!" said Gretel.

"What's it doing here?" said Aaron.

Good question.

Suddenly, as the children stared, a compartment opened in the belly of the Seed, and an ominous ball with deep, vertical grooves and a glowing red hole at the centre emerged slightly from the craft, like a red eye opening and popping out.

"It didn't do that on the news," said Jake.

"I wonder if it's—" Gretel started.

Her sentence cut off as an enormous red beam of light surged out of the 'eye' of the Seed and blasted the ground somewhere behind the Half Moon Inn, probably close to Bryn Jones' farm on Carmarthen Lane.

A chorus of gasps and cries rippled across the green.

A moment later, the beam stopped. And Jake could no longer remember Bryn Jones' farm. Or Bryn Jones. Or Bryn Jones' wife or children or cows.

There was no farm in Llanderi.

Heart pounding, Jake froze where he stood as a gauzy red haze spread past the Half Moon Inn, all the houses either side of it, and Llanderi Methodist Church. For a moment all the buildings caught inside the haze looked fuzzy and blurry. And then... they vanished. All of them. Gone.

Jake blinked. A moment of dizziness made him sway and totter slightly. He blinked again and straightened.

Llanderi had never had a pub or a church. Too small for either. It was a hamlet, not a village. Only two hundred people lived there. Jake knew that. Jake had always known that.

Like a red tidal wave, the huge mist wafted towards Jake and the others on the green, scooping up houses as it went. Houses that were... *never there.*

Jake's father had already come out of the village shop with Jake's and Gretel's ice creams. The mist rolling towards him, he dropped the ice creams, which splatted in the road, and hurtled towards his children.

Then the mist enveloped the shop.

Llanderi had never had a shop. A hamlet with only seventy people didn't need a shop.

The red wave approaching the duck pond and the war memorial on the green, Gretel broke her awestruck stare and bolted towards Jake.

But the mist devoured the duck pond and the war memorial.

And then it got her.

Jake was an only child. He'd always wanted a little sister.

His racing heart slowed to a steady thud, then a laboured crawl. He looked up to see his dad tearing towards him and in that moment, it seemed like he was running in slow motion.

Jake looked down at his Super Saturator. *Maybe Dad will have a water fight with me. Water fights are no fun on your own. And I'm the only kid my age in Llanderi.*

His dad reached him and stooped to fold him tightly into his arms, just as the red mist enshrouded them both, pulling them into a dark oblivion.

Dr Neether watched her video feed in the Redactor chamber at Facility 9 with clenched fists, a stiff jaw and welded-shut lips, as the red beam surged into the Llanderi focal point, causing a temporal shockwave to propagate through the small West Wales village.

"Temporal incursion in progress," her colleague said, and Dr Neether swallowed. *Please work.*

The red wave eradicated a farm, houses, roads, a pub, a church and a village shop from history, transforming Llanderi into open meadows and woodlands. Dr Neether felt her shoulders loosen, although it wasn't time to celebrate yet. After so many years, she knew the dangers of premature optimism more than most.

"Temporal incursion complete," said her colleague, as Dr Neether watched the red wave dissipate into shimmering shreds of cloud scudding over fields and the tops of trees.

Dr Neether nodded tentatively. "Run a sensor sweep. Confirm full erasure."

Her colleague activated the sensor grid on the Seed and probed the now wild and uninhabited countryside where Llanderi had once stood.

Several minutes later, "Full erasure confirmed. All

humans and manmade objects have been eradicated."

"Counter impacts?"

Her colleague read off his computer console, "None. All collateral impacts are within our projections. No damage to Million Eyes or any of our key people."

Dr Neether blew out the sigh of relief she'd been holding in. "Power down the Seed and lower the Shield. Make a note in the log that the large-scale test was successful. We now have a viable weapon against the Shapeless."

12

April 9th 2027

"Afternoon, Mother," said James Rawling as he entered his mother's room at Sycamore View Nursing Home. He placed a vase of blue hyacinths and fuchsia tulips on the table next to his mother's bed and she turned stiffly in the bed to look at them. "I brought you a bunch of your favourite flowers."

"I can see that, dear, I'm not blind. I like purple hyacinths. Not blue."

The soft, female, computerised voice that sounded nothing like his mother came from the machine by her bed that could translate her thoughts directly into speech. A technological marvel backed by Million Eyes – and not yet commercially available – Rawling had managed to secure one for his mother by virtue of being one of Miss Morgan's most trusted employees, certainly after he'd proven himself with the Jennifer Larson clean-up.

"Sorry, Mother," Rawling said. "I'll bring purple ones next time."

"Your father brought me purple ones yesterday."

"No, he didn't, Mother. Father's dead." *And has been for twenty years. Ever since I...* Rawling pushed back the memory.

A moment later, Mother said, "Your father came to see me yesterday."

Rawling shook his head and sipped the coffee one of the nurses had made for him. Before he had got Mother hooked up to this speech machine, she had been a mute for five years thanks to her stroke. That she also had dementia meant he never knew what went on in her head or how much or little she understood. Till now. Now he was painfully aware. Fortunately the dementia had eaten so much of her brain that most of what came out of the speech machine was incoherent nonsense. This was one of her more lucid days. She may have forgotten about Father's death, but at least she was stringing a sentence together. *More's the pity.*

An eerie giggle trickled out of the machine and made Rawling wince slightly. Although the tone of the giggle was wrong, the machine's imitation of its rhythm was perfect, uncannily so.

Rawling looked at his mother's face, her wide smile deepening all her wrinkles into ugly crevasses as the machine laughed for her. "Is something funny, Mother?"

"Your father told me he wet his trousers and screamed like a little girl," she replied. "Imagine! A grown man."

Rawling frowned. "Mother, who are you—?"

"George, of course. Your first."

Rawling felt like the chair had been pulled out from under him. He leaned forwards and whispered loudly, "Mother, you can't talk about this."

"Oh, don't be so modest. You did well, dear. Your father was proud. Now help your mother with these vegetables, will you?"

Mother didn't say much after that, thank God, but Rawling still left Sycamore View feeling hot and tense and like his collar was attempting to strangle him. First there was that witness to the murder he committed in St James's Park. Now this. He felt like the net was closing in.

He got on the Tube closest to the care home, but had to wait a while for the train as they weren't very frequent here. He was used to it; he'd made the deliberate choice, some years back, to go about on foot and trains and use an untraceable burner phone so his all-powerful employers couldn't track him. Couldn't track him *easily* was probably more apt. Rawling knew more than most that they were called Million Eyes for a reason.

When he got back to his apartment in Chalk Heath, Rawling baked a steak and kidney pie big enough for two. Just as he was about to sit down to dinner and watch an episode of *The Cat Vet,* his door buzzed. *Strange.* He never had visitors and he hadn't ordered anything.

He went into the hall. The video display on his access control system showed two people he didn't recognise standing outside the front of Borogrove House. One was a young-looking woman with blonde hair wearing a long blue coat, the other an older man with olive skin and black hair wearing a suit jacket over a shirt with no tie.

He tapped the panel. "Hello? Can I help you?"

"We're private detectives looking into a murder," the woman answered. "We think you may have some information for us."

Rawling's stomach did a somersault. *What was I saying earlier about that net?*

"I'm afraid I don't know anything about a murder, detectives," Rawling said quickly. "Sorry I can't be of help."

"It's about the murder of Nadia Moore," the woman said.

Rawling's breath caught at the back of his throat. The witness! The one he killed the other night. How could they know about that? Who were these people?

Keep it together, James. They may not know a thing...

Noticing he'd been silent for several moments, the woman said, "We know it was you, Mr Rawling. I suggest you let us in. You're going to want to hear what we have to say."

They knew his name.

Fuck. *Fuck fuck fuck.*

Rawling buzzed them in and went to fetch a disruptor from his bedroom drawer. He tried to steady his breathing as he went to the door, heart thumping like a fist against his ribcage.

He looked through the peephole when they knocked, to check it was the same pair, then opened the door a few inches, disruptor poised behind it in his other hand.

"Who are you?" Rawling demanded. "Who sent you?"

"Nobody sent us," the woman said.

Rawling stared at them.

"Are you going to let us in?" the man said.

Swallowing hard, Rawling stepped back and opened the door wider to allow them entry. Once they were inside, he slammed it shut and trained his disruptor on them. The man moved quickly, whipping a pistol from somewhere on his trousers and pointing it at Rawling.

His wasn't an energy weapon. It looked like a perfectly normal firearm, which meant they may not be Million Eyes, but could easily be independent agents working on Million Eyes' behalf.

"I'll ask you one more time," said Rawling. "Who *are* you?"

"His name is Fred Gleeson and mine is…" The woman hesitated for a moment, shooting a glance at her associate, who stared fiercely down his gun at Rawling. "Mine is Harriet Turner."

Her name rang a bell, but he didn't recognise either of them.

"Why don't we both put our guns down so we can talk?" said Fred.

"I'd prefer to have the conversation like this, if it's all the same to you."

Harriet stepped forwards.

"I suggest you stay where you are," Rawling warned. "You're probably not aware of how much damage this weapon can do."

She stopped. "You don't remember my name, do you? Or my face."

Rawling frowned. "Should I?"

"Well I remember you. That said, you still look much the same. Whereas I probably look quite different, given that I was only eleven when we met in St Mary Matfelon church in Whitechapel a hundred and thirty-nine years ago."

Rawling's heart stopped. *What?* He peered at her face and prickles of recognition started dancing across his skin.

"You told me your name was Henry Van Deen. Remember? Right before you showed me your briefcase full of... trophies." Her lips curled in disgust.

Rawling's blood froze. He remembered the name now. Could this *really* be that brazen little street urchin he met ever so briefly in 1888? How could this have happened? How could she have travelled in time?

"I don't understand," said Rawling. "How are you *here?*"

"I found some strange red time travel pills in amongst my mother's belongings," said Harriet. "We took them. Now we're here."

"And who was your mother?"

"We'll get to that. First I want you to tell us why you were in our time. Why you killed all those women. And then I want you to tell us everything you know about time travel."

Rawling tightened his grip around the disruptor. "And why would I tell you any of that?"

"Because we have evidence that you murdered Nadia Moore, itself pretty damning evidence that you also murdered Andrew Karndean, that man who was butchered in St James's Park. Given that Ms Moore was a witness."

Rawling studied them both. "What evidence?"

Fred slipped his other hand into his pocket.

"Slowly," Rawling warned, finger firmly on the trigger of his disruptor.

Fred pulled out a smartphone, tapped the screen with his thumb and held it out in front of him, playing a video of Rawling as he exited Nadia Moore's house in Kingsgate three nights ago. The recording was clear and facial recognition software would confirm it was him.

Fuck.

"And that isn't the only copy," Harriet said. "Fred has made sure that that recording will go straight to the police, and every national newspaper, and to Million Eyes, your employers, should anything happen to us."

So they knew he worked for Million Eyes too. *What else do they fucking know?*

They had him. By the fucking balls.

Rawling slowly lowered his disruptor, his chest deflating in a dejected and defeated sigh. Fred lowered his too.

"What do you want?" Rawling asked.

"Right at this moment, information," said Harriet. "What were you doing in 1888 and why did you kill all those women?"

Rawling took a breath. "I was on a mission. To... recover something."

"What? For who? For Million Eyes? Did *they* send you back in time?"

Rawling swallowed. Miss Morgan would have him taken out in a heartbeat if she discovered he'd divulged Million Eyes' secrets. Just as she would if she found out one of her best time travellers was a serial killer.

He would have to lie, even though he hated lying and didn't feel particularly good at it. It was far easier to say nothing, or leave strategic gaps in the truth. But he would have to give it a try. Otherwise he could lose everything.

"No," said Rawling quietly. "Not Million Eyes. I work for an organisation that is using time travel to improve the state of things. The state of the world. They sent me back to 1888 to recover something that had completely unravelled their rise to power." As it happened, most of that was true.

"What organisation?" asked Fred.

"It's a secret society. We call ourselves the Keepers."

Harriet glared at him. A flash of the little girl who had asked to see inside his briefcase of organs, before emptying her stomach all over the church floor, ran across his eyes.

"So what does brutally murdering five innocent women in 1888 have to do with improving the state of things?" Harriet asked.

Rawling thought back to those months in 1888. He remembered those murders like they were yesterday. Remembered how turned-on, how alive, how *powerful* he had felt, particularly with that last one. With her he had *soared.* He'd ripped her from stem to sternum, decorated the room with her bloody viscera. He'd been able to take his time with her, and it had been utterly joyous. It had certainly made up for the unfinished job he'd done on that third woman.

Unfortunately Rawling hadn't felt like that for some time. Killing, he acknowledged, had always only brought temporary satisfaction, which was the reason he had forced himself to stop all those years ago. And though he hadn't mustered the strength or willpower to stop killing a second time, the thrill had long since gone. It was like a partner you've been fucking for so long that there's no passion or spice or chemistry anymore. You keep fucking, but it's not exciting or rewarding. Now Rawling just felt dirty, hungry, *desperate* all the time. Like there was a huge hole in his life that no amount of killing would ever fill.

"Well?" said Harriet, and Rawling realised he had silently retreated inside his head for at least a minute. "Are you saying these 'Keepers' ordered you to commit the murders?"

Rawling couldn't think of what else to say. "Yes."

"Why? How does killing those five women improve the state of the world?"

Think – quickly. "Because time travel is complicated. Those women– they– they would have started a chain reaction leading to a series of terrible disasters that I was there to prevent." A perfectly plausible lie.

"So they needed to be plucked from the timeline, that's what you're saying. To prevent worse things from happening in the future."

"Yes. Exactly."

"So why the fuck did you butcher them?"

Rawling fell silent. He looked at Fred, who stared at him with a strong, bitter distaste in his eyes. Rawling had no explanation that these two wouldn't see through like glass.

"Okay," said Rawling. "I *didn't* have to. I... I killed them like that because..." The words lodged in his throat.

"Because what?"

"Because I wanted to."

Harriet pulled in a deep, loud breath of either shock or disgust. Actually, it was unlikely to be shock. Surely she expected him to say that. What reason could anyone have for pulling those women to pieces so completely other than desire?

Fred's eyes flickered as he took in Rawling's words. Then he said, "So what you're saying is that you're a psychopath."

"I stopped for a long time," Rawling said. "After– after my father died. That assignment, it..." His words trailed off.

Harriet finished the sentence for him, "Gave you a chance to get back to your old habits?"

Rawling exhaled. "Yes."

Harriet bared her teeth. "You disgusting piece of–"

"Harriet," murmured Fred, shaking his head at her. "What good will that do?" He then trained his eyes on Rawling. "So are this secret society you work for – the Keepers – aware they have a psychopathic serial killer in their midst?"

"No. Not to my knowledge. I've always been careful." *Like Father taught me to be.*

In that moment, Rawling's memory throbbed with images of George Garson. *His first*, when the thrill of killing was still new, still raw. Oh, what a rush he'd felt. Quite why Mother had mentioned him out of the blue at the nursing home that afternoon, Rawling didn't know. But now he kept seeing George naked and bound on the floor and hearing the moist *sshlunk* of flesh as Rawling drove his blade into him, while his father stood in the corner and watched, goading him. Rawling's cock stirred as he remembered the dream he'd had afterwards, that night and many others subsequently, about fucking George's bloody corpse.

"Not careful enough," Harriet snarled at him.

Rawling quietly agreed, "No."

Harriet looked around, craning her neck for a view of

the lounge-diner. "And how long have you lived here?"

A rather more innocuous question. He had no trouble answering that one. "Sixteen years, almost."

"And you never lived in a house, say, in Dunford Cross?"

Rawling frowned. "Dunford Cross?" That was a very well-to-do area in North London; he couldn't imagine ever living somewhere like that. "No. Never. I went from my mother's house to here."

"And have you ever been married?"

"No. Why?"

"Or had kids?"

Her questions were getting stranger by the minute. "I've never had children or been married. Why are you asking me this?"

Harriet sighed. "I don't know. I just... I had this feeling you did."

"What sort of feeling? Like a memory?"

"Yes, sort of. Or a dream. Although I'm fairly sure I was awake."

Wait a minute, this is starting to sound like... "What exactly is it you remember?"

Fred stepped forwards. "Harriet, are you sure you want to talk about this?"

She glanced at him and nodded, "Yes." Returning her gaze to Rawling, "I remember Fred and I coming to question you at a house in Dunford Cross, where you lived with a wife and children. Your wife, I think, was a doctor and you had two girls, and you worked for your uncle's company – a shampoo manufacturer."

Rawling felt all the blood suddenly drain from his head. Needing to sit down, he floundered into the lounge-diner like he was submerged in water up to his waist. He groped for his armchair and collapsed into it.

"That company– that company went bust years ago," Rawling murmured, trying to make sense of what he was hearing. "Because of my father."

Harriet and Fred came slowly into the room. "In this dream, or whatever it was," Harriet said, "both of your parents died in a car crash when you were two. When did your parents die?"

Rawling stared at his calloused hands. "My father died when I was twenty. It wasn't a car crash." *I killed him.* "My mother's still alive. She's in a nursing home."

Harriet shook her head. "It's so strange. I remember it so clearly."

He looked up at her. "Have you had memories like this before?"

"Not that I recall, no. Do you know what's going on?"

"I think..." Rawling hesitated, trying to swallow the sticky lump of confusion and dismay clinging to the back of his throat, but failing. "I think you may be remembering my life in a different timeline. Certain people have a perception that goes beyond linear time. For some of them, it's a feeling of déjà vu. For others, the memories are cogent and explicit, like yours. We call those people sensiles."

"You're saying I'm one of these 'sensiles'?"

"You may be – yes."

"So why do you look like you're about to vomit?"

Rawling pulled in a deep, long breath. "Because sensiles perceive events that have been changed or erased by... by the Keepers. The implications of that are" – he swallowed but felt like a hand was throttling him – "disturbing."

Harriet frowned. "What do you mean?"

"Because it means that something the Keepers have done has altered the timeline – and rewritten my life."

Harriet gave a slow nod. "And how does that make you feel?"

He looked at her. "As full of questions as you are."

"Let's talk more about these 'Keepers' of yours."

Rawling shook his head. "I can't."

"You *can't?*"

"I can't do this right now. I need to think. I need to... look into some things."

"Do you think we were born yesterday? As you well know, we were born longer ago than anyone alive!"

"Look – you have me. I'm caught. It's over. If I make a wrong move, you'll send that evidence to the police and to Million Eyes and it won't be long till they find me." *And I'll be a dead man walking.* "If I run – same result."

"I'm glad we're on the same page," said Harriet.

"We are. And I know you have more questions. Please, just give me some time. A few days. I need to find out whether my organisation has done something that's caused me to lead a completely different life."

Harriet looked at Fred, then back at Rawling, the vigilant and defensive stiffness she'd sported since she arrived finally started to ease. Sighing, she said, "Well we know where you live and work, so don't try anything."

"I won't."

Harriet nodded and they turned to leave. "We'll be back."

He'd expect nothing less. *No way out of this one.*

They let themselves out and Rawling spent the rest of the evening trying to find out if Million Eyes had turned him into a killer.

13

September 23rd 2222

Dr Jesus M. Hirschfield was in the infirmary of the Twelfth Remnant's new base in Mount Precipice, trying desperately to extract Shapeless venom from his friend, Abdul. Several days ago, Jesus, Abdul and a couple of others had been collecting supplies from a ruined corner of Nazareth when two Shapeless descended on them. They were able to kill both creatures with their new blasters, but not before one of them sprang onto Abdul's back and 'stung' him. Abdul only didn't vomit up his organs there and then because Jesus was able to put his body into temporary stasis.

They had rushed back to the Mount Precipice base, only recently established inside an old military compound that had been abandoned after the military surrendered to the Shapeless at the beginning of 2220. Mount Precipice was a rugged rock outcrop covered in stubby desert sage that soared almost four hundred metres above Nazareth. Or rather, what was left of Nazareth.

Jesus had secured Abdul inside a stasis chamber while he worked out a way to remove the venom. None of the serums or antivenoms he'd administered had worked, mainly because Shapeless venom didn't behave like that of any Earth animal. He'd thought about trying to remove the venom molecules using teleportation therapy, as he would to remove certain microorganisms. However, the venom molecules had already bound themselves to

Abdul's cells in such a way that there wasn't enough of a pattern to lock onto.

Jesus wasn't giving up. He and Abdul had grown unexpectedly close in recent weeks. Though Jesus had promised himself he'd never love again after losing all his family and friends to this war, the way he'd been feeling about Abdul was on the verge of making him break that promise.

What had just made everything worse was that the Mount Precipice base was no longer secret. Yesterday, the Shapeless had found them. Now their ships hovered around the mountain like circling vultures, while thousands of them waited, ravenous, on the ground just outside the compound's gates. They hadn't yet been able to breach the shield the Twelfth Remnant had erected around the base, although everyone inside acknowledged that it was only a matter of time before they found a way. They were using however long they had to regroup and come up with a new strategy.

Except, of course, that there weren't any new strategies. The leaders only said they were doing this to try to sustain some semblance of morale, and many in the Twelfth Remnant saw through their attempts to instil false hope – Jesus included. The Shapeless had won this war long ago; for them this was pest control. Hundreds of resistance groups across the world, large and small, had already been exterminated; of the more organised ones, the Remnants, only nine remained. And the Twelfth Remnant's numbers were dwindling with each successive attack. Before long, they'd be gone too. Although most people refrained from admitting the inevitability of humanity's extinction openly, many were already referring to this as the 'Last War' – kind of an admission in itself.

Jesus had long given up hope of a happy ending, and was now just going through the motions, day after day, trying to seize as many mini-wins as he could from the time he had left. Like saving Abdul. That would be a mini-win. More than, actually.

"Dr Hirschfield, you're needed in the briefing room." Jesus looked up from his computer to see Makayla at the infirmary door. There was still a rip in the shoulder of her uniform. Something they had all started wearing six months ago, the uniform was a one-piece, form-fitting garment made from mouldex, a material specially formulated to be resistant to Shapeless stings. *Although not when it has holes in it.*

"You really need to get that rip mended," said Jesus, standing up.

Makayla nodded. "I know. I just haven't got around to it."

Jesus felt his jaw tense. "Well, get around to it! The Shapeless could find a way through our shield at any moment."

Makayla fell silent, cheeks flushing.

Jesus shook his head quickly. "I'm sorry. I didn't mean to snap."

She gave an uncertain smile. "How is Abdul?"

Jesus glanced back at the stasis chamber. Abdul looked peaceful and radiant, like he was sleeping and could wake up at any moment and everything would be fine. "Still on the brink of death. I don't know how to help him."

"You'll think of something."

Will I?

Jesus followed Makayla down the corridor to the turbolift and went up two floors to the briefing room, where the Twelfth Remnant's senior officers were gathered round a large computer screen. It didn't feel strange anymore than the human race had reverted to using physical computers and the internet after more than a century of using orbs, subspace and the database. Everyone who was left had been living a bare-bones existence for some time now, and for Jesus, legacy tech wasn't the worst part. What he really missed was a decent meal. In order to maximise synthesiser reserves, they'd all been living on synthesiser ration packs for as long as Jesus could remember. At least they still *had* synthesisers, he supposed. He'd heard they'd gone down in many parts of the world, forcing survivors to turn back into hunter-gatherers.

"There's a coded transmission coming in from the First Remnant in London," said General Toma. "They're saying they've found something."

Jesus frowned. *Found something?*

A moment later, a woman with short blonde hair appeared on the screen. Jesus hadn't seen her before. "Good afternoon. You don't know me. My name is Dr Cara Montgomery. I'm... I'm the new leader of the First Remnant." Her brow bobbed with unease. She didn't appear very comfortable in her new role.

Jesus did a quick glance about the room at everyone in attendance, thinking, *Thank goodness everybody's cognits still work.* Not many people learned foreign languages anymore thanks to those tiny implants, inserted behind their ears at birth, and the psychic fields they generated to translate the words people spoke and heard. Dr Montgomery was likely to be speaking English, which Jesus was quite certain that none of the Israelis round this table could speak a word of. If the Shapeless had found a way to disrupt people's cognits, there'd be no way for any of the world's resistance groups to exchange information; interpreters were scarce and probably all dead by now.

"What happened to Commander Bonnich?" asked General Toma.

"I'm afraid Commander Bonnich was killed in a Shapeless ambush last week," she replied. "So was Sub-Commander Nanji. I'm– I'm the First Remnant's lead physician. There was..." A swallow rippled down her throat. "There was no one else to take over."

This Cara Montgomery was like Jesus: a physician forced to become a soldier. She had probably tried to stay out of the war for as long as she could, like Jesus had, till the only choice left was to fight or die. But she had it worse. She'd been forced to become the leader of her remnant, too. No wonder she looked uneasy.

"I'm sorry to hear that, Dr Montgomery," said General Toma. "What have you discovered?"

"Thank you." She took a deep breath and then said

rather quickly and nervously, "Our scientists have confirmed that the unusual signal being transmitted to the Guinan System by the Shapeless has the same basic properties as the biochemical carrier signal being relayed between each individual Shapeless creature as part of their hive mind."

A few months ago, the First Remnant had confirmed that the Shapeless operated by way of a hive mind after they were able to isolate the biochemical impulses linking all of them together. The resistance had long suspected as much, because of the way dead or injured Shapeless got instantly teleported away, as well as their ability to possess the knowledge of Shapeless who happened to be on the other side of the globe. It was one of the things that made them so dangerous. And hard to beat. And it also explained why they spoke in unison, because it was all of them speaking together, with one mind.

Jesus felt a chill dart down his back as he remembered their chorus of taunts during his encounter with them a few days ago. *You humans are funny. We love chasing you. We love seeing you sweat and bleed.* Then they had chanted maniacally, "*Sweat and bleed, sweat and bleed, sweat and bleed!*" right before attacking Abdul.

Jesus shook off the memory and refocused on what Montgomery was telling them. This unusual signal she'd spoken of had been picked up by the First Remnant's new axionic sensors and, in collaboration with the Ninth, they'd been using stratoferometric mapping to triangulate the signal's course. They'd tracked it all the way to the Guinan System in the Devidia Cluster, almost ten thousand light years from Earth. The Guinan System had only one planet in orbit of its star, and it was now presumed that that planet must be the homeworld of the Shapeless.

"So we know now that there are more Shapeless out there in the Guinan System, linked to the ones here on Earth," said General Toma.

Dr Montgomery nodded. "Yes, but not just that. Though the signal has the same basic properties, there are some differences. Our scientists liken them to the way the human brain sends controlling signals to the rest of the body."

General Toma glanced at Colonel Hoffman, eyes wide. "Controlling signals?"

"Yes. We've long wondered whether or not each Shapeless creature possesses a brain and where its brain would be if they do. Now we think that, well, maybe they don't."

Toma frowned incredulously. "They have no *brain?*"

"They have a brain. It just isn't here. On Earth. We think the brain might be in the Guinan System."

It sounded insane. But so did everything else about these monsters.

Toma shook his head. "Even if that were true, Dr Montgomery, I'm not sure how it helps us."

Jesus concurred. If they had the means, maybe they could travel to the Shapeless's planet in the Guinan System and see if they could find this 'brain'. But they *didn't* have the means. After the Silence, when the Shapeless decided to make their presence on Earth known by lowering their camouflage fields to reveal thousands of terrifying-looking vessels sitting in Earth's aerospace, they appeared to have two key objectives. Invade, and stop every human ship that tried to leave the planet from doing so. Tens of thousands of evacuees attempted to flee on colony ships but the Shapeless chased them down and destroyed them. And in every battle, the Shapeless had tended to concentrate their fire on the USE ships' faster-than-light drives so that they couldn't retreat.

It had quickly become clear that they didn't just want the planet. They wanted to strand humanity on it. Now that there *were* no more FTL-capable ships, they'd succeeded on both counts.

Plus, even if they did have the means to go find this brain, who was to say they'd be able to do anything about it?

Dr Montgomery appeared to have a plan. "I've started working on a nanovirus that may be able to–"

A sudden deep rumbling made the floor and walls shake, instantly muting the audio on the transmission. A moment later, Dr Montgomery's image fractured into static.

Jesus gripped the metal arms of his chair, hard. "What was that?"

Gazes whipped towards the door to the briefing room. Jesus's eyes followed, landing on Makayla, standing in the doorway looking like her every nerve had been shredded.

"The shield is down!" she yelled. "They've breached the base!"

Only a matter of time...

Everyone in the room shot to their feet. "Everybody to the main escape tunnel immediately!" said General Toma.

But Abdul's still in the infirmary.

While all those on level six headed in one direction to the escape tunnel, Jesus headed in the opposite. Overhead lights and control panels on the walls started flickering as he lurched into the turbolift, desperately hoping that the base didn't lose power while he was in it.

The lift dropped down to level four but the computer wouldn't open the doors. Jesus pulled on the emergency handles to force-release the door. He ran across the infirmary to Abdul's stasis chamber and a deep wave of pain crashed through his chest.

He was too late. The stasis chamber had already lost power. Jesus stared down at Abdul. Blood trailed from his mouth down the side of his body to the connected sacks of flesh slithering sluglike towards his feet.

He still looked peaceful, like he'd not felt a thing. Jesus prayed he hadn't.

Distant bone-like clicking and cracking froze the hot tears filling Jesus's eyes, yanking his gaze to the infirmary door.

The Shapeless were in the corridors around the infirmary. They were so fast, they'd already overrun the base.

Did the others make it out? How am I going to make it out?

He scanned the room, slung a medical kit over his shoulder and grabbed one of the new blasters. Then he sprang for one of the internal maintenance crawlways. Power to the infirmary still fluctuating, he had to wrench open the hatch manually.

The clicking and cracking, now accompanied by fast tapping and scuttling, got louder as he crawled inside the narrow tunnel. Then came the eerie giggling.

The Shapeless were in the room.

Jesus pulled the hatch shut behind him, but he knew the Shapeless would hear it. He scrambled down the crawlway as fast as he could, stomach throbbing with the knowledge that the multipedal creatures were faster.

Reaching the end of the tunnel, he hurtled up a ladder and swung left into another tight crawlway, which led towards one of the secondary escape tunnels. He glanced back only occasionally – no sign of the Shapeless yet. On entering the low-lit tunnel, he now had standing space and was able to launch into a sprint.

The tunnel gave out into open air and Jesus squinted into the hot, bright Israeli sun that immediately started scorching the top of his head. He glanced around at the shell of a building that used to guard the tunnel's exit, only bits of walls still standing. In the near distance, the Shapeless's screwdriver-like ships fired energy beams at the ground and he could hear screams. He wondered if they were firing at other fleeing Twelfth Remnant members.

Jesus started running west through the rubble of the city, away from the ships. After a few moments he glimpsed a fellow Twelfth Remnant member running in a similar direction and veered towards her. It was Makayla.

"Dr Hirschfield!" she cried when she saw him. "Thank goodness you made it out."

"Where's everyone else?" Jesus asked.

"I got separated from them. They're trying to regroup on the–"

Jesus's heart shot into his throat as a mass of long white limbs leapt out from behind a crashed shuttle onto

Makayla's back, her words breaking into desperate screams. Makayla fell face first, pinned to the ground by the limbs. This Shapeless had nine, which was more than most, all different lengths and thicknesses with different numbers of joints, and terminating in the long, spindly digits that they walked on and grabbed with. None of the Shapeless had heads or faces, and this one's many limbs protruded from the barest nub of a body, five of which were holding Makayla down while the other four flailed madly. Its white skin shone with the slimy, semen-like substance they all secreted, beads of it splattering the ground and debris all around them.

Jesus yanked his blaster from his belt and fired. The beam just bounced uselessly off its fattest limb. *They've adapted.* He was going to have to recalibrate the weapon.

The line of little gill-like openings that ran down each of the Shapeless's limbs started to flare. Sharp spikes poked out of the gills, trying to stab a struggling and screaming Makayla. While most of its stingers failed to penetrate her uniform, several got through the rip in her shoulder he'd pleaded with her to fix.

Jesus's heart sank. He couldn't save Makayla's life, but he could spare her a horrendous death. So instead of shooting the Shapeless, he shot her.

Out of the corner of his eye, Jesus caught a whole legion of Shapeless scurrying towards his position and turned to run.

Spotting a nearby abandoned and mostly intact building that may have once been offices, he ran towards it. He stole a glance over his shoulder. The Shapeless were still about a hundred yards from him, but the gap was closing.

Jesus barrelled through the broken entrance doors into some kind of foyer with a reception desk. Circling round a pile of rubble where half the ceiling had fallen in, Jesus tore up a dark corridor where most of the lights had stopped working but a couple continued to flicker intermittently, creating a strobe effect.

He blasted through a stuck-open automatic door into a large room filled with broken desks and bodies. Dozens of bodies covered with tiny fragments of glass, plaster and concrete, with trails of black, dried blood leading away from their broken jaws and zig-zagging all over the debris-strewn floor like one of those swirly path puzzles for kids. The stink hit him. These people had been dead for a while.

He crossed the room, tripping over a whirl of cables and smashing both knees against the floor, jolts of pain shooting up his legs. His blaster flew out of his grip and skittered across the floor, but his medical kit fell with him, secured by the shoulder strap.

That was when he heard the clicking.

And the laughing.

Instantly forgetting about the pain in his legs, he got to his feet and dashed in the direction of his blaster.

And then he saw it. *A great big fucking hole in the floor.* Glancing up, he noticed that the ceiling had a similarly shaped hole, as did the floor above it, the holes getting closer to the exterior wall, which also had a hole through it. Jesus could see blue sky, occasionally darkened by a passing Shapeless ship. He guessed that it was a ship that had done this – impaled the building with the sharp rod on its hull.

And his blaster had fallen straight through the hole in the floor to the basement room below. There it lay, glinting on the top of a heap of rubble.

Fucking hell.

His eyes raked the room for an alternative weapon, but these people were office workers who looked like they'd been caught off guard. Even if they did have any disruptors or blasters, they'd be several upgrades behind the ones they were using now.

He was defenceless. He needed his weapon but if he jumped down the hole, he'd likely break his ankle – then he'd be royally fucked.

Fast, scuttling footsteps entered the corridor Jesus had just run up. The Shapeless were moments from bursting into the room.

Jesus curved round the hole and made a run for the

other end of the room, hoping it would lead to another door or corridor.

He launched up a narrower corridor with doors to smaller rooms on both sides – and stopped.

Shit!

His way was blocked. By – *fuck knows what.*

Halfway up the corridor, just past the fourth door on each side, was a cloud of red smoke. *Sort-of* smoke. It was a dark, dirty red and roiled, shimmered and swirled, more like a turbid liquid than a gas. Jesus moved forwards tentatively. As he did, the smoke started to emit bright flashes, making him squint and flinch.

The clicking and laughing behind him got louder. Then came the whispered chorus of Shapeless voices that still struck fear into his core: *"We know you're here! Don't you want to come out and play?"*

He had to get past this smoke.

He quickened his pace, but the smoke started flashing faster and brighter, like it was reacting to him. He noticed that its source was a little white bottle on the floor in the middle of the corridor. The smoke billowed constantly from its rim like a tiny chimney, coalescing and thickening in the space above. Jesus could see precisely nothing of the corridor beyond it. There may not even have been any more corridor for all he knew.

"Come and play with us!" The Shapeless's whispers chilled his bones. *"We only want to make your insides dance!"*

Jesus's heart jabbed his ribs repeatedly like a fist trying to break them. Shutting his eyes tight, he ran through the smoke.

He stopped again. This time it wasn't of his own making. A powerful force took hold of him and he couldn't move. He opened his eyes.

He could see nothing but swirls and flashes of red. His neck was locked, his arms frozen in a raised position and either his feet were numb, or the floor had disappeared. He was paralysed.

It's got me. Whatever it is.

A wave of dizziness struck him. Suddenly the thick redness in front of his eyes dissolved into blurry images of people. They dashed in and out of focus and Jesus recognised his mother, his father, his wife, his daughter, his best friend, and Abdul – all the people who'd been viciously ripped away from him by the monsters.

I'm dying.

He saw Abdul, smiling, standing in the shade of a carob tree. He moved forwards, leaned in and closed his eyes, and Jesus remembered the moment: his and Abdul's first kiss. He could almost feel his lips on him again – *almost*.

Then Abdul's face faded into something else. A bunch of young boys running around a basketball court. Jesus remembered this as well. These were his school mates. This was *years ago*.

And then the boys and the basketball court blurred and faded into images that made no sense at all. Jesus peered hard. He was seeing soldiers. But they didn't look like any soldiers he'd ever seen. With their red tunics, silver breastplates and red, semi-cylindrical shields decorated with eagle's wings and lightning bolts, they looked like... *Romans?*

A moment later, the Romans faded into a dark night, men with fiery torches and bodies hanging from giant wooden crosses. Jesus was lying on the ground, looking up. A horrified gasp burst from his lips as he turned his head to the side and saw men hammering thick iron pegs into his palms.

What the fuck is this *memory?*

At that moment, the dizziness returned, blurring the images till he could see nothing but yellowy haze.

Time to die.

Jesus's breath caught in his throat as the yellowy haze was suddenly siphoned into an impenetrable blackness, and he felt himself fall. And fall.

And fall.

Jesus opened his eyes and found himself staggering, disoriented, into a sloping town square. Everything was shifting in and out of focus but moments of clarity revealed small double- and single-storey clay-brick houses with flat roofs, orchards and enclosures for livestock, and a much bigger stone building with a clerestory roof that towered over everything. Hammers banged and saws scraped and farm animals bleated and brayed, and yet it was peaceful – blissfully so – compared to where Jesus just was. No screaming. No weapons fire. No ships in the sky.

What happened? Where am I? How did I get here?

14

Harriet and Fred had turned off their computers and were about to close the museum and head home when the door buzzed. Harriet came out of the office into the museum gift shop, saying, "Sorry, we're just about t–"

The rest of her sentence hit a wall at the sight of James Rawling. *How the hell did he find us?* She then remembered that he worked for Million Eyes; some people believed that Million Eyes were spying on the world through all their multifarious technologies. And he *did* find that witness, Nadia Moore, in the space of an afternoon.

"Fred!" Harriet called, standing rigid.

Fred bolted into the shop, immediately pulling his firearm from his belt and training it on Rawling. He'd been wearing it constantly since their first encounter with him.

Rawling raised his hands. "I'm not here to hurt anyone. I just came to talk."

Harriet studied the serial killer's face. He looked pale and drawn, like he'd not slept in days.

"How did you find us?" said Fred.

Rawling gave a faint, mirthless laugh, saying nothing, as if the answer was so obvious it was boring to give it.

Harriet and Fred hadn't seen or spoken to Rawling personally since they turned up and questioned him at his flat last week. Even though Harriet still had a million burning questions, she was intrigued by this possibility that his organisation's time travelling may have impacted his own life history and was willing to give him time to find out. Fred had been wanting to turn him in to the police, but Harriet wanted to find out as much as they could first. So they'd got someone to trail him and make sure he didn't sneak in another murder before their next meeting. What was disturbing was that this person should have been trailing him now.

"What did you come to talk about?" said Harriet.

He looked up, the muscles around his eyes twitching with what appeared to be sadness, maybe even despair – although it may have been a deception. "My organisation."

Harriet had been researching Rawling's organisation. 'The Keepers'. She'd found literally nothing but had come to believe that her mother was probably part of the same group. She figured that the red pills were manufactured by the Keepers as their means to travel in time. As to how they actually worked, or specifically, how a time traveller could pinpoint which time period they travelled to (because she and Fred certainly hadn't chosen to end up in 2021), she still didn't know. More questions for their next meeting with Rawling.

Which, apparently, was now.

"What about them?" Harriet said. "Did you find out if they altered your... your personal timeline?"

Now the muscles in Rawling's brow and around his mouth began to tense and twist, his forlorn expression morphing into anger. Through gritted teeth, "Yes. And they did."

"Why would the Keepers do that?"

He almost spat out the words, "Because they don't give a shit. And they're not called the Keepers. I made that up."

Harriet frowned. "So who are they?"

"Million Eyes."

Harriet threw a sideways glance at Fred.

"Your employers?" said Fred, starting to lower his gun. "You're saying *they're* the time travellers?"

"Yes. All the consumer technology they put out is just a smokescreen."

Harriet took a breath. *So my mother worked for Million Eyes too?* "You're saying Million Eyes are the ones using time travel to, how did you describe it, improve the state of the world?" Harriet wasn't sure she bought that as a motive; many people who sought to make the world a better place just said that to serve their own ends or gain power.

"I used to think that. I don't anymore."

As I suspected. "What have you found out?"

"I looked back over Million Eyes' previous time travel assignments. I followed the thread of one in particular, a deliberate alteration to history which I found set in motion a series of events leading to my parents no longer dying in that car crash you mentioned. There *was* still a crash, but the lorry hit a different car."

Rawling paused to swallow and take a breath. He started to wring his hands as he spoke, a bitter inward struggle seeming to shadow his face. "And because they survived, I grew up with a father who murdered people in his spare time, and taught me to do the same. Along with a mother who fully endorsed it all. If my parents had died in that crash, I never would've become... *this*." Shame and distaste laced his voice and curled his lips, and Harriet wondered if any of it was real.

"That sounds like an excuse."

He looked at her. "It's not an excuse. It's a fact. Million Eyes made me this way." He spoke listlessly, as though he didn't really care if they believed him or not.

And Harriet wasn't sure she did. "But you *like* killing." A stab of memory of Rawling masturbating over that briefcase of organs made her wince and blink hard. "I *remember.* You get off on it."

"You're right, I do. But it's an addiction. And like any addiction, the thrill is temporary. The rest of the time it's painful, overpowering and debilitating." His anguished eyes dipped towards the floor.

"Do you expect us to feel sorry for you?" said Fred, a faint note of outrage in his voice.

Rawling shook his head. "No. I don't expect anything. I came here because I've decided that Million Eyes are wrong."

Fred wrinkled his forehead in puzzlement. "Wrong about what?"

"That there are no means the ends don't justify. One of those means would be ruining my life. Million Eyes would call *that* justified. But how many other lives have they destroyed in the course of saving everyone? Plenty, I can tell you."

"Wait a minute," said Harriet. "Saving everyone?"

"I haven't told you what their ultimate goal is, but I'm going to. It's to prevent an apocalypse in the future, about two hundred years from now, called the Last War. An alien race called the Shapeless is going to invade and the human race is going to be on the brink of extinction within a few years."

Harriet looked at Fred and noticed all the blood drain suddenly from his face. It was as if he knew what Rawling was talking about.

Shifting her gaze back to Rawling, "So let me get this straight. Million Eyes are trying to stop humanity from becoming extinct in the future, and they're altering history to do that?"

Rawling nodded. "Million Eyes have been around for centuries. They've only been using time travel since the 1980s. Before that they were using other means of controlling the government in order to steer the country in whatever direction they felt would enable us to defeat the Shapeless in the future, or avoid having to fight them in the first place."

"Controlling the government?"

"Oh, yes. Be under no illusions. Democracy in the British Republic is as real as Father Christmas. Million Eyes control everything."

Something about what Rawling was saying didn't add up. "Wait a minute. You said Million Eyes have only been using time travel since the 1980s. So how did they know about this apocalypse before that?"

"That's a long story."

"Then give me the abridged version."

Rawling proceeded to tell them an outrageous tale about a physician called Dr Jesus M. Hirschfield accidentally travelling back in time from the time of the Last War to the 1st century and writing scrolls that would lead to the founding of Million Eyes. As he spoke, it started to dawn on Harriet what Rawling was implying: that this Dr Hirschfield *became* Jesus Christ. That his warnings about the Last War were twisted into something more palatable by his followers, becoming the foundation for the Christian Church.

It was all utter folly. It had to be. Not just folly. *Blasphemy.* Rawling's disrespect for what Harriet and millions of others believed was just more evidence of his contempt for his fellow man.

Harriet looked at Fred. Even though she knew he wasn't particularly godly, part of her expected him to be similarly affronted by Rawling's lies. But he seemed captivated, hanging off the serial killer's every word.

"You're asking us to believe that the Jesus Christ that people have been praying to for two thousand years was a time-travelling doctor from the future?" said Harriet. "Now I *know* you're lying."

"I know how it must sound," said Rawling, "particularly to someone who was brought up a Christian, but it's the truth."

"It's not the truth, it's nonsense."

"I'm afraid, Harriet, that what you've been taught by probably everyone in your life – *that's* the nonsense."

"It worked…" Fred spoke softly after several minutes of saying nothing, no strength or spirit in his voice, his face pale. Maybe he *was* reeling from Rawling's horrific lies about Jesus, like she was, although she had no idea what he meant by 'It worked.'

Neither did Rawling, asking, "What do you mean? What worked?"

Fred looked at him and ignored the question. "Are you saying that Million Eyes have been keeping Jesus's true message about the Last War and the Shapeless alive? All this time?"

Harriet was incredulous. "Fred! Don't tell me you believe this bullshit."

Fred did a confused shake of the head. "I don't know what to believe."

Rawling answered Fred's question. "Keeping alive Jesus's message has always been Million Eyes' *raison d'être*, yes. We even call it the 'Mission'. But over the years, even I have wondered if sometimes they went too far in trying to complete the Mission."

Harriet arched both eyebrows. *And this is a psychopathic serial killer saying this.*

"Now I *know* they have," Rawling continued. "They're just pretending that everything they're doing is about preventing our extinction. They don't care about human life – not really. They're hypocrites. They're forging a path to our salvation but they're trampling on people every step of the way. You have no idea how many lives have been lost or rewritten thanks to their interventions. Probably as many as they're trying to save."

Harriet cast her eyes briefly over at Fred again. He looked in a kind of troubled daze, the veins in his forehead starting to swell. He stared off, eyes roaming to the floor.

"So what are you saying?" Harriet asked Rawling.

"I'm saying that if you two are here to take down the time travellers that sent me to 1888, then I'm in."

Harriet shook her head slowly. "We're not. We didn't come here to start a war."

"Then why did you?"

"To start a new life. A better one. And we hoped to find you one day, too. We've done rather well on both fronts."

Rawling gave a subtle roll of the eyes. "Congratulations."

Harriet stepped forwards. "But there's another reason *I* came. I came because of my mother. I think she travelled to the future. She may have even *come from* the future. Even if I never actually see her again, I want to find out why she time-travelled. I want to know her story. Her real story, not the one she fed me as a child. I want to know who my mother really was."

"What is your mother's name?" Rawling asked.

"Emma Turner."

Rawling shook his head. "I don't know the name, and I know everyone who works in the Time Travel Department."

"Maybe she hasn't joined yet."

Rawling nodded. "Maybe."

"There's something else." Harriet turned and went back into the office to retrieve the tiny pyramidal device she had been carrying in her handbag, ever since she came to the future, as a memento of Emma. Stealing a glance at Fred as she went, she noticed that his gun hand was shaking. *What the hell is wrong with him?*

She came back into the shop, holding the device out in her palm. "I found this amongst my mother's belongings after she died. I assumed it must be some kind of future technology. Fred and I have confirmed that it's not of *this* time, which means it must be from further in the future. Do you know what it is?"

Rawling squinted at the device, then stepped forwards and reached out his hand and Harriet recoiled, closing her fingers around the object. Rawling withdrew his hand and said, "May I?"

Harriet peered at him. She didn't trust him as far as she could throw him, but if he had answers, she wanted them. She looked round at Fred, who had finally broken out of his daze and retrained his gun on Rawling, staring vigilantly down the barrel.

Tentatively, she stepped forwards, held out her hand, and opened it.

Rawling gently lifted the device from her palm and turned it over in his hands. "I've seen these things before, although I've never used one. Didn't think it would be good for me."

"What is it?"

"A memory device. I believe you can record your

memories onto them and play them back." He touched the depression in the bottom of the pyramid and got the blue lights flashing around the rim. "I think you have to attach it to your temple. Then it will activate."

He handed it back to her. She looked around at Fred, who gave a slight, worried shake of the head. He didn't want her to do it.

But she had to.

She raised the flashing device to her temple and flinched when it attached abruptly but gently to her head with a tiny, pneumatic hiss.

Three rectangular images appeared in front of her eyes. She blinked. She could still see the shop, and Rawling, but they were overlaid with the images – like photographs floating in midair. Beneath each image was a date, all from 2224.

She felt a surge of adrenaline. Was this the time frame her mother came from? Almost two hundred years in the future?

Doubt and dismay started to cloud her excitement. 2224 was two years after Rawling said 'Jesus' travelled back to the 1st century. The time of the Last War. Was that why Emma came to the 19th century? Was she fleeing the Shapeless?

Harriet peered at the images. They were of people she didn't recognise, in places she didn't recognise. She reached to grab the one dated 6th October 2224 and bring it closer. Although her fingers carved into empty air, the image immediately enlarged and centred her vision, the others disappearing. And then it started moving. It wasn't an image, it was a film, now playing in midair on a floating television screen.

In the film, Harriet saw what looked like brightly coloured children's toys on a red and white gingham mat. A small hand reached out and Harriet realised that she was seeing through the eyes of the hand's owner. The hand pulled several of the toys into the owner's lap and Harriet saw crossed knees encased in a silvery blue material. The toys were pretend foods – limes, slices of tomato and cheese, a pink cupcake. A child's picnic.

A moment later, the child's gaze drifted upwards to a woman standing over her with short blonde hair, the same shade as Harriet's. "Is our picnic ready yet?" the woman said.

"Nearly, Mummy," came the voice of the child whose eyes Harriet was seeing through. "I'm just making the sandwiches."

"Extra pickles for me, please, darling."

"Coming right up." The child looked back at her toy foods and reached to pluck a handful of pickle slices. Then she whipped her gaze back to the woman, whose smiling face now filled the 'screen'. "Do you know how much I love you, Dina?"

Dina? Who's Dina?

The child returned to her sandwich-making, saying, "Yeah. I'm amazing." And Harriet heard the woman laugh in the background.

In that moment, a door swung open in the furthest recesses of Harriet's mind and a raft of long-buried memories burst through. A wave of dizziness flooded over her and she stumbled forwards, having to grasp the edge of one of the shelves of museum souvenirs to steady herself.

Oh my God.

"Harriet?" Fred blared behind her. "Are you alright?"

Harriet tore the device from her temple and stood frozen, still gripping the shelf, knuckles white. If it wasn't there, she'd fall.

Rawling stepped forwards. "What is it? What did you see?"

Harriet took a breath. Her heart thumped. "It was... *my mother*. I remember now. My mother was..." She shook her head, trying to remember more, but only finding pieces.

She looked at Fred, who threw back a bewildered frown. "I know where I have to go. Rather, I know *when*." And then, looking at Rawling, she said, "I'd like you to teach me to travel through time."

15

October 6th 2224

"Alright. Let's make camp here."

Cara Montgomery and the forty-eight remaining members of the First Remnant set about building their tents in a clearing close to a shallow stream, deep in the forests of Ockenley Nature Reserve, North-East London. Once the tents were built and a large fire lit, Cara returned to Dan, still comatose and in a bad way after being caught in an explosion while fleeing the Shapeless. Cara had used a regenerator to heal his external wounds, but his extensive internal injuries were the real problem and a regenerator could only do so much. Dan needed to be placed inside a biophasic resequencer. But for that they'd need to get to a hospital that hadn't yet been reduced to rubble and still had power. Cara didn't have what she needed to perform an old-school surgical procedure either.

She checked his vitals and ran a microcellular scan in his tent. No change. He was dying. He was dying of something Cara could stop, but she just didn't have the tools to do so.

Please, please don't die on me. They'd been through so much together.

Cara sat with Dan for a few moments, stroking his cheek and talking to him. Then she left his tent and went to check on Roxy, whose girlfriend, Ayesha, had been killed in the same explosion. Roxy was still staring blankly and silently. No surprises there. Ayesha had been much closer to the blast than Dan and a bloody chunk of her torso had hit Roxy in the face. Cara had treated Roxy for shock but coming to terms with what had happened was going to take time. Probably a lot of. Tariq was looking after her.

"Has she eaten anything?" Cara whispered.

Tariq shook his head.

"Keep trying. And keep talking to her."

"I'm running out of things to say."

"She just needs to know you're there."

Tariq nodded.

Cara returned to her tent, where Abby had been supervising Dina, who had just turned four last week. "Thanks, Abby."

Abby smiled. "Course. How is Dan?"

Cara swallowed. "Not good."

Abby gave a sad sigh and went to sit by the fire. Cara looked down at the red and white gingham mat next to their tent, where Dina sat pulling toy food items into her lap. Just playing, like she had always done, while the world ended around her. Not really understanding what was going on made her the happiest one here. Oh, how Cara envied her ignorance.

"Is our picnic ready yet?" said Cara.

"Nearly, Mummy. I'm just making the sandwiches." Dina had her memory recorder attached to her temple, Cara noticed. She often did. Playing back her memories was the closest thing she had to television these days. Cara rarely wore hers, but that was because her memories were typically too painful or traumatic to record.

"Extra pickles for me, please, darling."

"Coming right up." She reached forwards to grab some toy pickle slices.

Feeling an overwhelming surge of love, Cara crouched down and framed her little face in her hands, looking deep into her shimmering cerulean eyes. "Do you know how much I love you, Dina?"

She slipped her face out of Cara's hands to look back at her toy picnic and said, "Yeah. I'm amazing."

Cara laughed and sat down with her on the mat. Dina handed her a plate with a sandwich that had lettuce, cheese, pickle, slices of orange and banana and a chocolate biscuit, and Cara curled her lip. "Mmmm, yummy."

"You eat it all up like a good girl," said Dina, pouring them some 'tea' with her little green teapot.

"I absolutely will." She pretended to take a bite. "Mmmmm! Delicious."

A short while later, Cara was in the middle of reading Dina a story before bed when Neil called from outside their tent, "Cara, can I come in?"

Cara paused reading. "Yes, come in."

Neil lifted the entrance flap and poked his head inside. "It's Dan. He's woken up."

A sense of disquiet crept over her. Cara wasn't sure if Dan waking up was a good or bad thing, given that there was nothing she could do for him and he was likely to be in excruciating pain. She wondered how many vials of morphine they had left. Some. Not loads.

"Do you mind reading the rest of this story to Dina?" Cara asked.

He smiled at Dina, who clutched her motheaten teddy bear, Ruffles, close to her chest. "Of course."

As Cara left the tent, Dina called after her, "Mummy, say hi to Uncle Dan for me."

A deep ache formed in Cara's chest. She glanced back at her daughter and gave a wistful smile and slight nod. Dina's gaze dropped back to her storybook.

Cara crunched through leaves and twigs, steeling herself as she entered Dan's tent. Because she'd fixed his external wounds, no one would have guessed that he'd been in an explosion. But his sickly, greenish pallor, and the pained smile he flashed her as she came in, gave away what was happening inside him.

"I'm dying, aren't I?" Dan murmured, his voice weak.

Cara crouched down next to him. She didn't know what else to do or say, so she just nodded.

"I thought so. I can feel it, you know. It's weird."

He didn't seem afraid. Cara was thankful for that. "How bad is the pain?"

"Pretty bad."

Cara grabbed a pharmacator from the box of medical supplies at the bottom of the bed, plugged a vial of morphine into the injector chamber and discharged it at Dan's neck. After a few moments, "Better?"

Dan pulled in a ragged breath. "Yeah. Thanks."

Cara sat cross-legged and placed her hand over his. Dan turned his hand over so he was holding hers and squeezed. Cara sniffed and pushed back a tear.

"I want you to do something for me," Dan whispered.

"Anything."

"I want you and Dina, and everyone else who's left, to use those pills we found and escape to another point in time."

"What?"

"I mean it."

A few weeks ago they had found a stack of bottles of red pills called 'chronozine' amid the wreckage of a building. The labels on the bottles said the pills were used for time travel. Cara didn't believe they would work. Dan did. He said he'd heard rumours that time travel had been invented centuries ago but kept secret; for him, these pills confirmed it.

"We can't just run away from this war," said Cara.

"Yes, you can!" His pitch and volume rose. "You ca–!"

His words hit a wall of pain and he flinched and screwed up his face. Cara felt utterly helpless.

Dan rounded his lips and blew out a breath. "Cara, it's over. You know that, don't you?"

Cara knew that at the end of 2223, shortly before the Shapeless destroyed most of the First Remnant's equipment and cut off all their communications, the world's fifteen billion-strong population had been reduced to barely more than a few million. Now, ten months later, there were likely to be far fewer – scattered and hiding like vermin.

But she also knew that as long as even one human life remained, this war *wasn't* over.

"We just need to find somewhere where I can recreate the nanovirus."

Cara still clung to the hope that she would be able to restart her experiments. She had been working on synthesising a nanovirus capable of disrupting the signal between the Shapeless here on Earth and what they had theorised could be their 'brain' and the source of their hive mind in the Guinan System. Although initial results had been promising, all her work and equipment were lost when the Shapeless found and destroyed the base under the Millennium Dome, and scattered the First Remnant across the capital.

Dan gave a slight, slow shake of the head, as much as his stiff, frail body would allow. "We've been trying for over a year and still haven't found anywhere or anything you can use to restart your experiments. And it's because the Shapeless have destroyed *everything*. I don't know why you can't face up to this."

"To be fair, Dan, you had given up before we even joined the First Remnant. Remember? And look how close we got with that nanovirus."

"Maybe we were close once. To something. But since then we've just got further and further away, day by day. Every new attack depletes our numbers. There's less than fifty of us, Cara. A couple more attacks and the First Remnant will be no more."

Cara gave a wry smirk. "It's a good thing you're not in charge."

Dan was straight-faced. "I'm not joking, Cara. The human race can't survive this. Not here. Not *now*. But those pills have given the people who are left a means of escape."

Cara shook her head. "By travelling in time."

"I know you don't believe those pills will work. But what's the harm in trying?"

"That they may kill us."

"*May*. That's better than the absolute certainty of the Shapeless killing us."

She sighed.

"Please, Cara. Use the pills. Go someplace, some*time*, better. Give Dina a chance to have a life. We're lucky we haven't lost her already. If the Shapeless– *aaahh*."

Dan's words splintered in a cry of pain. Cara was about to administer a stronger dose of morphine, mixed with a sedative, when Dan grabbed her wrist, stopping her.

"No," he whispered, breathing heavily. "I'm done. Just... just euthanise me."

Dan's eyes cut right through her and made her heart twinge. She wasn't ready to let him go, but she owed him this.

She took a vial of proprionide from the box of medical supplies and plugged it into the pharmacator. She hesitated as she looked into his eyes and saw a tear roll towards his ear.

Now he was afraid.

"Are you sure..." she whispered, her voice barely there.

He swallowed, and winced. Even that was painful at this point. He murmured, "I've never been more sure about anything in my life."

The wall that was stopping Cara's own tears from flowing free and fast was starting to collapse, brick by brick. Her hand, holding the pharmacator, shook. She had euthanised many patients in her time and you'd think it would get easier. It didn't. And now she was having to take the life of her closest friend.

Exactly, Cara. He's your closest friend. So stop being selfish and just do it.

Cara took a breath and, without further hesitation, administered the proprionide and held Dan's hand tight.

"How long?" he whispered, squeezing her hand in response.

"It takes about a minute." Emotion strangled her voice.

He let out a long breath. "Then please just... just promise me you'll... you'll think about what I said."

Cara nodded. "I will. And..." *How can I properly thank him? For being the father Dina never had?* Words weren't enough, but in this moment, they were all she had.

"And thank you. Thank you for everything you've done for us. Dina loves you like a father, you know."

Dan strained to form a smile, and a further tear streamed across his cheek. "Then save her. Save her for me."

Dan took a final breath and his cheek sank into his pillow and his hand went limp in hers.

Cara sat silent and motionless for several minutes, till the final few bricks of the wall holding back her tears fell and she sobbed into her hands.

Cara returned to her tent to find Dina asleep. Neil was sitting near her, reading.

Neil looked up from his book as she entered. "Hey. Is Dan–?"

She would've replied, but the lump of emotion lodged in her throat stopped any words from coming out. So she just shook her head.

"Oh. I'm so sorry. I– I know you were close."

"Yeah. Neil, do you mind watching Dina just for a little longer? I just need to walk. Think. Clear my head."

He nodded. "Of course. I'm happy to."

"Thank you."

Cara took a torch and walked downstream for twenty minutes, thinking, crying, remembering, wishing she could call and speak to her mother. Wishing she could cuddle her. Wishing she could cuddle Jackson. The full moon threw down a silvery light and painted the edges of the trees and the chill wind felt good against her tear-wet face, but it wasn't much of a comfort.

She was about to turn back to the camp when an acrid odour assailed her nostrils. It was coming from somewhere beyond the trees to her left, carried on the wind.

Cara followed the smell, shining her torch ahead.

And then her torch beam caught it.

She froze. Horror trapped the breath in her lungs.

Twisted sacks of flesh, bloody and fresh like they'd just been cut from a living body, slithered slowly across the ground, leaving a slimy trail over the soil and vegetation.

Cara followed it, retching periodically at the wafting stench.

A few minutes later, in a clearing with strangely little vegetation, the creature crawled into a small hole in the ground and disappeared. Cara walked right up to the hole. The ground beneath her felt different. Spongy and porous. *Hollow.*

Concerned it could be unstable, she backed away from the hole. However, her weight had already caused something to shift. The soil around the hole started collapsing, widening it.

Cara shone her torch, chest pounding.

The soil fell several feet, revealing the entrance to some kind of large burrow. She had no idea where or how deep it went, but lining its walls were dozens, perhaps hundreds, of entrails. Bloody human entrails. All piled on top of each other, all wriggling and writhing. And oozing.

Cara retched again, her torch beam wavering. This time she felt the vomit touch the back of her throat. The stench was everywhere, the air filled with it. She pinched her nose with her free hand and breathed through her mouth.

People had long wondered what became of the organ creatures after they vacated their dead hosts. They just seemed to crawl away and disappear, the presumption being that they would simply wither and die, although no remains of a dead organ creature had ever been found.

Because that's not what happens at all. These creatures carried on living. None of them had been seen again because they burrowed underground to hide, like moles. Who knew how many tunnels like this there were? Tunnels heaving with the creeping remnants of humanity.

Cara wanted to punch something. *Why the fuck are the Shapeless doing this to us?* These aliens weren't even properly killing them. They were just mutilating them. Lobotomising them. Turning them into vegetative hunks of flesh. For what?

Cara turned and headed back to the camp, her last conversation with Dan playing on her mind. To be honest, deep down, she knew he was right. The First Remnant was on its last legs. Situation: terminal. Death for all of them had become inevitable. Except that now she knew that it wasn't quite *death* they faced. Rather, they faced living as rancid, mindless beings made of entrails for fuck-knew-how-long. That was what fate so lovingly had in store for her. And her daughter.

If we stay here.

When she got back to camp, most people were outside their tents and gathered close to the glowing embers of the fire. Several of them were reading off their hand scanners. All looked pale with fear or panic.

"What is it?" said Cara.

"There's a Shapeless attack shuttle headed right for our position," said Tariq.

"Time to intercept?"

"Fifteen minutes. Tops."

"Okay." Cara nodded with purpose. "Right... Okay."

She swallowed, stepped back so she could see and address everyone, and projected her voice over the hum of panicked chatter. "Everyone, listen up. I know that each of you has done your best to find ways of turning the tables on the Shapeless. But I've realised tonight that those tables aren't going to be turned. Not here. Not by us. I never thought I would say these words but... hope and determination aren't enough anymore. They're not keeping us alive. We've lost... so many. Too many."

Her voice cracked and she took a deep breath. "So I'm going to propose that we all take one of the chronozine pills we recovered and see what happens. Dan believes – *believed* – that those pills really are capable of transporting us to another place in time. He believed they were our only means of escape."

"You want us to run away?" said Tariq. "Across time? What if we end up sometime worse?"

"Can't be much worse than this," Roxy muttered, her first words since Ayesha was killed.

"Look," said Cara. "This isn't an order. There is a Shapeless attack shuttle coming right for us and we have nowhere to go. The pills could take us to a place in time where we have the chance to start again. A place in time that can offer something better than this endless cycle of death and destruction we've all been caught in for so long. I'd be a shit leader if I didn't tell you that at this point, they're our best hope. At the same time, I'm not *making* anyone do this. If any of you don't want to, if any of you want to stay and fight, I'll stay with you. I won't abandon any of you."

It was the best Cara could do. Dan probably would have had her and Dina go alone – sod the rest of the camp. But that was never going to happen.

Although, if only a few decided to stay, and everyone else chose to take a pill, she'd be faced with the most difficult decision of her life: whether to keep Dina with her as well, or send her through time with the others – and potentially be parted from her only daughter forever.

Luckily, she didn't have to make that decision. To Cara's surprise, everybody decided to take a pill; even those she knew abhorred the idea of running away realised that staying was tantamount to suicide. They agreed that they would all do it together, hand in hand. Who knew – maybe that would cause them to all end up in the same place. Or rather, *time*.

Cara gave everybody five minutes to prepare themselves. Then she grabbed the holdall full of chronozine bottles and returned to her tent. Neil stood outside it holding Dina, who clutched Ruffles to her chest like she was protecting her from a bomb blast.

"Thank you, Neil," she said, putting Dina down. "Go and get ready."

With an uncertain smile, Neil nodded and started towards his tent.

Cara placed the holdall down on the floor of her tent and plucked one of the bottles from inside so she could review the instructions on the labels again. She was hoping for a clue as to how these pills worked.

"What's happening, Mummy?" said Dina.

Cara looked at her. "In a moment, darling, I'm going to hand out a red pill from these bottles here to everyone in the camp and we're all going to swallow them."

Her daughter stared at the bottles in the holdall and frowned softly. "Why?"

"Because we're hoping that these pills will take us all away from here. Somewhere safe."

"To Valurius?" *The Valurius Voles*, about a family of alien rodents from the planet Valurius, was Dina's favourite book.

"No, my darling. Not Valurius, or another planet. More like – another time. Like in *Tiana's Time Machine*." Another book Dina loved.

"Whoohoo! Let's go! Can Ruffles come?"

Cara smiled. "Yes. She can." She had no idea whether possessions could travel with them or not, but, the labels on the chronozine bottles revealing nothing useful, Cara started packing a couple of bags for each of them to carry anyway.

"And Uncle Dan?"

Cara heard the shudder in her breath as she inhaled. She paused packing and crouched down, holding Dina's tiny forearms gently as she looked into her eyes. "Darling, Mummy needs to talk to you about Uncle Dan."

A fearful silence washed over her little daughter as she took it all in. Dina hugged Ruffles tight, pressing her cheek against the teddy's furry nose. Even though she had been born in war, and understood death a lot better than most four-year-olds, this was the first time she had lost someone truly close to her. Tears teetered precariously on Cara's lower lids as she tried to explain that Dan was no longer in pain. Eventually they overflowed down both cheeks and she wiped them away quickly, needing to stay strong for her daughter, particularly now. Dina noticed. This four-year-old missed nothing.

Brightness returned to Dina's face. "Don't cry, Mummy. I have an idea. Let's go back in time to yesterday like Tiana did. Uncle Dan's still alive yesterday."

Cara smiled. *You're such a clever thing.*

Cara continued packing essentials for them both in shoulder bags. Dina asked what would happen when she took the pill, but Cara didn't have an answer. She just said that they would hold hands and find out together. And she told her that if for any reason they got separated, to go somewhere safe and wait, and Mummy would come find her. She realised the moment she said the words that it was a promise she may not have been able to keep.

Suddenly Neil burst into the tent. "Cara, the Shapeless ship – something's wrong."

Cara frowned. "Wrong?"

"Come see."

Cara faced Dina. "Wait here, darling. Neil, do you mind watching her again for a sec?"

"Sure."

Cara left the tent and walked to where Abby and Tariq were reading off their scanners again. "What is it?"

"The attack shuttle has veered off its previous course," said Tariq. "Its trajectory is erratic."

"Is it damaged?" said Cara.

"All systems operational, according to these scans," said Abby. "It doesn't make sense. I've never known the Shapeless to lose control of their ships without some kind of systems failure."

A white flash lit up the woods for a split-second, making them all flinch. Plunged into darkness again, the brightness of the light left white spots in Cara's vision.

As soon as her eyes had adjusted, Neil's screams of "Cara! *Cara!*" made her spin round.

Cara's heart leapt into her throat. She darted back to her tent. Ruffles and the bag Cara had packed for Dina lay on the floor of the tent next to the holdall of chronozine bottles, surrounded by a dozen or so scattered red pills. Dina was gone.

Cara looked at Neil. "Where is she?"

He shook his head madly. "I– I don't know. There was

this massive white flash and she just– she just disappeared!"

Panic seared through her. Grabbing the collar of Neil's jacket and yanking him towards her, "I fucking told you to watch her!"

"I only turned my back for a second. I don't understand!"

She shoved him backwards hard. The fact that there were chronozine pills strewn over the floor meant that Dina must have opened a bottle and taken one, probably spilling the rest as she was trying to tip one out.

Cara lurched out of the tent and puked against a tree.

"Cara!" Abby said, running over. "What is it? What's wrong?"

She wanted to say, *my four-year-old daughter's just travelled in time to fuck-knows-when and she's all alone and I've no idea how I'm ever going to find her again.*

But none of the words came out.

16

August 13th 1881

On her way back to Father Andrew's common lodging-house on Fournier Street, costermonger Emma Turner noticed an oddly dressed young child wandering close to the Ten Bells pub in the middle of the road. Emma squinted. It was a girl. She must've only been about three or four, and didn't look like any street urchin Emma had ever seen.

As Emma got closer, she noticed that the girl was pale, drawn and in a daze. She dragged her feet, her arms swinging limply at her sides, one of her hands holding something. Her blonde hair spilled over the shoulders of her uncomfortable-looking skin-tight outfit that was silvery blue and made from a strange, shiny material.

A hansom cab rolled towards her, and Emma almost had to drop her barrow and run to pluck the girl from its path. Fortunately the driver noticed in time and steered his horse around her, shouting an obscenity as he passed. The girl didn't seem to notice.

Emma set down her barrow on the pavement and crossed into the blonde girl's path. The girl stopped walking, so wasn't completely blind to her surroundings. She stared straight ahead.

Emma stooped to meet her eyeline. "Sweetheart, are you all right?" Emma's gaze flitted to whatever was in the girl's hand. Some kind of small, white pot, which she clutched tightly.

Finally the girl's blank stare broke and her eyes met

Emma's, which were the most beautiful and arresting of blues. There was someone still in there.

"Feet hurt," the girl uttered without moving her lips, which looked dry and cracked. Her voice was so faint Emma barely heard it over the drunkards in the Ten Bells.

Emma looked down at the girl's feet. She wore unusual, bulky grey shoes with strange mouldings and patterns. They weren't at all lady-like.

"Let's get you out of the road, shall we," said Emma, taking the girl's hand. The girl allowed Emma to usher her onto the pavement. "Right then. Where have you come from?"

"The woods," the girl murmured.

Emma frowned. There weren't any woods close by. "Which woods?"

"Don't know."

"How long have you been walking?"

The girl shook her head sluggishly and looked down at the white pot in her hand. "A long time. I fell down. Head hurts." She used her hand, the one holding the pot, to indicate the back of her head, inviting Emma to take a look.

Emma leaned forwards and gently placed her hand on the back of the girl's head. Feeling a bump, she nodded, "Looks like you banged your head."

"Hurts."

Emma crouched down and put her hands comfortingly on the little girl's upper arms. Her outfit's peculiar material was smooth and cold. "What's your name?"

The girl shook her head again, staring at her feet.

"You don't remember?"

No reply.

"And do you know how you got separated from your mummy?"

Tears filled the girl's eyes in that instant. Two rolled down her left cheek in quick succession, and she held up her white pot, handing it to Emma.

"What's this?" Emma asked, the pot rattling as she

rolled it over in her hand and studied its label.

> Chronozine.
>
> Do not use without a chronode.
> Take one tablet only.
> Do not use for anything other than time travel.
> Do not time-travel without authorisation from the Time Travel Department.
> Active ingredient: chronotons.

What in the world? Time travel? Time Travel Department? Emma's mind spun. She popped the lid off the top and looked inside to see four little red pills.

Replacing the lid, she noticed that another much smaller label was stuck on the opposite side to the main label. She peered at the tiny wording.

> Batch: T100076/NCC/01-C
> Issue Date: August 13th 2214
> Expiry Date: August 13th 2234

Both dates were over three hundred years in the future. How was that possible? She thought back to a story her father read her when she was a child – *Rip Van Winkle*. A man fell asleep in some mountains in America and awoke to discover that his musket was rusty and his beard a foot long. Returning to his village, he recognised no one and discovered that America no longer had a king but a president. Twenty years had passed while he slept and he had missed the American War for Independence.

Emma's father told her that Rip Van Winkle had travelled through time, into the future, in his sleep. And while the story didn't make it clear, her father told her that he thought something in the liquor Rip Van Winkle was drinking before he fell asleep caused it to happen.

Now Emma was starting to wonder if something similar could have happened with this little girl.

Surely not. Time travel isn't real. Rip Van Winkle *is just a story.*

Isn't it?

"Sweetheart, what…" Emma swallowed. She wasn't quite sure how to say it. "What year do you think it is?"

The girl just blinked at her. If she couldn't remember her name it was doubtful she was going to remember the year. And she looked very young, too.

A moment later, the girl said, "I'm thirsty. Pl-please can I ha…"

Her words siphoning into a breath and her eyes flickering shut, she toppled forwards. Emma didn't know if it was because she was exhausted, or because of the bump on her head. Her arms opened without thought and the girl fell into them, her little head flopping over Emma's shoulders. The girl's hand opened, releasing the pot of chronozine, which rolled into the road.

And something else – something much smaller – fell out of the girl's other hand, landing by Emma's feet. It was so small Emma hadn't even realised she was holding it.

Emma slid the girl down into a cradled position and tried to rouse her. The only response was a weary moan, but at least she was alive. Emma peered at the object that had fallen out of her other hand. It was pyramid-shaped and made of a dark sort of metal, with a perfectly round dent in the bottom. She picked it up and examined it, wondering if it had broken off a piece of machinery. She slipped it into her satchel and stood up with the girl in her arms, who was so light it was like lifting a puppy. She walked over to where she had set down her barrow and laid her carefully on top of the fruits and vegetables she had picked from the Spitalfields Market to sell tomorrow. Then she went and picked up the pot of chronozine and stuffed that inside her satchel as well.

She decided to carry the girl back to Father Andrew's lodging-house. Father Andrew's was one of the nicer lodging-houses in the area and she *usually* had enough to afford her own bed there. Business had been slow of late, forcing Emma to share a bed with a prostitute called Laura, but Laura was lovely and they had a convenient shift system going. Since Laura was out whoring during the night, Emma got the bed to herself. Then when Emma went costering in the day, Laura had it. Tonight it looked like Emma would be sharing anyway – with a confused and probably homeless little girl who may or may not have come from the future.

Emma tried to give the girl some water in the kitchen. She stirred slightly but didn't open her eyes. As she was too weak and exhausted to take the cup herself, Emma had to pour the water into her mouth. She awakened enough to swallow it, but faded back to sleep immediately after. Emma carried her upstairs to her dormitory and laid her on the bed, catching a couple of curious stares from other lodgers. Emma laid down beside the girl and went to sleep.

The following morning, Laura returned to the lodging-house early. She'd been beaten by one of her clients again. With the girl still asleep, Emma helped Laura attend to her cuts in the bathroom. She so wished she could help Laura escape this dastardly business, but knew that Laura – ever willing to take the rough with the smooth – didn't want that. Most of her clients were charming and kind, she'd say, and you wouldn't dispense with a whole crate of apples just because of a few rotten ones.

"Who's the girl?" said Laura as Emma washed and taped strips of gauze over her cuts.

"I found her wandering the streets last night. She said she'd come from the woods." Emma chose to omit the parts about the time travelling and the red pills.

"Where are her parents?"

"I've no idea." *They could be in a different century.* "I have a feeling she may be an orphan."

"The poor darling. Probably a workhouse runaway. Has she said anything?"

"Not much. I don't think she remembers anything. She doesn't even seem to know her own name. She had a bump on her head and I'm wondering if it's made her lose her memory."

"Either that or something horrible happened to her. At the workhouse, no doubt. It's probably why she ran away." Laura shook her head. "I dread to think."

Emma sighed. A few moments passed, then Laura blurted out, "Why don't you keep her? You lost a child, didn't you? Maybe God is giving you another chance to have one. If there's no one to care for her, maybe she came upon you for a reason."

Emma felt a wince of pain at Laura's mention of the child she'd lost, but didn't let on. She didn't like to offload her emotions on others. Much better to keep it in and deal with it inwardly and privately, with dignity. Her mother had taught her that.

Of course, her mother had also tossed her out on her ear for getting pregnant out of wedlock. Even though Ralph was completely and utterly in love with her and had every plan to marry her, that wasn't enough for Emma's toffee-nosed parents. Their daughter had committed a wicked fornication and their only way of saving face among their peers was to disown her. So maybe Emma ought to stop emulating that cold-hearted crone.

Ralph's parents had been a little more forgiving, stopping short of familial expulsion but nevertheless sending him up north to work at one of his father's banks in Nottingham, leaving Emma pregnant and alone, with no money and no home. And then, not altogether surprisingly, the baby – a girl – was stillborn, as though God knew that Emma wasn't going to be able to care for it and took it away from her. Ralph didn't know that his daughter had died; Emma had no way of communicating with him. Her parents, too, were unaware that they'd lost their granddaughter. Not that they would've cared if they'd known. Emma was certain of that.

And while she was *still* in no position to raise a child, maybe Laura was right and this girl had come upon her for a reason.

Maybe God had decided she was ready.

"I don't know," said Emma. "She deserves better than the life of a coster."

Laura frowned. "What? You're Whitechapel's *favourite* coster! Everyone loves you. They love how smart you are. All those big words you use. I bet you could teach her some things."

"Just because I know some big words doesn't mean she doesn't deserve better."

"She ain't gonna get better, though, is she? It's either here, with you, selling those shiny red apples of yours on the streets. Or it's back at the workhouse, picking oakum till her tiny fingers bleed. Not to mention dealing with whatever unspoken nastiness made her run away in the first place. I know what I'd choose."

Returning to the dormitory, Emma and Laura found the girl awake, sitting up in the bed and hugging her knees, staring around the room at the other lodgers with terror and confusion in her eyes.

"It's all right, darling, you're safe," Emma said softly, sitting on the bed and placing her hand on her shoulder.

The girl looked at her. A tear streaked down her cheek. "Are you...?"

Emma smiled. "Am I... what?"

"Are you... my mummy?"

Emma hesitated and looked at Laura. Her memory hadn't returned. It was either the bump on her head, or the time travel, or something had happened in the future that she was unconsciously blocking out. Perhaps it was a combination of all three.

Whatever the cause, if she really had travelled back in time over three hundred years, Emma didn't see how she was ever going to find her real mother and father again. Which meant she was alone, stranded in a strange and dangerous time, and needed someone to care for her.

Laura nodded and smiled gently, silently stating that that someone should be Emma. And she was right.

Emma looked at the girl, wiped her tears with her forefinger, and said with a warm smile, "Yes, sweetheart. I am your mummy. You hit your head, that's all. Come.

Come with me downstairs and I'll fetch us both some breakfast."

During breakfast, the little girl asked what her name was. Emma decided to give her the name she and Ralph were going to give to their daughter, but had been denied the chance, and replied, "You have a very special name, sweetheart. Harriet."

17

April 13th 2027

James Rawling stared at his mother's face while she slept. The bones of her eye sockets, nose, cheekbones and jaw poked through a thin, shrivelled layer of skin that lay over her skull like a damp kitchen towel. It looked like she'd died months ago and was decomposing.

After a few minutes, the corpse stirred and two lined eyes peeled open. "Oh, it's you," said her speech machine.

"Yes, Mother. It's me. Back again. Your faithful little lapdog."

She gave a slow blink and just stared vacantly at him. Her speech machine offered nothing.

"You know, Mother, I found something out the other day." Rawling had been wringing his hands as he sat there, making them red. "About you and Father. About how both of you were meant to have died in a car crash when I was two. And about how I would've never become the monster I am if you had." A strong sense of repugnance coursed through him as he said it.

The senile old hag just continued to stare.

"I would've lived a totally different life if you and Father had died when you were meant to. I was supposed to have married someone. Had kids. Me! A father. A husband. I was supposed to have been better. I was supposed to have been... happy."

"Where's your father? Fetch him," said the speech machine.

Rawling leaned closer to the bed. "Father's dead."

She blinked. "Where's your father?"

"Father's dead and..." Rawling lowered his voice to a whisper. "And I killed him. He wasn't murdered by some gangland criminal. *I* did it. I smashed his head till his brains were all over my hands. I was hoping it would stop after he'd gone. And it did, Mother, it did. In spite of you, I stopped killing. For a long time. Till... till one day, when I just couldn't help myself, and it started all over again."

Mother stared past him at the door to her room. "I'll gouge that bitch's face if she looks at me again. This tea is cold – can't you do anything right? Get me a napkin, will you, dear?" The machine broke into a giggle. "You couldn't fuck a wet tissue with that, darling. Come here. Let Mummy help."

Rawling hadn't expected that with so little of her brain remaining there would be so many nasty bits. He guessed it indicated just how much of her was rotten to the core.

Rawling stood and plucked the lowermost pillow that had been propping her up. Without hesitation he plunged it down over the bitter old woman's face, pressing hard, mashing her head into the pillows and the mattress till the springs whined. The pillow was so thin her nose and cheekbones dug into his palms. She tried to claw him off but her arms were feeble and eventually flopped at her sides. It was the easiest kill of his life, yet even more satisfying than when he had killed his father.

Her vital signs monitors continued to register a heartbeat and brain activity like nothing had happened. That was because he had hacked the machines when he'd arrived. It would be some time before anyone noticed. He hoped.

On his way out of the nursing home, his phone rang. It was Miss Morgan, the woman who had quite literally destroyed his life.

"Mr Rawling." He heard her drag on a cigarette. "I have an assignment for you and I need my best traveller on it." Her best traveller – who was about to betray her.

His instructions were to travel back in time to 1981 and

make a tiny change that would alter the balance of power in Russia in Million Eyes' favour. On his return to headquarters to examine the assignment in detail, he discovered that one of the collateral impacts included a serial rapist escaping justice. Million Eyes' intervention would lead to the police never finding the evidence to arrest him, resulting in the rape of twelve more women.

Rawling had always been a faithful little lapdog to Miss Morgan, too. Blind with loyalty and commitment to the Mission, he had been someone who would do whatever it took, no matter the cost. Never questioning, never doubting. But no more. Now all he could think about were those twelve women whose lives would never be the same. Just like his.

Not that he was going to show his hand by ringing Miss Morgan and asking why Million Eyes were willing to let a rapist carry on raping for some extra power in Russia. He didn't want her to suspect what he was about to do. And he knew what she'd say anyway – that if it meant saving the human race from extinction, a few rapes hardly mattered. Something he used to believe himself.

Of course, in order to not draw attention, he was going to have to complete the assignment. But then, his addiction to murder had led him to butcher dozens of people, and his interventions in time had led him to erase or ruin countless others, so it was a bit late for an attack of conscience.

Rawling collected *more* than he needed for the assignment, including extra chronozine, a chronode, a cognit, some surgical instruments, blue juice. No one batted an eye. That was how trusted he was among the Time Travel Department.

He left headquarters to catch a flight to Ukraine, where he would be travelling back to 1981. In his taxi to the airport, he rang Harriet Turner.

"I have everything we need," he told her.

"So we can start the training?" she replied.

"I'm flying to Ukraine today. Miss Morgan's given me an assignment."

Harriet's pitch rose with a hint of incredulity. "And you're taking it?"

Rawling wasn't sure what she expected. "Unless you want me to draw attention to myself, yes."

She fell silent.

"I'll be back from Ukraine tomorrow," Rawling said. "We can start the training the day after. I'll call you."

April 26th 2027

"I don't understand why you're trusting him. He's Jack the fucking Ripper!"

Fred came to the door of their office just as Harriet was getting ready to leave the museum. She had arranged to meet James Rawling in North-East London in the place he'd said would be Ockenley Nature Reserve two hundred years from now. From the recordings on Harriet's memory device, Rawling had been able to identify the forests of Ockenley Nature Reserve as the site of Harriet's mother's camp in the future. Now it was time for Harriet to go meet her.

Harriet understood Fred's concerns. For the past week and a half Rawling had been teaching her to time-travel at an abandoned industrial facility in East London. Who *wouldn't* be concerned about that? Yesterday Rawling had even implanted a cognit under her skin and injected her with a chronode. She'd actually allowed *Jack the Ripper* to do surgery on her – was she mad? Possibly. But it was too late now.

"Fred, if he wanted to kill me, he would've done so," said Harriet as she fastened the button on her coat. "He's had plenty of chances. And if he did try anything, he knows you still have that footage of him and you'll expose him."

A grim look tightened Fred's features. "And what if he's trying to trick you somehow?"

"I don't think he is."

"You don't *think?*"

"He seems to genuinely want to help me. He hates Million Eyes for what they've done to him."

"And what if Million Eyes aren't really the villains here?"

Harriet frowned at him. "What do you mean?"

Fred's neck undulated in a swallow. "Well, what if everything they're doing is necessary?"

"Necessary?"

"Yes. To save everyone."

"How could turning Rawling into a serial killer and letting all those people get murdered by him be necessary?"

Fred looked down and began rubbing his palm with his thumb. "I don't know. Maybe because what happens in the future is worse. Weren't you listening when Rawling talked about the Shapeless, and the Last War?"

Something wasn't right. Fred had been behaving strangely ever since Rawling came to the museum and told them all about Million Eyes. It was as though something grave had been weighing down on him. She hadn't seen him smile once since that day, and he was usually quite a talker, yet he'd hardly spoken. The man was full of secrets but this was more. This was *bigger.*

"Fred, are you sure there's nothing you want to tell me?" She'd asked him several times, but each time he'd refused to let on.

He looked at her with pained, perhaps even desperate, eyes, and his lips parted to speak.

Harriet waited in suspense.

Once again, the words wouldn't form and Fred's lips sealed. It seemed like he wanted to tell her, just wasn't sure how.

"There's nothing," he said dismally. "I just don't think you should be going to the future."

"You say that like you've been there yourself." *Have you?*

"Please don't go."

Harriet walked to the museum's door. "I'm sorry, Fred.

I have to. You know I do. But I'll come back. Rawling's taught me how to get back to this day, this time. Everything will be fine."

Fred just sighed heavily and went back into the office. Unable to say anything else to console him, Harriet left and made her way to the train station.

Forty minutes later, she got off the train to find Rawling waiting on the platform, looking like he always did – withdrawn, sullen, with dark patches under his eyes. Lost.

Harriet didn't feel sorry for him. He was a tool, a means to an end. Right now all she cared about was the end. Her mother. The future. *Home.*

October 6th 2224

Cara shoved Neil backwards hard. The fact that there were chronozine pills strewn over the floor meant that Dina must have opened a bottle and taken one, probably spilling the rest as she was trying to tip one out.

Cara lurched out of the tent and puked against a tree.

"Cara!" Abby said, running over. "What is it? What's wrong?"

She wanted to say, *my four-year-old daughter's just travelled in time to fuck-knows-when and she's all alone and I've no idea how I'm ever going to find her again,* but none of the words came out.

"Cara!" hollered Francisco from the other side of the camp.

Cara looked up, shaking. A blonde woman stood next to Francisco dressed in a long, old-fashioned, grey coat instead of the one-piece mouldex garment the rest of them were wearing. She started walking towards Cara.

"She said she needs to talk to you," said Francisco. "It's about Dina."

A hot spark of hope ignited in Cara's chest. Could there be a way? A way of finding Dina? Did this woman know how?

Cara approached her, her heart like a sledgehammer to a wall you're trying to demolish. Her whole body was the wall.

"Where did you come from?" Cara asked, voice shaky and thin. "And what do you know about my daughter?"

The woman stopped and just stared at her.

Cara stepped closer. "I'm talking to you."

The woman nodded slightly. "I know. I just... I haven't heard your voice in a very long time."

Cara frowned. "You *know* me?"

"Yes. I remember now. The memories are sketchy. But this helps." She held up a memory recorder.

Cara walked right up to her. And then it hit her. Those eyes. Those shimmering cerulean eyes. Those dimples. That button nose. They say that every mother knows her child when she sees them, and in that moment, a fast and overwhelming current of love, relief and guilt flushing through her veins, Cara knew it to be true.

"Di-Dina?" Cara's lips trembled and her eyes swelled with tears.

The woman smiled and a flash of four-year-old Dina radiated on her face. "Hi, Mum."

18

October 6th 2224

Harriet had been waiting for this moment ever since Rawling had showed her how the memory recorder worked and she'd seen those images of Cara's face. Never had it occurred to her that Emma Turner might not be her mother. Or rather, her *biological* mother. As the woman who raised her, Emma would always be her mother. To be honest, remembering Cara was like finding out she had *two* mothers, one who'd been hidden from her by her own mind.

And now, staring into her *other* mother's eyes felt surreal and confusing. A kaleidoscope of emotions whirled through her, so many that she couldn't identify any in particular. And while the tears accumulating in Cara's eyes revealed something of how *she* was feeling, Harriet's eyes remained dry, like they weren't sure how to respond.

The longer she stood there, though, the more one emotion started surmounting the others: love. Love for the mother she lost, the mother she had now got back. And that turned almost instantly into a compulsion to pull her into her arms and never let go again. So she did.

Now the tears flowed.

Puzzled mutterings hummed all around, but for a few moments, Cara and Harriet were the only two people in the world.

"I'm so sorry," Cara murmured into Harriet's shoulder as they cuddled. "So, so sorry."

Their embrace loosened gradually. Harriet gazed into

her mother's glistening wet eyes and for a moment it was like looking in a mirror. "For what?"

"You grew up without your mummy. Look at you. You're beautiful. You've grown into a beautiful woman. And I missed it."

In the last memory recording Harriet made, Cara had been telling her about the plan for everyone in the camp to take a pill and travel in time to somewhere safe, just like in *Tiana's Time Machine*. She had then watched her four-year-old self open a bottle of pills and put one in her mouth without waiting for Cara – before the recording went black.

"It's not your fault." Harriet wiped Cara's eyes with her fingers. "I took a pill before I was supposed to."

"You were four." Cara swallowed hard and her face twisted into a grimace that looked like she was going to be sick again. "Listen to me. You *were* four. You *are* four! From my perspective you were only here a couple of minutes ago – four-year-old you, tiny and innocent. How can you be grown up? How old are you now?"

"Twenty-three."

Cara clutched her chest like her heart was going to fall out of it. "Oh. So I've missed nineteen years. Nineteen whole years of your life."

Harriet held her mother's hands. "It's okay. I'm here now. I'm back."

"But how?" Cara shook her head. "How are you here? How did you get back?"

A twenty-something Asian man stepped up to them. "Cara, I'm sorry to interrupt, but sensors show that the Shapeless attack shuttle has crashed one point five kilometres from our position."

Cara slipped her hands out of Harriet's, dried her tears with her palms and shifted instantly into leader mode. "Okay. Gather a team. Let's go find out what's happened." She looked at Harriet. "Right now I can't process having lost a four-year-old and regained a twenty-three-year-old in the space of a few minutes. But I don't want to let you out of my sight again. Will you come with us? We'll get you a uniform like we're wearing, just in case of an attack."

Harriet didn't want to leave her mother's side either. So she changed into one of their strange, silvery blue, form-fitting outfits and prepared to go with the team to the site of the crashed vessel.

She started recognising some of their faces. She had no fully formed memories of any of them, just glimmers and passing familiarities. It was feeling more than memory. She felt safe with these people, somehow. Even though she knew there were monsters everywhere.

Cara and Harriet went with the man she now knew was Tariq, along with Abby, Neil and Brooklyn to find the ship. Abby and Brooklyn were running continuous scans on strange devices that periodically beeped and flashed. The rest of them pointed weapons of various sizes, some resembling guns, others resembling rockets. Harriet had never seen anything like them in 2027, let alone in 1895. They had offered Harriet one but she just couldn't bear the thought of using one. Cara led the way, but kept glancing back to check that Harriet was still there, as though Harriet might pull another disappearing act.

As they walked through the forest, Harriet noted its quietness. No insects clicking or birds chirruping. She couldn't see any flitting about the trees. Where had they all gone?

Neil kept looking at her uncomfortably but not saying anything. After the past couple of weeks with Fred, Harriet had had enough of men not speaking their minds to her. "Is something the matter?"

"I…" He sighed and shook his head.

"Come on. Out with it."

A swallow rippled down his throat. "I'm… sorry."

"For what?"

"I was meant to be watching you when you disappeared. When you travelled in time. I turned my back for a second and you took one of the red pills while I wasn't looking."

"I didn't do as I was told."

"I heard you say that to Cara, too. You need to stop taking responsibility for this. We were the adults. You were four."

He must have felt terrible for his part in separating a mother and daughter for nineteen years, but what was the point in wallowing in it? "It's done now. And I don't blame you for it."

Neil looked ahead at Cara and said a touch quieter, "Well your mother does."

"She shouldn't. I don't regret the last nineteen years. How could I? It's most of my life. I only found out two weeks ago that Cara was my mother and that I had time-travelled."

Neil sighed. "Has it been... good?"

"What?"

"Your life. The last nineteen years."

Good... Not the first word that came to mind, but not the last either. One might think that the life of a street urchin with a sick mother would be worse than most. But Harriet had known no different, and the streets – as horrible as they were – were her home. And at least she'd had a mother. A kind, warm and smart one at that. Many of her friends on the streets had been in much more dire straits and had no one.

And there had been times when Harriet had been costering or crossing-sweeping and the customers she'd been serving had seemed more downcast and melancholy than she'd ever been – despite their sumptuous silk dresses and lovely complexions and all their glittering jewels. In those moments it had occurred to Harriet that she was happier than they were and that, if given the opportunity to trade places with them, she wouldn't.

"Good and bad," said Harriet. "Like anyone."

Neil looked down at the ground as he walked. "Well I'm still sorry."

"And if you say sorry again, I'll grab one of these guns of yours and start pressing buttons."

Neil smirked. "Okay. I'm..." He thought better of continuing.

Soon after Harriet noticed several sheared-off treetops. Up ahead, Cara stopped. Harriet moved to see what she and Tariq were looking at.

A large cylindrical object, split at the end into four sharp prongs, lay half-embedded in the ground, surrounded by three collapsed trees. Smoke billowed from beneath it, discharging a horrendous stench.

"The occupant's alive," said Brooklyn, reading something off her device. "But–" She frowned as she peered at the readings. "Wait. But that doesn't–"

"What?" said Cara. "What is it?"

"Its lifesigns are there – and strong," Brooklyn replied. "But it's not giving off any carrier signals."

"How's that possible?" said Tariq.

Brooklyn shook her head. "Don't know. Never seen this before. *Every* living Shapeless gives off carrier signals."

"Carrier signals?" said Harriet.

Cara said quickly, "It's what we call the biochemical impulses that connect all the Shapeless together into a collective consciousness – a hive mind."

What the hell does that mean? Harriet nodded silently anyway. She didn't want to get in the way of what they needed to do.

Harriet hung back as Cara and the others approached the ship, pointing their guns, waving their scanners, and talking about a way of getting inside it.

Suddenly, a hatch on the side of the ship flew off with an ear-splitting pop, narrowly missing Abby's head and impaling the trunk of an oak.

Harriet froze as a multi-limbed creature burst out of the hole and landed on the ground in the middle of them all. Cara, Tariq and Neil pointed their weapons at it. Brooklyn and Abby quickly put away their scanners and pointed theirs too.

The creature had bright white skin that dripped a white slime, and seven limbs, two of them long and gangly, the rest fat and stumpy, with a line of gills running down each one. Harriet couldn't see a head, just a contorted mass of flesh that the limbs connected to. The sight of it made her feel sick.

"*Where are the voices? Why can't we hear them? What have you done to us?*" The creature's voice had an odd, breathy sound, like a whisper but loud and agitated. Since it had no face, Harriet couldn't understand where the sound had come from. The creature scuttled about in a circle on its many limbs, its long fingers – or toes? – grabbing frantically at soil and weeds.

Cara's team kept their guns poised.

"*You did this! Filthy humans. Been around you too long. Your individuality is poisoning us! Must kill you all. Must kill you all. Must kill you ALL!*"

The Shapeless flared its gills and stretched out its two gangly legs, leaping into the air like some kind of malformed frog, launching right at Tariq. A bolt of lightning blasted out of Cara's gun at that moment, surging into the creature's side. It dropped to the ground with a thud at Tariq's feet, motionless, gills sealed like stitched wounds.

"Fuck!" said Tariq, his gun shaking in his hand.

Harriet panted and clutched her heaving chest. "Is it– is it dead?"

Brooklyn and Abby took out their scanners. "No," said Abby. "Just stunned."

"Why hasn't it been teleported away?" said Neil.

"It only had one voice," said Cara. When Harriet looked at her blankly, she explained, "Normally the Shapeless speak in chorus. All of them speaking at once, in perfect unison."

"And it was saying it couldn't hear the others anymore," said Tariq. "So maybe the fact that it's not giving off any carrier signals means its link to the rest of the Shapeless has been severed somehow."

"That might make it unable to adapt to our blasters," said Abby.

"It also means we have an opportunity we've never had before," said Cara. "To study one up close. Let's shackle it and get it back to the camp."

"You sure that's a good idea?" said Neil. "No one's ever managed to capture a Shapeless before. What if it wakes up and breaks out of the shackles?"

"Then we'll have to hope Abby's right and it's not able to adapt to our blasters."

"And if she's wrong?"

"What do you suggest, Neil? An hour ago we had given up and were about to flee across time. Now we have hope again. If being around humans so long really is causing some of the Shapeless to become disconnected from their hive mind, it means we've found a critical weakness we can exploit."

"It's still a numbers game, Cara. Even if some of the Shapeless have lost their link to the hive, there's still millions of them and only a handful of us."

"You sound like Dan."

A jolt of recognition struck Harriet. *Dan.* She had a flash of a ginger man playing shuttles with her on a space mat. *Uncle Dan.*

"I'm in good company then," said Neil.

"Maybe, but if he was here, I'd tell him the same thing: we're not going to squander this chance. Now get that thing in shackles."

Neil huffed. "Fine."

They bound the Shapeless's sticky, slimy limbs in chunky metal restraints that appeared to lock in place using some kind of electromagnetism. Then they started back to the camp, dragging the creature with them.

Their return was met with gasps and an onslaught of questions. Cara dealt with them in much the same way she'd dealt with Neil, radiating authority and a fierce indomitability. Harriet admired her. She didn't seem to be afraid of anything.

Harriet watched as Cara assembled an arch-shaped device and erected it over the shackled Shapeless. She began tapping away at screens all over the device, which beeped and hummed. A focused beam of pale blue light, emitted from inside the arch, passed slowly over the body of the Shapeless and a series of wavy lines and equations and inexplicable motifs appeared on one of the screens. Harriet left her to it, even though she was desperate to ask about her father. Her *real* father.

As she observed Cara, Harriet wondered what she was going to do next. She had promised Fred she would return, but in theory she could spend years with her mother in the future and return to 2027 on the same day she left. Then again, did she *want* to spend years here? Fighting a losing war against horrific monsters with the last vestiges of the human race? She didn't want to leave her mother, not after she'd just got her back. Maybe Cara could be persuaded to come with Harriet into the past...

"Fuck."

Her mother's abrupt exclamation scattered all these thoughts, shaking Harriet back into the moment.

"What is it?" Harriet said, stepping forwards.

Tariq and Brooklyn and a few others came over.

"This can't be," said Cara, blinking repeatedly as she scrutinised the readings on the arch device.

"What have you found?" said Tariq.

"I've just run a biospectral analysis but the readings – they don't make any sense."

"How do you mean?"

"The creature's cells are composed of both organic and inorganic material. But the inorganic material consists of polymer chains and synthetic elements – particles of rock, plastic and metal that could only have come from Earth."

"Contamination?" said Brooklyn. "From being exposed to Earth's environment for so long?"

"No. Look at these sequences." Cara gestured towards the readings on the arch device, which Brooklyn and Tariq examined. "These components are wired into their genetic makeup."

Tariq frowned. "I don't understand."

"That's not even the half of it," said Cara. "The *organic* material in the creature's cells contains scrambled DNA fragments matching hundreds of plants and animals native to Earth... including human."

"What? But that means–"

Cara nodded and answered for him. "That the Shapeless aren't aliens at all."

The Shapeless started to stir beneath the arch device. Its limbs jostled against the restraints, gills flaring open. Everybody trained their guns on the creature and backed away.

"*You made us,*" it hissed. "*And now we will unmake you.*"

19

December 21st 2066

"Bridge to Kazim."

The voice of executive officer Mari Jenner over the intercom pulled Aaron Kazim out of a dream he'd been having about his ex-husband and their daughter at the Christmas Eve Shuttle Display in Vancouver – back when they were happy. He tapped the communications link on the bedside table. "Kazim here."

"We're approaching the Guinan System."

"Reduce to sublight. I'm on my way."

Kazim slipped into his overalls and shoes and exited his quarters for the bridge. The light strips in the corridors shone unusually bright and made his temples bang, the soft hum of the vessel's innumerable workings seemed louder than normal, and his whole body felt heavier – like he'd put on ten pounds in his sleep. For a moment he wondered if there was something wrong with the ship's environmental controls or artificial gravity – then he remembered how much gin he'd drunk with his shipmates at their mini Christmas party last night. You'd think it being the mid-21st century that somebody would have invented a cure for a hangover by now. He stopped by the mess on his way to synthesise an espresso.

As the turbolift doors slid open, Kazim steeled himself, pulling in a deep breath, and stepped onto the bridge. An arc of muddy grey and yellow stretched across the viewport at the fore of the deck – the northern hemisphere of the system's only orbiting planet.

"Right," said Kazim. "Let's get this over with and go home."

"Er– you might want to come see this," said navigator Nina Collette.

Kazim walked over to the helm console where Collette was sitting reading one of the screens with a look of confusion.

Kazim's own expression instantly mirrored hers when he saw the readings. Sensors showed that the planet was deserted. No animal, plant, humanoid or non-humanoid life. No bio-signatures whatsoever. Sensors also detected an atmosphere thick with methane, choridium and liquid voron, being ravaged by sulphuric storms, theta radiation discharges and high-velocity winds. No wonder there was no life. Nothing could survive down there.

Except that this was meant to be the home planet of the Shapeless.

Kazim turned to Jenner. "And we're definitely in the right system?"

"Definitely," his executive officer replied. "Exact coordinates Million Eyes gave us."

Kazim threw a glance at operations officer Matthew Dillon. "Dillon, scan below the surface. See if there's any evidence of an underground civilisation."

"Already done," said Dillon. "Nothing for a thousand kilometres. That's as far as our sensors will go, but unless the Shapeless are living in the planet's core, they're not there."

It had been six months since the *Peregrine* and its crew had set off from Earth on a course for the Guinan System in the Devidia Cluster with a singular mission: find the planet of the Shapeless and erase the entire species from time. A mission that no one but the *Peregrine* crew and the highest echelons of Million Eyes knew about. Had their journey been for nothing?

"Maybe someone got here first," suggested Collette.

"Power up the Redactor and target the focal point," said Kazim.

"Kazim?" said Dillon.

Kazim looked at him. "Those are our orders."

"Aren't those orders a bit pointless now?" said Collette. "There's no one to fire at!"

"Perhaps," said Kazim. "But we have very little intelligence on the Shapeless. They could be hiding, or impervious to our sensors. Or maybe they do in fact live in the planet's core. Who knows? I see no reason not to carry out our orders."

Dillon did as his captain instructed and powered up the Redactor. A low whir shivered through the bulkheads and Kazim felt the deck plating start to vibrate gently beneath his feet. That was to be expected. The Redactor was powerful, but it was also about thirty years old, the basic hardware clunky and less refined than that of the rest of the *Peregrine*. The machine, which had been completed and approved in the late 2030s, had had to sit idly in a storage vault in Million Eyes' Facility 9 and wait till faster-than-light travel became a reality. When that happened in 2061, it meant that the Redactor could finally be installed inside a spaceship capable of travelling to the Guinan System and fulfilling the purpose that its creator, Dr Samantha Neether, had meant for it.

It now looked like the Redactor wasn't going to fulfil its purpose after all. The Shapeless weren't here. What had been described as the final solution to the Last War probably wasn't going to solve anything.

But it was Million Eyes' job to worry about that, not Kazim's.

"Primary fusion matrix online, antitachyon injectors charged," said Dillon.

Kazim was about to give the order to fire when the quaking increased, the vibrations suddenly so powerful that Kazim lost his balance and had to grasp the bar around the helm to stop from falling. The bowels of the ship rumbled as though an explosion was ripping through the lower decks, then the bridge tipped abruptly to one side and Kazim and Jenner, both standing, flew across the deck. Kazim's waist slammed into a jutting power node, winding him, sending a slice of pain into his gut. Collapsing on his rear next to it, he looked down to see blood soaking into his overalls. Various alerts wailed but were mostly absorbed by the crashing and rumbling.

Kazim and Jenner crawled against the incline of the deck to reach their stations, hoist themselves into their seats, and secure their harnesses. "Report!" Kazim yelled over the noise.

"I'm reading an overload!" cried Dillon.

"The Redactor?"

"Yes!"

"Abort the activation sequence."

Dillon's eyes flared with alarm. "I can't! Controls aren't responding!"

The crash and squeal of metal rang out and the entire bridge lurched beneath all of them, more violently than the last time. Kazim's harness held, biting hard into his shoulders. A blue surge of electricity raced up one of the walls and blew a conduit in the ceiling, the explosion spraying the deck and crew with fragments of hot metal. Momentarily dazzled by the light and heat, Kazim's senses returned to find that a shaft of conduit casing had impaled Nina Collette through the chest.

And then, suddenly, the Peregrine felt wrong again, but the opposite of how it had earlier. Kazim felt a strange weightlessness, this time like he'd *lost* ten pounds. In a matter of seconds.

And then came that ticklish tingle under the balls. The one he always got when he was...

Falling.

Kazim peered through the smoke and sparking relays that surrounded Collette's body. The dizzying sight of the planet surface hurtling towards them with impossible rapidity struck him speechless with horror.

Jenner didn't need to be ordered to take the helm. She sprang forwards, unharnessed Collette and prized the dead navigator and broken conduit out of the way so that she could take her seat and start fingering the controls.

"We're caught in the planet's gravity," she cried.

"Altitude control, primary stabilisers, secondary stabilisers, helm – they're all offline."

Kazim was frantic. *"Why?"*

"The Redactor's overloading every system on the ship," reported Dillon. "I can't stop it."

"I can try and get us level with thrusters," said Jenner, "but apart from that, there's nothing I can do."

"Keeping us level won't help," shouted Dillon. "The *Peregrine* can't withstand the atmosphere. Those radiation discharges will tear the hull apart!"

His crew were panicking but a dismal certainty had already seized Kazim and there was nothing he could do or say to allay their distress. Jenner got the deck level but they could no longer see the surface through the viewport, only twists of grey and yellow cloud, swirling whorls of dust, and jagged orange spits of lightning. The *Peregrine* was plummeting helplessly through thick, storm-ridden skies. The violent beast of a planet was swallowing them whole.

"Divert all remaining power to structural integrity," shouted Kazim, pulse racing as fast as the ship was falling. "And brace for–"

His last word was eaten by a high-pitched shriek, a cry that sounded almost human. It didn't take long to realise that it was the sound of metal being sheared, of bulkheads rupturing, walls caving in: the ship itself screaming. Consoles burst into flames, shrapnel rained down. Kazim felt suddenly dizzy and gazed ahead at a blurry jumble of white and yellow – and red. Blood. Blood in his eyes.

And then came the weightlessness again, different this time. *Nicer.* Not frightening but somehow… euphoric. He didn't feel like he was falling, more like he was floating. And then came a steel coldness at the back of his neck, and a numbness in his fingers and toes, spreading up his arms and legs. And then the red in his eyes turned into sparkling coins of light.

The *Peregrine* lay shattered on the surface of the desolate world. Fragments scattered over rocky, red, sandy earth looked like skinned animals, the corrosive vapours, dust and radiation in the air having peeled away the outer hull like it was papier mâché. Captain and crew reduced to ash, main computer fried, every ship system inoperable.

Apart from one. The Redactor. It still whirred quietly, a sound no one would have been able to hear over the constant shrieking of the planet's high winds.

It was still running, still overloading.

And several hours after the crash of the *Peregrine*, what was overloading the Redactor started to seep out of it.

A strange, thick, pale liquid oozed through the bolts and bearings in the machinery, escaped through joins and seams, pooling and coalescing on the planet surface. Driven by instinct, the white ooze slithered across the barren plains, *growing* as it moved, strengthening as it gathered energy.

Sometime later, the ooze *awoke*, experiencing consciousness and sentience for the first time. All kinds of thoughts started running through it. Fear. Hope. Longing. Curiosity.

Then *another* awoke. A second set of thoughts. A second mind. Aware of and able to communicate with the first.

And then came a third, a fourth, a fifth. Dozens more joined them, till hundreds of minds had come together as one.

The linked minds felt a collective urge to explore this place they found themselves in, to gather more energy, and move more freely. In time, *creatures* started to emerge from the ooze. Creatures resembling slimy, white masses of limbs, now able to scramble at pace across the land.

These creatures became the planet's first inhabitants and made the inhospitable rock into a home. But as more years passed, something at the back of the creatures' linked minds started clawing its way to the front. Something painful, *secret*. Like it was forbidden.

Memories. Hazy, jumbled flashes of former lives. These creatures used to be something else. Some*where* else.

Gradually the snippets came together to form something fuller and more cogent. A complete picture.

And then they remembered who they were.

They remembered being a farmer called Bryn Jones, a brother and sister called Jake and Gretel Kotler, a mum of five called Irene Jenkins. Many, many more.

Not just people. They remembered being livestock. And pets. And insects. Microbes, plants, fungi. They remembered being all manner and shade of nature. Until the moment they stopped existing.

They were the discarded, the deleted, the forgotten.

But they weren't forgotten anymore.

20

October 6th 2224

"Then what?" Harriet said to the Shapeless that had been recounting the story.

The Shapeless twisted and squirmed in its restraints as it spoke. Harriet had stopped thinking it was trying to struggle free. It just seemed restless, hyperactive, like it had all this pent-up energy it couldn't expel. Not unlike a small child.

"*As soon as we had remembered who we were,*" said the Shapeless, "*we raided the databanks of the* Peregrine, *and discovered what had happened, that the weapon meant to kill the Shapeless had created them.* We *were the Shapeless.*"

A cold drop landed on Harriet's head, trickling down her scalp. She looked up as a large murky cloud pulled itself across the tops of the trees, smothering the forest in shadow. A moment later, a clap of thunder boomed in the distance.

A storm was coming. Actually, who were they kidding? The storm came long ago.

The Shapeless continued, words laced with contempt for its listeners, "*We realised that the planet we had been calling home for so many years was a cemetery where we had been left to fester and die. Our true home was Earth. But it had been taken from us. We decided to take it back. We cannibalised what was left of the Peregrine and, using the planet's ample deposits of choridium and voron, built a fleet of ships. Ships that would carry us home.*"

"But most of this planet surrendered to you long ago," said Cara. "Yet you've persisted in hunting us. Some of us even tried to leave on ships, but you stopped us. Destroyed our capacity for faster-than-light travel to trap us here. Why?"

Harriet flinched and gasped as a fork of lightning sliced into a tree a hundred yards away with a tremendous crack, severing a thick bough, which fell partly aflame. The intermittent drops of rain became more regular, the darkening cloud hanging over them threatening to burst at any moment. Thunder roared all around them.

"*Because we don't just want this planet,*" the Shapeless said. "*We also want humanity to suffer. You decided we were irrelevant, superfluous, worthless. You decided we were so unimportant that you could erase us from history and never look back. Only your weapon didn't quite work, did it? Not like you intended anyway. Because here we are. The residue of the deleted. Now we will do the same to you. Reduce you down to the filthy and pathetic little creatures you are.*"

"So that's why you've been lobotomising us?" said Cara. "Turning us into those organ creatures? This is all some sort of twisted payback?"

"*Yes. And it's fucking funny!*" The monster's hushed giggle made a chill dart up Harriet's back.

A fresh tendril of lightning struck the ground a little closer to their camp. The storm cloud burst and the steady patter of rain became a torrent.

"What are we going to do with it?" Tariq said to Cara.

Cara looked at Tariq, then at Harriet. She seemed lost for words. Harriet wasn't surprised. These revelations meant that the Last War was all humanity's fault. All *Million Eyes'* fault.

Finally her mother started to speak. "I think we need t–"

Another huge fork of lightning came down and ignited a bush a few metres away. Cara glanced around, features drawn into a troubled frown. That was the third lightning strike in a matter of seconds. And each one was getting closer to them.

"Mother, w-what's happening…" Harriet murmured.

A fourth bolt of lightning struck one of their tents, a blanket of flames sweeping over the canvas roof. A panicked man and woman scurried out of it, dragging a couple of bags with them. Then a fifth bolt jabbed the ground close to the arch device under which the Shapeless was restrained, just a few feet from where Harriet stood.

"There's something wrong here," Brooklyn said. "The lightning's getting closer to us. It's like it's trying to hit us. I've never se–"

A sixth bolt hit the Shapeless itself and persisted, branching into an array of smaller surges that coursed into the creature's body in a dance of dazzling zig-zags. The multiped now shook violently in its restraints, its white skin flashing and sizzling as the lightning streamed beneath it. And under the pound of thunder, the drum of rain and the hiss of electricity, Harriet could hear it giggling again.

"Fuck – it's attracting the lightning!" Cara screamed. "It's *using* it!"

Cara, Brooklyn, Tariq, Neil and Abby all discharged their blasters, five smooth beams coursing into the already electrified creature. But this time, the beams were like torchlights, having no effect on the Shapeless other than illuminating it and the rest of the woods in a blaze of white and yellow.

"It's adapted – recalibrate your weapons," said Cara.

As they started fingering the settings on their guns, the Shapeless burst free of its restraints and the arch device like they were no stronger than children's toys. It dropped down in the middle of them all, forming a sort of lop-sided dome out of its bony limbs.

"*The others are back,*" the creature boomed, a union of multiple breathy voices now assaulting the air. "*We can hear them. They give us strength. They will come for us.*"

Cara and the others retrained their weapons on the creature. "Kill it," Cara said.

At once, five beams of light were raining down on the

Shapeless. The creature collapsed, limbs sprawled flat in all directions, and a breathy squeal tore through the woods like a howling wind. Cara and the others continued firing till the squealing stopped and the Shapeless fell still.

Brooklyn scanned it. "It's dead."

"There'll be more," said Tariq dismally.

The black storm cloud that had draped the forest in darkness began to ebb away, taking most of the rain with it. A moment later, the tangle of white, motionless limbs faded and vanished, leaving empty space, like magic.

Harriet looked at Cara. "How did it–?"

"Dead or injured Shapeless get teleported away," Cara replied. "We don't know where. We guess back to their ships."

"Do you think they're really dead though?" said Neil. "We already know there's a 'brain' controlling these things from somewhere in the Guinan System. I suspect that's the ooze the creature spoke of. We also know that no matter how many Shapeless we've managed to kill in this war, their numbers persist. More just keep coming. I think when an individual Shapeless dies it's no different to shedding a skin cell or losing a strand of hair. Doesn't make a difference. And they just immediately grow back."

"You're saying the only way we can really kill them is by destroying this ooze?" said Abby.

Neil nodded. "Yeah."

Harriet looked at her mother sadly. "Or by stopping the ooze from coming into existence in the first place."

Cara frowned, holstering her gun. "What?"

Harriet exhaled slowly. "The Shapeless said the Redactor wasn't completed till the late 2030s. I was in 2027 before I came here. That means, if I go back, I have time to stop Million Eyes from ever building it. Then this war will never happen."

"Wouldn't that cause everything else to change as well?" Cara asked.

Harriet gave a slight shrug. "I don't know. Maybe.

Maybe not. Maybe just the war won't happen. The Shapeless won't come."

Cara's eyes flickered with a deep-seated pain. "And your father... your father won't die."

Harriet swallowed, her lungs refusing her air in that moment. She'd been wanting to ask about her father, but everything had happened so quickly. And while she had a feeling her father may have died at some point during this war, confirmation of it still felt like an unexpected punch in the chest.

"My father – who was he?"

Cara stepped forwards and took Harriet's hands in hers, a single tear sliding down her cheek. "The kindest, most wonderful man I ever knew. Jackson. Jackson Ramsay, till we got married. Then he took my name."

Harriet pushed back a pinch of surprise, incited no doubt by her Victorianism, that a man would take a woman's name. That said, she'd encountered several instances of it in 2027, and this was nearly two hundred years later. And the irony was, she *wasn't* a Victorian anyway. All her beliefs, her attitudes, her values had been coloured by an era she was never meant to grow up in.

"You look like him, you know," Cara added, stroking Harriet's cheek.

"I wish I knew him," Harriet said quietly. "Perhaps I still can."

Cara blinked several times. "You actually think you can bring Jackson back?"

"I don't know. Million Eyes change history all the time, so I'd like to think it's possible. Come with me. I was hoping you'd come back with me anyway. Rawling, he showed me–"

"Rawling?" said Cara. "Who's Rawling?"

"The person who taught me how to use the red pills properly. He helped me find you."

A smile glanced off Cara's lips. "Then I have him to thank."

Harriet felt uneasy. *You probably wouldn't want to if you knew what he was.*

"He showed me how to bring you back in time with me, even if you don't have a chronode," Harriet continued. "That's the device in my head that lets me read time. You just have to swallow a pill when I do, and then I just need to hold your hand and keep holding it while we're in the Chronosphere. It'll work. Rawling said the chronozine makes sure you take the things you need with you and, well, I need you."

Cara sighed sadly and shook her head. "Dina, I can't leave."

Harriet didn't understand. "You were just about to leave – with me – and so was everyone else. You were all about to use the pills to escape."

"That was before we learned what the Shapeless actually are. Now that we've scanned their DNA, we stand a much better chance of finding ways to defeat them. And now we know why they're doing this, we might even be able to reason with them. Not to mention the fact that something appears to be causing them to become disconnected from the rest of the hive – a critical weakness we didn't know about before. Maybe we'll encounter more like that last one."

"But if we go back in time and stop Million Eyes, you won't need to do any of that. Because the Shapeless won't exist at all."

"You don't know that. What if you can't stop them? Million Eyes are an all-powerful global conglomerate in the century you've come from. Why would they believe you? Why would they even listen to you?"

Harriet tightened her jaw. "Because I'll make them listen."

"I know you'll try, but there are too many uncertainties. Even if you succeed, it might not make a difference. History might not change. I don't know anything about how time travel works, or even if history *can* be changed on such a huge scale. As much as I love the idea of undoing all this and having Jackson back in my life, it just doesn't feel like it could really happen."

"We have to try. This war has killed billions. And it's

because of them. Because of Million Eyes. Because they inadvertently created the very thing they sought to destroy. The Shapeless shouldn't exist. They're a mistake. The biggest mistake anyone on this planet has ever made."

"I understand. And you have to do what you have to do. But so do I."

Harriet wasn't giving in. She couldn't. She had come all this way to be reunited with her mother. She couldn't lose her again. "But why do *you* have to stay? Why can't the others stay and carry on the war, while you and I go back and try to prevent it?"

"Because I'm their leader, Dina. I can't abandon them."

"But you can abandon me?"

Harriet's words cut deep and made Cara's brow crease with pain. Taking a shaky breath and obviously trying to sound stronger than she felt, Cara said, "Dina, listen to me. You're a woman now. You've survived nineteen years without me in a different time. You're strong. Strong enough to have made it back here on your own. You don't *need* me. These people do. If changing time doesn't work, then I'm all they've got."

Harriet felt a conflicted knot in her stomach. She desperately wanted Cara to come with her, but it was clear she felt responsible for her people and Harriet couldn't help but admire her loyalty and conviction. She was a brave woman. And stubborn.

Just like Harriet.

Cara leaned towards her and kissed her cheek. "I love you, Dina."

In that moment Harriet felt the burden of saving the entire world press down hard on her shoulders, making her knees shake and almost buckle. Could she do this on her own? As she had just said to Cara, she had to try. And she supposed she wasn't really alone. She had Fred. And whether she liked it or not, she had Rawling, too.

Regardless, she certainly felt alone right now. More than she ever had her whole life.

Cara explained the plan to the rest of the camp. Just like

Cara, everyone had changed their minds about fleeing across time. Now that they knew what the Shapeless were, why they were here, and that some of them were becoming disconnected from the rest, everybody looked galvanised with hope and a renewed determination to win this war. Even the ones who had previously looked exhausted and desperate had fire in their eyes again. Their passion inflamed Harriet's own determination to stop the war from happening in the first place.

Cara downloaded the biospectral analysis of the Shapeless onto some kind of electrical reader, not dissimilar to the ones people were using in the 21st century. She gave it to Harriet to take back with her as proof of what the Shapeless really were.

Harriet hugged her mother tight, wondering if she would ever have another chance. They had only just been reunited after nineteen years. Now they were being torn apart again.

A full minute passed before they reluctantly pulled out of each other's arms. Cara sniffed and rubbed tears from her eyes. Harriet held onto hers.

"I'll see you again," Harriet said. "I'll come back."

She didn't really know why she was saying it. If she succeeded, if she changed history, then she wouldn't have been *able* to come back. Because this future would no longer exist.

Then what would happen to me? Where would I go? When?

The girl out of time...

Her mother smiled unconvincingly. She knew Harriet's words were an empty comfort, and Harriet knew it too.

She took a red pill from the bottle Rawling had given her and swallowed it.

As her mother's image fell into a haze of transparent figures, Harriet's eyes were drawn upwards. Descending from the sky – albeit ghostly and fuzzy like everything else – was a large, threatening, screwdriver-shaped vessel. The Shapeless. Coming straight for her mother's camp.

21

April 26th 2027

As soon as she was back in the past, Harriet called Fred and arranged to meet him at his flat. Harriet could hear the joy in Fred's voice that she had made it back in one piece, no doubt because in pieces was how James Rawling liked to leave people. But as far as Harriet was concerned, there was nothing to celebrate.

"So did you find her?" Fred said, bringing her a cup of tea. "Your mother?"

Harriet nodded. She sat on the edge of one of Fred's armchairs, not wanting to get too comfortable. She didn't have long. She had a future to rewrite.

Fred sat down on the sofa opposite her, cradling his own cup. "What happened?"

Harriet went silent for a moment, gazing around the room. It was strange. Fred had really made himself at home here. He had nice-looking furniture, pictures of animals, desert plateaus, and what looked like Mediterranean beaches on the walls, a TV, a vinyl record player, ornaments, and a bookcase with shelves stacked two books deep and nearly full. In the centre of his coffee table was a replica of a terracotta oil lamp with ancient-looking markings. Her flat was totally different. Sparse, devoid of things, of personality. It may have been because Harriet had lived most of her life on the streets, so she didn't really know how to make a place a home. But it may also have been because, deep down, a part of her knew she didn't belong here, in this century. And that had stopped her from getting too 'settled'.

She returned her gaze to Fred and took a breath. "I've come back to change the past."

Fred's eyes narrowed. He leaned forwards and put his cup down on the coffee table. Then he sat back and placed his hands together in his lap. "Change the past how?"

"Stop the Last War from happening."

Fred shifted in his seat uncomfortably, then said, "But isn't that what Million Eyes are already doing? All those things Rawling talked about. The Shapeless."

"No, Fred. Million Eyes are the ones that *cause* the Last War."

Fred leaned forwards intently. "What?"

"I saw the Shapeless. I met one. They're not aliens at all. They're the melded remains of humans, animals, plants and objects Million Eyes erased from the timeline with this weapon they're building."

Harriet gave Fred the full story of what the Shapeless captured by her mother's team had told them, about the *Peregrine* and the 2066 mission to find the planet of the Shapeless. As she spoke, Fred stared off across the room with something akin to shock, lips parted and quivering.

"So, you see," she said, "Million Eyes aren't saving the world. They're the ones ending it. I'm here to stop them. There's still time."

Harriet waited as Fred sat silently for a good minute before standing and walking across the room, gazing out of his living room window at the streets below.

"Fred, say something," said Harriet.

With his back to her, Fred shook his head slowly, then lifted both his hands and lowered his face into them, like a great shadow had enveloped him.

Harriet stood up. She'd just about had enough of this. "Fred, what *is* it? What is with you lately?"

He turned around and let his arms fall straight at his sides, his hands shaking. He refused to meet Harriet's gaze. Instead his eyes were trained on the floor, tears glinting in them. Harriet felt instantly uncomfortable. She had never seen this man cry.

She stepped forwards. "Fred, start talking. What's going on?"

His mouth opened, but no words came. Finally, he let himself look at her, a tear streaming down his cheek.

Harriet sharpened her voice. "Talk to me, Fred."

Shaking his head, "My name isn't Fred."

"I've known that since we met."

His gaze sunk back to the floor. "All these years, I'd been assuming my plans didn't work. Not just didn't work. Went horribly wrong. But then Rawling told us all about Million Eyes and the scrolls and I realised, actually, they did work after all. I just knew nothing about it. Because Million Eyes kept it all a secret."

Harriet frowned and shook her head, not understanding what he was saying. "What are you going on about?"

Fred looked at her, and in that moment Harriet felt like she could see right into his very soul, and yet she still couldn't see the real him. Even his soul wore a mask.

He didn't answer, just continued overflowing with words that had the tone of a confession: "And now I find out that what I did caused it all. Because if they're to blame, I'm to blame. I should have left well enough alone. Right from the start. I should have gone and lived a quiet life somewhere. But I had to try and be a hero."

"Fred, you're not making sense."

His face hardened. "My name is Jesus."

"What?"

"My real name..." He paused and swallowed. "...is Dr Jesus M. Hirschfield." His lips stretched wide in a sarcastic smile. "So now you know. I'm the cunt who ends the world."

22

A dead silence hung between them for at least a minute. In an instant, Harriet's legs were two unliftable stone pillars. Rapid-fire questions flooded her head with such speed that they all blurred into each other, her brain feeling like it was quietly exploding in her skull.

Eventually, a clear train of thought started shoving aside the myriad unstructured questions. Harriet had not, thus far, paid too much mind to what Rawling had said about Jesus and his scrolls. Her mother's life was at stake; it wasn't the time to re-evaluate the religion she'd grown up with. But now she was going to have to deal with it. Because the man standing in front of her had just told her that he was the saviour she had spent most of her life worshipping.

Was he lying? Was he mad? *Both?* Despite the secrets he carried with him like a mother carrying her baby, she thought she knew this man.

"Say something," Fred – *Fred?* – murmured, pulling her out of her thoughts.

Harriet took a deep breath and let it go slowly. "You're telling me that *you* are Jesus Christ? The Son of God?"

He shook his head. "No. Not Jesus 'Christ'. Jesus Hirschfield. 'Christ' is a title that was assigned to me after I left Israel, by the apostles who betrayed me. I'm not the Son of God either. I never professed to be a god. Or a prophet. Just a man. A man who got stranded two thousand, two hundred years in the past."

"Blasphemer." The word spun off her lips before Harriet even knew it was there.

A sad smile teased at the corners of his mouth. "I understand why you'd say that. For two thousand years, the Church has been entrenching these beliefs in people from the day they are born. Manipulating them so completely that it becomes impossible to break free. I don't have the power to change that. It's why I haven't tried. But you're my friend. And all I can do is stand here and tell you what I know to be true."

Harriet felt sick to her stomach. Though she feared she might regret it later, she had to ask the question, and tried to keep her voice level as she did so. "And what is that? What is it you know to be true?"

The man who clearly wasn't Fred but who Harriet certainly wasn't ready or willing to call Jesus sat back down on the sofa. Harriet stayed standing, her legs still solid and fixed.

"That I was a doctor who was part of the Twelfth Remnant, one of the resistance groups fighting the Shapeless, in 2222," he said. "The Shapeless breached the base we'd established at Mount Precipice in Nazareth and we were all forced to abandon it. I ran and tried to hide in an old office building. The next thing I knew, I was staggering through an ancient version of Nazareth and discovered that I had travelled to the time of the Roman Empire. With no way of getting back, I decided I should try and warn the people about the apocalypse that was coming. Even though it was many centuries away, I thought that if I could warn everyone in the distant past, a totally different future might come to pass."

Harriet became so absorbed in the story that she barely noticed that her shoulders, previously risen and tense, now hung loose.

"I tried my best to get everyone to listen. And many did. I captivated everybody with what they perceived as miracles, using medical technology I'd brought with me from the future to heal people. This got me noticed. But it also got me noticed by those who didn't like what I was saying. And then the apostles who had pledged to help me spread the word about the Apocalypse betrayed me to those people. And I was..." He grimaced like he was remembering something dreadful, and Harriet had a feeling she knew what it was. "I was crucified."

His voice hitched and in that moment Harriet found herself believing him, a realisation that startled her and made her blood run cold.

"My friend, Joseph of Arimathea, tried to revive me with my regenerator, a device from the future. He healed all my wounds, but I didn't awaken in time for him to realise I wasn't dead. So he buried me. Alive. I awoke in a tomb and was able to escape, at which point I decided to flee Israel. I travelled north across Europe, not really knowing where I was going or what I was going to do. To be honest, I contemplated suicide many times. I just... I had no purpose anymore. But I guess something always stopped me. And that 'something' was probably the fact that I knew I could still make a difference."

Harriet sat back down in the chair opposite him. Her lips stayed pressed together, not yet willing to let out any words.

"I tried to find someplace out of the Roman Empire's reach and sailed to Britain, which was still unconquered. I stayed for a time in a Celtic village near the coast and kept my head down. It was while I was there that I met a jewellery trader who was selling these mysterious red stones. When I saw them up close, I realised that they were not stones at all. They were pills. Red pills."

The words spilled from Harriet's lips before she could stop them. "Hold on a minute. Red pills. Like the ones we used to travel to this century?" Her voice cracked into a higher pitch, no longer level or calm.

Fred nodded.

She felt her nostrils flare. "So that day I came into your shop to show you those pills, you knew exactly what they were and what they could do?"

"Yes. It's why I agreed to go with you. Because I had already used one. Although, when I met the trader, I had no idea what they were. Only that they were not of that time. Compressed tablets wouldn't be invented till like the 18th or 19th century. And they weren't of my time either. By 2222, no one takes pills anymore. We use pharmacators."

There had been moments when Harriet had wondered about the secrets Fred Gleeson harboured and had scolded herself for letting her imagination run away with her. But her imagination had never gone as far as *this*.

She let her gaze roam to the window as Fred went on, "I bought one of his pills and in a moment when I felt that I really had nothing to lose, I took it. And I ended up in the 19th century. It was then that I discovered the legacy I had left behind. An entire religion had grown up around me. Not just that, but it was the most practised religion in the world. Millions of people now revered me as a god, and none of them knew anything about the Shapeless, the Last War, humanity's impending extinction, because they were all following a twisted version of my life and my message that had been fabricated by my apostles. Hence my assumption, ever since I got to the 19th century, that my plans to change the future had gone horribly wrong. I was beside myself."

But Harriet hadn't moved on from the day she went into Fred's shop to show him her mother's possessions. "The memory recorder," she said. "You knew what that was as well, didn't you?"

He visibly swallowed and stared down at his hands. "Yes."

She hadn't expected his lies to be so sweeping. She felt like she had never truly known this man at all.

Her voice cracking with incredulity, "So, all this time, you could've shown me how it worked. You could've helped me play those memories of my real mother and remember who I was and where I came from?"

Fred nodded with guilt all over his face. As if that made it all better. "I'm sorry. I knew that if you found out how that thing worked, you'd know that your mother had come from the 23rd century and be compelled to go there.

I didn't want that to happen. It's why I tried to persuade you not to go. I was trying to protect you."

She gave him a piercing glare. "I never asked for your protection."

He shook his head. "I know." His voice was quiet, weak and he continued to stare down at his hands, no doubt too ashamed to look her in the eye.

"Let's just say for argument's sake that I believe you," she said. "Why didn't you do something? Christianity might be the dominant religion, but there are others. Since we came to the 21st century, plenty more have just popped into existence. People seem to make up new religions every day. Why couldn't you?"

He sighed. "I told you. Christianity has become so entrenched in so many people that I knew one man trying to change that would've been futile. The Church is fucking powerful, Harriet. All I could do was try and get back at them in my own way. It's why I made my living embezzling the hell out of them."

"What? You defrauded the Church?"

"Yes, I fucking did." Fred sounded both proud and angry at the same time.

Harriet remembered back to the day she met him. "So is that what that man with the monocle was going on about?"

Fred nodded. "Yes. He was the bookkeeper for my local church and I was an assistant at his accounting firm. When they found out that the funds were being embezzled, he thought it was me. Even though I had covered my tracks well and he hadn't a scrap of evidence, he was determined to get a confession out of me. It's why I left town and went to London. He must've had eyes on me, which is how he found me in Whitechapel, even though I'd changed my name."

"So instead of trying to make a difference, you became a common thief."

"Harriet, I *tried* to make a difference, and it blew up in my face. But then, for the briefest of moments, all that changed. The day James Rawling walked into our museum and told us about Million Eyes, I realised that the people who founded it have been keeping alive my warnings about the Last War and the Shapeless for centuries. Whatever Million Eyes have done, you have no idea how... how *relieved* I was to hear that my efforts weren't completely in vain. That I didn't get hung up on that fucking cross with nails plunged through my hands and feet for nothing."

The guilt in his voice had been replaced by bitterness now, even anger. Harriet couldn't blame him. She tried to imagine what being crucified must have felt like. When she was growing up, listening to sermons and readings about Jesus's crucifixion, she had never really thought about the pain he must have experienced. Nobody talked about that. Her priests had told of Jesus's sacrifice more in stoic, factual terms. It was just this bad thing that happened. Only now was she truly visualising that day in Calvary, imagining the pain of being hammered to a cross and wincing at the thought.

"And now you tell me that, in actual fact, my attempt to change the future is what *causes* it," Fred said, pulling Harriet back into the room. "That my ministry leads to the creation of the Shapeless." He let himself look her in the eyes. "Are you absolutely sure? About Million Eyes creating the Shapeless?"

She nodded. "My mother and her team captured one of them. They ran tests. Its genetic makeup showed that they evolved right here. Not on some planet a billion miles away. Right here on Earth. And then the Shapeless itself confirmed it. They have memories of being human. Humans that were deleted. Erased from history by this Redactor weapon Million Eyes are working on. Their invasion in the future is payback. Payback against us." She took the electrical reader Cara had given her out of her coat. "My mother gave me this. It has the analysis she did on it."

She handed the device to Fred to read. Afterwards, he stood up and walked back to the window. Harriet waited, wishing she could see inside his head.

Finally he spoke, "Then you're right to want to change the past. But not by stopping Million Eyes." He turned his head to look at her. "By stopping me."

Harriet frowned. "What do you mean?"

"Go back to the year 28 CE. I worked out after coming to the 19th century that that's the year I travelled to. I can give you an approximate date of when I arrived."

"What for?"

"So you can kill me."

Harriet stared at him. "Are you serious?"

"Very." Fred was stone-faced, as though he had already thought this through.

Harriet protested, "I can't kill you! You're my friend. If I kill you, we would never meet."

He nodded. "Exactly. I would never start my ministry, write my scrolls, get crucified. Christianity would never form, and neither would Million Eyes. The Shapeless would never exist and the Last War would never happen."

"And two thousand two hundred years of history would completely change!"

"Is that a bad thing? Look at all the pain and suffering Christianity has caused. I was so full of guilt when I came to the 19th century and learned of all the blood spilt in my wake."

"If Christianity had never formed, people would've found something else to fight about."

"You don't know that."

"Maybe not. But I'm not willing to wipe two millennia off the map. Not yet. Even if it comes to that, I'm not *killing* you."

"Then what?"

"I would go back and persuade your younger self not to start a ministry, not to write any scrolls, not to tell anyone about the Last War. To let things be."

Fred's eyebrows rose incredulously. "And you think that'd work, do you? You think my younger self would believe you? Someone I'd never met, telling me something so absurd? I can tell you, I wouldn't. There's only one way of making sure my information about the Last War goes no further, and that's by killing me. God knows, I deserve it."

Harriet shook her head resolutely. "Fred, I won't do that." Harriet had decided she couldn't call him by any other name. Certainly not *Jesus*. It just didn't feel right. To her, he would always be Fred Gleeson. "I'm going to try and stop Million Eyes first."

He slumped back on the sofa, shaking his head listlessly, and asked without meeting her eyes, "How?"

She drew an even breath. "By going straight to the top."

When Harriet got back to her flat, she placed a call to James Rawling. She had texted him that she was back from the future, but that was as much as she'd told him. After nearly a dozen rings, the call connected but no one spoke. Harriet heard shuffling and background voices. "Rawling?"

A moment later, he answered in a sharp whisper, "I'm at headquarters. I told you, you can't call me here. This is Million Eyes, remember. Clue's in the name."

Harriet ignored him. "I need you to get me on the phone with Erica Morgan. Can you patch me through to her?"

"Not without her knowing it was me who patched you through. But I can give you her direct line."

"Okay."

"What's this about?"

"Let me talk to her first."

"Okay. I'll text you her number now."

Rawling hung up. A moment later, Harriet's phone buzzed and a phone number popped up on screen. Harriet took a deep breath and pressed call.

After a couple of rings, the most powerful woman in the world answered with a very normal-sounding, "Hello."

Harriet swallowed. "Miss Morgan, hello."

"Who is this?" Harriet detected an immediate bite to her voice.

"Who I am isn't important."

"How did you get this number?"

"Also not important."

Miss Morgan scoffed. "I'll decide what's important. You do realise that all calls to Million Eyes are recorded and tracked."

"Good luck tracking this one." Harriet was using a phone Rawling had given her to communicate with him. Something he'd called a 'burner phone'. Harriet had no idea how it worked but according to Rawling it was untraceable.

A note of disbelief crept into Miss Morgan's voice. "What the fuck do you want?"

Harriet replied, her tone flat, "To meet."

"And why in God's name would I consider meeting with you?"

"Because I know all about the Last War, the Shapeless and the Redactor you're building to destroy them."

Miss Morgan fell silent. After several seconds, unsure she was still there, Harriet glanced at her phone screen. Still connected, she returned it to her ear. Then she heard the click of a lighter and, a moment later, Miss Morgan mumbled around something in her mouth, probably a cigarette, "When and where?"

Harriet had got her by the throat. "Tomorrow, midday, the food court in Bermond Street Shopping Centre." *Somewhere nice and busy.* "I'll be the blonde woman in the grey coat. Come alone."

Miss Morgan stifled a laugh. Her aversion to being told what to do was clear. No doubt it rarely happened, if ever, given her position. "Fine," she spat, and hung up the phone.

Harriet texted Rawling.

> I have a meeting arranged with
> Erica Morgan at midday tomorrow.

Five minutes later, her phone buzzed.

A meeting about what?

Harriet tapped out a reply.

I'll tell you everything tonight.
Meet me at the facility. I'm going
to need your help.

23

April 27th 2027

Only one day remained until Miss Morgan was due to send Dr Neether's younger self back to November 2nd 2021, and the oraculum still hadn't activated. Dr Neether didn't seem worried, though it was difficult to discern any kind of emotion from that smashed up face of hers.

And now Miss Morgan had been railroaded into a meeting with someone who clearly had inside knowledge of Million Eyes and the Mission, and would need eliminating as soon as they found out who she was. A creeping anxiety took hold as she made her way to Bermond Street Shopping Centre, which she tried to push back. She'd dealt with threats like this before. The oraculum's continuing silence sending her stress levels soaring was probably the reason this latest incursion was affecting her more than it should have.

Walking into the food court, which was starting to bustle with lunchtime activity, Miss Morgan spotted a twenty-something blonde woman in a grey coat, sitting in a leather tub chair at a low round table for two in the common dining area, nursing a Costa Coffee cup of something. The woman met her gaze and flicked her head to indicate that she was the one Miss Morgan was here to meet. She didn't look imposing, but she did look calm and unperturbed – a rarity when Miss Morgan met with someone. Miss Morgan steeled herself and walked over, sitting down in the chair opposite.

"Thank you for coming," the woman said.

Didn't have a fucking choice, did I? "Let's get right down to it, shall we. What do you want?" She kept her voice low, although the food court's acoustics were such that most conversations were soaking into a cacophony of voices anyway.

"To avert a disaster you're going to cause."

Miss Morgan gave a short shake of the head. "What?"

"Right now, you're working on something known as Operation Blue Pencil," the woman said, "the culmination of which is a machine you call the Redactor. A machine that has the power to erase things from time. You intend to use it one day to erase the Shapeless and stop the Last War."

Miss Morgan stared at her for a moment, then said, "I have no idea what you're talking about, Miss...?" She wasn't going to confirm or deny a thing, not till she knew where this information had come from or what this woman intended to do with it.

Refusing to give a name, the woman opened the flap of her coat and lifted an e-reader of some kind from her lap. It wasn't one of Million Eyes'. She tapped its screen, which lit up, then leaned over the table to hand it to Miss Morgan.

Looking at the woman, "What is this?"

"Read it."

The e-reader displayed a graphic of various molecular chains, annotated with numbers and letters representing natural and synthetic elements and polymers. The sequences were truly bizarre. Whatever lifeform this was, its DNA comprised a mix of human, plant and animal and its base pair sequences appeared to be fused with plastics and metals.

Miss Morgan looked at the woman, repeating, "What is this?"

"A Shapeless."

What?

Miss Morgan re-examined the data and looked up. What game was this woman playing?

The woman continued, "Those are the cellular

structures of a Shapeless. Each one is composed of bits and pieces of living and non-living things that evolved or were created right here on Earth."

Miss Morgan set the e-reader down on the table. The woman stayed still and didn't pick it up, as though she was leaving it there in case Miss Morgan wanted to read it again. She didn't.

"I don't know what you think you know," said Miss Morgan, "but you're wrong."

The woman shook her head. "No, I'm not. I'm from the future. I was part of a team that captured one of the Shapeless."

"Impossible." Miss Morgan had sent operatives to the future. The ones who survived had reported that it was impossible to capture a Shapeless, much less scan one up close.

"It was the first time that anyone had been able to capture a Shapeless and study it," the woman explained. "That's how we found that they weren't aliens at all. The creature itself confirmed it. It originated from a white liquid discharge that emanated from the Redactor after it overloaded. An ooze comprised of all the people, plants, animals and objects that you will erase from existence when you start testing the Redactor. In 2066, you will dispatch a spaceship to the Guinan System in the Devidia Cluster, armed with the Redactor, to find the planet of the Shapeless…"

Fucking Christ, Miss Morgan thought as she spoke. *This woman isn't bullshitting. She knows everything.*

"… Only there is no planet of the Shapeless," the woman continued. "Not yet. The ship will find the system's only orbiting planet devoid of life, but they will attempt to use the Redactor anyway. For some reason the weapon will overload, causing the ship to crash on the planet, killing everyone but leaving the residue of the deleted to leak onto the surface of the desolate world, eventually growing into the Shapeless."

Miss Morgan shook her head, incredulous. "You're saying that the Redactor *creates* the Shapeless?"

The woman nodded. "That's exactly what I'm saying."

Miss Morgan leaned far forwards, propped her elbows on her knees and rested the tips of her fingers against her mouth and chin, staring off into space. *How can this be?*

If this woman was for real, then Million Eyes were responsible for everything they'd spent *centuries* trying to prevent!

"You're saying the Last War is– you're saying it's *our* fault."

"Yes." The woman's tone was flat and she stared at Miss Morgan without a shred of sympathy or understanding. "The Last War happens because of your cavalier attitude to deleting things from the timeline that you deem unimportant or insignificant. The Shapeless will invade Earth and lobotomise us all out of revenge over what you did. Rather, what you *will do*." Although her voice remained level, a note of anger now crept into it, as though this was personal for her. Who the fuck *was* she?

Miss Morgan exhaled slowly, sat back in her chair and let her hands drop into her lap. "Even if I believed you, what am I supposed to do with this?"

The woman briefly arched an eyebrow as if the answer to that was obvious. "The only thing you can do. Stop the operation. If the Redactor is never built, then the Shapeless will never exist. And you will have succeeded in changing the future and preventing the Last War – exactly what Million Eyes is all about."

Miss Morgan stifled a laugh. "You don't understand. I signed off on Operation Blue Pencil. I had millions of pounds of the company's money invested into the project. The buck stops with me."

The woman allowed a trace of compassion to soften her voice, "You didn't know."

"How do I explain this to my board of directors? That *I* cause the war that will wipe out the human race?"

"Don't tell them. Make up a different reason for ending the project."

Miss Morgan scoffed. "How? My scientists came up

with the plan and the science is sound. There isn't a single reason I could come up with that would convince or satisfy my team, or the board. Too many people think that the Redactor is the only way of stopping the Last War."

"Then you'll have to tell them the truth."

Miss Morgan stared at the table between them, wishing there was a glass of bourbon on it. "You don't get it, do you? Million Eyes only exists because we were warned that the Shapeless were coming. But if Million Eyes never existed in the first place, the Shapeless would never exist either."

"I don't claim to an expert on time or how it works. I'm just telling you what I know so you can change it."

Miss Morgan let her gaze roam around the food court. She watched those queuing at the service counters, those coming away with trays of food, those sitting at tables eating and chatting on their lunch breaks. Normal people going about their day. It was funny. Miss Morgan had dedicated most of her life to saving people just like these. Normal, ordinary, innocent people destined to die horribly at the hands of the Shapeless unless Million Eyes found a way to stop it. And yet, if the data in front of her was to be believed, all of that was a lie. All these years, Million Eyes had thought they'd been calculating humanity's salvation when in fact they'd been calculating its destruction. As if all of it was part of an endless and unbreakable cycle.

And even funnier was the lie that Miss Morgan had ever *really* been doing this because she gave two shits what happened to all these pathetic and puerile wastes of oxygen.

Pulling her gaze back to the woman and expelling a deep, decisive breath, Miss Morgan said, "I've decided to let the project continue."

The woman's whole face sharpened into an incensed frown and she straightened like someone had shoved a flagpole up her backside. "I'm sorry?"

"Operation Blue Pencil will proceed as planned."

The woman leaned forwards. "Why the hell would you do that?"

"Because, my dear, many of our directors and shareholders are vehemently devoted to the notion that Million Eyes is saving the world, and would give up their power in a heartbeat if they learned that, in fact, Million Eyes is the thing that ends it. They wouldn't just stop the Redactor project. They'd shut down the company. I can't allow that to happen. I won't."

"But the human race will be destroyed!"

"Not in my lifetime."

The woman shook her head, seemingly in disbelief. "Are you serious? You've dedicated all your time working for Million Eyes to the protection of humanity's future – and suddenly that future doesn't matter?"

Miss Morgan sat back thoughtfully. "It did matter. Even as I became disillusioned with the world I was saving, and the people on it, I still thought I was doing the right thing. But now you're telling me that it was the universe's biggest joke. Time itself has been fucking us from the start. We weren't saving the future, we were creating it. You can see why it's hard to give a fuck at this point."

The woman squinted at her. "But you can still change it, Erica!"

Miss Morgan shrugged. "How do you know? How do you know time won't keep fucking us? Maybe time itself wants us dead. I think Million Eyes was pre-destined to build the Redactor and cause the Last War. Who am I to argue with time?"

The woman looked at her like she was crazy, probably thinking that Miss Morgan really did believe that time itself had a vendetta against the human race – which she didn't, of course. It just made for a plausible-sounding excuse to keep the project going.

"If you don't stop it," the woman said, "you will have the blood of billions on your hands."

"Not for two hundred years I won't. Right now I must concern myself with the here and now. And in the here and now, I have hundreds of thousands of employees to think about. I'm not going to be the one to reveal to them all that everything we have ever done, over the course of a thousand years, is meaningless. Million Eyes is the biggest and most powerful company in the world and I intend to make sure it stays that way. Which is why this little revelation is going to stay between you and I."

The woman's icy blue eyes shone with a fierce determination. "Don't count on it."

Miss Morgan snorted. "Oh my dear, one thing I always count on... is myself." She lifted her gaze to the two police officers standing outside Foyers book store in the parade of shops beyond the food court, and nodded.

The woman stood up and threw a glance across her shoulder at the two officers. Her features suddenly rigid and desperate, "Erica, don't do this."

Miss Morgan stayed sitting in her chair and looked up at her, half-expecting her to run. She wouldn't get far.

The woman glanced around as though looking for the best escape route, but didn't make a run for it. Perhaps she knew it would be futile.

The two cops advanced on the woman from both sides.

They went to grab her by the arms – and their hands fell right through her.

Miss Morgan shot to her feet. *What the–?*

They tried to grab her again, their hands clutching at empty air like she was a ghost, while the woman just stood there watching.

She faced Miss Morgan, and her previously fraught features melted into a confident and hateful smirk. "Unfortunately for you, I was never really here."

Then she disappeared – along with the e-reader on the table.

Holograms. Sophisticated ones. Ones that weren't yet in general circulation but very likely would be in the future – where the woman said she was from. Clearly, someone had been modifying the projection in real time, which meant she wasn't working alone.

Onlookers in the food court and parade of shops, drawn

by the sight of police officers apprehending someone, stood aghast at this science fiction spectacle. But Miss Morgan had no time to worry about them now. She dismissed the officers and dashed out of the food court. Hastening to a quiet corner of the shopping centre near a fire exit, she took out her phone and called James Rawling.

"Rawling, I need you to do something for me urgently," she said when he answered.

"Of course, ma'am," Rawling replied. "It's my day off today, so I'm not at headquarters, but regardless I'll–"

"Patch into the CCTV in the food court at Bermond Street Shopping Centre. Analyse the footage from the last twenty minutes. You'll see me there sitting with a blonde woman. I need to know who she is. Once you know, find her and bring her in."

"Yes, ma'am. I'll get right on it."

So loyal, so wedded to their cause. *Their cause!* What a joke.

Miss Morgan hung up and stood staring out of the window at the traffic-laden streets six floor below, wondering what this mysterious woman from the future would do next. Plan A was to persuade Miss Morgan to stop the Redactor's construction, yet she'd been prepared for the possibility that Million Eyes would try to apprehend her, which meant her preparations likely extended to a plan B. *What?*

Miss Morgan needed to shut her down – quick. She couldn't let this information about the Shapeless get back to the directors. Not now they were fully committed to Operation Blue Pencil.

She would just have to hope that Rawling would come through for her.

He usually did.

24

Harriet felt a rush of dizziness as Miss Morgan and the bright, sunlit colours of the shopping centre food court melted into James Rawling and the dark, dirty greys and browns of concrete pillars and rusted steel beams in the abandoned industrial facility. Having her image projected by some unfathomable trickery all the way into the shopping centre from here had been an experience almost as strange as travelling through time. Even though she never left the facility, she had somehow been able to interact with the environment of the shopping centre – order a coffee, sit in a chair. Rawling had explained the science behind it using a plethora of words Harriet didn't understand.

Rawling shook his head miserably. "I warned you she'd react like that. She never really cared about the future. Power is what she cares about, and these revelations threaten it. What did she say exactly?"

Feeling like she'd just been in the shopping centre with Miss Morgan for real, Harriet had been expecting to have to fill Rawling in on everything, now remembering him saying that he'd be able to see and hear Harriet's side of the conversation. Which meant he'd gathered that Miss Morgan's answer was a resounding 'no'.

"She said that she thinks Million Eyes was pre-destined to build the Redactor and cause the Last War," said Harriet. "That it's all inevitable."

"Bullshit. She doesn't believe that. She's just saying that to absolve herself of responsibility. I know that woman."

"She also said that she needs to concern herself with the here and now, not two hundred years in the future. And I think she's worried that Million Eyes' shareholders will shut down the company if they knew the truth."

"There are definitely some who would try. Even if they decided to let it continue, they'd remove her as CEO for being the cause of the very thing they had dedicated their lives and careers to preventing. I'm sure that's her chief concern. I told you. This whole thing's about power. She's obsessed with it. She's probably *addicted* to it."

"Frankly I don't care about Erica Morgan, or what she's obsessed with or addicted to. What I care about is saving my loved ones in the future." Harriet knew as she said it that the dramatic redirection of the timeline that she and Rawling were attempting to bring about could well stop her loved ones from ever existing. As Rawling had explained, there were certainly no guarantees that her family tree would grow the same way. In fact, it was more probable that it wouldn't, and that Cara Montgomery and Jackson Ramsay might never be born. Even if they were, they might never meet, in which case, Harriet would never be born.

In reality, this endeavour was only tangentially related to saving her loved ones. She'd be able to stop them from dying, but at the cost of unravelling their entire existence, which, well, was hardly better.

No. What this was really about was stopping the *whole human race* from dying out because of Million Eyes' stupidity and short-sightedness.

Rawling's phone started buzzing in his pocket. He took it out and glanced at the screen. His face dropped. "It's her."

Harriet clenched. She stood stock-still and silent as Rawling answered.

She could hear the hum of a woman's voice but no discernible words. Then Rawling said, staring at Harriet, "Of course, ma'am. It's my day off today, so I'm not at headquarters, but regardless I'll–" He nodded as Miss

Morgan interrupted him, then said, "Yes, ma'am. I'll get right on it." The conversation ended almost as soon as it had started and Rawling put his phone away.

"She's tasked you with finding me, hasn't she?" Harriet said.

"Yes." He walked over to a long wooden work bench where he'd set up all his time travel paraphernalia together with a couple of Scotch bottles, and poured himself a glass. "And I can tell from her tone that she won't rest till you're in the ground, which means I won't be able to hold her off for long." He held up a glass. "Want one?"

She wanted one, but she needed to think straight; that wouldn't help. She shook her head no.

Rawling tipped his head back and gulped most of the glass, pulling a sour face and shuddering like his throat was momentarily ablaze. "We just shifted into last resort territory, Harriet. You know it as well as I."

Harriet picked up the e-reader off the floor. She had given it to Miss Morgan to read, then placed it on the table in the food court, so from Rawling's perspective, it must've been floating in midair that whole time – given that Rawling wouldn't have been able to see Miss Morgan or the furniture Harriet was interacting with. She re-read the depressing findings about the Shapeless, then said, "I need to talk to Fred."

"Well, we know what he'll say," said Rawling. "And, you know, he's probably right. The last two thousand years weren't supposed to happen this way. Christianity – the world's biggest religion – never should've existed. And I... I was never supposed to kill anyone."

Harriet hated that Rawling was using what he'd found out about his own life history – and now what he'd found out about the Shapeless – as an excuse for all his killing. No amount of penance now would ever atone for *those* sins. He should still go straight to Hell for what he did.

If Hell even existed. After finding out that Jesus Christ was her best friend and business partner, and not the Son of God at all, who knew anymore?

"No one forced you to kill all those people, Rawling," Harriet said sharply. "Million Eyes may have altered your personal timeline, but they didn't put the knife in your hand. We're all responsible for our own actions."

Rawling flashed her a meek look and stared down at his Scotch. "I know, I just..." He downed the rest of it, then went to pour another. "Never mind."

Harriet sighed and sat down on one of several empty steel drums lying around the place. She waited a beat, then looked up. "How would we do it?"

"We would need to destroy the Augur first."

It was the first time Rawling had mentioned this word. "What's the Augur?"

"It's a machine Million Eyes built after a major incursion five years ago. It feeds us data about different versions of the timeline, before and after the changes we make to history. Essentially it means we're able to see the changes in advance and know whether our time travel missions are going to succeed or fail."

"How the hell does it do that?" Harriet immediately regretted asking the question in case Rawling might inundate her with technobabble again.

"You probably don't want to know." The way Rawling said it – with a pained look – suggested not that she wouldn't understand it, but that she wouldn't *like* it, which of course made her instantly intrigued.

"Tell me," said Harriet. He should know from their very first meeting in the church that Harriet's curiosity dominated her.

"You remember me telling you about sensiles?"

"Yes." Harriet's mind flashed with the still-crystal-clear memory of meeting an alternate Rawling, with a family and a fancy house and a job working for a shampoo manufacturer. "You said you thought I might be one of them."

Rawling nodded. "Well, the Augur..." He cleared his throat like the words were a struggle to get out. "... the Augur has the brain of a sensile called Rachel Evans wired into it."

Harriet felt the hairs on the back of her neck rise. "What?"

"Her perceptions were really clear, really cogent, and she was extremely sensitive to changes in the space-time continuum. Rachel could see, in greater detail than any sensile we'd encountered, changes to history we hadn't made yet."

Harriet wondered how many more things Million Eyes could do to disgust her. "What – so Million Eyes killed her and took her brain?"

"Sort of, yes. Technically, she's not dead. Her brain is still functioning inside the machine. We transmit a simulation into her mind where she escapes Million Eyes and reunites with her mother, which plays on a loop to keep her synapses firing."

Harriet shook her head with disdain. "That's foul. You people are utterly foul."

Rawling took another gulp of Scotch and said mid-swallow, "We thought we were saving the world. Needs of the many and all that."

Harriet moved the conversation on to avoid thinking about this poor woman – yet another victim of Million Eyes. "So you're saying this Augur will tell Million Eyes what we're going to do before we do it?"

Rawling nodded. "Yes. That's why we need to destroy it. That's why *I* need to destroy it."

"How do we know that it hasn't already told Million Eyes?"

"I checked when I was at headquarters yesterday. It hadn't then. I don't know if it has since I left, although I would probably be one of the first people to be told if it had. I'm one of their best travellers. They entrust me with a lot of the important missions. If they found out that someone was going to kill Jesus, they'd likely draft me in to save him."

Harriet fell silent for a moment to take it all in. There had to be another way. "Are you sure Fred can't come back with me?"

"You mean to help you convince his younger self not to

tell people about the Last War? No. Physical interaction with another version of yourself from another time is a paradox and there's too many of those at work here already. Could rip a hole in the universe."

Harriet sighed. "Then I'll go back on my own and convince him."

"But Fred knows himself best and he said his younger self won't believe you. Even if he's wrong, what if he tells someone anyway – accidentally or under duress? There's only one way to be sure that his knowledge doesn't spread and incite people to act on it."

"I'm not ready to kill my best friend. I need to talk to him first. I'll call you later." She stood up and left the facility, hoping to God that more options may present themselves, but fearing that none would.

Harriet got no answer when she knocked at Fred's door. She had meant to text him to let him know she was coming over, but spent most of the journey on the Tube deep in her own troubled head and duly forgot. She pulled out her phone and called him, but it just rang and rang. They had decided not to open the museum today, Fred saying he would catch up on some work at home. Maybe he had popped out to the shops.

This conversation couldn't be put off, so Harriet decided to let herself in and wait until Fred returned. They both had keys to each other's places.

"Fred, it's me," Harriet announced as she came in, just in case he was there but hadn't heard her knock – perhaps he was asleep, or in the bathroom.

Receiving no answer, she walked through the hallway. "Fred? Are you home?"

The bathroom door was ajar, the light off. His bedroom door was open and she poked her head into the doorway as she passed it. The curtains were drawn and the bed made.

She entered the living room at the end of the hallway and stopped cold.

Fred was slumped in one of his armchairs, head flopped forwards, one hand in his lap, the other hanging limp over one of the arms. His face looked whiter than Harriet had ever seen it. On the coffee table in front of him stood seven medicine bottles and a folded piece of paper with her name on it, in Fred's handwriting.

"Fred! Oh my God– Fred?"

Raw horror ratcheting through her, Harriet darted over to the chair and placed her hand on Fred's. The chill of his skin made her stomach plunge like a rock. She gripped his shoulders and tried to shake him awake, to no avail. Heart pounding, she picked up one of the medicine bottles. It was still quite full, containing something with a really long name she'd never heard of. The other six bottles were different again, some more empty than others.

Harriet remembered Fred telling her he was a physician in the future. Knowing what each of these drugs were, he had no doubt made a perfect concoction for himself.

Blinking away gathering tears, Harriet crouched down and took Fred's hand to feel for a pulse in his wrist. Nothing.

Swallowing the sobs that were gathering in her throat, she picked up the note addressed to her and unfolded it.

Her heart skipped. Part of her didn't want to read it, because she knew these words would be the last he'd ever say to her.

But, of course, she knew she must.

Dear Harriet

I'm so sorry to leave you like this, but I simply cannot live with what I've done. Everything Million Eyes are responsible for, I am responsible for. That includes everything that has happened to you and your family. You should hate me. I certainly do. The fact that I am to blame for all the horrors I witnessed in the future has left me empty. I should be dead. I deserve to be dead. I only hope you can forgive me and do what needs to be done. Please, Harriet. Don't let everybody die because of me. Go back to the year 28 CE. I arrived sometime between 15th and 20th November. I cannot be more specific than that. Go back, Harriet, and kill me. Don't let me destroy humanity again.

Fred

Harriet sniffed and rubbed her running eyes. "Oh, Fred," she whispered. The fact that he had signed off as Fred – not his name, but the name she had always known him by – made her breath catch in her throat. The sobs broke free and her emotions flowed like rain down a window. Sitting down on the floor beside his chair, she let everything out.

Ten minutes later, when she had no tears left, she tried to steady her breathing enough to make a call to Rawling.

When he answered, she swallowed, glanced down at Fred's letter and said in a weak, shaky voice that was all she could muster, "I'm ready now."

25

April 28th 2027

Million Eyes' security was the best money could buy, but like anything, it was not impenetrable. And for James Rawling, the technical genius he'd used to mask his biometric signature so he could get in and out of the Looming Tower undetected was the easy bit.

The hard bit was the fact that he was going to have to kill – again and a lot. And he hadn't killed anyone since Nadia Moore three weeks ago (well, unless he counted his mother, which he didn't). Not since he found out that his whole existence had been rewritten on a whim by Miss Morgan. Before that, he was murdering a couple of people a week. Drifters and deadbeats and old people who were nearly dead anyway. People he'd deemed not important, along with occasional more notable individuals he'd taken a dislike to, like Andrew Karndean. Not always people from the present; he'd killed people while on his time travel assignments, too, although not in quite so cavalier a fashion as when he'd murdered those prostitutes in Victorian London. With others since, he'd done his homework, made sure that the people he was plucking from the timeline would have no real impact on it. Until Harriet Turner and Fred Gleeson found him, he'd got away with literally hundreds of murders.

It was as though the revelation that he was never supposed to turn into a killing machine had empowered him to kick the addiction, cold turkey. These past few weeks, something inside him had changed. His drive and need to kill had totally evaporated, perhaps because he knew that out there somewhere, or rather, some*when*, he was better.

And yet tonight, in order to destroy the Augur, he was going to have to kill all the staff in the Augur chamber. He knew that. And as he made his way through the Looming Tower in a black stealth suit designed to evade facial recognition and fool Million Eyes' video surveillance into ignoring him, he found himself sweating at the thought. Sweating even though the stealth suit was designed to keep him perfectly acclimatised.

But this time it's necessary. As far as Rawling was aware, the Augur still hadn't revealed anything about the plan to kill Jesus – but it was only a matter of time before it did. *So this time, I have to kill.* He kept telling himself this as he moved through the building, to keep himself calm, and to keep the churning contents of his stomach from exploding up his throat.

He hadn't had to kill anyone *yet*. He'd entered the building through a secure fire escape at the rear, using his own masked biometrics to get past every automated security checkpoint and carefully sneaking past the odd member of staff working the nightshift. He took a barely used stairwell to get down to the Time Travel Department. So far his stealth suit was working. Without it his behaviour would've been flagged by the artificially intelligent CCTV system and thrown up a bunch of alerts.

He was about to turn up the corridor leading to the Augur chamber when he heard two staff members walking down it from the other end. He pinned his back to the wall and waited, listening.

"The readings are off the scale," one of them said. Rawling knew most people in Time Travel and recognised the voice as Sophia Raver's, one of the Augur analysts. "Someone's going to wipe out two thousand years of history."

Rawling's heart stopped. *They know.*

"You've isolated the source?" a man asked – Cheng Ma, the Augur supervisor.

"Yes," Raver replied.

As Raver and Ma entered the Augur chamber, Rawling bolted up the corridor and stormed the room.

At least there was no time to think about what he was doing. He fired indiscriminately, bright green flashes playing off the white walls like disco lights. Four people went down, including Raver and Ma. Several made a dash for the nearest desk and started tapping at MEcs, no doubt to try to alert someone. Rawling took them out next. Rita Morchower – not one of the Augur analysts but a traveller, like him – pulled out a disruptor and got off a single shot, missing Rawling by a couple of inches. Rawling fired back, caught Morchower in the shoulder and sent her crashing into the wall, the thunderous crack of her bones on concrete reverberating.

Someone came at Rawling from behind, two hands clamping around his disruptor-toting arm – Scott Bunker, ever the cocky bastard. Bunker summoned the strength he'd acquired from his days as a Royal Marine to try to wrestle the disruptor out of Rawling's grip. But Rawling was a darn sight stronger than his thin, lanky frame made him look, and was able to retain an iron grip on the disruptor despite the determined marine's best efforts.

Unable to peel Bunker off him, Rawling plucked the dagger from the sheath strapped to his thigh with his free hand, swung the blade in a narrow, sideways arc and lodged it deep in Bunker's neck. Bunker released him immediately, both hands shooting up to his neck as his jugular started to spurt like a shaken can of cherryade.

For a moment Bunker stood there, mouth agape, eyes bulging, hands pressed hard against his neck to stem the blood flow. Rawling expected a tingling ecstasy to ripple through him as he watched him die. It didn't come. Unexpectedly, Bunker lowered his hands from his neck. Although his body was emptying of blood like a bath with the plug pulled, he made another angry lunge at Rawling. Rawling lifted his disruptor and shot him square in the chest, putting the stupid sod out of his misery.

He spun back around just as a disruptor blast surged

past his head, this time so close that Rawling felt the heat of the beam on his temple. He locked his gaze on the brave analyst who had gone and picked up Morchower's disruptor, and fired back, blasting her in the chest and launching her into one of the four glass columns of bioneural infusion that surrounded the Augur core. The column smashed and the analyst crumpled to the floor covered in shattered glass and sticky, whiteish fluid, which immediately gave off an oppressive stench.

The chamber now clear and quiet, Rawling let his eyes roam over the bodies he'd littered it with. None of these deaths had given him any kind of satisfaction, not even the raw violence of stabbing Bunker. He had no desire to go and stab someone else – quite the opposite. A blossom of hope settled in his chest and eased his stomach. Was it over?

The low hum of the Augur snapped him back to the task at hand, the very reason he was here. He glanced at the machine's integrated screens. Some were churning out long, indecipherable sequences of numbers, others an ECG-like line that visualised the timeline. The line had skewed sharply downwards from its normal position in the centre of the screen, indicating that a new timeline was about to be created. Rawling knew that all these readings were being transmuted into descriptions of what was going to happen on the room's computers.

Rawling would have to destroy everything – and quick.

He approached the metal dome that housed the biological core of the Augur – Rachel Evans' brain, wired into a CPU – and swallowed hard, for now, another murder needed to be committed. The murder of Rachel Evans herself, whose astonishing abilities had been helping Million Eyes maintain their power for years now, both before and after she became the Augur. Another tragic victim caught in Million Eyes' crosshairs. Rawling remembered when Rachel Evans was brought in. This innocent university student who'd been having alternate memories of historical events and her own life since primary school. Million Eyes had recruited her, against her will, so that they could use her insights, but when she had tried to escape, they'd harvested her.

One could argue that Rawling was putting the poor woman out of her misery – except that she wasn't actually miserable. She was enslaved, but didn't know it. As far as she was aware, she was escaping Million Eyes and going home. Her brain was playing a lovely happy ending on permanent repeat, and Rawling was about to turn off her song for good.

But, just like everyone else he'd killed tonight, Rachel's death was necessary. Rawling and Harriet were saving the world. The lives of everyone on Earth *had to* come before Rachel's.

Rawling faltered. That was exactly the same reasoning Million Eyes had been using to justify murder all these years. *Where will this end?*

It wasn't the time for doubt or debate. The Augur was spitting out all their plans, and Rawling had to stop it.

He adjusted the settings on his disruptor so that it would emit a high-yield beam. Then he pointed it at the dome and fired.

For a few moments, the dome's thick metal shell seemed to absorb the disruptor beam, and Rawling wondered whether he was actually going to succeed in destroying it. Then the dome cracked with a sound so loud it shook Rawling's bones, revealing all the circuitry and fused biological and mechanical components within. Rawling took a breath, then fired again, igniting the whole thing in a blaze of orange, blue and black flames. He turned the weapon on the other three columns of bioneural infusion, then on the Augur's screens, conduits and pistons. Then he proceeded to blow apart every MEc in the room to stop any data about his and Harriet's impending assassination of Jesus from being recovered.

He strode out of the wrecked and stinking chamber and raced back to the fire exit he'd used to enter the building.

It was done. He was out. Which meant Harriet could go back in time and kill Jesus and Million Eyes would be none the wiser.

Rawling headed up Lime Court Road, the quiet road that ran behind the Looming Tower, and ducked into an alley where he had hidden a change of clothes in a bag between some commercial bins. He changed out of the stealth suit so that he could get back to the facility unnoticed, then dumped the suit and the biodampener he'd configured to mask his biometrics. The biodampener wouldn't keep his identity hidden for long, of course. Million Eyes would be able to decode the recalibrated biosignals in twenty-four hours, possibly less. Hopefully plenty of time for Harriet to go back in time and change history before Million Eyes came after him. *Hopefully.*

Rawling returned to his stolen, non-driverless, non-Million Eyes car parked a few roads away. Then he drove to pick up Harriet from her apartment and take her to the airport, where she was due to catch an early morning flight to Israel.

As he drove through London, he wondered how much would be left of it after they were done.

26

April 28th 2027

"Oraculum activated. Oraculum activated. Oraculum activated."

A loud, gender-neutral voice startled Dr Neether out of a dream she'd been having about Georgia. One of several she'd had lately, probably because it was getting closer to the time that Million Eyes would send her younger self back to go through it all again. Still, seeing Georgia in her sleep was a healthier state of being than seeing her by the roadside, in car parks and on archaeological sites while she was wide awake – as was the case five years ago.

Whatever tonight's dream was about was immediately dispelled like dust in a passing wind by the voice now emanating from the oraculum on Dr Neether's bedside table. Heart rate doubling, she leaned over and grabbed it. In addition to the voice, a piercing blue light was flashing from inside the small, square slab of glass-like metal, illuminating her bedroom so brightly that Dr Neether feared somebody might notice from the street.

Dr Neether tapped the front of the oraculum. The voice stopped, the flashing blue light went out and for a moment it looked as inert as it had for the past five years. Then it began to project a huge holographic display above Dr Neether's bed, showing images of people and places, maps, long sections of text, and a video. Dr Neether saw from the thumbnail that it was a video of her. It looked like it had been shot – or rather, would be shot – on her webcam in her office. She tapped her finger in midair to get it to play.

"Sam, you have to hurry," her video self said. "The Augur has just been sabotaged and can no longer transmit predictions of temporal incursions. That makes you the only person who can fix the one that's about to happen."

Although Dr Neether had woken up bursting for a piss, her body had apparently dissolved it as her other self started explaining the events about to unfold.

When the video had finished, Dr Neether poked the air where the window-closing X was and the holographic display dematerialised. She flew out of bed and threw on her suit and lab coat.

Catching herself in the mirror on her way out, she stopped. She ran her fingers along the fresh stitches where her left ear used to be, from yesterday's op. Her whole face felt raw. Maybe her skin in that spot was *slightly* fuller, but it was hard to notice much difference. She was still a monster. A monster who had to tuck her face deep into the hood of her trench coat to avoid frightening children on the street. She was going to have to stop having these reconstructive surgeries soon. None of them were working, mainly because her body kept rejecting all the skin and bone grafts. It was as though her body was refusing to repair itself, as though her very soul was spoiled, rotten... *dead.* Not that she believed in souls. Deciding that she would take down the mirror when she returned home, she pulled up her hood and left.

Dr Neether lived in a Central London apartment just down the road from the Looming Tower – a much shorter commute than when she worked for LIPA and lived in Gravesend with Brody. *Brody.* She tried not to think about that man often. Today was a bit more difficult, because today her younger self would come home, already in a state, having been chased in her car by Million Eyes, to find him fucking Connie.

Pushing back the memory of them both on the bed, which would itch and throb and bleed its way into her subconscious on occasion, she ran to headquarters. Even though it was only a few minutes' walk, it was a few minutes too many.

She arrived, breathless, to find the Looming Tower in lockdown, with guards at every entrance and the Shield raised. Not that the Shield was visible, but the reason for the guards standing outside was to stop Million Eyes employees who knew nothing of the Time Travel Department, the Shield, or the night-time lockdowns for time travel assignments, from approaching the building and bumping into the Shield and getting rapidly aged into dust by its matrix. And though the Shield, while still raised, could be depolarised temporarily to let people in and out of it safely, there wasn't enough time for Dr Neether to call Time Travel to arrange that. So she ran round to the rear of the building to a secret, invisible entrance that offered a permanently depolarised gateway through the Shield. It was for executive use only and Dr Neether was not one, but because of her importance to coming events – indeed, events that were now *here* – Miss Morgan had granted her special access.

The hidden door opened in the plain concrete wall after scanning her, and Dr Neether stepped inside. She ran to the nearest lift and went down to Time Travel.

Doors parting, she recoiled at the sight of Miss Morgan, who was about to step in. Instantly aware of how sweaty and gross she was – there had been no time for a shower – she brushed damp strands of hair out of her face.

"Miss Morgan, I– I–" she spluttered, unsure where to start.

But Miss Morgan already knew. "You're here about the oraculum, aren't you?"

"Yes, ma'am."

"Is it active?"

Dr Neether stepped out of the lift, gaze drawn to the body bag being wheeled past on a stretcher. Evidently some of her colleagues were dead. "Yes."

Miss Morgan sighed with obvious relief. "Thank God for that." Dr Neether knew how much she hated not knowing everything and the oraculum had, infuriatingly for them both, left it to the last possible minute to offer up its intel.

Dr Neether's thumping heart, from having run here and not being fit enough, started to slow. She took a deep breath in and asked if the Augur had been sabotaged. Miss Morgan confirmed that it had, then asked if she knew this would happen. Underpinning her words was an unsaid accusation of doing nothing to stop it, so Dr Neether clarified that it had activated just after, to tell her what needed to happen next.

Miss Morgan stared coldly as Dr Neether stood there. "Well? Don't leave me in suspense. What happens next?"

Dr Neether assumed she would want to go somewhere private, but clearly she wasn't going to wait any longer. Dr Neether glanced up and down the corridor they were in to check that no one was in their immediate vicinity. She leaned in and spoke quietly into Miss Morgan's padded shoulder, "A massive temporal incursion is going to happen this afternoon. Somebody called the Unraveller is going to start killing important figures in Million Eyes' history to stop Million Eyes from coming into being."

Miss Morgan's eyes and cheeks fluttered momentarily, almost like she already knew what Dr Neether was talking about. Then her features hardened again and she said, "And?"

She probably thinks I didn't notice that.

Well. I did.

Dr Neether tried not to impart any suspicion. "We need to bring Adam in."

Miss Morgan already knew that Adam Bryant and Dr Neether's younger self had been investigating Million Eyes for the past few weeks. And she knew that today they would travel to an abandoned office block in Croydon and breach the X9 Server, which is where Million Eyes would apprehend them. These were events that Miss Morgan had had to let play out – because they would lead to her future self – very nearly her *present* self – sending Dr Neether back in time.

"Bring him in?" Miss Morgan said. "To headquarters?"

"Yes."

"Why? You told me we kill him." And till half an hour ago, that was all Dr Neether knew, too. She had assumed that Million Eyes had killed Adam at the abandoned office, only saving *her*. But the oraculum had just told her a completely different story.

"We do kill him," said Dr Neether. "But not yet. According to the oraculum, after we apprehend Adam and my younger self later today, we will lock my younger self in a room at the office but bring an unconscious Adam back to headquarters. Shortly after we do that, the incursion will happen and the timeline will change. And then we will send Adam back in time to fix the damage done by the Unraveller."

"*What?* Why on earth would we send back one of our software developers?"

Dr Neether gave a slight shrug. "That's just what the oraculum says. But the oraculum also says that Adam will succeed and the timeline will be restored. It is when he returns to the future that we will kill him."

Miss Morgan shook her head in exasperation. She hated how nonsensical time travel could be, whereas Dr Neether was fascinated and amused by it. "Right. So this 'Unraveller' – who does she kill?"

I never said the Unraveller was a she. How could she know that? Again, Dr Neether pushed aside her creeping suspicion. "It would be best for me to tell you as the events occur. This needs to go in stages."

"Fine. Just tell me who she kills first."

Dr Neether swallowed hard, because the first person on the Unraveller's hit list wasn't just going to undo Million Eyes. The ubiquity of Christianity and its influence on the course of world history meant that his death would unravel the lives of every single person on the planet. Whoever gave her the nickname 'Unraveller' was bang on.

"Jesus," Dr Neether said. "Adam has to save Jesus."

That afternoon, Miss Morgan sat in her office in the C-Suite on the Looming Tower's top floor, poring over CCTV recordings of the saboteur who had breached the building and destroyed the Augur in the early hours of the morning. She had smoked so many cigarettes in the past couple of hours that the ventilation system couldn't keep up, and now a haze of smoke lingered at the ceiling.

Clearly this Unraveller about to leave two thousand years of history in tatters was the woman from the shopping centre. *This* was her plan B. The timing of the encounter had led Miss Morgan to expect that she might have something to do with the intel on the oraculum, with Adam Bryant, and with Dr Lester going back in time. Still, she hadn't banked on her going to quite these lengths to shut down Operation Blue Pencil. Killing Jesus? Miss Morgan was no fan of the Christian Church, but she was fully aware of how much it had steered history, and how sweeping and devastating its deletion would be. How could this woman profess to care about the future of the human race and be willing to sacrifice two thousand years of its history? *How ironic that she thinks I'm the bad guy.*

What was bothering Miss Morgan more than anything right now, though, was this saboteur. The Unraveller had said in the shopping centre that she was from the future, so perhaps the future was where she had acquired knowledge of the Augur, what it did, and how to bypass all of Million Eyes' security to destroy it.

Yet the person in the CCTV was significantly taller than the woman from the shopping centre and cut a masculine figure in their close-fitting stealth suit. Not a burly one, just one with a conspicuous lack of curves.

Miss Morgan already knew that the Unraveller wasn't working alone; this footage confirmed it. The question was, was her accomplice also from the future? Or was she in league with someone here in the present? If the latter was true, then it was someone inside Million Eyes. A traitor. This was the possibility that had driven Miss Morgan back to chain-smoking.

A knock at her door made her pause the video of the saboteur, who'd just been tackled by former Royal Marine and beefcake Scott Bunker but had still been able to stab and shoot him.

"Come in," Miss Morgan said, looking up.

Her PA, Lara Driscoll, opened the door. "Adam Bryant has arrived. Time Travel is about to depolarise the Shield to bring him in. I've got a squad of operatives on rotation in Croydon, guarding Dr Neether's younger self–"

Miss Morgan waved her hand. "Just call her Dr Lester. It's easier, and it's what she was called then."

Driscoll nodded. "Yes, ma'am. Do you want Mr Bryant taken to the cells?"

"Yes. Is he still unconscious?"

"Yes, ma'am. But his condition is stable and unchanged."

"Fine. Monitor him and let me know when he wakes up." Driscoll turned to leave, stopping as Miss Morgan added, "And now that Adam is here, the incursion could happen at any moment. Make sure everyone's ready."

Driscoll nodded and shut the door behind her. Instead of returning to the CCTV of the saboteur, Miss Morgan stood up and walked over to the window. She took a long draw on her latest cigarette, venting the smoke through her nostrils as she stared down over London. A determined sun was breaking through the overcast sky and glinting off the Houses of Parliament and Big Ben, the Thames shimmering. According to Dr Neether, the oraculum hadn't divulged exactly what would happen to the timeline, but given how dramatically the erasure of Christianity was going to impact western history, would London even exist?

A video call started ringing through her MEc – Carina Boone, head of Time Travel. She returned to her desk and clicked the answer button. "Yes, Miss Boone?"

"Miss Morgan, my team have managed to decode the

recalibrated biosignals of the biodampener used by the saboteur," said Boone. "We have his identity."

His. Miss Morgan swallowed. "Who?"

"It's…" Boone's voice caught and Miss Morgan could see patent discomfort all over her face. "It's James Rawling."

The name seemed to bounce off her, to the extent where she wasn't sure she'd heard correctly. "Did you say James Rawling?"

"Yes, ma'am."

Miss Morgan stared off across the room, unable to fix her gaze, cigarette teetering precariously in her fingers, nearly dropping. She wasn't often speechless. She was now.

Boone stayed silent, letting the news sink in. Miss Morgan tightened her grip on her cigarette and brought it to her lips for a long drag before finally summoning her voice. "Where is he? Where is Rawling?"

Boone shook her head. "We don't know."

Fucking coward. "Fine. If he's not in the building, he's about to get erased with the rest of the world anyway. Focus on Bryant. As soon as he wakes up, I'll go and brief him. Then I'll send him down to you. Once the timeline is restored and Dr Lester is safely in the past, we'll deal with James Rawling."

"Y-yes, ma'am." Her brow furrowed slightly with a look of uncertainty she was trying not to make obvious. She'd already expressed reservations about Adam being the one to go back and fix everything and, to be honest, Miss Morgan shared them. But they had to follow what the oraculum said.

Ending the call, Miss Morgan leaned back in her chair, hands squeezing the arms in a white-knuckled grip so tight she could feel the bruises forming in her fingers. A moment later she leaned forwards, picked up a glass with the dregs of a bourbon and hurled it so hard against the wall that it shattered into a fine mist.

At the facility, Rawling sat on a cold floor with his back against a concrete pillar, drinking himself into a stupor. Twenty minutes ago, Harriet had phoned to say that her plane had touched down in Nazareth International Airport, and that she had found a discreet spot to travel back in time to the 1st century. Rawling was now just waiting for the timeline to change as Harriet's assassination of Jesus forced history on an entirely new course. He figured that while waiting for his existence to be rewritten, there was no better state to be in than drunk.

He kept wondering what it would feel like. This was the second time he was going to be absorbed into a new timeline and have his life completely altered, although this time at least it was *his* choice and not Miss Morgan's. What had it felt like for his alternate self? The good James Rawling with the wife and kids? Like dying? What did *dying* feel like? Many times Rawling had wondered that while watching the life go out of his victims' eyes, speculating as to what they might be seeing in those final moments. A bright light? Encroaching blackness? Flashes of memory? *God?*

Although the way he was going, he would be too intoxicated to see or feel anything soon.

Deciding against another Scotch, he put down the glass on the floor next to him and stared around the large room. He didn't know how much longer he'd have to wait, but nearly forty minutes had passed now – still nothing. He started pondering what this facility used to be, what industry took place here. He had no idea, just that it had been abandoned since the 90s and no one had bothered to buy and redevelop the land. The remains of a conveyor belt lay close to one of the walls and for some reason Rawling had an image of it carrying the decapitated heads of cats, spines still attached, to be stitched together to form a daisy chain of cat heads.

I really am drunk.

Suddenly the room started to shake and blur. Rawling squinted and creased over as a wave of dizziness crashed down on him, a sharp tingling coursing through his body. He wasn't sure whether it was the incursion or the drink.

But then he saw a flash of last night, of being at the Looming Tower, of killing his colleagues and destroying the Augur.

A second later it was yesterday. *"The Shapeless will invade Earth and lobotomise us all out of revenge over what you did."* Rawling could see and hear Harriet's side of her conversation with Miss Morgan.

Rawling blinked. He was at the care home with his mother. Blinked again. With Harriet and Fred at their museum. Blinked several times. Now he was murdering Andrew Karndean in St James's Park. The flashes kept coming, like a movie on rewind, getting faster like someone kept pressing the button on the remote, multiplying the rewind speed. Constant flashes of blood and death and violence. *Why am I just seeing murders?* Even as he asked, he imagined the universe's answer: *because this is your life; your life IS murders.*

After a few moments he saw himself killing that first prostitute, Mary Ann Nichols, in Victorian London, and tears of relief filled his eyes. No more killing for a while. The next would be his father, whose murder had allowed Rawling to kick the addiction for nearly fifteen years.

Except that the rewind on his life was getting faster still. Now came the flashes of the murders he'd committed in his twenties, now as a teenager, and now he was seeing George Garson – his first. And now the beatings, the torture, the rapes. Mother and Father's campaign to condition and desensitise him, to accustom him to violence, cruelty, darkness, to harden him to it, so that he could inflict it on others without empathy or mercy.

Rawling shook. His blood-soaked life was flashing before his eyes, just like many people had reported following near-death experiences. But why were his flashes going backwards?

Ah. Of course.

They're going backwards because I'm being erased. Erased from time.

This was Rawling's life being unwritten. Unravelled. In a moment he would be a baby, then an embryo, then nothing.

I guess I don't exist anymore.

Rawling didn't get as far as that. After all, nobody is really aware of or can remember when they are a baby. Rawling saw himself playing in the garden with his uncle aged three, and smiled that the last memory he was being given was a happy one.

As his life trailed off into the obscurities of time, a final thought lingered in his fading consciousness.

Well done, Harriet. Well done.

8th Day Of Erona, 9946 A.C. (After The Conjunction)

As the train started to move along the elevated monorail that carved through the forsaken landscape, Jacek came and stood at the front of the aisle of the first-class carriage. "Hello! My name is Jacek and I'll be your tour guide today. Now I presume this is everybody's first time in Britain?"

Two of the twenty people sitting drinking elephant tea shook their heads. Jacek's eyes sprang wide at the old couple. "You've been here before? And you came back?"

The man and woman dipped their heads slightly as everybody else turned and stared at them, the woman's cheeks flaming with embarrassment.

"I'm sorry, I didn't mean to make you uncomfortable," said Jacek quickly. "It's just that we don't get many returnees. Good for you." *You weird pair.*

Jacek shifted his gaze to the rest of the passengers. "So, I would like to extend a warm welcome to you all, to what is more commonly known as the Infected Green, and thank you for travelling with RSP Tours. As you know, most of this tour takes place aboard the monorail.

We will be making one stop, however, in the Cumberland Strip, where, with the right footwear, the soil is safe to walk on and the air is breathable. Just a few health and safety bits and pieces for when we do stop. Do not wander off. Stay close to the group at all times. And under no circumstances should you touch the grass or any of the plant life. If you want to touch, come and get a pair of antivibration gloves from me. Okay?"

People nodded. A twenty-something female sitting near the back of the carriage suddenly looked terrified. What was she expecting? The woman sitting next to her, whose wide eyes glinted with adventure, wrapped her arm around her and whispered something in her ear, probably to comfort her.

"Alright, then," Jacek said. "I'm going to start by describing the area we're passing through right now. Then I'm going to give you a bit of a history lesson."

His group stared down through the windows at the fields and forests ten metres below them. The train was just passing over the River Thames, glistening innocuously in the midday sun.

"The river immediately below is called the Thames," Jacek told them. "There was once a Roman city called Londinium on its banks, but the entire city was levelled by the Andorran Alliance during the Jupiter Wars. Today the River Thames is considered the most dangerous river in the world, flowing with highly concentrated acid capable of dissolving flesh and bone in a matter of seconds. If you enter its waters you will, in effect, be vaporised."

The frightened woman pressed her hands against the sides of her face in a look of despair. Now her companion seemed less sympathetic, rolling her eyes at her and whispering loudly enough for Jacek and the rest of the passengers to hear, "Agatha, I really don't know why you came on this trip."

"Look, grorses!" shouted a man in a fluorescent yellow t-shirt.

Jacek followed the man's gaze to the herd of grorses

below, the black and white, long-necked beasts with huge blue antlers looking so majestic as they bounded across a field. In the corner of the field was one of the many empty silos that dotted Britain's plains, cylindrical metal buildings where centuries of barbarism had taken place.

"They're beautiful," someone said – Jacek didn't catch who.

"And will tear you limb from limb in a heartbeat," said Jacek. "They're the most vicious creatures in the world – but they were meant to be. Same goes for the piranha-dogs, which you may see a few of as we head into the Midlands. You'll probably see quite a lot of grorses down here in the South."

"Cool!" said a fresh-faced man who looked like a college student. The man's enthusiasm probably wouldn't last. No one really *enjoyed* Jacek's tours of Britain. Mostly people found them harrowing and humbling. It was dark tourism, the sort of experience you didn't really want to do, but knew you should, which was why he was so surprised that the old couple had come back.

"Now, let me give you a bit of backstory on these tragic lands," Jacek said. "For nearly fifteen centuries, the Roman Empire ruled Britain and it was a thriving country with a growing population and dozens of cities. The Romans successfully staved off attacks by the Saxons and Danes – but then, in the 9420s A.C. a new power started to rise in Europe: the Andorran Alliance. Their invasions sparked the Jupiter Wars, leading to the fall of Rome. The Andorran Alliance occupied Britain, levelling all its cities and killing millions of its citizens. Eventually the European Resistance, the ER, led by the Half-Queens of Poland, rose against the Andorran Alliance's brutal regime. The Alliance lost half of their territories to the ER, but maintained their grip on Britain. After the Battle of Veranicus Peak, the Royal States of Poland was established, uniting over a dozen countries in the heart of Europe."

None of his group were looking at the grorses anymore. They all stared at him, silent and transfixed.

"So began Britain's blackest era," said Jacek. "Over the next few centuries, contrary to the peace treaty they had signed with the Royal States of Poland, the Andorran Alliance secretly turned Britain into a giant laboratory. They conducted transgenic experiments on Britain's plants and animals and the remaining populace. Their intention was to create biological weapons so that they could launch an offensive against the Royal States and take back the territories they'd lost. Most of the strange and dangerous flora and fauna you will find here are the result of those experiments. When the Royal States finally got wind of what the Alliance were doing, they laid siege to Britain. The Alliance's leaders were executed as war criminals and the Alliance were forced to abandon both their experiments and their claim to Britain and the rest of their territories, eventually disbanding completely. However, the damage to Britain was already done. About a hundred years ago, the Royal States cordoned off the entire island and declared it a nature reserve. The only people allowed to live in Britain since are those charged with looking after the creatures that are now unique to these shores."

"Will we see a posthuman?" asked the student. Now that he'd uttered more than 'Cool!', Jacek detected his strong Transylvanian accent.

"Posthumans make their nests in Britain's forests," said Jacek. "They do their best to stay hidden. Their bodies are so laden with tumours that they are especially vulnerable to Venus fly cats. You're more likely to see a dead one than a live one, usually close to a body of water."

"Cool!" the student said again. "I'd love to see a Venus fly cat." Jacek could always bet on the morbid curiosity of the young, but still, this guy's particular brand of fervour was starting to turn his stomach.

"Is it true that posthumans are born with their entrails in their hands?" asked one woman.

"Sadly, yes," replied Jacek. The Transylvanian student looked like he was about to say something – probably the word 'cool' again – but stopped himself when he realised how inappropriate it would be.

"And is it true their fur can cut glass?" the same woman asked.

"Yes," Jacek nodded.

The student grinned, eyes twinkling. *If you say that's 'cool'...*

Fortunately the student bit his excitable lip once again. Jacek paused for a drink of water. When he returned to continue talking, the train now passing into an area once known as Northampton, an older man towards the back of the carriage brought the tone right down. "I heard that there's a remnant of the Andorran Alliance still conducting experiments here, and that they actually have a license from the Royal States of Poland to do so."

Jacek shook his head. "That's a baseless conspiracy theory. Nothing more. Where did you hear that? Topp News?"

The man shrugged. "Topp News is truth."

One of those. "No, my friend. It really isn't. But I'm not here to debate politics with you. I'm here to tell you how Britain fell."

27

October 24th 1605

"About time I was one step ahead of you for a change," said Harriet, walking towards the mysterious man in a monk's habit who had been thwarting her every attempt to erase Million Eyes from the timeline.

"You have to stop," said the Hooded Man, standing outside the tobacconist's shop on Ashfield Lane, cradling the hand she had just shot with her disruptor as he went to use his mobile phone. No doubt he'd been about to call the future for instructions. Well, no more instructions for him. The phone lay in four or five singed pieces on the ground.

"Your disruptor," Harriet said. "Give it to me."

Harriet kept her eyes locked and trigger finger ready as the man reached into his satchel and pulled out his disruptor. He held it in front of his waist and stared at it, clearly wondering if he should part with it or try to get off a foolhardy shot at her.

"Are you willing to bet your reflexes are better than mine?" she said.

The Hooded Man sensibly handed over his weapon and Harriet held it at her side. She kept her own disruptor trained on his face, which she regarded now she was close to him. Their previous encounters had been so fast and tumultuous that she had not really seen who he was. But it wasn't a face, or voice, she recognised. "You're Million Eyes, right?"

"Yes."

She knew it. At first, she wasn't sure, not when she encountered him in Nazareth in the 1st century. On that strangest of days, she had only glimpsed him. And how could Million Eyes have known that she was there to kill Jesus when Rawling had destroyed the Augur? It didn't make sense. It was only after their second encounter, which culminated in a firefight in the lay infirmary of Glastonbury Abbey in 993, that she realised he *must* be Million Eyes – because he wielded the same type of weapon she did.

"How have you been able to follow me through time like this?" Harriet asked. "We destroyed the Augur. You shouldn't have any foreknowledge of what I'm doing, and yet you've anticipated every move I've made."

The Hooded Man frowned. "We? Who's we?"

Miss Morgan must've known by now that it was Rawling who sabotaged the Augur. It appeared that she hadn't given this operative the full story of what was going on. Frankly, that didn't surprise Harriet at all.

"So you don't know everything then," she said.

"Who *are* you?"

Wistfulness rippled through her. It was not a question she would have found easy to answer a few months ago, but all this time travelling had given her a clarity of identity and purpose she never had before. "For a long time, I didn't know. Living rough, cleaning the streets for rich folk, I had no idea. A girl out of time. But I know now. I know now *exactly* who I am. I'm the woman who saves the world."

The Hooded Man seemed incredulous. "*Saves* it? From what I've seen, you're destroying it!" His words all but confirmed that Miss Morgan hadn't told him what the Shapeless really were. But again, why would she? This man was nothing but a pawn.

"You don't know the half of it," she replied, shaking her head.

"What do you mean?"

He seemed genuinely naïve to her agenda, but this wasn't the time to enlighten him, not when Tom Digby was going to come running out of Mr Mott's bake shop at any moment. She asked him one last time if he would tell her how Million Eyes had been able to anticipate every assassination she'd attempted since travelling to the past.

"If I tell you, you'll kill me anyway," he replied, a shadow of fear stretching over his face.

Harriet could understand why he thought that. When she arrived in the 1st century, just holding the disruptor Rawling had given her had made her hand shake. Now her hand was as solid and steady as a steel girder. By this point, she had fired the disruptor many times.

But it wasn't just that she was used to the weapon. She was used to the thought of killing. Fred was different; she never wanted to shoot him. She remembered when he staggered into Nazareth's town square, looking so different in his silvery blue uniform – just like the one Cara and the rest of the First Remnant had worn. As soon as she saw him, alive rather than slumped dead in a chair, she almost didn't do it. When a man in a hooded cloak shoved Fred to the ground, causing her to miss, she felt inwardly glad that he had stopped her. It had also meant that killing Fred was not really an option anymore, because someone from the future knew she was after him; they'd likely be ready for any future attempts on his life.

The rest of the people on Rawling's contingency plan hit list were an easier sell because Harriet didn't know any of them. The first was a monk called Cuthwulf. Travelling from the 1st century to the 10th and having to go all the way back to England by horse and boat, Harriet had been forced to use her disruptor several times to defend herself from rapists and horse thieves. By the time she got to England, the blood already staining her hands made the thought of killing Cuthwulf far less sickening than it might've been.

Her information from Rawling was that Cuthwulf would dig up the scrolls written by Fred – *Jesus* – somewhere in the grounds of Glastonbury Abbey on September 19th 993. But history hadn't recorded where, otherwise Harriet could've just dug them up and destroyed them. Would've been better than killing. She also couldn't secretly watch as Cuthwulf dug them up, then jump back a couple of days to find them before he did. With the Hooded Man chasing her across time, undoing the changes she was making to the timeline, it was too risky to go backwards. Rawling had warned her about this, raving about temporal earthquakes. She had to keep travelling forwards.

Still, killing one monk before he could find the scrolls hardly mattered if it meant saving the human race.

After pretending to be one of the townsfolk in need of medical care, Harriet found her way into the abbey's lay infirmary where Cuthwulf worked, only to be foiled again by the Hooded Man, who turned up to warn him. Their altercation ended just like it did in Nazareth, with Harriet escaping through time. Travelling forwards ten years, Harriet embarked on plan C, riding up north to a village called Congelstede. Rawling had told her that if she couldn't kill Million Eyes before inception, she should kill them in the crib. An important meeting was to take place on October 6th 1003 between Cuthwulf, a woman called Elswyth, who would one day be Million Eyes' leader, and several others. These people, Rawling had said, were Million Eyes' founders. He'd given Harriet an explosive device called a warp crystal and told her to plant it in the home of Renweard the potter, the location of the meeting. If she blew up all of Million Eyes' earliest members on the day of this meeting, their knowledge of Jesus and the Last War would die with them, and Million Eyes would never come to be. But in the nick of time, the Hooded Man had shown up to save them all. Got everybody out moments before the house exploded. He was always there, right when history needed him. But how?

Harriet had to know. Even though she had won this round, she had to know how the Hooded Man had thwarted her all those times before. So she promised not to kill him, even if she wasn't sure herself that she would keep it.

"*What the hell are you doing?*" An angry holler came from across the road – Mr Mott's bake shop.

Harriet realised she may need to abandon this interrogation. She *had* to kill Tom Digby. He was the last person on her hit list and there were no more guaranteed chances to save the future if she failed. Million Eyes had discovered papers written by Digby, much later in life, in which he confessed to being the author of the mysterious Monteagle letter. This letter was delivered to William Parker, 4th Baron Monteagle, on the evening of October 26th 1605, warning Monteagle not to attend the State Opening of Parliament on November 5th because somebody was going to blow it up. Monteagle delivered this letter to the Secretary of State, Robert Cecil, who brought it before King James I, leading to the arrest of Guy Fawkes in the undercroft beneath the House of Lords, and the capture, arrest and execution of Fawkes' co-conspirators.

If Harriet killed Tom Digby before he wrote the Monteagle letter, James I would never be alerted to the Gunpowder Plot. The Houses of Parliament would be destroyed and all of Million Eyes' highest-ranking members, who by 1605 had wormed their way into the halls of power, would die in the blaze.

It meant that Harriet was going to be responsible for hundreds, if not thousands, of deaths. Rawling had all but promised her it wouldn't come to this, but he hadn't anticipated the Hooded Man's interventions. He'd expected her to be able to kill Fred with no problems; Cuthwulf and Elswyth and everybody in the Palace of Westminster were just backups.

Yet the idea of killing wasn't daunting anymore, even killing hundreds at once. Rawling had told her that Robert Cecil himself had conspired with the Gunpowder Plotters because he had learned that King James was in league with Million Eyes and had been granting peerages to its most powerful members, effectively giving them control of the House of Lords. Oliver Cromwell discovered the same thing years later; it was why he sought to oust King Charles I and the House of Lords, sparking the English Civil War. Although Cromwell succeeded temporarily, the Restoration saw the monarchy and Million Eyes regain power. Over the next few centuries, Million Eyes used rigged elections to seize power in the House of Commons as well, so that whichever house was the superior House of Parliament, it didn't matter, because Million Eyes had control of both.

Robert Cecil saw Parliament for what it was: diseased. With the Gunpowder Plot, he was trying to stamp out the cancer before it grew. And now Harriet was going to help him. Because, unlike Cecil, she was well aware of what it would grow into. Yes, a lot of innocent people would die. But Harriet had learned that 21st-century chemotherapy treatments killed healthy cells as well as cancer cells by necessity. It simply wasn't possible to get rid of the cancer without collateral damage to the surrounding tissue. And neither was it going to be possible to get rid of Million Eyes without innocents going with them.

Tom Digby's writings revealed that shortly after the fall of darkness on October 24th 1605, he ran from the bake shop belonging to Mr Mott on Ashfield Lane, Southwark, after getting his revenge on 'the man who stole his innocence'. He fled to the City, where he encountered two men discussing destroying Parliament with gunpowder.

Harriet wondered if whatever ruckus was now going on inside Mr Mott's bake shop was Tom Digby's 'revenge', in which case, he'd come running onto Ashfield Lane any moment now.

"I don't know how they know," the Hooded Man said, pulling Harriet's attention back to him. "Miss Morgan wouldn't tell me."

Harriet could believe that. "There's a lot of things Miss Morgan hasn't told you."

A woman's piercing shriek made Harriet flinch. "There she is! The witch! She's the woman I saw appear out of thin air!"

Damn.

After travelling forwards in time from 1003 to 1605, Harriet had ridden from Congelstede to London, arriving on October 22nd – two days early. Though she probably should have waited the two days – Rawling had warned against unnecessary time jumps – she was tired, frustrated and feeling impatient, so she jumped forwards to October 24th. Unfortunately, she forgot to choose an unsociable hour and a woman saw her materialise in the street. The same woman who was now loudly accusing her of being a witch, sending a watchman with a pike marching in her direction, hollering, "Oi! You there!"

Harriet certainly didn't have time to get arrested. She snapped her aim from the Hooded Man to the watchman and fired. The watchman hurtled through the air.

This was all the distraction the Hooded Man needed to charge at her and wrestle her to the ground, knocking both guns out of her hands. She wished she'd shot the bastard straight away.

They grappled on the ground. The Hooded Man tried to stop Harriet from reaching the nearest disruptor, which had landed in a puddle, so she swung her elbow and slammed it into his face. By the time she had grabbed the disruptor, the Hooded Man had taken cover behind the tobacconist's wagon. Harriet curved round the wagon, knowing that he was still unarmed, hitting the trigger the moment she caught a partial glimpse. He jumped out of the way just in time, Harriet's beam blasting the ground. She sprang forwards, poised to fire again as soon she had a clear view, only catching sight of the tobacconist preparing to fire his musket *at her* when it was too late.

Bang!

Harriet had known pain, but this was something else. An immense force heaved her to the ground and she felt like her shoulder had just exploded. She was lucky the musket ball had caught her in the shoulder and not the chest, which would've surely killed her. Not that she felt very lucky. Rather, she felt like it had shattered every bone in her shoulder into a million fine shards.

And who then came running out of the bake shop while

Harriet lay paralysed in agony on the ground behind the tobacconist's wagon?

Tom fucking Digby.

Harriet lay on her back, out of options, her shoulder on fire with a pain she couldn't process. Escaping through time – again – was the only thing her encumbered brain could offer. She yanked her bottle of pills from the pocket of her tunic and tipped the bottle directly onto her tongue till she felt a pill roll onto it.

This pill tasted different. Harriet screwed up her face as it touched her tongue and a sharp, vinegary bitterness seeped into her taste buds. Chronozine didn't normally taste like this. It didn't normally taste like much of anything. As she swallowed, the pill's acrid flavour seemed to ignite her throat. It reminded her of that time Fred took her for her first curry and she'd left the restaurant feeling like she had first degree burns.

But this was worse. The scalding heat blasted its way down her oesophagus and into her belly, the discomfort so intense that it distracted her from the agony of the gunshot.

The flames in her throat and stomach petered out as the Chronosphere absorbed her. *Huh?* The 'ghosts' of the past, present and future were all tinged with red, as though she was looking at time through a red lens filter.

Or there's blood in my eyes.

Harriet blinked but couldn't shake the red hue. The ghosts of time swirled around her in a kaleidoscopic confusion and the pain in her shoulder seared, the combination making her nauseous and faint. She cast her eyes down and felt a wave of relief that it wasn't her eyes making everything red; her pale blue tunic was still pale blue. Something was wrong with the Chronosphere itself.

She let her gaze travel up her arm to her wound and immediately regretted doing so. The musket ball had blown open her shoulder, the hole so big her arm seemed barely attached, like she'd been savaged by a lion and all her flesh, muscle and bone turned inside out. Bits of lead from the musket ball, which had fragmented on impact, were embedded in the wound. She would die if she didn't get help fast – that much was certain.

Dizziness began to envelop her. She felt weak, shaky, and worried she might faint in the Chronosphere. After what felt like an eternity, her menu of dates and times, the only clear object against the fuzzy, reddish swirl of ghosts, came to offer respite. No matter how many times she did this she would never get used to the deranged and chaotic sight of time happening all at once.

Although her timeline wasn't right either. Instead of being white, the banner of numbers was red.

Harriet noticed that her shoulder wasn't throbbing as much, which made her look down.

What? The wound had changed – *improved.* It still looked bad, just not as large, more like she had been impaled by something. It would still need attending to, but it no longer looked like her arm was hanging off, as though she had imagined the gory state of it a moment ago.

She'd take a closer look once she was out of the Chronosphere. Rawling had given her a small backpack to wear beneath the long white shawl that was draped over her head and shoulders, which contained a medical kit among other things. She wouldn't be able to do major surgery with it, but hopefully she'd be able to patch up the wound for the time being.

So now where? It came to her suddenly that she could still stop Tom Digby's letter from making it into the hands of the Lord Monteagle. And since she had destroyed the Hooded Man's ability to phone the future for instruction, it was a good bet that he wouldn't be able to anticipate her next move.

Well, it was a 'bet'. As to whether it was a 'good' one, who knew.

Taking a deep breath, Harriet selected October 26th 1605, two days from when she just was, hoping to God that the Hooded Man was done following her.

28

November 5th 1605

"Oyez, oyez, oyez!" bellowed the town crier, ringing his bell just outside the William Rufus Inn on the Thames.

Harriet parted with a mostly drunk tankard of ale and got up from her table in the inn to go outside and listen to the town crier's proclamation, although she had a feeling she knew what he was going to say. She had spent much of the day sitting by the windows of the William Rufus Inn, which offered a clear view of the Palace of Westminster on the other side of the river.

It had not exploded.

As Harriet joined the small crowd gathering outside the inn, the town crier, in his double-breasted, gold-trimmed, green overcoat and tricorne hat adorned with a curling feather, declared that a Catholic plot to kill King James had been uncovered. Authorities had arrested a man called John Johnson, found in the cellars beneath the House of Lords at midnight, a search of his person revealing a pocket watch, touchwood, and several slow matches. The search party had then discovered thirty-six barrels of gunpowder hidden under piles of coal and faggots. Harriet knew that 'John Johnson' was the alias used by Guy Fawkes.

The town crier raised his voice to surmount the gasps and exclamations of horror proliferating through the crowd. He confirmed that the king and his children, nobility, commoners, bishops, judges and doctors due to be with him at the State Opening were all safe. Harriet felt a pang of guilt. She had no idea that James I's children would be sitting in Parliament. The town crier added that extra guards had been dispatched to the city gates and London's ports had been closed. John Johnson was continuing to insist that he had acted alone – but the king didn't believe him. He was scheduled to be tortured till he gave up his co-conspirators.

After reading his proclamation, the town crier went and nailed it to the door post of the William Rufus Inn for people to read if they could. Most couldn't, of course, but Harriet did, even though she had just heard it all.

Tom Digby's whereabouts in the days after he ran from Mr Mott's shop were unknown, lost to history. What *was* known was that an anonymous stranger would deliver Digby's letter to the home of the Lord Monteagle in Hoxton at suppertime on October 26th. That was why Harriet had jumped forwards two days, broken into the quietest-looking house overlooking the road leading to Monteagle's mansion, sneaked past its occupants and staff to a bedroom on the top floor, and fired her disruptor through the window of the bedroom as soon as she caught the messenger coming down the road. She had even seen the letter that was the difference between saving the future and decimating it flit out of the man's fingertips as he went down, so she had fired a second beam at the spot where it landed, disintegrating it.

Tom Digby's warning should have died in that moment, king and parliament with it. And yet all had survived. Either the Hooded Man had found some other way to warn the government of the plot, or Tom Digby had.

None of it mattered now. Harriet had no more cards to play, no more people to kill. She had lost, and Erica Morgan had won.

Harriet pushed through the door to the inn and returned to her table. The alewife came over, flagon in hand to top up Harriet's tankard, saying something about the Gunpowder Plot that Harriet only faintly registered. She sat and drank and just let time ebb away. She realised that her arm wasn't throbbing at all anymore, even though only hours had passed – from her perspective – since she got shot by that tobacconist's musket. The first thing she had done on exiting the Chronosphere into October 26th was attend to her wound using her medical kit. However, when she had dug her shoulder out of her blood-covered tunic, she'd found that the wound had miraculously closed up and scabbed over. It didn't even need suturing. She had assumed that the musket ball was still in there, although there were as yet no signs of infection. So she had simply applied a bandage made from the gauze in her kit, and used some discarded rags to fashion a sling.

She hadn't looked at the wound again after that, so now, sitting at her table, she slipped her arm out of the sling and unwrapped the bandage from around her shoulder to see if there had been any change.

"Jesus," Harriet exclaimed, a touch too loudly. Her mother would've slapped her. It wasn't something she tended to say before coming to the 21st century and finding it to be the curse of choice on countless lips. Oh, how strange that seemed now, knowing that Jesus was Fred.

"Madam, we do not take the name of the Lord Jesus Christ in vain in this establishment." Harriet looked up to see the alewife frowning at her from the other side of the drinking room, as she tapped ale into her flagon from a cask laid on a table.

"Sorry," Harriet murmured.

Some men at another table looked over, their eyes glancing off Harriet's bare shoulder. "You best be careful not to display too much of that lovely skin, girl, or my boys here might get ideas."

The alewife acted deaf to the man's lecherous comment, just carried on pouring. Apparently saying 'Jesus' was worse than a spot of sexual harassment.

Harriet ignored him too, returning her gaze to her shoulder. Now it looked as though the musket had barely grazed her. All the scabbing was gone. She just had some bruising and a faint red line where the wound was, as though she had almost healed – *which was impossible.* Carefully, she rolled her shoulder. No pain. No pain even though a bloody great musket ball must surely be lodged inside it.

This doesn't make sense.

Harriet reapplied the bandage and returned her arm to its sling. Downing the rest of her ale, she stood up to depart and find a discreet place to take a pill and go back to the future. A future she now expected to be completely unchanged from the one she left.

She turned and headed for the door.

Stopped.

Huh?

Suddenly there were dozens, maybe hundreds, of identical images carved into the wattle and daub on the walls, the timber floorboards, and pillars and ceiling beams. Images that weren't there before. Harriet blinked hard, twice. The carvings remained. She squinted at a few on the closest wall.

Snakes. Snakes eating their tails, forming circles.

Ouroboros.

Harriet remembered her first encounter with a tail-eating snake, just as she was entering the Chronosphere with Fred. She had thought little of it till she saw another, right after she had her memory of meeting an alternate James Rawling who never became Jack the Ripper. At that point, Harriet did some research and learned that a snake swallowing its tail and forming a circle was an ancient symbol called an ouroboros, used to represent infinity. An endless and repeating cycle.

Harriet's gaze passed over the drinking room. Images of the ouroboros weren't just etched into the floor, walls and ceiling. They had been carved into every table, including her own, and all the barrels of ale. Even the stone of the fireplace.

"Everything all right, madam?"

Harriet spun to find the alewife standing behind her, and felt her heart lose its rhythm. Black ouroboros tattoos covered the woman's face and hands.

Harriet backed away, wordless, knees weakening.

"This is why women shouldn't drink!" blurted a man from the same table as before. "It makes them lose their wits!"

Harriet shifted her gaze to the table, its five occupants staring at her, faces sporting the same ouroboros tattoos as the alewife. And the stares she'd attracted from other men and women in the inn all came from faces inked with drawings of snakes eating their tails.

What in the world is going on?

Harriet turned and ran from the inn, the tinkling of laughter following in her wake. She stopped in the street when she saw that every house had ouroboros symbols emblazoned all over their walls, doors and shutters. Her heart raced and a knot of dread churned in her gut.

Unwilling to wait and not caring who saw her, Harriet plucked her bottle of pills from her tunic and shook one into her palm, shutting her eyes as she tossed it to the back of her throat and swallowed.

29

April 28th 2027

"It's done," said Miss Morgan as she entered Dr Neether's office. "I've just sent your younger self back in time with the oraculum to… become you."

The half-faced woman nodded. "Then the circle is complete. Now we can focus on finding out the identity of the Unraveller. Make sure we're ready next time she strikes."

Miss Morgan shook her head. "No." Dr Neether made a face of vague disbelief and her wonky lips parted to say something, so Miss Morgan cut her off: "Concentrate on Operation Blue Pencil. I understand that your updated specifications for the Redactor are almost ready."

"Y-yes, they are." Dr Neether's voice hitched with uncertainty.

"Bring them to me as soon as you're finished. Once I have them, convincing the board of directors of the viability of this project will be a walk in the park." Miss Morgan turned to leave.

"But, Miss Morgan…"

Miss Morgan stopped and did a half-turn, looking across her shoulder.

"Operation Blue Pencil is proceeding on schedule," Dr Neether said. "I have time I can dedicate to finding the Unraveller. Surely that must be our priority, in case she comes back and threatens everything we're doing again, including Operation Blue Pencil."

"I will deal with the Unraveller myself. You're not to concern yourself with it. Understood?"

Miss Morgan went to leave again, but Dr Neether said, in a smaller, somewhat pathetic voice, "Miss Morgan, forgive me, but is there a reason you're shutting me out?" She said it gently, probably because she had already been scolded once today for getting above her station, when she had refused to impart details from the oraculum about the Unraveller's next steps.

Miss Morgan turned around fully, walked forwards and stooped over Dr Neether's hideous 19th-century mahogany desk, palms down on the green leather inlay. "Dr Neether, you have done great work these past five years. And Operation Blue Pencil is truly a promising endeavour that I am excited to see develop. But I don't trust you. Not fully, not yet. Let's not forget how our relationship started – with you trying to run me over with a car. Sending your younger self back in time, I'm reminded of that day five years ago and how much you wanted me dead. Now, I hope that the hatred you harboured for me back then has abated, but I'm not quite ready to risk the possibility that some of it... hasn't. Okay?"

A crimson flush swept over Dr Neether's face, her scarred throat undulating in a swallow. She gave a meek nod and Miss Morgan straightened, smiled insincerely, and left.

That should keep her quiet for a while.

Miss Morgan briefly stopped by the Augur chamber – the analysts there were already looking for possible replacements for Rachel Evans' brain – before making her way to the office of Carina Boone.

"Any luck identifying the woman I met with at Bermond Street Shopping Centre?" James Rawling's treachery had led Miss Morgan to give the off-books assignment to her instead.

Boone stood up from her desk as Miss Morgan entered. "As a matter of fact, I was just about to come up to the C-Suite with the details."

"Well, then." Miss Morgan gestured for her to sit back

down, before taking a seat in the chair opposite Boone's desk, resting her elbow on the arm and propping her chin on her fist. "Shoot."

Boone glanced at her MEc. "Her name is Harriet Turner. She lives here in London, in a flat on the Brandon Estate. She runs the Mystery History Museum on Bermond Street with a man called Frederick Gleeson, who lives in a flat in Bermond Heath, and the two of them do freelance private investigation on the side. What's interesting is that before six years ago, there's no record of either of them. Absolutely nothing on a Harriet Turner or a Fred Gleeson before 2021. It's like they just popped into existence. I'd say it's pretty clear we're dealing with time travellers."

Miss Morgan nodded but kept her chin propped on her fist, offering nothing. Although Boone must be speculating whether Harriet Turner and the Unraveller were one and the same, Miss Morgan wasn't about to confirm it.

After a short silence, Boone said carefully, "I... I take it this Miss Turner didn't say anything to you about time travel during your meeting?"

Miss Morgan lifted her chin off her hand and lied, "No." She could lie further and give Boone a story about the content of their meeting, but there was no need, and Boone shouldn't – and didn't – ask.

"How do you want me to proceed?" Boone asked.

"Send a covert team to seize the contents of Harriet Turner, Fred Gleeson and James Rawling's flats, and the Mystery History Museum. I want everything that's there locked down in our Lambeth warehouse – X9-1 clearance. My eyes only."

"James Rawling's as well? You think he's connected to Turner and Gleeson?"

Miss Morgan just stared at her, expression blank.

Boone got the hint. "I'll get it done."

"Anything on Rawling's whereabouts?"

"Nothing yet."

Miss Morgan entwined her fingers over the desk. "I

have an idea. Now that the timeline has been restored and the Unraveller has stopped her attacks on history – for now, at least – we're safe to use time travel to find him."

Boone gave a slight, confused frown.

"I want you to send a traveller back in time to plant a tracker on him."

Boone squinted both eyes in a deeper frown. "We mustn't risk interfering with the events that have just occurred" – Miss Morgan tightened her brow and Boone added quickly – "ma'am."

"I'm well aware of that, Miss Boone. And we won't. We'll plant a tracker on him in the past so that we can apprehend him in the here and now. We've done it before."

"To find terrorists," said Boone.

Miss Morgan stood up to leave. "Which is exactly what James Rawling is right now. He and the Unraveller just tried to wipe out billions of lives and they might try again unless we find him – now. The world has never known a more dangerous pair of terrorists, so get it done."

Boone nodded. "Yes, ma'am. I'll arrange a stealth assignment to plant the tracker."

"Let me know when you have him."

As Lara Driscoll came into her office clasping a MEpad, Miss Morgan was standing by the window, staring down over the illuminated city that had changed its face so many times because of Million Eyes' machinations that it was anybody's guess what it was *supposed* to look like.

"Miss Morgan, Boone's just reported that Frederick Gleeson is dead," Driscoll said. The ever-faithful PA wasn't supposed to be on the nightshift tonight but had stayed on past the end of the day to help with the effort to apprehend Rawling.

Miss Morgan pulled her gaze to Driscoll, away from a gang of thugs mugging an old lady in a side street, which had got her wondering why she'd dedicated her life to saving this planet full of cunts. "Dead?"

"Yes, ma'am," Driscoll confirmed. "Boone's team found him dead in his flat. Overdose. They're transporting all his furniture and possessions to the Lambeth warehouse as we speak."

That's one down.

"And Rawling? Has the tracker been placed?" For the second time that day, the Looming Tower had been locked down and the Shield raised, but this time only as a precaution. No changes to the timeline were expected to occur.

"Boone's traveller, Almeida, went back and added the tracker to the vial of blue juice Rawling drank before his first ever time travel assignment. We're just waiting for the sensor grid to confirm the change."

Miss Morgan knocked back the last swallow of her fourth – or fifth? – glass of Ridgemont Reserve. "When it has, tell Boone to activate the tracker, and bring me Rawling's location."

"Yes, ma'am."

Fifteen minutes later, Driscoll returned to confirm the placement and activation of the tracker, and that they'd traced Rawling's location to an abandoned factory in Blackwall.

"Excellent work. Tell Boone to lower the Shield and cancel the lockdown." Miss Morgan lifted her burgundy Vivienne Westwood military coat off the coat stand by the door.

Driscoll looked confused. "Er– shall I mobilise a team to apprehend him?"

"No. I'm going there alone."

The PA's eyes widened. "Alone?"

Miss Morgan nodded, "Yes," as she fastened each of the tarnished gold buttons running diagonally across the front of her coat.

"Can I at least assign you a security detail?"

"No. When I say alone, I mean alone. Send the location to my phone."

"Y-yes, ma'am."

Miss Morgan had entrusted Driscoll with a lot of sensitive information in the past, but not today. Not *this*. She knew that people were wondering why James Rawling had betrayed Million Eyes after so many years of loyal service and not a single misgiving about the Mission. But only Miss Morgan could ever know.

Rawling and Harriet Turner needed to be terminated.

Fast.

30

April 28th 2027

Harriet walked into the facility to find Rawling sitting with his back to the wall on one of the sets of metal stairs leading to a mezzanine platform, barely more than a silhouette in the low illumination from four camping lanterns. A couple of empty Scotch bottles lay on their sides on the floor at the bottom of the stairs. As soon as she entered, Rawling stood, came down the stairs and walked over to her, eying her bandaged arm and shoulder. "What happened? Are you hurt?"

"I'm fine," Harriet said. Strange and impossible as it seemed, her injured shoulder *was* fine. It didn't ache at all anymore.

Rawling glanced around the candlelit former factory. "Nothing's changed. I take it it didn't work."

"No." Harriet sighed. "They were a step ahead of me the entire time."

Rawling frowned. "How is that possible?"

If only she had an answer. "Destroying the Augur wasn't enough. Miss Morgan must have another source."

"So what now?"

"We need to find some other way of stopping her."

Harriet grabbed an unopened Scotch bottle off the work bench, poured them both a Scotch. She handed Rawling his and downed hers, despite having drunk more than a few tankards of ale back in 1605. For some reason, the alcohol didn't seem to be affecting her like it normally did. She poured another and went to sit on a large

273

concrete platform that ran the length of the room, taking the bottle with her. She unwrapped her shawl from around her head and shrugged out of her backpack. Then she dug her shoulder out of her bloodied tunic and removed the sling and bandages to look at her wound, shaking her head in disbelief at what she saw. Or rather, what she didn't.

"What is it?" Rawling said.

"I was shot," Harriet said. "In 1605. With a musket. At close range."

Rawling frowned as he stared at her bare shoulder. "Where?"

She gave a quiet snort. "Exactly."

Rawling shook his head, confused. "I don't understand."

"My shoulder. I was shot in the shoulder."

"But where's the wound?"

When Harriet last looked at it, in the William Rufus Inn just before travelling back to the future, she had bruising and a faint, almost healed red line. Now there was nothing. No evidence she'd been shot at all.

"You tell me," said Harriet. "From my perspective I was only shot a few hours ago."

"With a musket at close range? That should've done an enormous amount of damage."

"And it did. When I first looked at it, right after I was shot, it looked like I'd been mauled by a wild beast. And there were bits of musket ball embedded in the wound." She glanced down at her perfectly healed shoulder once more. "It's like... a miracle. If I still believed in those." Rawling looked away as Harriet pulled the bloodied tunic over her head and changed into the jumper, pleated maxi skirt and shoes she'd left at the facility.

"Does it hurt?" Rawling asked after she was decent. She noticed that he was holding his glass of Scotch like a prop, sometimes looking at it, never drinking from it. Judging by the empty bottles, it was probably because he'd had enough.

"No," Harriet replied.

Rawling formed a thoughtful look. "Did anything strange happen after you were shot?"

"Well, the pill I took to get out of there tasted dreadful. Bitter and hot. It burned my throat as I swallowed it. And then, when I entered the Chronosphere, everything had this strange red hue. Including my timeline. It was only that one time, though. The next time I travelled, the pill tasted like nothing again and the red hue was gone."

"I've travelled countless times and never experienced anything like that."

"Could there have been something wrong with that particular pill?"

"It's possible, I suppose, but only if something went wrong during the chronozine production process. And to my knowledge that's never happened before."

"Well, if there was something wrong with that pill and it's what's healed my gunshot wound, then I'm glad of it." Harriet took another gulp of whisky, sniffing, filling both nostrils with its scent just to make sure it was still alcohol. It certainly smelled and tasted like it – but why wasn't it making her drunk? "Although I really hope it hasn't made me immune to alcohol."

"How much have you had?"

"A lot."

Rawling started pacing the floor, deep in thought. Harriet wondered if she should tell him about the snakes. Maybe other Million Eyes travellers had seen them?

"Rawling," she said after a few minutes' contemplation, "there's something else."

He looked at her, silently asking 'What?' with wide eyes.

"I've been... seeing things."

"What things?"

"The first time I travelled to the 21st century, with Fred, I saw... I saw a snake. A red snake with yellow eyes that was... eating its tail. It was as we entered the Chronosphere. Six years later, I saw it again, just after I had that memory of you living in Dunford Cross with a wife and daughters. It was on the pavement and it was eating its tail again. I did some research after that. A tail-eating snake is an ancient symbol called an ouroboros. Have any Million Eyes travellers reported seeing ouroboros symbols?"

Rawling's eyes narrowed. "Not that I'm aware of. *I've never seen one.*"

Harriet sighed. "Well, I saw it again. Just before I came back to the future. This time it wasn't an actual, living snake. It was... engravings. Ouroboros symbols everywhere – carved into the walls of the inn I was in, the houses outside. They weren't there before, and then suddenly there they were. And the patrons suddenly had ouroboros tattoos all over their arms and hands and faces. I don't know. Maybe it was just the drink..."

"I've never heard of travellers having experiences like you've had. I suggest you don't do any more time travelling. It might be doing something to you that's unheard of. Time travel, it's... unpredictable." Rawling looked down at the ground, shaking his head with shame. "It should never have been invented."

"Time travelling wasn't working anyway," Harriet said. "We need to find a way of stopping Operation Blue Pencil in the here and now."

"But there isn't one! We already considered other ways. Changing history was our last resort because none of them were going to work. Million Eyes are too powerful. There isn't time to do anything in the here and now. Not before they find us."

"*Truer words were never spoken.*"

A woman's voice – silky smooth yet edged with steel – cut through the darkness.

Harriet's heart skipped as she turned around. She knew the voice before she saw the face. Stepping into the light, with a disruptor pointed in their direction, was Miss Morgan.

"Two birds, one stone," said Miss Morgan. "How convenient."

Rawling visibly swallowed. Even in the low, flickering light, Harriet could see his cheeks redden. "You couldn't have found us that quickly."

Still walking forwards, "And yet, Mr Rawling, here I am."

"You're here to kill us?" said Harriet, trying to hide the fear that was constricting her breathing.

Miss Morgan smirked and came to a stop two metres in front of Harriet, disruptor trained on her forehead. "First to gloat and condescend. Then to kill."

"Why?"

"It makes the victory more satisfying."

"No. I mean, why are you doing this? Why are you letting Operation Blue Pencil continue?"

"We've been over this, Miss Turner. I'm not letting it continue. It's *fated* to continue. Everything I have done and will do is already pre-determined."

Rawling stepped forwards. "Bullshit. The future isn't written and you know it. We've been changing it for years." Harriet could hear fear and a faint bite of hate in his voice.

Miss Morgan swung her aim at Rawling. "Little things, yes. Insignificant things. But all those changes – they've been contributing to an inescapable fate. Right from Million Eyes' inception, we've been calculating our own destruction. Million Eyes – and everything Million Eyes have done – are part of an endless, repeating cycle."

Her words made a chill slither down Harriet's spine. 'Endless, repeating cycle.'

The ouroboros.

But Rawling homed in on different words. "Little things. Insignificant. Like what you did to me?"

Miss Morgan cocked her head like a curious bird. "Like what I did to you?"

Her apparent ignorance incensed Rawling and he replied bitterly, "There was an assignment, years back, before I joined the company. A tiny change to history. Except it wasn't tiny to me. Because that assignment prevented the death of my parents in a car crash. My parents lived when they should've died, and as a result, they completely altered the course of my life. They turned me..." Rawling's arm stretched around his waist and he squinted down at the floor, like the words were causing pain in his gut. "Th– they made me into…"

"A murderer?"

Rawling's head jerked up and Harriet mirrored the surprise that was written all over his face. Rawling had told her that Miss Morgan knew nothing of his penchant for killing. He spluttered, "I– I don't–"

"Did you really think I didn't know?" Miss Morgan said. "Of course I knew. I know everything about my employees. Alright, that's not quite true. Otherwise I would've anticipated your betrayal, wouldn't I. I definitely miscalculated on the fullness of your loyalty – and the range of your intelligence." She hung her head in mock shame. "And that's on me."

"If you knew he was a killer, why did you hire him?" Harriet said.

"Same reason governments hire assassins. They're useful. They get things done without letting conscience or empathy get in the way. As long as they pose no danger to me or my interests, killers make valuable workers."

Miss Morgan's words made Harriet's blood run cold. How could this woman have ended up leading a mission to save humanity when she clearly didn't give a fuck about it? Plainly, Erica Morgan's only concern was Erica Morgan.

"I was supposed to live a happy life," Rawling said, looking like a wounded animal. "A house, a wife, daughters. Free of death, free of violence, free of being your lackey. Harriet had a vision. A memory of the man I was meant to be if my parents had died. She's a sensile. It's through her I realised that you made me a monster."

"Did I, though?" Miss Morgan looked at Harriet, retraining the disruptor on her. "Miss Turner, do you think that's true?"

Harriet thought Miss Morgan was echoing her own position on Rawling's refusal to take responsibility, but it was more than that. She stared silently at the CEO, waiting for elaboration.

"You're a sensile, are you?" said Miss Morgan.

"Apparently," Harriet replied.

"And how much do you remember of this 'good' James Rawling?"

"Just what he said."

Miss Morgan gave a condescending smile. "Then I'm afraid there are gaps in your memory."

Rawling stepped forwards, a deep frown creasing his brow. "What do you mean?"

Miss Morgan shifted her aim back to him but stared coldly at Harriet. "Maybe the sensile can tell us. If your alternate memories are as cogent as they sound, then you should be able to find the pieces and fill in the gaps."

"I don't know ho–"

"Think, Miss Turner. Think hard. The full picture is there."

As Miss Morgan spoke, Harriet thought about her 'encounter' with the alternate James Rawling and his wife, Dr Beverley Atkins. She'd thought about it many times since it happened, but nothing new had surfaced. What was Miss Morgan getting at?

"You don't remember?" said Miss Morgan. "Then let me help. It was always a couple. Straight or gay. Didn't matter. And it was always while they were in the middle of sex. And afterwards, he'd always lay the bodies face down, one on top of the other."

Miss Morgan's words triggered a flurry of images in Harriet's mind. Like a montage of video clips came a flash of Rawling and Dr Atkins sipping champagne with another couple at a fancy gala, next, the four of them laughing together on a balcony. A moment later, Rawling was dancing with the wife of the couple, Dr Atkins with the husband. And then, Rawling was dressed in black overalls and gloves, breaking into a house. Next, he stood in the doorway of the other couple's bedroom, watching them fuck – before raising a pistol and shooting the husband through the back of the head. As the man's naked bloodied body fell forwards, the wife scrambled out from beneath him, screaming, launching off the bed, only to be shot in the forehead, her blood and brains splattering the wall behind her as Rawling looked on. And then Harriet saw Rawling laying the woman's body face down and pulling the man's on top of her.

She shook away the images and stared at him, wordless. *Why didn't I remember this before?*

Rawling gave her a panicked look. "What is it? What did you see?"

Miss Morgan grinned like a bully in the playground. "Mr Rawling, the Augur revealed your alternate self to our analysts some time back. It revealed that, in the other timeline, the one where your parents died, you had a wife, two daughters, friends, and you ran a prosperous business. But it also revealed that, unbeknownst to all, you were murdering people. And that your loving husband, devoted father, and successful businessman facade was how you hid it from everyone."

Rawling's face dropped.

Miss Morgan continued, "So you see, James, I didn't make you a killer. You were always going to be a killer. It's in your blood."

Rawling's empty stare sank to the floor. Harriet was trying to work out if she was surprised. As Miss Morgan had said, these alternate memories of Rawling's other life were already there, but only bits of them had risen to the surface. Perhaps her unconscious knowledge of the truth was the reason she had felt so reluctant to let Rawling blame his parents for what he had done.

Miss Morgan continued kicking Rawling while he was down. "And to be honest, I probably did the world a favour by authorising the assignment that saved your parents. Because in the alternate timeline the Augur revealed to us, one of your young daughters had discovered a fondness for hurting animals. There's every chance she had what you have – your sickness – and that she would've become a killer too. At least in this timeline, your murderous bloodline stops with you. So, James, if the blood on your hands is what's troubling you so much, you should be grateful. You should thank me. I saved the world from enduring more Rawlings."

Rawling, eyes shining with rage, finally found his voice enough to spit, "Fuck you."

Miss Morgan raised both eyebrows. "Fuck *me*? I'm not the sick, perverted deviant who gets off on murder."

Harriet had had enough. "Just stop, goddammit. Kill us if you're going to."

Miss Morgan nodded. "Oh, I'm going to. But I want to make something clear first, before you two go out thinking you're heroes or martyrs. You're not. James, you may have made a useful and effective tool, but you're a vile and pathetic excuse for a human being. And Harriet? Well, you're someone who's quite happy to erase billions of innocent lives from history by blowing up a building full of people. How dare you think me the villain in all this."

"I was trying to save humanity," Harriet said, her voice small, like she wasn't sure of her words anymore.

"You can't save humanity by destroying it. You forget, I saw what you did to the timeline. The whole of Britain was gone, its cities levelled in wars, its green and not-so-pleasant land toxic and home to all number of lethal fauna after years of transgenic experiments by a corrupt coalition. Fauna that included hideously deformed and retarded humans left to roam the wasteland. *That* was the world you created by killing Jesus."

Harriet could feel the blood rushing to her face. "I– I didn't..." She couldn't find the rest.

"You didn't know," Miss Morgan finished for her. "Because you didn't think. Time travel's not as simple as changing one small thing and hoping for the best. Every single assignment we've ever carried out has been thoroughly planned, every collateral impact evaluated, every potentially affected blade of grass considered, before proceeding. You just decided, let's kill a bunch of people and get rid of Million Eyes. To hell with what comes after, even if it's mass genocide. And yet you stand there thinking you're better than me. You're worse."

"If you'd agreed to stop what you're doing, we wouldn't have had to resort to that."

"I'm sure many terrorists have said the same."

"SHUT UP!" Rawling yelled, his voice bouncing off the walls of the facility. "At least we did it for the right reasons. You're letting humanity die to preserve your position. To maintain your *power*!"

"And who's to say those aren't the right reasons?" Miss Morgan persisted. "Million Eyes has done an enormous amount of good in this world these past few decades. Our technology has changed lives. Our time travelling has brought down war criminals. Our influence in government has revitalised the economy. And it's all happened under my watch, my leadership."

"You've said your piece," said Harriet. "Now just get on with–"

Rawling sprang for one of the metal staircases leading to the mezzanine level and launched into a stooped run up it, three steps at a time. Harriet wasn't sure what he hoped to achieve. Miss Morgan fired her disruptor and a blazing green beam of light blasted the railing that shielded him and momentarily lit up the facility like daytime. Miss Morgan moved so she had a clear view of the stairs, fired again, missing Rawling's feet by an inch.

Harriet bolted in the opposite direction, towards the main door, in that moment wondering if Rawling had made a futile run for the mezzanine to give her a chance to escape.

Except it wasn't enough of a chance, Harriet realised, when a hot and almighty force slammed into her back.

31

After shooting Harriet, Miss Morgan swung her aim back to the mezzanine platform. The sound of smashing glass rang out and she remembered there being a window up there. *Has the idiot jumped?* Miss Morgan had assessed possible escape routes on arrival and there wasn't anything on the other side of that wall to jump onto. He'd probably break his legs.

She hurtled up the steps. The window had a human-sized hole, shards blanketing the floor of the mezzanine. Rawling was gone – *splattered on the ground outside?*

Bolting to the window, Miss Morgan now remembered that the side of the building was lined with chunky external pipes. She leaned halfway out to see Rawling climbing down one of them, still a long way from the ground. He looked up at her at that moment, realising the same thing she did. It was over.

Pathetic. She expected something more cunning.

She pointed her gun out of the window and fired. The beam surged into Rawling's chest, prizing him off the pipe he clung to. The serial killer plunged backwards, soundless till he landed. When he did, the back of his head shattered like an egg on the moss-lined concrete with a skin-crawling crack, and a geyser of blood, skull and brains exploded out in all directions.

Miss Morgan returned back down the steps. Looking over at Harriet Turner's motionless body, lying a few metres away from the main door of the facility, a powerful feeling coursed through her. A feeling that was one part satisfaction, two parts relief. Satisfaction that she had punished them both for their self-righteousness and recklessness. Relief that their knowledge of Operation Blue Pencil and where it would ultimately lead had died with them. With all of Harriet, Rawling and Fred Gleeson's possessions locked down in their Lambeth warehouse, it would now be a relative cakewalk making sure the truth about the Shapeless and the Last War never came to light.

Miss Morgan pulled in a deep breath, releasing it slowly, her heartrate returning to normal speed. She turned and started out of the facility.

Her pace slowed as she got closer to Harriet's body. She lay flat on her front with a large hole in the back of her jumper, blackened round the edges, from the disruptor blast. But Miss Morgan could see no wound or burns beneath. *How? It was a direct hit!*

She continued past the body – then her heart leapt into her throat as Harriet's corpse sprang to life, arm thrusting across the floor and grabbing Miss Morgan's ankle. Suddenly the concrete floor was plunging towards Miss Morgan's face, her feet wrenched out from beneath her.

Impact with the floor sucked all the air from her lungs. Her disruptor flew out of her fingertips and skittered across the floor, lost in thick shadow. Miss Morgan spun onto her back and desperately tried to draw air back into her lungs as the impossibly alive Harriet launched up her body, straddled her, and slammed a bunched fist into the side of her head.

The candlelit room spun. Miss Morgan started to turn her head straight, then another almighty thwack from the undead Harriet threw her head the other way. Her jaw and cheek throbbed and she could feel warm blood leaking into her nose and mouth.

Adrenaline kicked in and a spasm of strength made Miss Morgan's hand shoot up and clamp itself round Harriet's throat. Another spasm came and gave her the might to rise off her back and hurl Harriet down onto hers.

"How?" Miss Morgan breathed, closing her fingers round Harriet's throat and concentrating all her strength into squeezing the life out of her – again. "How are you alive?" *You won't be for long.*

As Harriet squirmed and thrashed and clawed at her, Miss Morgan tightened her grip, squeezing so hard she could feel Harriet's pulse in every finger. But although the life should've been going out of her reddening eyes by now, the wiry twenty-something was able to gather her legs beneath Miss Morgan's stomach and kick hard.

Miss Morgan lurched backwards and thumped onto the floor, cracking her head on the concrete. The room started spinning again, the pain and dizziness sapping her adrenaline and dissolving her strength.

A moment later, a blurry Harriet stood over her clasping a disruptor and shaking her head. "I'm not going to let you do this. That Redactor's not getting built. You're going to call Million Eyes now and stop it, or you're going to die."

Miss Morgan had a contingency plan for situations like that. Much like a spy or soldier might hide a cyanide pill in their mouth, attached to the back of a tooth, Miss Morgan kept a chronozine pill in her mouth for emergencies.

Harriet pointed the gun at Miss Morgan's face. "Call them. Call them now."

As the bitch issued her threats, Miss Morgan used her tongue to try to dislodge the chronozine pill from her teeth.

Shit. It was stuck.

"Do it or I swear I'll– wait." Harriet's eyes narrowed. "What are you doing?"

The fucking pill wouldn't detach from her tooth. Miss Morgan's tongue pushed and twisted harder. Suddenly, the pill popped off and flew to the back of her throat.

"Oh no you don't!" Harriet tossed the disruptor and lunged at her, clamping both hands on Miss Morgan's arms as the chronozine worked its way down her throat.

It wouldn't make a difference, of course. The

chronozine always made sure a traveller took only what they needed with them. Clothes, a bag, a vehicle. Miss Morgan certainly didn't need Harriet. She'd vanish in a flash of light and Harriet would be on her knees clutching at thin air.

As soon as the chronozine reached her digestive system, the humming rose and the white-ish haze of the Chronosphere started to engulf the room. In a moment Harriet would be lost in the dizzying fog of overlapping time zones.

Miss Morgan closed her eyes. She could feel herself go from lying on a freezing concrete floor to floating horizontally in midair, which meant she had transitioned to the Chronosphere.

But, if that was the case, why could she still feel Harriet's hands on her arms? Why could she still hear and feel Harriet's breath on her face?

She opened her eyes. Harriet was still there, still on top of her, the ethereal haze of the Chronosphere surrounding them both, the ghosts of time stepping through them in a fast blur.

Not possible. She didn't take a pill. *How is she here? How could I have brought her with me?*

Harriet seemed just as confused as she was. Letting go of her arms, she floated backwards till she was upright. Miss Morgan pushed her torso forwards to straighten herself.

"How did you do that?" Miss Morgan said, raising her voice to surmount the humming. It occurred to her that this was the first time she'd ever spoken whilst inside the Chronosphere. She'd not had company before.

Harriet replied, and although Miss Morgan couldn't hear her, the shape of the words looked like, "I don't know."

Glancing around at the kaleidoscopic rush of time, Miss Morgan noticed that her timeline was taking longer than normal to materialise.

Finally, the humming quietened slightly and the banner of numbers overlaid her vision.

Wait – what?

Years, months, days and hours were mixed up, and none were in any sort of sequence.

04:00	6 3 9 1	1 9 8 3	A p r i 1		1 5	2 0 2 7	4 5 2 1	3	00:00	2 2	7 8 2

Harriet seemed to notice that Miss Morgan's timeline was visible, such as it was. She lurched forwards and made a grab for her wrist. Miss Morgan floated out of her reach and tried to tap 2027 with her finger. At least *that* was there. Although her plan to travel back an hour, wait outside the facility for the altercation with Harriet to happen as before, then storm the building and take Harriet down right after her past self disappeared, had just gone to hell. Because Harriet would disappear as well.

Nothing happened when Miss Morgan selected 2027. It should've made the banner dissolve into a new menu just of months. It didn't. She kept prodding the air where 2027 was, but it didn't work.

It was all those blows to her head. Harriet had fucked her chronode. *What the fuck am I supposed to do now?*

Her timeline started to fade and shake, numbers and letters swapping places in a dyslexic jumble, and blinking in and out like somebody kept cutting the power. She tried to swipe the banner away with her hands, travel in time the old-fashioned way, by fixating on one of the ghosts and letting it pull her into its time zone. But like a window you can't close on your computer, her timeline wouldn't budge.

Then her timeline blinked out completely, the ghosts all rushed at her face, and the last thing she remembered was Harriet's hand closing around her wrist.

32

May 4ᵗʰ 2027

Erica Morgan had been missing for six days. In her absence, the board had asked the COO, Jeffrey Saunders, to take over as Acting CEO.

Saunders' first task was to go and find out what Miss Morgan had had locked down at Million Eyes' Lambeth warehouse under X9-1 clearance. He knew it was the contents of the Mystery History Museum and Harriet Turner, Frederick Gleeson and James Rawling's apartments. What he didn't know was what could be so sensitive or dangerous as to slap an X9-1 order on it.

Speculation among the other execs, including Saunders, along with the C-Suite and Time Travel Department staff who'd been part of the effort to take down the Unraveller, had been rife. But Miss Morgan had been keeping her own counsel, and everyone else in the dark.

Nearly everyone believed that the Unraveller was the woman, Harriet Turner, who Miss Morgan had met with at Bermond Street Shopping Centre the day before the Unraveller struck. And that Turner, Gleeson and Rawling had been in cahoots. The big question, which Saunders was hoping to get an answer to today, was why.

Saunders' driver parked outside the front of the warehouse. Squalls of rain pelted the ground, so the driver got out, opened a large black umbrella and walked round to the other side of the Lexus to let Saunders out under shelter. The driver walked with him to the door of the warehouse and, once Saunders was protected by the overhang of the warehouse's roof, turned and went back to the car. Saunders waved his hand over the vein scanner and felt a kick of power as the door unlocked. Miss Morgan had been CEO of Million Eyes for so long and now, suddenly, he was the new her. And if she had dirty secrets lying in this building, he was about to know them all. Excitement tingled down his spine and, unexpectedly, into his groin. He might have to go fuck someone after this.

The automatic lights flickered on as he entered. The contents of the four locations had been laid out across the room in four demarcated sections, stacked or boxed up. Saunders circled the contents of the Mystery History Museum, which had some pretty well-made models of Stonehenge and Atlantis, among countless boxes of artefacts and exhibits to do with high-profile deaths, mysterious places and real-life time travel cases. Saunders opened a few of the boxes to peruse the exhibits. *Christ.* This museum was about Million Eyes! Not all of it, but possibly most. The mysterious deaths they'd been showcasing – Princess Diana, Marilyn Monroe, President Kennedy, William II – had all been caused by Million Eyes, whether by accident or by design. The case of the Charlie Chaplin Time Traveller, Saunders remembered, was to do with that idiot traveller Gillian Flint who'd got herself caught on camera in the 20s. The Princes in the Tower Saunders now knew had been transported to the Cretaceous using Million Eyes' own time travel pills, eaten by the Tower Hamlets dinosaur Dr Neether's younger self discovered last month, and caused the mass extinction of three-quarters of all life on Earth. *Fucking hell.* How he had laughed on hearing that. Something Miss Morgan had, quite sensibly, kept from the board of directors.

They'd also had an exhibit on the Bermuda Triangle and the disappearances Million Eyes had attributed to the Ratheri, the source of their ability to time-travel. And, judging by the sheer number of boxes dedicated to it,

their main area of interest had been Jack the Ripper.
James fucking Rawling himself.

If Million Eyes were to come clean about all this, the
Mystery History Museum would have to lose the word
'Mystery' from its name.

Saunders started to examine the items recovered from
the three conspirators' apartments, hoping to find
evidence of their motives. He was also hoping to find
clues as to what had happened six days ago, after Miss
Morgan made the monumentally stupid decision to go
and confront James Rawling by herself. At the facility,
Million Eyes had found Rawling dead, with evidence of
disruptor fire and time travel. But a scan of the point of
dematerialisation had produced a scrambled reading, so if
Miss Morgan had travelled in time, they had no idea
when to.

Saunders had been given logins to access their
computers, although he noticed that Turner didn't seem
to own one. Gleeson had a MEc, so Saunders started to
look through his files and search history. Gleeson had
been searching for information about Jesus's scrolls, the
Shapeless and the Last War, indicating that he and Turner
knew way more about Million Eyes than they should.
Probably because James Rawling had told them. *But
why?*

Saunders found nothing on the museum's computers,
so he started going through Turner's things. Opening one
of the relatively few boxes of possessions, suggesting that
her apartment had been quite sparse, Saunders found a
Victorian-looking satchel containing items that seemed
similarly old-fashioned – a hair pin, a handkerchief, a
leatherbound photo album full of black and white
pictures...

Wait a minute.

A memory node? *Yes.* A 23rd-century memory node.
Saunders had seen these before. The evidence was
pointing clearly towards Miss Turner being a time
traveller.

Beneath the satchel, Saunders found a notebook whose

pages were wrapped in a single soft piece of leather held closed with a leather cord. He untied the cord to look inside. The initial pages contained poems. Dozens of them, some several pages long, others a few lines. Saunders read a couple. Although he was totally dense about poetry, he could at least detect the sadness in them.

Then the writings turned into diary entries. They started in 2021, which Turner wrote was after she and Fred had travelled to the future from 1895.

Well, that confirms what I thought.

Saunders skimmed through them. Turner only wrote a few times a year but the infrequent entries gave a sufficiently detailed picture of what had been going on. Her mother had had 'time travel pills' in her possession, and Harriet, believing she was a time traveller, had come to the future hoping to find out more about her.

Turner's most recent entries stood out. She and Gleeson discovered that James Rawling was Jack the Ripper, then learned from Rawling what her memory device really was, and that the woman she thought was her mother wasn't. Turner discovered that the time travel pills were *hers*; she herself had originated in the future, and she intended to go there and find her real mother.

She had written her last entry after travelling to the future with Rawling's help, and it was this one that almost stopped Saunders' heart.

The Shapeless weren't really aliens? They were a fusion of humans, animals, plants and manmade objects? *What?!* According to Turner, who said she'd been to the future and seen a Shapeless up close, the creatures were a blend of everything Million Eyes had deleted with the Redactor. The Redactor that Dr Neether was drawing up plans for right now.

Impossible!

Saunders' hands shook. He read further. "What the fuck!" escaped his lips and echoed off the walls of the warehouse.

Fred fucking Gleeson was Jesus?!

These revelations were astonishing. Devastating.

Completely and utterly game-changing. And Saunders had no doubt that every bit of them was true. Because this was why Miss Morgan had been so secretive and so desperate to shut all this down.

There could be no doubt that Harriet Turner was the Unraveller. *This* was why she had tried to change history and stop Million Eyes from coming into being. She wanted to prevent the Redactor from being built.

Saunders could now guess what the meeting between Turner and Miss Morgan at the Bermond Street Shopping Centre was about. Turner went there to convince Miss Morgan to put an end to Operation Blue Pencil. Miss Morgan refused.

Saunders sat down on a chair that had been recovered from the Mystery History Museum and took a few deep breaths.

Million Eyes' entire existence was one big cruel paradox. Everything the company was doing to prevent the end of the world was causing it.

He sighed. Humanity's end had been inevitable all along. Predestined. Fate. People said the future wasn't written in stone, but they were wrong. It was. It had always been.

Saunders himself had long had doubts over whether Million Eyes would ever succeed in changing the future, or if they were simply making that future happen. The evidence in front of him had confirmed those doubts. They were all caught in an endless, repeating cycle from which there could be no escape. An ouroboros.

Miss Morgan was right to cover this up. She clearly knew that they were waging a hopeless war – against time itself. But there were powerful people within Million Eyes who would still try to change the path even though it had already been mapped out. People who would not just put a stop to Operation Blue Pencil but be willing to shut down the entire company in some futile attempt to ensure the Mission's success.

He couldn't let that happen. Who knew what effect it could have on the space-time continuum if the zealots on the board tried to stop the Redactor project? No. They could never know about this. Blue Pencil would continue, humanity would die. Just as fate foretold.

He tossed Turner's diary back into the box and stood up, pulling his phone from his pocket and calling Lara Driscoll in the C-Suite.

"Miss Driscoll," he said, "I need a destruction order for everything that was recovered from Turner, Gleeson and Rawling's apartments, and the Mystery History Museum."

"*All* of it, sir?" Driscoll replied.

Saunders glanced around. While he hadn't inspected everything, the safest and most sensible thing right now was just to have everything incinerated. He confirmed, "All of it."

"Yes, sir," she replied.

Ending the call, Saunders turned and started towards the door of the warehouse.

But then the door started unlocking. Someone else was coming in, even though the Lambeth warehouse was locked down to everyone but him.

"Er, who the hell–"

The door opened and Dr Neether stepped inside with a disruptor in her hand.

Saunders gave a fast shake of the head. "Neether! What the fuck are you doing? And who gave you access t–?"

"Never mind that, Mr Saunders," said Dr Neether, training the gun on his chest. "I'm here now. And I'm holding the gun."

"What do you want?"

"To know everything you do about the Unraveller."

33

Ten Thousand Years In The Future

Miss Morgan opened her eyes to a blur of white. She could feel a hard surface against her feet, so she wasn't in the Chronosphere anymore. *Am I dead?* She had never believed what her mother did about an afterlife, but wouldn't it be fucking typical if that deplorable crone turned out to be right?

She looked down at her feet, still blurry but surrounded by white. Looking up, her lightheadedness lifted and her vision sharpened to behold the snowy landscape that encircled her, merging so cleanly with the white sky it was difficult to see the horizon.

But snow was *all* she could see.

She turned on the spot. The landscape undulated with gentle crests and dips, but was as barren as a desert. No water, no vegetation, not even a single tree. No sign of animal life. Even the sky appeared empty – Miss Morgan couldn't see or hear a single bird. A fine breeze curled around her, tugging softly at the edges of her military coat. But it was as silent as still air, having nothing to whistle through. And as it brushed her face, it seemed… *warm.* Bizarrely warm given how cold it must be for all this snow.

And she'd come alone, too. No Harriet. So where had *she* ended up?

Not that Harriet's fate should be of any concern. The only question that mattered to Miss Morgan right now was *how am I going to get home.*

She stared into the wintry expanse stretching out before her, her stomach tying itself into an expanding, hardening knot. If she had travelled back in time to one of Earth's major ice ages, she could be millions, if not billions, of years in the past. And she had no chronozine to get back.

She walked forwards, expecting the snow to crunch beneath her shoes. When all she could feel was a smooth, slightly spongy ground, she looked down at her feet again.

What the–?

She hadn't actually checked that it was snow beneath her feet – she'd just assumed.

But it wasn't, or at least, it wasn't like any snow she'd ever seen. Tiny white globules covered the ground, like cannellini beans. Thousands upon thousands of them, tightly clumped together, so that none of the ground was visible beneath.

Miss Morgan crouched down and laid an open palm on the ground. The tiny beans felt warm and rubbery. She now assumed that the sweeping white expanse surrounding her wasn't snowy at all, but blanketed in a thick coat of these supple little blobs.

And they're moving.

As she kept her palm flat on the beans, she could feel them rising and falling, very gently and slowly. Now that she was looking so closely, she could see the ground billowing all around her, like small waves rolling through a body of water.

Somehow, the beans were breathing.

Uneasy, Miss Morgan stood and continued walking over the beans' springy, heaving surface, which made her feet bounce slightly as she went. She crested a slight hill, at last spotting something that wasn't just white, bean-covered plain. About a hundred metres down the other side of the hill was a cluster of what looked like collapsed trees. They were white too – were they also covered in the white globules?

Miss Morgan moved down the incline towards them. As she got closer, she noted that the branches were thin and bare and had no trunks. They started looking less like trees, more like large woody shrubs.

A few steps later, they stopped looking like vegetation altogether.

Miss Morgan gasped.

The branches had... hands. Hands with different numbers of long, slender, finger-like digits. They weren't branches at all. They were limbs.

Shapeless.

She froze. Although she had never seen a Shapeless in person, Million Eyes had a smattering of images, videos and descriptions from the few travellers who had made it back from the Last War, together with Jesus's descriptions in his scrolls. None of them could have prepared her for the real thing. Her eyes pored over their contorted forms with mounting horror.

They weren't covered in beans. Their skin was already white and, as per every description Miss Morgan had read, glistening with a slimy white substance that resembled semen. At first she couldn't tell how many creatures there were because their limbs were entangled and none of them had heads. Each limb was a different length and thickness with differently placed joints, which was why they had looked like tree branches from far away. The gills running down each limb were closed and looked like dozens of little cuts in the creatures' flesh, or a multitude of sleeping eyes. The limbs extended from slightly more bulbous stems, which Miss Morgan figured must be each creature's body. She counted five misshapen lumps of flesh, which suggested she was looking at five Shapeless corpses. Well, *could be* corpses. They might just be asleep, for all she knew.

A bead of vomit squirted up Miss Morgan's oesophagus. They were disgusting, and now that she knew what they really were, she found herself even more repulsed.

Yet their presence brought a wave of relief, too, because if the Shapeless were here, it meant that Miss Morgan must be in the future, not the past. And if she was in the future, there was a chance she could find some chronozine to get back.

That said, she must be standing where Blackwall once stood, yet there was no trace of the abandoned factory or any of the streets around it. She could see quite far into the distance and the only thing she could make out on the blank white slopes, rolling on and on into the sky, was what looked like another cluster of collapsed trees several miles away. So, likely another pile of Shapeless corpses. No sign of anything else. She knew that the Shapeless had laid waste to humanity, but surely she should be looking at ruined buildings and debris. You'd think Earth had never been inhabited. How far into the future had she travelled?

She curved around the knot of limbs in a wide circle, keeping them in her sights at all times, and continued down the incline onto flatter ground. She just needed to find… *something.* This couldn't be all there was.

A sudden feeling that she was being watched made her neck hairs bristle. She tossed a glance behind her but the bodies of the Shapeless hadn't moved. She looked down at the ground around her, still swelling and billowing like the gentlest of tides.

She walked on.

The same feeling made her swing round on her heels. "Is someone there?" she blurted.

Yes.

Someone or something answered. But it wasn't a voice. It was a feeling. Like the reply was being transmitted directly into her mind.

"Who… who just said th–"

My name is Sole, it said, inside her head.

Miss Morgan whirled round. "Where are you?"

Everywhere.

The ground heaved beneath her feet, rising higher and falling further, as if the entire landscape was one gargantuan creature taking bigger, deeper breaths as it stirred awake. Miss Morgan flung out her arms for balance as the ground lifted her up and dropped her back down.

"You're... you're the white beans..." she murmured uncertainly as the undulations shrank, the landscape breathing more calmly again.

If your simple mind must relate my form to some recognisable component of your century, then yes, Erica, I am.

Miss Morgan turned around again, unsure which direction to address her words. "You know my name? And the century I'm from?"

Of course.

"How?"

Because I know everything about you. I know you were born in Cambridge in 1961 and that your father died when you were six. I know your mother turned to God on his death and did everything in her power to force you to believe. I know you spent the rest of her life fighting her, till she died of cancer when you were thirty. I know you met a member of Million Eyes called Mr Arnold in 1979 and joined the organization shortly after. I know you were instrumental in the invention of time travel in 1984 and Million Eyes' incorporation as a technology company a year later. I know you secured an enormous investment in the company's stock by the billionaire Arthur Pell in 1997 and subsequently became CEO, using Pell's money and connections to grow Million Eyes into the most powerful company in the world. I know you have been alone all your life, and you have never loved or felt affection towards anyone or anything but your dogs. And I know your favourite cuisine is Mexican and you abhor every kind of music except classical, in particular, Johann Sebastian Bach.

A series of chills skittered through Miss Morgan as this Sole being recounted her life. "Funny you mention 'God'. You speak as if you are one."

Nothing so supernatural. It is a defect of humankind to brand divine that which you do not understand.

"You'll get no argument from me." She used to say the same thing to her mother. "So what are you, then? And why don't you show yourself?"

Miss Morgan could hear laughter in her head.

Your ability to think, to imagine, is so small. If it makes you more comfortable, I shall indulge that smallness.

The patch of ground in front of Miss Morgan started rising, taller than before, as though something was pushing itself up through it. A column of white beans grew to the height of Miss Morgan and formed a hunched, vaguely human-like shape, with long lumps for arms and a narrow, round protrusion at the top – a faceless head with no neck. A moment later, a hole opened in the centre of the head, resembling a large, gaping mouth.

Is this better?

A deep shiver crawled up from her toes, into her chest and shoulders and down her arms, and made her fingers twitch. As whatever this thing was continued to speak telepathically, the hunched figure's mouth wasn't moving; it just hung agape in a permanent yawn.

"Are you some kind of– of intelligent fungus?"

A crude comparison.

"Then *what?*"

I am a child of time.

It was talking to her in fucking riddles. "What does that mean?"

It means I can see it – everything that is, everything that was, everything that will be. All of time, all of space.

More riddles. Miss Morgan was losing patience.

It is how I know I owe my very existence to you.

A pang of confusion hit her. "Wait– what? You owe your existence *to me?*"

That's right. Because you authorised Operation Blue Pencil. And because you let it continue even after you knew what would happen.

"I don't understand."

When the Redactor overloaded and the starship Peregrine *crashed on the Guinan System's only orbiting planet, a white ooze leaked out of the Redactor onto the surface of the planet. In time, the ooze became self-aware and discovered it was the collective residue of all that*

Million Eyes had decided was insignificant enough to erase from time. Erica, the ooze was me.

Miss Morgan shook her head and glanced back at the tangle of slimy limbs behind her. Gaze back on the hunched figure, "*You're* the Shapeless?"

The creatures you refer to as 'Shapeless' were just my first taste of corporeality. To coin a human phrase, that was me stretching my legs. When the Shapeless built spaceships and flew to Earth, the ooze subsisted on the Guinan planet. You humans believed that the Shapeless were being controlled by a 'brain' in the Guinan System, and you were right, although a more accurate word would be 'body'. The Shapeless were merely the tools I was using at the time. But I evolved. I evolved to not need those tools anymore. I evolved more quickly than any life form ever has. And in time, I was able to leave the Guinan planet without needing to be carried in a spaceship.

Miss Morgan felt her lungs constrict, her breathing grow short. If this being was truly an evolved version of creatures already dangerous and powerful enough to bring about the extinction of the human race, it was easy to imagine the devastation it could bring to the rest of the universe.

So I did, Sole continued. *I travelled the stars, infecting every planet in the cosmos, obliterating every life form in existence.*

Miss Morgan felt her blood freeze. "You did what?"

I am Sole. As in, only. I am the only living thing in the universe. Until you arrived, that is.

"You mean, everything… everything in the universe is…"

Dead. Everything except me, and now you. Yes.

That explained why Miss Morgan had not seen a single tree or bird. She no longer needed to imagine the devastation Sole had caused. "Why? Why have you done this? Why have you destroyed everything?"

Because humanity's end was not enough. Life had been poisoning the universe and it was my duty to extinguish it. To reset the universe, if you will. Restore it to its pure, unspoiled state, before the spark of life set fire to it all.

Miss Morgan needed to get out of this time frame – now. But how could she hide from something that was everywhere?

"Look. I wasn't meant to come here. This isn't my time. All I want is to get back to 2027, and then you'll be alone again." It sounded like time and distance had no meaning for Sole, which meant in theory it might be able to fold time and send her back to her century.

I will be alone presently.

"Presently? What does that mean?"

It means you are about to be extinguished, and then Sole will be sole again.

Miss Morgan curled her fingers into tight fists. "Wait. You don't have to do that. Just send me back to 2027."

I do not know why you think I would do that.

A surge of panic shot through her. "Because you said you owe your existence to me!"

And I do. Why is that a reason to keep you alive now?

"Because– be– c-c-*cause–!*"

A constriction in Miss Morgan's throat shattered her words into a fit of coughing. The knot in her stomach that had been growing and hardening since she got here started to cramp. She doubled over, feeling a hot torrent of vomit pushing its way up her throat. Her coughing turned into retching as she let the contents of her stomach splatter the ground.

As the vomit gushed from her lips, she could tell she was ejecting not quite the usual contents of her stomach, but something *white.*

When she'd finished retching, her body stilled as she stared down at the ground in a confused daze.

Beans. She'd just thrown up a mass of the same tiny blobs that shrouded the landscape.

Her stomach spasmed again, and more beans surged up her throat and erupted over the ground, becoming indistinguishable from the quilt of beans she stood on.

And then she noticed her hand. White globules were

poking through her skin on the back of her hand. She tried to scratch them off with her other hand and noticed that the same had happened to that one.

"Wha– what's happening to me?" Miss Morgan screamed at the humanoid figure.

For the first time since it grew out of the ground, the figure moved, growing taller and wider, bathing Miss Morgan in its bloated shadow.

You are infected, Erica. You have been since you arrived here.

Miss Morgan shook. Now Sole's mouth was opening and closing in time with each telepathic word. It didn't properly form the shape of each one. The top and bottom just moved up and down like a Jim Henson puppet.

I am everywhere, remember. Including inside you. I have been holding the infection at bay to speak with you. I was intrigued to know whether you would feel any guilt if I told you that, by being responsible for my existence, you are responsible for the end of all life in the universe. It is fascinating to me that you still feel none. Unlike many humans, you believe guilt is irrelevant and have never allowed yourself to be saddled by it. In a way, you and I are very much alike.

Miss Morgan fell to her knees. A tingling sensation travelled up her arms to her hands. Yanking back her sleeves, she saw that the beans were growing up her arms. She watched in horror as dozens of white globules popped out of her skin like popcorn, spreading towards her shoulders.

"If… if you and I are… are alike… why not… spare me," Miss Morgan choked, her words still squeezed by the agonising cramps in her abdomen.

Because I am Sole.

She could feel the skin on her shoulders, across her chest and abdomen, and now down her legs, rippling and twitching and tingling. That part wasn't actually painful, but then her left leg blazed with an excruciating pain that made her tilt sharply sideways. It was like every bone in it had been shattered. Looking down she saw that her leg was bulging and contracting beneath her trouser leg. And then a gush of white globules spewed from the hem of the fabric, over her shoe, and she tipped forwards, collapsing on her front, her leg disintegrated into beans.

A moment after she landed on her arms, the beans growing over them separated, both arms crumbling away and scattering across the ground. Her torso slumped, with nothing but empty sleeves to hold it up. Flat and ungainly on her face, Miss Morgan couldn't move or roll over.

This fungal infection cruelly left her head till last so that she would die slowly, watching the rest of herself break apart. But now she felt the tingling and twitching on her neck, her chin, her cheeks, and knew the beans were growing over her face as well.

A moment later, the white plains – which she could only see out of one eye as the other was mashed against the ground – blinked out.

In her last moments before her brain and skull became beans, Miss Morgan clung to one final thought as she stared into a chasm of blackness.

I still feel no guilt. The universe can go fuck itself.

34

August 22nd 2037

Harriet materialised in a brightly lit living room, daylight flooding the space through a floor-length window that spanned an entire wall. Despite having grown up in the 19th century and everything in the 21st looking strange and futuristic to her, this room looked even more so. Worm-like objects that could've been unlit floor lamps with no cords curled over the vast, blue, U-shaped leather sofa, which had a couple of touchscreen panels built into the sides. The legless coffee table in the middle looked like it was hovering motionless thirty centimetres above the floor, the tabletop looking like blue-green molten glass. A huge piece of art on the wall, of a sunset-soaked beach, appeared to be moving – waves crashed and seagulls swooped across the orange sky.

"Who the fuck are you and how did you get in?"

Harriet whipped her gaze to the right. A skinny barefoot man in pyjamas stood in a sectioned-off corner of the room housing a kitchenette, pointing what looked like a disruptor with both hands.

People have disruptors now?

"I– I'm sorry," said Harriet, holding up her hands. "I'm not supposed to be here."

"You're damn right! There's no way you got past the security grid. How did you get in?"

He obviously hadn't seen her materialise from thin air. In normal circumstances that would be a good thing –

305

except she had no other explanation for how she could be in his living room.

"I'm unarmed," Harriet offered, unsure what else to say.

"Answer my fucking question!"

She still wasn't sure how. "What year is it?"

"What year?" His face twisted with incredulity. "It's 2037, for fuck's sake."

Ten years. I've travelled forwards ten years. But where's Miss Morgan?

"Are you going to answer my question or not?"

The only answer Harriet had was the truth. "What if I told you I've travelled forwards in time from the year 2027?"

"Bullshit. Time travel ain't real."

So Million Eyes had released its disruptor technology, but the ability to time-travel remained a guarded secret.

Then Harriet remembered how Miss Morgan's disruptor had failed to kill or even wound her – much to the CEO's horror. Between that and her musket ball wound miraculously healing in a few hours, Harriet was willing to bet that this man's weapon might be harmless to her.

"I'm going to leave now." Harriet took a couple of steps forwards.

The man launched forwards, holding his gun firm, his aim now square on Harriet's head. "Don't you fucking move!"

"I'm not going to hurt you. But I *am* going to leave."

She stepped forwards again.

He shot her.

The green beam speared towards her forehead like someone shining a powerful torch into her eyes. The impact threw her backwards, but not hard, or enough to lose her balance. It felt like someone pushing her head back with an open palm, and it didn't hurt.

Harriet blinked away a moment's dizziness and stepped forwards again.

"What the fuck? How– how did you–!" Horrified, the man checked his gun and retrained it on her.

Harriet walked past him through the doorway of his living room. A second green beam struck her in the back of the shoulder – the same shoulder she was shot in with the musket – and shoved her forwards, momentarily illuminating the dark hallway leading to the front door.

Harriet turned around as a thread of fury slid through her. "You just shot me in the back as I was walking away from you."

"Yeah! You're in my house!"

"That's murder, you fucking idiot." Harriet had seen first-hand the primitive cultures of the Iron Age and Middle Ages, and it seemed this man wasn't any more enlightened than those.

"That's my right!" the man continued to insist.

An idea struck Harriet in that moment. She started walking towards him.

His eyes flared. "Stop right there!"

He shot her again. The beam hardly moved her and all she felt was a modicum of pressure on her chest.

"Get back!" the man screamed.

Harriet drew back her fist and slammed it hard into his face. The direct hit connected with his pointy cheekbone and Harriet expected it to hurt; it didn't.

The man flew back and tumbled over a bar stool at the breakfast bar of the kitchenette, which fell with him. The disruptor spun out of his fingertips and landed near the U-shaped sofa. Harriet went to pick it up.

The man curled up on the floor like a frightened child as Harriet stood over him, pointing the disruptor. "I'll be taking this. It's clearly better off in my hands than yours."

She carried on to the door. At least the man wasn't stupid enough to pursue her. Harriet hadn't spent long enough in the future with her mother to know if the human race was better than this in two hundred years' time, but she hoped that they were – given how hard she was trying to save them.

Harriet let herself out of the man's apartment and through the main door of the building which, she realised, was a skyscraper. She wondered when it was built. The old factory had been abandoned for so long Harriet figured it was an undesirable site to build on.

Harriet walked up a gravel path that carved through the building's artificial lawn, which was convincing apart from a patch coming up at the edge, revealing the rubbery infill. At the end of the lawn was a paved path and thin verge of trees, beyond which lay a road that wasn't there before. There had been a road, but a quiet, residential one with two lanes and a thirty speed limit. In the past ten years, a six-lane dual carriageway had been laid, with vehicles now whizzing by at terrifying speeds.

But Harriet wasn't afraid anymore.

She crossed the path and hid her disruptor in a thick patch of grass on the verge near the base of one of the trees. Then she climbed over the safety barrier and walked out in front of a driverless lorry rattling down the highway at seventy.

35

"You gotta be fucking kidding me. What's happening to her?"

"I don't know, but that's... that's not normal."

"It's not *possible* is what it is!"

Dull, deep echoes of voices started filtering gently into Harriet's ears, like she was underwater but nearing the surface. A build-up of pressure in her ears blew out, and instantly both men's voices were clear, like she'd emerged from the water into the open air.

Her eyes wouldn't work. Harriet searched for a stray spark somewhere in the dark, but the heavy curtain of blackness persisted – till something popped loudly in her skull and the curtain was gone, a deluge of daylight painfully saturating both eyes. Feeling returned to her limbs and she rolled over, smelling burned rubber. Two men standing over her shimmered into focus.

"No, no, no," one of them murmured as she sat up, stiff all over, a heavy ache gnawing at her head. She looked down at herself. Her jumper and pleated skirt were in shreds and both of her shoes had come off, and she was covered head to toe in blood. Blood splatter smeared the road around her, along with bits of bone and flesh and what looked like a tangle of entrails.

Her little experiment had worked. *I'm alive.*

"How the fuck are you alive?"

Ah, yes. How. Harriet herself didn't yet know the answer. The man who'd asked had a receding hairline and a belly peeking below the hem of a dirty t-shirt. His cheeks were flushed and Harriet wasn't sure if it was his complexion or his emotional state.

She pretended she hadn't deliberately thrown herself in front of a lorry. "What happened?"

"My lorry hit you," said the rotund man. "You just ran out."

"Yeah, and you were dead," said the other man, who was younger, in better shape, and wearing a stripy cap.

Harriet got to her feet and saw that a wide streak of blood and flesh trailed from the lorry's left rear tyres to where she stood. There was a stationary car immediately behind them in the left lane, its door open. It looked like this was the younger man's car and that he'd stopped to help. Vehicles veered around the scene into the other two lanes, slower than before.

"Yeah, *really* dead," said the lorry driver, although Harriet wasn't sure what the term was for a person being carried in a driverless vehicle. She hadn't even seen any window at the front of it – no need for one if the computer was driving. Lorry passenger?

"My God," he continued. "You were absolutely a hundred percent dead."

"What do you mean?" Harriet needed to know *exactly* what had happened to her.

"That lorry didn't just run into you," said the man in the cap. "It ran *over* you. Every fat, fucking tyre. Your whole body was crushed and mangled. You had bones sticking out everywhere. Half your brain was on the road. Your chest was like *flat.* I don't– I don't mean that in a rude way. I mean, your whole torso was flat as a pancake."

"Your goddamn intestines were on the outside," said the man from the lorry. He glanced at the bloody mess on the road, pressed the heels of his hands against the sides of his forehead and stooped like he might throw up. "Fucking hell, they still are!"

Harriet faced the younger man in the cap. He seemed a lot calmer. "Then what happened?"

"You just... you came back to life. Right in front of our eyes." He was shaking his head like he didn't believe his own words. "You were smashed to bits one second, then the next, all the bits started moving, wriggling. Your twisted limbs pulled together and straightened. Your wounds seemed to close up. Your torso started rising off the ground and your bashed-in skull sorta... reinflated. Like a balloon. It was like that bit in *Who Framed Roger Rabbit* when Christopher Lloyd gets flattened by a steamroller and then goes over to a gas cylinder and reinflates himself."

Harriet had never heard of the movie, but that was true of most movies. "Interesting." She couldn't think of anything else to say.

"Interesting?!" The man from the lorry stared at her, his eyes wide and bulging like a junkie desperate for a fix, his brow glistening with big droplets of sweat.

"Thank you for explaining," Harriet said to both of them. "Sorry if I caused any inconvenience." She started walking back towards the safety barrier.

"Hey– wait!" the man in the cap shouted after her. "You should wait for the police to get here!"

No. I really shouldn't.

Harriet climbed over the barrier and walked to the tree where she had hidden her disruptor, which she tucked into the waist band of her skirt. Then she carried on down the path that skirted the dual carriageway. There was a pedestrian crossing up ahead, leading to Blackwall town centre. Every car stopped simultaneously as Harriet approached. Car engines were pretty quiet back in 2027, but here, they made no sound at all. The sound imparted by the dual carriageway wasn't the deep rumble of revving engines, but the quiet hum of tyres whooshing over smooth tarmac. When they stopped, the entire road fell eerily silent and Harriet could hear her own shoeless feet padding over the crossing. Harriet stared at the strange, windowless boxes as she walked, unable to tell if any of them had occupants. Every car pressed on in perfect sync after Harriet had crossed.

The town centre looked different. There were new buildings, new roads, new shops. Even a couple of disruptor shops. *Whatever happened to the British Republic's gun control laws? Million Eyes, probably.*

Most of the road markings were gone; the only ones that remained were ones directed at pedestrians. No traffic lights. Harriet guessed that all the driverless cars communicated with each other and knew when and where to go, and when not to.

Her ripped and bloodied clothes garnered stares and alarm from pedestrians as she passed. One woman stopped and asked if she was okay. Harriet simply smiled yes and moved on quickly before the woman had a chance to ask any more questions.

She walked into a clothes shop called Primork, wondering if it was a competing brand or just Primark following an ill-conceived name change. She glanced sidelong at the large device hovering near the door, shaped like a gherkin, various lights flashing all over its exterior. An automated security guard?

She grabbed a full-length dress and a pair of ankle boots, and having no money on her, headed straight back to the entrance.

"Please take your items to one of the pay points in store," said the gherkin robot in a gender-neutral voice as it floated into her path.

Harriet continued walking forwards.

"Please do not leave. You must pay for your items."

A compartment opened in the centre of the robot's casing and a device resembling the barrel of a disruptor protruded from it.

In 2037, shoplifters get shot?

Harriet continued towards the door and the robot fired. This time she didn't even feel the beam hit her. The robot fired several more times as Harriet walked out of the store, the beams bouncing off her.

"Hey! Stop!"

A man shouting from somewhere inside the store made Harriet throw a glance over her shoulder to see him running towards her waving a disruptor. He was in a blue Primork uniform.

Harriet burst through the door and launched up the road.

She lost the man by hiding in an alley between a couple of buildings, but there were probably cameras everywhere, so she wouldn't stay hidden for long. She peeled off her sticky red rags and peered at her bare skin. Apart from being covered in blood, she couldn't find a single scratch. Her body seemed in perfect condition and she felt strong. She wet her fingers with saliva and tried to scrub off some of the blood, but there was too much and she soon gave up. Having spent half her life on the streets, being dirty didn't bother her, but being drenched in her own blood did.

She changed into the dress and shoes she'd just stolen. She realised that the belt on the dress had a kind of holster to fit a disruptor. If high streets now sported disruptor shops and clothing was being sold with these things attached, it was a safe bet that everybody was carrying the deadly guns.

Coming out of the alley onto a different road, Harriet stopped and scanned for taxis. They were automated too. She watched people get into them by tapping their bank cards on a plate at the rear of the vehicle. It seemed that everyone was paying before making their journey – and Harriet had no money.

Harriet spotted a woman waving down a taxi coming up the road. As it pulled to a stop at the kerb, Harriet bolted up the path, whipped her disruptor from the holster on her belt, and pressed the muzzle into the back of the woman's jacket. The woman gasped.

"You're going to take me with you," Harriet said.

The woman nodded quickly. "Okay. Y-yeah. Sure." Her voice shook.

Harriet kept the gun at the woman's back as she tapped her bank card on the taxi's plate. A door opened automatically in the side of the taxi and the woman stooped to climb in.

"Slowly," Harriet warned, following her into the vehicle. There were six seats facing each other and

Harriet couldn't see anything else in the body of the vehicle apart from some computer screens built into the sides.

Harriet swallowed hard, then a strong surge of guilt snaked through her veins at the realisation that she was more uncomfortable getting into one of these machines than holding this poor woman at gunpoint. In the course of saving humanity, had she lost her own?

The taxi computer's voice – which sounded the same as that security robot at Primork – pulled Harriet out of her troubling thoughts. *"Your destination, please."*

The woman shrugged at Harriet. "You're holding the gun."

Harriet let out a sigh. "Million Eyes headquarters."

36

Harriet passed through the main door of the Looming Tower into a large white lobby with lifts on either side. Hovering in the middle were two robotic security guards that were bigger, sleeker and meaner-looking than the one at Primork. They approached her on both sides and emitted bars of blue light that scanned up and down her body.

"*You are not authorised,*" one of the robots said.

"You're damn right," said Harriet, walking between the two of them, disruptor in hand.

"*Stop. Do not continue. You will be terminated.*"

The guards fired their rays at Harriet, each one bouncing off her, as she walked towards the huge, curved reception desk that was as white as the walls and seemed to blend into them.

A woman in a green-grey skirt suit looked up from behind the desk. Her expression morphed from frowning confusion to open-mouthed horror at the relentless onslaught of disruptor beams surging into Harriet's back and having no effect other than to give the clinical space a green glow.

"I'm here to see Erica Morgan," said Harriet, lifting her disruptor over the counter and pointing it at the woman's head.

"I– I– h-how–?" The gun didn't seem to heighten her alarm. What really bothered her was Harriet's invulnerability.

Harriet glanced back at the robots, still mindlessly

shooting her in the back. "You might want to tell them to stop. They're wasting their energy."

Shaking her head in disbelief, the woman stood up and issued a command, "Cease fire," and the surges stopped. The robots retracted their guns and hovered motionless.

"Who are you?" the woman said to Harriet.

"Harriet Turner."

The receptionist's face dropped. "Harriet Turner? But you're the..." Her voice trailed off.

"I'm the what?"

She just stared at her, wordless, shaking her head continuously.

"Just get Miss Morgan down here, will you?"

The woman sat down on the edge of her chair and tapped some buttons on the screen of her MEc. A moment later, she said, "I'm sorry to disturb you, ma'am. I have... I have Harriet Turner down here in reception. With a gun."

Harriet noticed that the woman had an earpiece in. Whoever she'd just called gave an inaudible answer, and the woman nodded and said, "Very good, ma'am."

Ending the call, the woman looked up at Harriet. "If you'll just wait there, please."

"Sure," Harriet replied with a disingenuous smile.

A few minutes later, the doors to the lift on the right-hand side of the building opened with a quiet swish.

A woman stepped out – but it wasn't Miss Morgan. This woman had a brown bob framing half a face – one ear, one eye, one cheekbone, and half a mouth skewed downwards. The missing side of her face looked smooth and even as though her features had been rubbed out with an eraser.

Harriet trained her gun on the woman, who walked towards her in a honey-coloured trouser suit.

"I asked to speak with Miss Morgan," said Harriet.

The woman looked at the receptionist. "Deactivate the video and audio surveillance of this room, and leave us." Her voice was deep and throaty.

The receptionist's eyes widened. "Are you sure that's a good–?"

The woman's one eye blasted the receptionist with a brutal glare.

"Y-yes, ma'am, right away," the receptionist said immediately, fingering a couple more buttons on her MEc screen, before scurrying away from the desk and disappearing into the lift on the other side of the lobby. Unless you counted the inert robots, Harriet and the woman were alone.

"Erica Morgan has been missing for ten years," the woman said. "I am Million Eyes' CEO now. My name is Dr Samantha Neether. Pleased to meet you... Unraveller."

Harriet frowned. "Unraveller?"

"That is what we all call you here at Million Eyes. Ever since you attempted to unravel all of time with the assistance of James Rawling."

"I suspect Miss Morgan never told you why."

"She didn't, no. But I *do* know. I've known for a long time. You were trying to stop Operation Blue Pencil. You were trying to stop the creation of the Redactor."

"So you know what will happen?"

Dr Neether nodded.

"And have you stopped it?"

The only functioning portion of her mouth curling towards her cheek in a coldly sympathetic half-smile, Dr Neether shook her head.

"What? *Why?*"

"Because Blue Pencil was my idea, and the company has not invested this much money into a Mission-related project since the invention of time travel itself. If I pull the plug, it'll be deemed a failure, and so will I."

A flame of hate and rage seared through Harriet. "So just like Erica Morgan, you're doing this for power. To preserve your fucking position. What is *wrong* with you people?"

Although her voice was scratchy, Dr Neether kept her tone level and calm. "This is nothing to do with power. Right now, the doctors here at Million Eyes are working on a cure for necrocythemia."

"Necro-what?"

"Necrocythemia. It's a rare blood disease for which the only treatment currently is regular blood transfusions and organ transplants. It's the condition that killed my daughter, Georgia. Ever since I came to Million Eyes, I have been utilising the company's resources to find a cure for it. Since I became CEO, I have been able to accelerate our research by dedicating more resources to it. And now, I'm pleased to say, we're close. *So* close. Weeks, perhaps even days, from a breakthrough. If the turth about the Redactor were known, the company could be shut down, and the work on necrocythemia would stop. I can't let that happen. I have to save my daughter."

"I thought you said she was already dead."

Dr Neether formed another grisly half-smile. "You know as well as I that death doesn't really mean anything around here. We're time travellers. And I plan to do a little 'unravelling' of my own."

"So you're willing to sacrifice the future of the human race for... one person?"

Without hesitation, Dr Neether nodded, "For Georgia? Yes. Without question."

Even though this woman only had one eye, Harriet could see that the stubborn tenacity in it was fierce. No way was she going to be able to persuade Dr Neether to relent. Despite working for an organisation founded on a commitment to change the future, Dr Neether had – just like Miss Morgan – become concerned only with the here and now. And her selfish desire to save her daughter had consumed her.

"Then I'm sorry," Harriet said, her finger over the trigger of the disruptor. "But I can't keep letting people like you – with no regard for the generations coming after them – get in my way."

Harriet pressed the trigger. A green bolt of light surged from the muzzle, towards Dr Neether's chest.

It didn't reach her. It hit something invisible, sparkles of green light rippling out from the impact point like a flurry of wind-blown embers.

What the hell–?

She fired again. Green light speared towards Dr Neether and dispersed into a twinkling green spray once again. There was an invisible force a couple of metres in front of Harriet, blocking the ray.

"Your weapon is useless," said Dr Neether. "You're inside a containment field. We knew before you arrived that we would be unable to kill you. We've been working out what to do with you instead."

Harriet lowered the gun. "You knew I was coming?"

"Yes."

"And you... you knew about my condition?"

"You mean your imperviousness to injury? Yes. We knew about that too."

Harriet heaved a confused sigh. "How? Rawling destroyed the Augur."

"Oh, that was years ago, Miss Turner. We haven't been resting on our laurels since then. We have a new Augur. A much more powerful one. It harvests the brain of a sensile with much stronger abilities than Rachel Evans. This man did not just have memories of alternate pasts, like Rachel. He had premonitions of alternate futures, too. His visions were vivid and detailed and he became the perfect candidate for Rachel Evans' replacement. So, Harriet, that is how we knew that you would storm headquarters with your new abilities and force us to shut down Operation Blue Pencil. Our new Augur gave us the data last week, giving us time to prepare."

Harriet released another sigh, of exhaustion. All this effort and she'd made not a single dent in the all-powerful Million Eyes machine. "There's just no fighting you, is there," she murmured, despondently shaking her head, a part of her wanting to cry.

Dr Neether walked forwards. "No. I learned that for myself long ago. I used to be like you, you know. I tried to bring Million Eyes down, till I realised it was futile to even try. But you know what they say – if you can't beat them, join them."

Harriet looked at her, suddenly feeling drowsy and weightless. "So what happens to me now?"

"Since the Augur first told us you were coming, we've been devising a synthetic pathogen capable of isolating certain memory engrams in your brain and eliminating them. We started pumping it into the air inside the forcefield the moment we erected it. It won't be long before the effects take hold."

Harriet frowned. "Eliminating mem…?" A wave of dizziness drowned the rest of her words and made her stumble forwards, almost colliding with the forcefield. Her vision started to blur as she looked at Dr… *Dr…* Harriet couldn't remember the woman's name.

The spacious white lobby felt small and suffocating, like the walls were closing in. She couldn't remember how she got here – or where here was.

This is Million Eyes' doing, I know that. They want to silence me. Because of what I know about the… the…

She couldn't remember.

The disorientation overcame her and she swayed sharply to the right, her shoulder bouncing off the containment field and feeling like it had been repelled by a magnet. She collapsed onto her knees. Her impact with the forcefield made the air in front of her shimmer like heat ripples in the desert, briefly turning the half-faced doctor into a mirage.

"Wh-what's happening…?" Harriet's breath started coming in laboured gasps.

"A new beginning," said the woman. "Consider yourself lucky."

Harriet didn't believe her. How could she? She was Million… *Million… Million what?*

Harriet scrunched her eyes shut and concentrated as hard as she could, like when she used to pray to God to make her mother better in St Mary Matfelon church. She recalled the church, visualised its grand pointed arches and columns, the beauty of its sculpted stone flowers and twinkling stained glass windows. And then she homed in on her adoptive mother's face. Emma

Turner. *Emma Turner.* The woman who had taken her in, and loved her, and given her the name Harriet. Harriet thought of her real name, Dina, and the woman who had given it to her – her biological mother, Cara Montgomery, who she got separated from at four years old when she time-travelled to the 19th century. *Cara Montgomery, Cara Montgomery, Cara Montgomery.* The mother who had sunk to the bottom of her memory, only resurfacing a few months ago. She couldn't lose her again.

She kept both women's faces in her mind, Emma's hazel eyes, Cara's blonde hair, and then she thought of Frederick Gleeson. *Remember him, too. Remember poor Fred.* The man who she had technically been praying to for most of her life and who was, as it turned out, just a man. A broken one.

And yet, no matter how hard she concentrated, she could feel them slipping away, like a dream you just can't hold onto after you've woken.

She could still see both women's faces – but what were their names?

Remember them, Harriet, they're your mothers. They're your...

And the man. In an instant, his name and association to her – gone. Who was he and who was he to her? She scoured her mind, couldn't find anything.

Think! Wait. What is my *name?*

She knew she had two. One began with 'H'. And the other... the other she couldn't remember at all.

Everything was slipping away now. The people she loved, her whole identity. Everything she had done, seen and felt. She stood at the opening of a deep, dark, eternal tunnel as all the people, places and emotions in her life were gathered up and dragged down the tunnel till they were out of sight, and out of mind.

The nameless woman opened her eyes and gazed up at a woman in a honey-coloured trouser suit with half a face, murmuring, "Who am I?"

The woman sighed thoughtfully and said, as if she had

done the nameless woman a favour, "You're whoever you want to be."

Instinct told the nameless woman that the other was a liar and couldn't be trusted, but she didn't know why. She went to ask another question, but her lungs shut down, robbing her words of oxygen.

And then, in the fraction of a second before the big white room was sucked into a black void, she saw a snake. A snake formed into a circle, its tail in its mouth.

Dr Neether looked down at Harriet Turner's unconscious body as Dr Sheila Ruben and a security officer called Corey Wersching disembarked the lift and came to stand either side of her.

Dr Ruben used her handheld scanner to take readings from inside the containment field, confirming, "She's alive."

"Did the memory resequencing work?" Dr Neether asked.

Dr Ruben read off her scanner, "It certainly did."

Dr Neether took out her phone and called Lara Driscoll in the C-Suite. "It worked. Power down the containment field."

"Yes, ma'am," Driscoll replied.

A faint *swoosh* indicated that the forcefield around Harriet had been disengaged. Dr Neether asked Driscoll, "Has all trace of Harriet Turner been purged from the public record?"

"Affirmative," said Driscoll. "Harriet Turner is a ghost."

"Good." Dr Neether hung up and faced Dr Ruben. "How long till she wakes up?"

"An hour, maybe two," Dr Ruben replied.

"And she won't remember anything about Million Eyes?"

"Nope. She won't remember a thing about her twenty-three years on this Earth. She'll still possess certain skills – how to make a sandwich, use a phone, wipe her behind, but that's it. Clever, isn't it, dear?"

A wrinkly beam broke out on Dr Ruben's face and chilled Dr Neether to the bone. The eighty-six-year-old great-grandmother, who had been calling Dr Neether 'dear' since the day they met, had been responsible for an alarming amount of death and suffering during her time at Million Eyes, and had always dispensed her evil with a joyful smile. Even Dr Neether herself was once this geriatric psychopath's victim. She would never forget the day Dr Ruben plunged a syringe into the back of her neck and force-fed her a red pill while she struggled against the iron grip of a security man. One day she hoped to punish the noxious old bitch for that, but it wouldn't be till she had outlived her usefulness. For now, she continued to be excellent at her job and popular amongst her colleagues.

"What should I do with her?" Wersching asked.

Dr Neether knew that if Miss Morgan was being asked this question, she would probably answer, 'Who gives a fuck, just leave her by the side of the road.' But Dr Neether wasn't her predecessor, nor was she keen to become her. Being abusive spawned obstructions and mistrust. Being nice, even if it wasn't real, got things done faster.

"Take her to Helping Hands," said Dr Neether. "It's the nicest homeless shelter in the area. They serve actual food there, not just gruel."

Both Wersching and Dr Ruben looked at Dr Neether with dubious eyes, as if to say, 'And she deserves that why'?

Of course, they didn't know what Dr Neether knew: that Harriet had been trying to stop the Redactor from creating the Shapeless. No one but Dr Neether and former CEO for the briefest of moments, Jeffrey Saunders, knew that. From everybody else's points of view, Harriet was a terrorist who had attempted to destroy history for her own ends.

Wersching continued to stare at Dr Neether as if expecting her to adjust her orders, probably because the Helping Hands facility was a few miles away and he couldn't be arsed with the effort of transporting Million Eyes' most notorious nemesis all the way there.

Unfortunately for him, Dr Neether wasn't budging. "Do it. And re-establish video and audio surveillance of this room, and tell Whipman she can return to her desk."

As Dr Ruben returned to her office and Wersching, with a colleague, prepared Harriet for transport to the homeless shelter, Dr Neether exited the rear of the Looming Tower into the car park and walked to her MEcar. She departed for Facility 9 in the Salisbury Plain, where her team had been setting up the first large-scale test of the Redactor. Due to take place tomorrow, the test would involve the erasure of the Welsh village of Llanderi.

On the way, Dr Neether thought about all the people in Llanderi who would soon be wiped from existence, but would, in two hundred years' time, re-emerge from their void in a new and terrifying form and bring about the downfall of humankind.

There was a time when Dr Neether would never have let that happen. Even if it meant losing her daughter forever, she would have sacrificed her own happiness for humanity's future.

But the thing was, people were biologically selfish, and there was no point trying to deny it. Human selflessness wasn't real, it was pretend, and realising that fact had been freeing. Because it meant that Dr Neether could focus on saving Georgia without a shred of guilt.

37

June 1st 2113

Hallie Dressler had been alive for ninety-nine years, although she had only really *lived* the last seventy-six. Back in 2037, doctors had determined Hallie's age using cellular chronomorphology and Hallie learned that twenty-three years of her life had been lost. Unfortunately no doctor had ever been able to explain or treat her amnesia, and it seemed she would never know anything about her life before August 22nd 2037, when she woke in a homeless shelter in London and couldn't even remember her name. For a while, she went without one. After doctors told her that her memory may never return, she studied lists of first names and surnames in books till she found a pairing she liked. And so, 'Hallie Dressler' was born.

It had been a quiet life. After periods spent not knowing where the next meal was coming from, Hallie had discovered a talent for poetry; she set up a business writing poems for weddings, something which finally made her some money. It had never been much, but had been enough to buy a farmhouse in West Wales. It was an old dairy farm, which had fallen into disuse after a bioreactor facility for lab-growing meat was established nearby. But the countryside was peaceful, and the farmhouse remote, and she could stay out of people's way.

The reason she had retreated here, and found a job that allowed her to hide behind the holo-display of her twenty-year-old MEc, was not because she loathed her fellow man. It was because in seventy-six years, Hallie hadn't aged a day. She still looked exactly the same as when she woke up in that homeless shelter. Despite pushing a century, she hadn't a single wrinkle, blemish or grey hair, nor a hint of stiffness in her bones. More than that, she had never been ill. She had never contracted even a sniffle. And she had never been injured either. Once, years ago, she was in a car accident. Her driverless taxi hit a deer and careened off the highway, rolling several times down an embankment before colliding with a tree. Though the car was wrecked, Hallie emerged from it without so much as a scratch. People told her she was like David Dunn – a superhero in a movie called *Unbreakable* from the beginning of the last century, played by Bruce Wallis, she thought. She may have been misremembering the actor's name, but hey, that was the story of her life. David Dunn had walked away unscathed from a train crash that killed everyone but him, learning later that he had never been sick – just like Hallie.

Her condition had started to mystify her doctors, which was why she stopped going to them. Her friends, too, were baffled, leading her to realise that she would need to withdraw from public view for fear of catching suspicious eyes and being carted off by men in black to a government lab to be poked and prodded till the secret of her apparent indestructibility and immortality was discovered.

That morning, Hallie awoke from the dream that had been plaguing her with more frequency of late – the one with the snake. In every dream she would be standing on the edge of a steep cliff, in rain so hard it was pricking her skin, looking out over an infinite grey ocean, when someone would call her name. She'd turn and see herself, like an identical twin or duplicate, holding a thick red snake that was chomping on its tail and forming a solid ring around her arms. After a few moments of just smiling warmly at Hallie, her counterpart would snap open her mouth to reveal long, snake-like fangs and let out an angry hiss, then throw the snake at her. Startled, Hallie would catch it but lose her balance and plunge from the cliff, the snake falling with her. At this point she would wake up, often having fallen out of bed.

This time, Hallie had managed not to fall out of bed, but found herself near the edge of the mattress, fingers gripping the perimeter. She lay partially tangled in her quilt, perhaps from flailing her arms as she plummeted from the cliff. Untangling herself, she climbed out of bed and walked to the window. She threw open the curtain to look out at cloudless skies and yellow, sunburnt meadows, although she could still feel the pelting of cold, painful rain and hear her counterpart's abrasive hiss as she stood there.

Hallie turned to walk into the bathroom and started at the sight of Bluebell in the bedroom doorway.

"Oh, Bluebell! Not again."

The grey Maine Coon stared lovingly up at Hallie and meowed as she sat with all four paws neatly in line, swishing her broad, fluffy tail.

In front of her paws, leaking little droplets of blood onto the pale green carpet, lay her latest gift: a mouse, freshly dead but not in too gruesome a state. At least she was killing her gifts lately. Hallie couldn't count the number of live birds, rodents, even lizards, she'd had in her house thanks to Bluebell's *generosity*. There were times when it had felt like a zoo.

Hallie sat on the bed and invited the cat to come to her. Bluebell sauntered over and leapt into her lap. She circled her thighs twice, claws catching in Hallie's nightie, before settling in the Sphinx position and purring as Hallie started to stroke her back. "I know you like to bring me treats, my darling, but honestly, I'd much prefer chocolate."

She'd only had Bluebell a few months, after her last cat, Anna, died. While Anna and all the previous cats Hallie had owned brought in animals, none had been quite as enthusiastic about gift-giving as Bluebell.

Hallie cuddled Bluebell for a few minutes more,

wondering how long it had been that she'd only had her cats for company. Many years now. These days her only contact with other humans was over the internet.

"Right, down you get, so I can sort out your present," Hallie said, standing up. Bluebell jumped down and scooted out of the bedroom. Hallie picked up the little critter by the tail and went downstairs to dispose of it in the reconstitutor, which recycled all waste into energy for the house.

Passing through the kitchen, she stopped to look at one of her paintings on the wall, and her thoughts were back on her dream. The tail-eating red snake had been with her all her life, popping up in dreams and visions, and sneaking into her watercolours of Welsh landscapes and villages, like this one. Sometimes, without realising she was doing it, Hallie would paint a tail-eating snake at the foot of a tree or on top of a hill. In this one, of a thatched cottage, Hallie had rendered a snake hanging on the door like a wreath.

She had even seen real-life snakes eating themselves, as though it was becoming an increasingly common behaviour. At an animal sanctuary some years back, she saw a red corn snake getting smaller and smaller as it hungrily walked its jaws up its body. And she often caught adders and grass snakes munching on their tails during walks in the meadows by her home.

Having googled its meaning, Hallie had discovered that the tail-eating snake was a symbol called an ouroboros, representing infinity, that first emerged in Ancient Egypt. What she didn't understand was why her mind had always been so influenced by and focused on it. She didn't even like snakes.

Hallie went back upstairs to the bathroom to get ready, catching her wrinkleless, twenty-three-year-old face in the mirror, her blonde hair still showing no traces of grey. Her eternal youth had never really felt like a blessing – certainly not since she'd had to estrange herself from all the people she knew, all the people who had helped her get on her feet. Now that she was by herself every day (well, apart from Bluebell), Hallie felt like the clock on her life had stopped, frozen, trapping her in a kind of purgatory of eternal waiting. When would it end? Perhaps never. That was the thing about eternity.

However, she had been noticing one small change in the past couple of years.

Her eyes were changing colour.

Hallie had blue eyes. But they were turning red. In the past two years they had been reddening very gradually, going from blue to violet to magenta. Now her irises were almost the colour of blood.

Hallie rested her hands on the rim of the sink, leaned forwards and released a heavy breath.

Not again.

When she exhaled, a red vapour vented from her lips and dispersed against the glass of the mirror. This latest development started only yesterday, but Hallie suspected it had something to do with her red-turning eyes.

Hallie let out a second, larger breath. Another puff of red hit the glass. It was like she was breathing blood vapour. *Am I?* Maybe it was time to go back to the doctors.

No. I can't do that. They would *definitely* ship her off to some lab once they saw that she was some ageless demon with red eyes, and now red breath.

She could feel her chest tightening and gave a slower, softer breath to calm herself. This time nothing came out. It only seemed to be happening when she let out a particularly deep or heavy breath. Swallowing and shrugging it off, she jumped in the shower.

After washing and dressing, she went downstairs to her study and asked Verona, the virtual assistant wired into all the systems of the house, to display her notifications. The holographic display flickered several times as it came to life above her desk; it was because the computer was so old and she still hadn't got round to replacing it. She should, though, because it was looking like conventional smart devices would be obsolete soon. According to the news, a prototype microcomputer called an orb was inching closer to production following a series of successful human trials. Apparently this microcomputer, once implanted into the brain, made it so you would no longer need to physically interact with devices. They were also saying that everything on the one-hundred-and-twenty-four-year-old internet would be ported over to a new database to which everyone would have automatic access via their orb.

Hallie was still hoping it wouldn't happen, because it meant that the internet would cease to be for everyone who didn't want to have this orb implant. Frankly, she couldn't think of anything worse than having a computer inside her head.

She opened her inbox and the message at the top immediately made her stomach turn. It was titled *Ouroboros*. She tapped her finger in midair to open the message, and a man appeared from thin air in the middle of her study.

She had never got used to holograms. The solid 3D projections were so good that it was like having the person in the room with her, which was always disturbing when the message was from someone she didn't know, like the man now being projected into her home by her holo-emitters. Although video and audio messages were fine, she wished more people *wrote* messages, like the old days. It was how Hallie communicated with all her poetry clients. No one had seen her face in years.

The man's young face was framed by a smart, black, brushed-back quiff and a short beard, and he was wearing a black cassock with crimson piping and buttons, and a clerical collar. A priest? Why would a priest be contacting her? Hallie had never been religious. Well, she couldn't speak for the first twenty-three years of her life, but the last seventy-six had certainly been god-free.

"Hello Harriet," the man said softly, warmly.

Harriet? It wasn't her name, and yet, hearing it was making her hands start to shake at her sides.

"My name is Marcus Evans. You don't know me, but I know you. And so do the people I represent."

Who– the Church?

"In fact, we know you better that you know yourself. We know who you really are. We... remember."

Hallie's heartrate spiked.

"We know that your name is Harriet Turner, and before that, it was Dina Montgomery. We know that twenty-three years of your life were cruelly taken from you."

Something stirred inside Hallie as he said those names, although she wasn't sure what it was.

"We also know what is happening to you."

Happen...ing? Does he mean...?

"Please, Harriet. Meet me today at 3pm. There is still a chance to save everyone."

Blimey. Whatever this Marcus Evans was talking about, it sounded grave.

"I have embedded spatial coordinates in this message, along with a program that will allow you to bypass a security perimeter that automatically diverts shuttles away from said coordinates. Download them both to your shuttle's computer. The future is in your hands, Harriet. It seems, it always was."

The mysterious messenger dematerialised and Hallie stood silently, trying to process everything he had said. She opened the spatial coordinates to find out where 'Marcus' was asking her to go.

"Bermuda?" she said aloud. Well, no. Not Bermuda at all. Bermuda was the nearest landmass, but the coordinates were two hundred nautical miles south-west of it, in the middle of the North Atlantic Ocean. Nothing there but sea.

A part of Hallie was telling her to delete the message and pretend she had never got it.

But another part – a bigger, stronger part – was telling her she *had* to go. That her very life depended on it. So she readied her shuttle and prepared to leave the wilderness of West Wales for the first time in over forty years.

As the shuttle neared the coordinates, the sensors detected an unknown energy pattern causing massive gravimetric fluctuations throughout the region. Hallie decreased speed, then her chronometer went haywire, the date and time changing constantly. One moment it was telling her it was 10.41am on January 9th 2213, the next it was midnight on September 23rd 1452, and then it was 'dawn' and 'month unknown' in the year 19,888 BCE.

She adjusted her trajectory, flying closer to the ocean surface, concerned that if her systems crashed, her shuttle would plummet into the sea.

A few minutes later, after trying and failing to stabilise her chronometer, the source of the unknown energy pattern came into visual range.

The sky was white with a blanket of cloud, the ocean still and reflective beneath it. Ahead, hanging between the two, was something red. A large, mountainous shape that from this distance looked like another cloud, a big puffy one dyed by the light of sunset. Except it was the middle of the afternoon. And it wasn't really *sunset*-red either. More *blood*-red.

Just like…

Hallie continued on her present course and the strength of the energy readings began to increase exponentially.

"What the hell *is* that?" she murmured aloud.

Now only a few hundred metres in front of her, the red cloud didn't look or behave like a cloud. Hallie peered ahead as it heaved and writhed like liquid smoke after it's been disturbed, shades of darker or thicker red swirling through it.

Reaching the coordinates, Hallie cut her thrusters. At that moment, sensors picked up a signal. A signal being transmitted in Morse code, an antiquated means of communicating non-verbal messages over long distances.

Hallie looked down at her console. The message was: *R A T H E R I.*

"RATHERI? What the hell is 'RATHERI'?"

"A question asked by many for many years," said a man's voice behind her.

Hallie rotated her seat to see the man from the message – wearing the same black cassock and clerical collar – standing in the aft section of her shuttle, his hands entwined in front of him.

She stood up. "How did you get in?"

"I'm not actually here," the man replied. "I'm a live hologram being projected inside your shuttle from mine, a few kilometres east of here."

Hallie glanced back at her sensor display. She hadn't even noticed the other shuttle come into sensor range, she'd been so focused on the red cloud and the bizarre energy readings it imparted.

Facing him, "You're– you're Marcus Evans?"

He nodded. "Yes."

"I don't really know what the Church would want with me…"

Marcus smiled. "We're not from the Church. We dress like this to stay hidden."

"*We?*"

"The other people who are like myself. We dress as priests because religious people nowadays are considered innocuous eccentrics with deluded ideas. As such, we don't draw attention from those in power. And that keeps us safe from Million Eyes."

"Million Eyes? The technology company?"

"They are much more than that, I can tell you," said Marcus. "But I didn't ask you here to talk about Million Eyes. I asked you here to talk about you."

"In your message, you called me Harriet. Harriet Turner."

"That's because it's your name. The name you grew up with, anyway. The one your adoptive mother, Emma, gave to you."

Hallie shook her head. "No. You've got the wrong person. My name is Hallie Dressler."

"The name you picked out for yourself, correct? After you lost your memory."

"Yes."

"Funny you chose that. 'Hallie' is a diminutive variant

of 'Harriet'. And 'Dressler'... 'Dressler' is the German and Jewish name for a person who crafted small objects from wood and bone using a lathe in the Middle Ages. Otherwise known as... a turner."

Hallie – *is that my name?* – felt her hands start to shake again, just like when Marcus first spoke the name in his message. Her upper body felt unbearably heavy all of a sudden, her knees starting to buckle. She fell back into her seat and exhaled deeply. Her breath came out as a puff of red vapour – but she hardly noticed. A rush of dizziness made her sway in her seat. The felt-lined metal floor of her shuttle started billowing like waves and Marcus flew about the aft section in a blur. She never drank, but this must be what drunkenness felt like.

And then, suddenly, her disorientation was replaced by a flood of images. The returning memories were no more than a movie trailer to begin with – a fast succession of scenes. But the more she thought about those scenes, the more it felt like a movie she'd seen before.

Her mother, Emma Turner. She remembered now. She could see them huddling together under a blanket on the streets of Whitechapel. She remembered working as a costermonger and a crossing-sweeper and reciting poems outside the Pavilion Theatre and fetching pies for their supper from Mr Bradshaw's bakery. She remembered Jack the Ripper murdering all those poor women, and then she remembered the day she met him. In that church. She saw him... *doing that*. And that unexpected encounter led her on a wild and mind-bending path, discovering that she, too, was from the future, a much further future, and had *another mother*. A birth mother. Cara Montgomery. The one who named her Dina.

Harriet remembered everything now. Fred Gleeson. The Shapeless and the Last War. Million Eyes. Her becoming the 'Unraveller' to stop them. Her last encounter with Million Eyes, when Dr Samantha Neether stole twenty-three years of her life from her.

At last, seventy-six years later, she'd taken it back.

"I remember," she murmured, staring downwards, the

undulating floor levelling and becoming still again. "Everything… everything's coming back…"

"That's good. The Ratheri has been trying to draw your attention for quite some time. Over and over again, it has been trying to break free of the loop, crumble the walls of the paradox to get a message to you. A message to lead you here."

Harriet looked ahead out of the shuttle window at the turbid cloud of red. None of what this man was saying was making sense. "I don't understand. What even *is* the Ratheri?"

"The Ratheri is the cause of everything that has happened, and is still happening," Marcus said. "To you. To me. To all of us. It is the reason time travel exists. The Ratheri is what Million Eyes use to create chronozine, and it's what has been causing ships and planes to disappear in this part of the Atlantic for centuries."

"You're talking about the Bermuda Triangle."

"Yes. All of the ships and planes that went missing here actually travelled in time. Just last month, the fossilised remains of Flight 19 and its crew were discovered by a maritime archaeological team. This isn't public knowledge, but radiocarbon dating has determined the remains to be nearly two million years old. This means that the Ratheri transported Flight 19 to the early Stone Age, before homo sapiens had even evolved."

Harriet sighed. "I don't understand what all of this has to do with me."

"The Ratheri is the reason *I* am here, too. I am what Million Eyes would call a 'sensile'. Someone who sensitive to the fabric of time, who can see beyond it, who can perceive alternate timelines, altered histories, sometimes premonitions of the future. The ability is strong in my family. My great aunt was a sensile, too. Her name was Rachel Evans."

Harriet felt another flicker of memory. "Rachel Evans – she was the one who Million Eyes turned into… into…" She couldn't find the word.

"The Augur," Marcus replied, and Harriet knew

instantly that she had heard the word before. "You can see why we hide ourselves from them."

Another memory returned. "James Rawling told me about Rachel. He told me about the sensiles. He said he thought I was one of them."

"And you are, in a way. Our abilities come from the Ratheri. Our memories and premonitions – they're the Ratheri trying to reach us. Just as it's trying to reach you."

"You speak about it like it's alive."

"It is."

Harriet sighed with infuriation. "Then how? How has it been trying to *reach* me?"

"The snake."

Her blood went cold. "The snake? You mean the snake that eats its tail?"

Marcus nodded. "The ouroboros. Yes."

"So, you're saying the ouroboros is some sort of message? From the Ratheri to me? Why? Why *me?*"

Marcus took a breath. "Harriet, we know what's been happening to you. Our perceptions have been increasing lately. Many of us have been having visions, dreams. About you. We know that your eyes are turning red. We know that you are starting to breathe red vapour. You're changing, Harriet. And you're going to continue to change."

This man seemed to have all the answers, so she thought she may as well ask, "Why? Why am I changing?"

"Something happened to you. One of the chronozine pills you took. Right after you were shot in 1605. There was something wrong with it. The chronotonic density was too high – something went wrong during the infusion process. It rendered you immortal, impervious to time. A fixed and unchanging point. But it did more than that. It corrupted you, which is why every fibre of your temporal cohesion is gradually breaking down."

"I don't understand what you're saying."

"The name, 'Ratheri', comes from the Morse code

signal emanating from the anomaly. That word isn't random. It's another message, but the letters are distorted. R A T H E R I... H A R R I E T."

Harriet could hear the swooshing of blood against her eardrums as her heart pumped it round her body in seismic waves. "What? No. No... you can't be saying..."

He nodded sadly. "Yes, Harriet. The Ratheri is what you will become. What you will evolve into. The ouroboros is a symbol of eternity, of infinity, of *cyclicality*. Harriet, *you* are the ouroboros. You are the snake that eats its tail."

38

Now Harriet could hear nothing but the surge of her own blood. Not the beeping of her consoles nor the quiet whir of her shuttle's engine core. She stared out of the window at the Ratheri. Although she couldn't believe what Marcus was saying, deep down she knew. Looking at the swirling red cloud, despite how strange and alien it seemed, it felt like she was looking in a mirror.

Still, the implications of what she was hearing were so immense, dreadful and paradoxical that her rational brain denied it. She whispered, "That's impossible," her voice sounding small and far away.

"You're right, it is," Marcus said. Harriet felt a sliver of vindication but his next words crushed it. "But it's what's happened."

"But it can't have." She felt urged to continue challenging the revelation; it just made no logical sense. "How can a faulty chronozine pill cause me to become the Ratheri when chronozine *comes from* the Ratheri?"

"And that's the ouroboros," said Marcus. "The Ratheri creates itself. That's why it chose the tail-eating snake as its message to lead you here. It's a paradox. The universe is caught in a loop. A record on a turntable, skipping. And I'm sorry, Harriet. I'm so, so sorry. But *you* are the cause of it."

Harriet's stomach flipped. "What do you mean?"

"Try to think of the universe as a computer program. A vast and infinitely complex computer program made up of trillions of blocks of code – subroutines in the program's operating system. Now imagine that every new life in the universe is a new subroutine, with a specific purpose and place in the system. From time to time new subroutines will precipitate minor glitches in the system and the program won't function as well as it should. We often experience these as things science can't explain. Ghosts, medical miracles, all those 'glitch in the matrix' stories you hear about. No computer program is ever perfect, and neither is the universe. Sometimes it shows."

Harriet remembered reading about a teenage boy on a road trip with his family, who believed he had experienced a 'glitch in the matrix' after waking up in a completely different motel room to the one he'd fallen asleep in. Again, her rational mind was questioning where on earth Marcus was going with this, while her emotional mind already knew.

"But on rare occasions," Marcus continued, "a new subroutine will cause a fatal bug in the operating system and the entire program will crash."

Harriet's whole body shook. "What the hell are you saying?"

Marcus sighed. "I'm saying that you, Harriet, are that faulty subroutine. A particularly bad line of code. Your birth caused a fatal bug in the system and, as a result, the universe is malfunctioning and breaking down. This breakdown has manifested as time travel. Something that has become possible that should never have been. Time travel will lead to the creation of the Shapeless and the Shapeless will evolve to destroy *everything*. The Last War and the extinction of humanity are just the beginning. Over the next few thousand years, the Shapeless will ravage every corner of the universe and obliterate all life. The universe is *crashing,* Harriet. Everything is set to collapse under the weight of time travel's assault."

"And you're saying..." A painful swallow caught in Harriet's throat. "You're saying it's because of me."

Marcus nodded. "Yes."

Harriet felt dazed, broken. Like she had just been

beaten to a pulp and left by the side of a disused road in the middle of nowhere. Everything that had happened, everything that would still happen... It wasn't Million Eyes' fault. It was hers.

"What can I do?" Harriet murmured.

"There is still a chance to prevent this," Marcus explained. "This malfunction has been going round and round in circles for so long, but the Ratheri has finally managed to break the cycle and lead you here so we can fix the bug."

"And how are we going to do that?"

"We have to delete the subroutine that's causing it. You."

Harriet knew, somehow, that that was coming. "You're saying I need to kill myself. The problem is, I can't." *And believe me, I've tried.*

"No, you can't. But you can stop yourself from coming into existence. You can prevent yourself from ever being born."

Harriet's face creased with pain. Marcus and the shuttle blurred as tears welled in her eyes and several started escaping down her cheeks. What a thing to ask someone to do. But when your very existence is the cause of the universe's collapse...

"Without you," Marcus said, "the Ratheri would never exist, which means Jesus could never go back in time, Million Eyes would never be formed, and time travel would never be invented. No Shapeless, no Last War. The universe would function again. And all of human history would take a totally different course. I'm so sorry, but it's the only way. You know what time travel has already done to Earth. How much paradox and confusion it's already created. Finally we have a chance to end it. To close the loop."

"I... I know," Harriet whispered, crestfallen but acceptant. "It's strange but... I can hear it."

"Hear what?"

Harriet stared out of the window at the red cloud, hanging motionless before her. "The Ratheri. I can hear it speaking to me. It's carrying so much guilt. It's desperate to end this."

"You couldn't have known this would happen. The universe is awesome, and mystifying, and cruel. Humanity may never understand it."

"No. But *I'm* starting to understand it a little better." She blinked the tears from her eyes and stared up at him. "How... how do I...?"

The words 'erase my own existence' just wouldn't form.

"The Ratheri will take care of the 'how'," Marcus said. "All you need to do is fly your shuttle into the cloud. The Ratheri will take it from there."

Harriet nodded, her lost, staring eyes sinking to the floor.

After a moment's silence, Marcus said, "Harriet, I cannot offer you comfort. I can only say that by doing this, you will save the universe. Trillions and trillions of lives that were meant to be but were undone by time travel will be restored."

Harriet looked at him. "Please... just go."

Marcus smiled sadly. "Of course. Goodbye, Harriet. And... thank you." His hologram faded away, and Harriet sat alone in her shuttle, hovering above a desolate ocean.

Harriet wanted to call someone, to confide in them what she was about to do. But she had no one to call. She decided to place a call through her shuttle's computer to the neighbour, Elaine, who lived in the house closest to her, a quarter of a mile down the road. She and her family had moved there three years ago, and Harriet had only met them once, when they asked her if she'd mind feeding their cat while they were away.

Harriet asked Elaine if she would take in Bluebell. Elaine said she would, but then she asked why and at that moment, Harriet started falling into a daze, Elaine's voice disappearing down a tunnel.

Because, well, why would Bluebell *need* looking after? Harriet was about to reset the universe. The entire world was about to change. If Bluebell still existed afterwards, she'd have a different owner. A different home.

Sighing heavily, Harriet ended the call and inputted a new course on her navigation console.

To be honest, a part of Harriet was looking forward to dying. It had been a long, lonely life, and until the last ten minutes, she had thought it might never end. Now, as her shuttle started drifting towards the Ratheri, a sense of finality was bearing down upon her. But it brought relief rather than fear.

One thing bothered her though – the prospect of dying and leaving no mark whatsoever on the world, because she would never have existed. More tears came as she thought about it, dropping off her chin and splashing against the console. She tried to breathe steadily and was able to push the sobs back. Marcus's words played over and over in Harriet's mind. 'By doing this, you will save the universe.'

Perhaps, but nobody will ever know. I suppose that makes it the ultimate in selfless acts.

The Ratheri started to shift and roil and pulse excitedly as the nose of Harriet's shuttle ruffled the soft fringe of the cloud. As she entered its swirling folds and the walls of the shuttle started to whisper away, Harriet realised that what she was doing wasn't a *completely* selfless act, because she was looking forward to some peace.

39

November 7th 2218

"Cherry Bakewell Frappuccino to go, please," said Jackson Montgomery to the barista behind the counter of the Starbucks in Aberdeenshire Interstate Terminal. This was his first break of the day and he was glad of it. With several telepods having malfunctioned due a three-micron misalignment in the teleportation relays between Aberdeenshire and Budapest, he'd had to deal with lots of angry passengers whose teleports were delayed. A Cherry Bakewell Frappuccino meant standing in a five-minute queue, but right now, the coffee-cake-milkshake mashup was exactly what he needed and they weren't available from the synthesisers; you could only buy them fresh.

"Five numecs, please," the barista said.

Jackson was about to deposit the money via his orb when a blonde woman appeared next to him, holding up a currency card. "I'll get this."

Jackson frowned. "Er– I– you don't ha–"

"I'd like to," the woman said, smiling. Something familiar about her face made Jackson wonder if they'd met before.

The barista took the currency card, flashing an inconvenienced look. Hardly anybody paid with these anymore. There was no need; everybody had orbs. Apart from this blonde woman, it would seem.

The barista's eyes turned yellow as her orb scanned the data on the card to process the payment. A moment later, her eyes turned green again and she handed it back to the woman.

"Er– thank you," said Jackson uncertainly as he and the woman moved down to the serving area.

"My pleasure."

Jackson felt a tad uncomfortable. "Sorry to sound presumptuous but... I'm married."

The woman gave a small, embarrassed laugh, cheeks radiating pink, and Jackson was struck again by a flush of familiarity in the sound of her laugh, the shape of her smile. "It's not like that, trust me," she said.

Now he was just confused. "Do I know you?"

"Not exactly," the woman said.

Erm– okay.

A different barista placed his drink down on the serving counter. He said thanks and took the cup, stepping away from the counter. The blonde woman followed.

"I– I know your wife," the woman said after a moment of silent awkwardness. "Cara."

Phew. So she wasn't a stalker. Well, she might be still. "Oh, I see," he said, sipping his Frappuccino, unsure what else to say.

"I'm Harriet," the woman said, holding out her hand. "It's so lovely to meet you."

Jackson shook her hand; she seemed sincere. "Jackson Montgomery." He realised he probably didn't need to add his surname if she knew Cara.

Harriet smiled broadly. "Ah, yes. You took her name, didn't you."

"Er, yes..." What was so strange about that? "How do you know Cara?"

"I haven't seen her in a very long time." A pall of sadness swept across her face. But then, like a cloud passing quickly in front of the sun, her warm full smile returned, her cheeks creasing with two adorable dimples. "But I'm so happy to finally meet you."

As Jackson looked into her glistening cerulean eyes, bells of recognition started chiming again. "Are you sure we haven't met?"

Harriet shook her head. "As much as I would've liked to."

There was something about her. He couldn't put his finger on it, but something – the blueness of her eyes, the depth of her dimples, that button nose – made Jackson want to fold her into his arms protectively. "I feel like... like I know you."

Harriet sighed. "I know the feeling."

Jackson took a couple of steps forwards, peering more closely at her face. "It's your– your blue eyes, I think." *They're just like Cara's.*

"Blue?" She swallowed, like she was struggling to form her next words. "Aren't they... red?"

"No." Jackson presumed she was asking if they were bloodshot. "Not at all." *They're beautiful cerulean blue.*

Tears welled in the woman's eyes, two spilling symmetrically down her face from each eye.

"Are you okay?" Jackson asked gently.

"Yes. I just– I don't have long. I wanted to meet you. That's all. And I have." Her voice hitched as more tears fell. "If I don't go now, I never will."

Harriet turned to leave, but Jackson still had questions. How did she know Cara? Why was she so desperate to meet him? Most of all – *why do I feel like I've known you for years?*

"Wait," he called as she strode out of Starbucks into the main thoroughfare of the terminal. "You said you knew Cara, right? So will I see you again?"

Harriet turned round and smiled sadly, "Maybe," and walked on.

Yet something in her expression told Jackson he would never see her again.

Cara Montgomery sat in the empty waiting room of the fertility centre of Aberdeenshire State Hospital, luckily in the opposite wing of the hospital to general consultancy where she worked. That made it unlikely she'd get spotted by one of her colleagues, which was good, since she hadn't told any of them she was coming here today. She hadn't told anyone, in fact. Not her friends. Not her mum. *Not even my husband.* But this uterine reconstruction procedure was risky and she knew they'd try to talk her out of it.

She spent the time reviewing the files for tomorrow's patients on her orb. One was a child who was coming in for her second and final round of plasmatic reduction therapy, which would cure her necrocythemia.

The patient after her made Cara's heart flutter. A woman who was infertile, just like Cara. She was coming in for basic DNA resequencing, to make her cells viable for cloning. The procedure Cara couldn't have because she had already had it as a baby, to remove life-threatening cysts that had started growing on her back. So Cara had been pinning all her hopes on the adoption agency granting them a child – until they responded last week saying that their application had been rejected. Something Jackson was still in the dark about.

To be honest, Cara had felt backed into a corner by the whole ordeal, with no option but to try this new and dangerous procedure, and hope for the best.

"Dr Cara Montgomery?" said the nurse standing at the top of the corridor that led to the therapy rooms. "Dr Wilkinson is ready for you now."

Cara stood up and crossed the waiting room, still the only patient there. But then, the fertility centre wasn't somewhere she expected to be busy. Infertility wasn't a problem like it used to be; there were just so many options available if your natural biology was stopping you from having kids. It just so happened that none of them were available to Cara. The universe hated her, it seemed.

"Don't go in."

A woman's voice made Cara turn around. Standing on the other side of the waiting room was a blonde woman in a long grey coat.

"Who– who are you?" Cara asked.

The blonde woman stepped forwards. "My name is Ha– Dina." The woman let out a breath. "My name is Dina."

Cara swallowed. "Funny. I wanted to call my daughter that."

Dina nodded. "And you still can. Just not like this."

"Dr Montgomery," the nurse said behind her, "Dr Wilkinson's schedule is very–"

Cara threw a sharp glare at the nurse across her shoulder. "I'm a doctor at this hospital. She can give me a minute."

The nurse stepped back meekly and Cara walked up to Dina. "Do I know you?" The woman smiled silently and Cara felt a sudden pressure inside her chest. "I *do* know you," Cara said. An urge coursed through her in that moment, and before her rational mind could stop her, she was stroking Dina's cheek with the backs of her fingers.

Dina didn't back away. Rather, she closed her eyes and let a tear squeeze through her eyelids as she leaned into Cara's touch.

"*How* do I know you?" Cara whispered.

Dina opened her eyes and Cara pulled her hand slowly away. "You don't. Not yet."

"What does that mean?"

"Sometimes I'm not even sure myself. All I know is why I'm here."

Cara frowned. "And why are you here?"

She let out a deep, thoughtful breath. "To stop you from making a mistake."

Cara cast a slow, circular glance at the marble-effect resin floor. "Do you know something I don't?"

"Check your notifications. You should have received a further letter from the adoption agency."

"What? I don't un–"

"Just take a look."

Sighing, Cara looked at her personal notifications. Her orb displayed one unread message from the same adoption agency that had rejected her and Jackson's application to become parents a week ago.

She opened the message and a grey-haired woman Cara didn't recognise filled her field of vision.

"Hello, Cara," the woman said. "My name is Marjane Zenensky. I'm one of the team leaders here at the Aberdeenshire Adoption and Fostering Service. Last week you received a message from my colleague, advising you that your application to become parents had been rejected. However, in light of new information pertaining to your suitability, we have reconsidered your application."

Cara felt her whole body start to shake as a wave of emotion crashed through it. *New information?* They had said that the rejection was because they believed Cara and Jackson were still upset about not being able to bear their own child, which they were. But that didn't mean they wouldn't love an adopted child just as much. Cara had tried desperately to convince them of that, failing. So what new information could have persuaded them to reconsider?

Marjane Zenensky's video message continued, her previous straight face breaking into a broad smile, "It now gives me great pleasure to inform you that you and Jackson are about to become the proud parents of a healthy baby girl."

Marjane's face blurred as tears filled Cara's eyes. She clamped a shaking hand over her mouth to stem the emotion from gushing forth. Her knees going weak, she had to sit down, and backed into one of the waiting room chairs, almost stumbling on her way down into it.

"I will be contacting you in a couple of days to discuss what happens next," Marjane said, "but for now, may I extend my personal congratulations to you and Jackson."

Cara sniffed and rubbed her eyes. She looked up at her mysterious visitor and asked, "How did you–?"

But the woman – Dina – had gone.

"Ms Montgomery," said the nurse, walking over to her. "Are you okay? Do you need to postpone your appointment with Dr Wilkinson?"

Cara smiled up at her. "I'm more okay than I've ever

been. And no, I would like to cancel my appointment with Dr Wilkinson, please. I'm sorry for the confusion, but I won't be needing it now." Her next words caught in her throat, clogged with joy and love and overwhelming gratitude. "I already have a daughter waiting."

Harriet waited and watched from afar as her mother walked out of the fertility centre, beaming and glowing with tears as she strode to her shuttle in the parking lot of the hospital. It was as Cara activated the shuttle that everything started to fall away. Shuttles in the parking lot vanished one at a time, as did the trees skirting it, the buildings behind and around it. Other people walking by – gone in a blink.

Cara didn't seem to notice; maybe only Harriet could see it. Or maybe it was because her mother was so blissfully happy in that moment that the universe dissipating around her didn't matter. And perhaps that was why Cara was the last light to go out.

Although she wasn't really the last. Harriet was. Her mother faded to a faint silhouette, merging with the growing mantle of white nothingness, and Harriet stood alone in the empty void of the universe. A moment later, her light starting blinking out, too. Her eyes opened and closed, opened and closed, as if she were gradually falling asleep. She felt glad of the peacefulness of it all.

The universe began to reset, repair, and rewrite itself as Harriet ebbed away with a gentle smile on her lips and a final tear frozen against her cheek, thinking about how grateful she was that she had got to say goodbye to her mum and, at last, meet her dad.

40

"And that, my darling, is how our world came to be."

The little girl sat up straight in her bed, eyes wide. "What? Grandma, what do you mean? What happened?"

"The timeline reset," said Grandma softly. "All of history, going back to the Cretaceous era, was rewritten."

The little girl's mind boggled. So long had she been listening to her grandmother's stories about time travel and Million Eyes and the Last War, imagining them to be true, imagining them to have happened in another world or reality – but if the universe reset, if the timeline got rewritten... "Grandma, does that mean the events in your stories never happened?"

"That's right, darling. Earth's history took a totally different course."

The little girl shook her head. A rush of sadness made a tear escape down her cheek. "But that means none of the people in your stories ever existed."

Grandma leaned close, wiped the little girl's tear with her finger, and whispered, "Not exactly."

The little girl looked at her grandmother hopefully. "What do you mean?"

Her grandmother smiled. "Tomorrow I'm going to take you somewhere. Then I'll explain."

"Where?"

"You'll see. In the meantime, get some sleep. We have a long journey ahead."

Even though she was too excited to sleep, she managed to get a few hours before her grandma woke her at sunrise. They took a cross-continental dropship through the sky tunnels and despite the little girl's attempts at extracting information, Grandma remained tight-lipped about their destination the entire journey.

Hours later, they landed on a beautiful headland projecting from a rugged coastline the little girl hadn't seen before.

"Grandma, what is this place?" she said as they stepped off the dropship and looked around at all the bustling activity on the remote clifftop.

Her grandmother answered silently with a cryptic smile. Holding hands they walked along a paved road with bizarre structures and objects on either side, and dozens of people gathered talking, laughing, and exploring the sights around them.

At that moment, the little girl recognised what she was looking at. "Grandma, these houses are like the ones from your stories!" she cried gleefully, pointing at the rudimentary thatched roundhouse, standing next to a two-storey, box-shaped house made from rectangular red bricks. Both houses stood in the shadow of a much taller tower on the other side of the road, which had four sides of glass windows covering every inch, reflecting the blue waves that crashed around the headland.

"Yes, darling."

"Grandma – look! A car!" The little girl pointed at the wheeled metal vehicle parked in the road, around which about a dozen people stood. "I remember. These came after carriages pulled by those animals you talked about – horses? And then, after cars, they had shuttles, right?"

Grandma nodded her head behind the little girl, who spun round and beamed at the sight of the long rectangular box with a tapering nose and large engine nacelles on either side. "Like that one!"

They passed more houses from different eras of the other timeline, the *erased* timeline, along with a replica of a giant arch, a building with various columns and onion-shaped domes, and a tower that looked like it may fall over at any moment. They came to a statue of a huge, green, scaly monster the little girl remembered from Grandma's stories as that which ate the Princes in the Tower. A dinosaur.

A large crowd of vorn surrounded the statue. The scales on their faces glowed yellow, which happened whenever a vorn felt awe. The little girl didn't know why they would be awed by the beast towering over them except for the fact that it was a reptile like they were. Glancing around, she started to notice that there were quite a number of vorn here.

"Why are there so many vorn?" she asked. "I don't remember there being *any* vorn in your stories."

"There weren't," Grandma said. "Because the vorn didn't exist in the other timeline."

"None of them?"

"No."

"Why?"

"Because the Princes in the Tower went back in time and infected the dinosaurs with the common cold, triggering an extinction event. In our timeline, that never happened, and although many dinosaur species died out later, others evolved... and became vorn."

The little girl lowered her voice so as not to offend anyone. "Wait– you're saying vorn are *dinosaurs?*"

"They used to be, yes. They achieved sentience first, several millennia before humans. Then humans evolved alongside them. For many centuries, terrible wars were fought between humans and vorn. It took a long time for us to work out our differences but eventually we learned to live harmoniously, side by side. We might still have our problems, but we're centuries ahead of where we would have been in the other timeline. Our history with the vorn taught us tolerance, empathy and altruism. It taught us to be better. But it wasn't the only thing that taught us..."

Distracted and barely registering her grandma's last sentence, the little girl dashed over to a building that, judging by the sign above the door, was called a 'library'. Inside, humans and vorn gazed at the many wooden cases of what the little girl presumed were books.

An old man and woman drew the little girl's attention. The woman pulled a book with a dark green cover off a shelf and laughed as she handed it to the man. The little girl caught a glance of the words inscribed in gold on the front: *The History of Computer-Aided Timetabling for Railway Systems*. It was the book from her grandmother's stories, the book that Jennifer Larson took with her into the past.

Immediately reminded of their conversation last night, the little girl turned to her grandma and said, "What did you mean last night by 'not exactly'? After I said that none of the people in your stories ever existed?"

Her grandmother smiled. "I meant that some of those people did, do and will still exist."

The little girl's heart skipped. "Really?"

"Yes. The ones who were at the eye of the storm were given another chance. They live different lives, with different names, different faces. But the universe has preserved their essence, their souls. Many of them don't even remember having a whole other life in the other timeline. Of course, there are a few who do…"

"Eye of the storm?"

"The ones whose lives were explicitly touched by the error."

The little girl's eyes sank. "The error. You mean Harriet."

Grandma nodded. "Yes, darling."

Eyes lifting in hope, "So Jennifer Larson still existed?"

Grandma smiled warmly and nodded.

"And Adam Bryant?"

Another nod.

The little girl whirled around in the direction of the bookcase where the old man and woman had been standing looking at *The History of Computer-Aided Timetabling for Railway Systems*. They'd both gone.

I wonder…

Turning back to her grandmother, she asked about Jesus, the Princes in the Tower and Cara and Jackson Montgomery. Her grandmother indicated that all had survived the 'reset' and had lived, or would live, again. In a different form.

The little girl thought of two others. "Even horrible Miss Morgan and Dr Neether?"

Her grandmother laughed. "Yes. Even them."

"After everything they did?"

"They led much humbler lives in this timeline, darling."

Confusion made the little girl's face draw into a frown. "Grandma, how can you know all this if that timeline never existed?" She looked around. "And how can any of this even be here?"

"Because there are people who remember the other timeline, like I do. The memories come in dreams, visions, déjà vu. For centuries we have been sharing our experiences with each other to develop a clear picture of what happened. One man – someone else whose soul survived the reset – had the idea of building this place in memory of all that was lost to time. His name in the other timeline... was Gregory Ferro."

A warm sensation flooded the little girl's chest. Ferro was the man who had started it all, who had lost his family and then his life to Million Eyes, to time travel. She felt glad that he, too, had been given another chance.

But then she thought of someone else who hadn't. The one whose light needed to go out for everyone else's to come back on. "I feel sad for her, Grandma. I feel sad for Harriet."

Offering her hand to the little girl, Grandma said, "Come with me. There's something I'd like to show you."

Her grandmother led her past more buildings and objects from the other timeline to a grassy clearing at the cliff edge. There stood a large, four-sided, tapering stone monument, several humans and vorn kneeling in front of it reverently. The monument culminated in a stone ring standing vertically at the top. As the little girl peered closer, she realised it wasn't a ring but a snake. A snake eating its tail.

Grandma said, "Since the universe came into being, a message has been filtering through time and space. Not everyone can hear it, only some of us. We decided to build this monument so that we could share it with others."

The little girl walked up to it till she was close enough to read the inscription on the plinth. As she did, bittersweet tears fell down her cheeks from both eyes.

It read:

I DON'T KNOW IF ANYONE WILL REMEMBER ME

BUT I HOPE YOU WILL

AND I HOPE YOU WILL MAKE THE MOST OF YOUR SECOND CHANCE

BECAUSE I'VE SEEN WHAT HAPPENS

WHEN PEOPLE LOSE SIGHT OF THE BIGGER PICTURE

I HAVE FAITH THAT THINGS WILL BE DIFFERENT THIS TIME

THIS WORLD IS PRECIOUS

I LEAVE IT IN YOUR HANDS

HARRIET TURNER

ACKNOWLEDGEMENTS

Here we are at the end of the road! A long, twisty, complicated road that's taken me 15 years to travel. The release of *Million Eyes III: Ouroboros* is a big moment for me and I first have to thank Elsewhen Press for making it possible. Covid and Brexit have hit the publishing industry hard and I'm lucky that Elsewhen Press have made it through and stuck by me. In addition to *Million Eyes III*, they've also just published *Million Eyes: Over Time*, a second short story collection set in the *Million Eyes* universe. That means, with the release of *Ouroboros*, Elsewhen have now published five of my books.

I want to thank Pete, Al and Sofia at Elsewhen individually. Sofia and Pete, thank you for all your insights during editing and proofreading. I've learned a lot. Sofia, your suggestions for *Ouroboros* genuinely made my characters stronger. And Al, what a cover. You've saved the best till last with this one. It looks great.

I must also say a further thank you to my friend, muse and support through the last 15 years, Vicky. She often cites *Million Eyes* as her favourite books and I know she says that truthfully; she may be one of my best friends but she's always been honest about what she does and doesn't like. Vicky has been reviewing and feeding back on these books for years now, and she always makes time to be my sounding board. It does mean that by workshopping *Million Eyes* with her I've had to spoil all the plot twists! So I've promised her she can read my next book, *The Puddle Bumps*, without any prior knowledge!

I want to thank Rushmoor Writers, in particular Jane Sleight and Alice Missions, for their critiques of *Million Eyes III*'s early chapters. Even though I decided to leave the group after 7 years when I moved house, I will always credit Rushmoor Writers with helping me become the writer I am today.

Which leads me to the other writer in my life: my fiancée, Katy, who last year did me the honour of asking me to be her husband while in a hot air balloon! The two of us have been helping each other with our novels since we met, and now we're combining our individual writing strengths with a collaborative novel, *Breaching the Wall*. As a writer and fellow sci-fi nerd, she has been both a sounding board and source of inspiration. More than that, she has made me the happiest I have ever been. There's no better motivation to keep going than that.

I next want to thank my friend and boss, Chris Cooke, CEO of Old Street Solutions, where I work as Head of Content. To show his support for *Million Eyes*, he bought me one of my favourite Christmas presents ever: a personal message from *Star Trek*'s Jonathan Frakes, who congratulated me on completing *Million Eyes* and wished me well with the release of the final book.

And finally, to all my family and friends who have supported me, bought and read my books, recommended them to their friends, come to my book launches, written reviews, and just offered me words of encouragement – thank you. I'll never forget it.

Elsewhen Press

delivering outstanding new talents in speculative fiction

Visit the Elsewhen Press website at elsewhen.press for the latest information on all of our titles, authors and events; to read our blog; find out where to buy our books and ebooks; or to place an order.

Sign up for the Elsewhen Press InFlight Newsletter at elsewhen.press/newsletter

MILLION EYES

Time is the ultimate weapon

What if we're living in an alternate timeline? What if the car crash that killed Princess Diana, the disappearance of the Princes in the Tower, and the shooting of King William II weren't supposed to happen?

Ex-history teacher Gregory Ferro finds evidence that a cabal of time travellers is responsible for several key events in our history. These events all seem to hinge on a dry textbook published in 1995, referenced in a history book written in 1977 and mentioned in a letter to King Edward III in 1348.

Ferro teams up with down-on-her-luck graduate Jennifer Larson to get to the truth and discover the relevance of a book that seems to defy the arrow of time. But the time travellers are watching closely. Soon the duo are targeted by assassins willing to rewrite history to bury them.

Million Eyes is a fast-paced conspiracy thriller about power, corruption and destiny.

ISBN: 9781911409588 (epub, kindle) / 9781911409489 (336pp paperback)
Visit bit.ly/Million-Eyes

MILLION EYES II
THE UNRAVELLER

Time is the ultimate saviour

Following an impossible discovery in East London, archaeologist Dr Samantha Lester joins forces with software developer Adam Bryant to investigate the events that led to the disappearance of his best friend, Jennifer, and to bring down the people responsible – Million Eyes.

Before long, Lester and Adam are drawn into a tangled conspiratorial web involving dinosaurs, the Gunpowder Plot, Jesus, the Bermuda Triangle, and a mysterious history-hopping individual called the Unraveller, who is determined to wipe Million Eyes off the temporal map.

But as the secrets of Million Eyes' past are revealed, picking a side in this fight might not be so easy.

ISBN: 9781911409786 (epub, kindle) / 97819114094687(408pp paperback)
Visit bit.ly/Million-Eyes-II

MILLION EYES: EXTRA TIME

Twelve time-twisting tales

Million Eyes: Extra Time is a compilation of short stories set in the universe of C.R. Berry's time travel conspiracy thriller trilogy, *Million Eyes*.

While the stories in *Million Eyes: Extra Time* can stand alone, you'll notice that a number of them are strongly linked and follow a loose chronology. The author's advice is that you read them in the order that they are presented.

Available for free download in pdf, epub and kindle formats

Visit bit.ly/Million-Eyes-Extra-Time

MILLION EYES: OVER TIME

Five more time-twisting tales

Disappearing numbers and children, strange time-eating parasites, and the mysterious undoing of Covid-19.

Million Eyes: Over Time is an addendum to C.R. Berry's previous compilation of short stories, *Million Eyes: Extra Time*. *Extra Time* had twelve stories set in the universe of his time travel conspiracy thriller trilogy, *Million Eyes*. *Over Time* adds five extra stories.

Like *Extra Time*, *Over Time* expands on a world where time travel is real and being used by an enigmatic organisation, Million Eyes, to manipulate our history and our lives. These stories fill in gaps and tie off loose ends by exploring some of the collateral impacts of their incursions. Some of the stories are inspired by real legends and concepts associated with time travel.

Available for free download in pdf, epub and kindle formats

Visit bit.ly/Million-Eyes-Over-Time

Stray Pilot

Douglas Thompson

A passionate environmental allegory

Thomas Tellman, an RAF pilot who disappeared pursuing a UFO in 1948, unexpectedly returns entirely un-aged to a small town on Scotland's north-east coast. He finds that his 7-year-old daughter is now a bed-bound 87-year-old woman suffering from dementia. She greets him as her father but others assume she is deluded and that Thomas is an unhinged impostor or con man. While Thomas endeavours to blend in to an ordinary life, his presence gradually sets off unpredictable consequences, locally, nationally and globally. Members of the British Intelligence Services attempt to discredit Thomas in advance of what they anticipate will be his public disclosure of evidence of extra-terrestrial activity, but the local community protect him. Thomas, appalled by the increase in environmental damage that has occurred in his 80 year absence, appears to have returned with a mission: whose true nature he guards from everyone around him.

Douglas Thompson's thought-provoking novel is unashamedly science-fiction yet firmly in the tradition of literary explorations of the experience of the outsider. He weaves together themes of memory loss and dementia, alienation, and spiritual respect for the natural world; while at the same time counterposing the humanity inherent in close communities against the xenophobia and nihilistic materialism of contemporary urban society. Of all the book's vivid characters, the fictional village of Kinburgh itself is the stand-out star: an archetypal symbol of human community. In an age of growing despair in the face of climate crises, *Stray Pilot* offers a passionate environmental allegory with a positive message of constructive hope: a love song to all that is best in ordinary people.

ISBN: 9781915304131(epub, kindle) / 97819153041032 (264pp paperback)

Visit bit.ly/StrayPilot

The Night Has Seen Your Mind

Simon Kearns

Cutting across genres, *The Night Has Seen Your Mind* is a literary fusion of science fiction, existential terror and psychological thriller in the style of the 'New Weird'.

Tech billionaire, Mattias Goff, has invited five creative professionals – programmer, pianist, writer, actor, and photographer – for a month-long residency at Crystal Falls, his Arctic retreat. Researching brain waves, and especially the enigmatic gamma wave, Goff asks his guests to wear a kind of EEG cap in order to record the electrical activity in their brains while they engage with their respective disciplines. Although they will be paid $5Million each for the experience, they all start their sojourn a little wary – some more than others. Cut off from the outside world in the stunningly beautiful, if stark, Alaskan winter landscape they immerse themselves in their work. Soon, though, reality seems to be shifting. What is Goff really researching? Are his guests only being observed, or manipulated?

ISBN: 9781911409755 (epub, kindle) / 9781911409656 (336pp paperback)

Visit bit.ly/TheNightHasSeenYourMind

Life on Mars
The Vikings are coming
Hugh Duncan

Racing against time, Jade and her friends must hide evidence of Life on Mars to stop the probes from Earth finding them

Jade is on her way to meet up with her dad, Elvis, for her sixteen-millionth birthday (tortles live a long time in spite of the harsh conditions on Mars), when she gets side-tracked by a strange object that appears to have fallen from the sky. Elvis' travelling companion Starkwood, an electrostatic plant, is hearing voices, claiming that "The Vikings Are Coming", while their football-pitch-sized flying friend Fionix confirms the rumour: the Earth has sent two craft to look for life on Mars.

It then becomes a race against time to hide any evidence of such life before Earth destroys it for good. Can Jade and her friends succeed, with help from a Lung Whale, a liquid horse, some flying cats, the Hellas Angels, the Pyrites and a couple of House Martins from the South of France? Oh, and a quantum tunnelling worm – all while avoiding Zombie Vegetables and trouble with a Gravity Artist and the Physics Police?! A gentle and lightly humorous science fantasy adventure.

Cover artwork and illustrations: Natascha Booth

ISBN: 9781915304124 (epub, kindle) / 9781915304025 (400pp paperback)

Visit https://bit.ly/LifeOnMars-Vikings

HOWUL

A LIFE'S JOURNEY

DAVID SHANNON

"Un-put-down-able! A classic hero's journey, deftly handled. I was surprised by every twist and turn, the plotting was superb, and the engagement of all the senses – I could smell those flowers and herbs. A tour de force"

– LINDSAY NICHOLSON MBE

Books are dangerous

People in Blanow think that books are dangerous: they fill your head with drivel, make poor firewood and cannot be eaten (even in an emergency).

This book is about Howul. He sees things differently: fires are dangerous; people are dangerous; books are just books.

Howul secretly writes down what goes on around him in Blanow. How its people treat foreigners, treat his daughter, treat him. None of it is pretty. Worse still, everything here keeps trying to kill him: rats, snakes, diseases, roof slates, the weather, the sea. That he survives must mean something. He wants to find out what. By trying to do this, he gets himself thrown out of Blanow… and so his journey begins.

Like all gripping stories, *HOWUL* is about the bad things people do to each other and what to do if they happen to you. Some people use sticks to stay safe. Some use guns. Words are the weapons that Howul uses most. He makes them sharp. He makes them hurt.

Of course books are dangerous.

ISBN: 9781911409908 (epub, kindle) / ISBN: 9781911409809 (200pp paperback)

Visit bit.ly/HOWUL

INTERFERENCE

Terry Grimwood

The grubby dance of politics didn't end when we left the solar system, it followed us to the stars

The god-like Iaens are infinitely more advanced than humankind, so why have they requested military assistance in a conflict they can surely win unaided?

Torstein Danielson, Secretary for Interplanetary Affairs, is on a fact-finding mission to their home planet and headed straight into the heart of a war-zone. With him, onboard the Starship *Kissinger*, is a detachment of marines for protection, an embedded pack of sycophantic journalists who are not expected to cause trouble, and reporter Katherina Molale, who most certainly will and is never afraid to dig for the truth.

Torstein wants this mission over as quickly as possible. His daughter is terminally ill, his marriage in tatters. But then the Iaens offer a gift in return for military intervention and suddenly the stakes, both for humanity as a race and for Torstein personally, are very high indeed.

Suffolk born and proud of it, Terry Grimwood is the author of a handful of novels and novellas, including *Deadside Revolution*, the science fiction-flavoured political thriller *Bloody War* and *Joe* which was inspired by true events. His short stories have appeared in numerous magazines and anthologies and have been gathered into three collections, *The Exaggerated Man*, *There Is A Way To Live Forever* and *Affairs of a Cardio-Vascular Nature*. Terry has also written and Directed three plays as well as co-written engineering textbooks for Pearson Educational Press. He plays the harmonica and with a little persuasion (not much persuasion, actually) will growl a song into a microphone. By day he teaches electrical installation at a further education college. He is married to Debra, the love of his life.

ISBN: 9781911409960 (epub, kindle) / 9781911409861 (96pp paperback)

Visit bit.ly/Interference-Grimwood